HOMEWARD THE SEEKING HEART

JANE PEART

Fleming H. Revell
A Division of Baker Book House Co
Grand Rapids, Michigan 49516

Scripture quotations in this volume are from the King James
Version of the Bible.

ISBN 0-8007-5374-7

Copyright © 1990 by Jane Peart
Published by Fleming H. Revell
a division of Baker Book House Company
P.O. Box 6287, Grand Rapids, MI 49516-6287

ISBN: 0-8007-5374-7

Printed in the United States of America

To the *real* "riders" of the orphan trains, the over 100,000 children who were transported by train across the country to new homes in the Mid-west, from 1854 to the early twentieth century, whose experience and courage inspired this series.

HOMEWARD THE SEEKING HEART

1

November 1888

The child stirred and moved restlessly on the makeshift bed, the worn velvet theatrical cloak thrown over her for a blanket slipping to the floor. The sound of loud music—the lively, foot-tapping finale of the music hall's evening's performance—vibrated through the open transom of the shabby dressing room.

With the rolling fanfare of the timpani, the last note merged with enthusiastic applause and echoed down the drafty hallway, soon followed by the sound of high heels clattering on bare boards as the chorus dancers came off stage. A minute later two young women pushed through the door.

"Well, that's it for tonight!" one announced breathlessly.

"My feet are killin' me!" sighed the other, a flashy blond, plopping down into one of two straight chairs before the spotted mirror and kicking off her red satin shoes.

"Shh, Mazel! You'll wake the kid!" cautioned the other dancer, jerking one thumb toward the sleeping child.

"Who, Toddy? Oh, she sleeps right through. She's used to it. Ought to be by now. I've been bringin' her to the theater every night on this run."

"Nobody to leave her with then?"

"Not without payin' a pretty penny. A penny, I might add, that I haven't got. It's all I can do to keep us alive, much less handin' out more for someone to watch her sleep!"

"Don't her father send anything?"

"Who? Him? Johnny Todd? Not on your sweet life, he don't," snapped Mazel with a toss of the brassy blond curls. "I'm not even sure where he is right now, to tell the truth. The last I heard he was with a troupe in Cincinnati."

"So, what are you goin' to do with her if we go on tour with this show?"

Mazel unscrewed the top of a big jar of cold cream and began smearing it over her boldly pretty face, now twisted in a sullen expression.

"Don't know. I haven't got that far with my thinkin', Flo." She spun around and faced her friend. "It's a chance of a lifetime, you know, and I'd hate to miss it. You heard what Barney said. We'd be 'playin' before the crowned heads of Europe' was his exact words."

"Well, you can't drag a little kid all over them foreign places, can you? I mean, you just can't tell what it'll be like"—Flo walked over to where the little girl lay and stood looking down at her. The long-lashed eyelids fluttered slightly. One small plump hand tucked itself under her chin; tangled golden ringlets spread against a tattered pillow.

"You don't need to tell *me* that!" Mazel retorted.

Flo reached down and gently touched a curl, then bent and absentmindedly retrieved the velvet cloak and tucked it around the sleeping child.

"How old is she anyway?"

"Five goin' on six come next June—"

"Well, what *are* you goin' to do?"

"I've thought of sendin' word to Johnny. Let him face up to his responsibilities for a change. She's his kid, too, after all."

"But if you don't know where he is—" Flo's voice trailed away questioningly.

"I've got his last address. They could forward a letter to him wherever he is now." Mazel shrugged.

"But that might take weeks and Barney said—"

"I *know* what Barney said, Flo. I got ears! We have to let him know by the end of the week if we're goin' on the tour!"

"You couldn't possibly hear from Johnny by then—"

There was a long silence while Mazel removed her heavy stage makeup with a cloth, then flung the cloth down impatiently. She looked at Flo's reflection in the smeared mirror.

"There's always the County Children's Home. I could leave her there, and Johnny could come and get her."

Flo gasped. "You wouldn't!"

"Why not? Ain't that's what we pay taxes for? To support that and the home for old people? That's what it's for, ain't it? For old people and kids who don't have any family—"

"But *she* has parents—you and Johnny. That place is for *orphans*, or kids that are left on the street—*abandoned! You wouldn't, you couldn't leave Toddy there, could you?*"

"Give me another idea then?" Mazel's tone was sarcastic.

Flo looked down again at the little girl, slumbering peacefully, her breath soft and even, unaware that her fate was being decided.

"It would only be *temporary*," Mazel said slowly as if the idea was catching hold more firmly.

"Temporary?" echoed Flo.

"I already made some inquiries. Under certain circumstances a child can be placed there *temporarily* if there's a family emergency or something that makes it impossible for the parent to keep the child. *Temporarily.*" Mazel kept repeating the word as though it confirmed something. "There's what they call a six-month-period *temporary* placement—that is, if it's a case of necessity—"

"No chance of them, say, puttin' her out for adoption would there be? I mean, in case your letter to Johnny got delayed or somethin', and he didn't come right away to get her?"

"Of course not. You sign papers and that sort of thing. Makes it all legal that it's just *temporary*."

Flo raised her eyebrows.

"If she was mine, don't think I'd take the chance. She's cute as a button, bright as brass. Somebody might just come along and think, 'I'll take this one home with me.'"

"Oh, for pity's sake, Flo. It ain't like a bakery where you go in and say 'I'll take the cherry tart or the chocolate eclair,' just because it strikes your fancy!" Mazel stood up and turned back and began taking off the red sateen costume with its tarnished gilt-trimmed ruffles. "Come on, hurry up and change! I'm starvin'! Let's go get somethin' to eat."

Flo took her blouse and skirt from the hook that served as a clothes closet, and began to get dressed. Neither woman said anything more until they were both ready to leave.

"What about Toddy?" Flo asked.

"We'll bundle her up and take her back to my room, then we'll go."

"Leave her there alone, do you?"

"My stars, Flo, you're a regular old fuss-budget, ain't you? I'll lock the door. She'll be perfectly safe. I do it all the time. Toddy's sound asleep. She'll never know I'm gone."

2

"Now, sit up straight and stop wigglin'," Mazel ordered as she dragged the brush through Toddy's mass of curls.

Toddy held on to the sides of the chair on which she was sitting and tried not to squirm, squeezing her eyes shut tightly as the brush caught in a tangle. She realized her mother was in no mood to be patient. Especially not after her argument with Flo the night before.

Not that the argument itself had been so unusual. She and Flo often had squabbles sharing the same dressing room. Arguments over costumes, face cream, or kohl, borrowing powder without asking—things like that happened all the time. But this time had been different. This time the argument had been over Toddy.

Having grown up among adults, Toddy had learned early in life to make herself scarce during grown-up conversations. That way she sometimes learned interesting things, although most of the time these discussions were mysteriously beyond her comprehension. Still, she had discovered that the best way to learn anything was to pretend to be playing with her rag doll, the one the costume seamstress had sewn for her, or to stick her nose in a book. In case anyone happened to notice her and remark, "Careful, little pitchers have big ears," she would appear to be preoccupied.

This particular argument had been going on between her mother and Flo for at least a week. Although most of the time it was conducted in lowered voices, last night at the theater, it had exploded.

"What do you know about the place?" Flo had asked Mazel. "I mean you haven't even gone to look at it, see what it's like. Don't you think it's kinda risky?"

"What's risky about it? A roof over her head, three squares a day, a bed to sleep in and other kids to play with— sounds like heaven to me after the way I was dragged around from pillar to post with my folks!" retorted Mazel, slamming down the pot of rouge and unscrewing the lid of the cold cream jar.

"Are you sure Barney won't let you take her along with us?"

At this Mazel spun around, hands on her hips. "I don't *want* to take along! Can you get that, Flo? This is the chance I've been waitin' for all my life. I mean to take advantage of it and I can't do that with a kid hangin' around my neck every step of the way."

"Well, *excuse me!*" Flo flung back sarcastically. "I'm just saying if she was mine, I couldn't go off to Europe and dump her in some orphanage!"

"Well, she *ain't* your kid, so mind your own business!"

Dead silence followed this exchange in the dressing room that was usually filled with cheerful chatter, joking banter and laughter. Toddy, sitting in the corner tying her doll's yarn hair with a piece of faded ribbon, hummed under her breath and wondered what an "orphanage" was. From under her long lashes she observed her mother, face flushed under the stage makeup, her lips compressed in a straight line.

Pretty soon the caller rapped at the dressing room door, yelling, "On stage, dancers. Cue two minutes." Flo and Mazel, still not speaking, hurried out.

Toddy heard the laughter that followed the exit of the comedian-juggler off stage and the music for the chorus's next set begin. She settled herself on the bench piled with pillows, cushioned by an old folded stage curtain, then hugging her doll, and drawing her favorite costume cast-off, a velvet cape, over her, she curled up and closed her eyes for sleep.

Toddy was accustomed to being left alone in theater dressing rooms. She had been carried into one in a wicker basket less than two weeks after her birth. Her lullabyes had been the tinny sound of a vaudeville band. Old playbills and theater posters had been her first books and pictures. She was "at home" in the backstage of a theater as other children were in a cozy nursery.

It was late when her mother, her face pale, with all grease-paint removed, appeared, bending over her and shaking her. "Wake up, Toddy! It's time to leave! Come on! Get up. You're too big for me to carry you anymore."

Sleepily Toddy roused herself and trudged after Mazel as they walked the deserted midnight streets back to the nearby boardinghouse. Usually Flo walked with them, the two young women laughing and chatting, complaining about the manager, Barney, or swapping gossip about other performers. But this night Flo must have left earlier and her mother seemed grimly silent and preoccupied the whole way. Angry. Toddy could always tell and as soon as they reached their room, she warily undressed and slipped right into the sagging brass bed.

From this vantage point, Toddy watched as Mazel, muttering to herself in some invisible dialogue, began packing. Finally, Toddy's eyes grew heavy and she fell asleep while Mazel was still doggedly making trips back and forth between bureau and trunk.

Early the next morning Mazel awakened Toddy, hurried her through a scanty breakfast of bread and jam and tea, then told her to get dressed. When that wasn't accomplished quickly enough to suit her, Mazel began helping, impatiently jerking arms into sleeves, shoving Toddy's feet into her shoes then struggling with the buttonhook to fasten them. She held out Toddy's coat for her, then jammed on her bonnet and tied the strings.

"Here, take this," she said, handing Toddy her small valise. Rushing to the door, she opened it and called over her shoulder, "Hurry up, we haven't got all day. I've got to meet the others at the train station at ten-thirty and we've got a long way to go before that."

With Mazel pulling Toddy along, they got to the trolley stop just as the streetcar rounded the bend. They climbed the high step up into the car and Mazel bought their tickets, asking the conductor to let her know the closest stop to "Greystone." Then they found seats in the nearly empty car. Toddy enjoyed the rocking motion as the car seemed to careen along the tracks, the bell jangling merrily into the morning air. When it jerked to a sudden stop, the conductor turned to look back at them. "Here's where you want to get off, lady!"

Stepping down from the trolley, they saw they were at the bottom of a steep hill. Mazel sighed heavily.

"Come on," she said and, tugging Toddy by the hand, they started up.

They were both breathless when they reached the top and stood in front of a large, stone building. Toddy looked at her mother curiously, wondering what kind of new adventure the two of them were about to embark on.

Mazel straightened her beribboned hat and adjusted her feather boa before ringing the doorbell. She glanced down at Toddy, then leaned over and, retying her bonnet strings, said brightly, "You're goin' to like it here, Toddy, you'll see."

Toddy ran a finger under her chin, loosening the too tightly tied ribbons a little and just nodded.

A few minutes later they were standing in a high-ceilinged room, opposite a severe looking woman seated behind a huge desk. She had introduced herself as Miss Clinock, head matron of Greystone, and was regarding both of them with a frown.

Much to Toddy's astonishment, her mother began to weep into her handkerchief.

"I have nowhere and no one else to turn to and no other way to support the two of us. We are absolutely alone in the world," she said between sniffles. "There's nothing I want more than to be able to make a home for my little girl. Something I can't do now. With the money I'll be paid on this tour, when I come back I'll—" she stopped and blew her nose. Then shaking her head sorrowfully, she continued, "But until then—"

"Yes, well, Mrs. Todd—" Miss Clinock interrupted, clearing her throat—"just so you fully understand the conditions under which we will accept your daughter." She passed Mazel a sheaf of papers. "Please read these over carefully before you sign them."

The room was very quiet for a few minutes; the only sound was the loud ticking of the wall clock, the tapping of Miss Clinock's own pen on the surface of the desk, and the rustle of papers turning as Mazel skimmed them. Then she stood up, placed them on the desk, and signed her name with a flourish. Miss Clinock took the papers and glanced over them.

"This seems to be in order. Except—" She looked up and the eyebrows over the pince nez rose inquiringly. "You have no address for the father? In case—?"

"No, ma'am, there's been no word from him in...well, in a long time...years, in fact."

"All right, Mrs. Todd, you can say goodbye to your daughter now, then we will see that she is taken up to her dormitory and settled in."

Mazel turned to Toddy, bent down, and gave her an impulsive hug. "Now, Toddy, you do as you're told and be a good girl. I'll bring you something nice back from Europe when I come, maybe a big French doll with real hair. You'd like that, wouldn't you?"

For a moment the two of them looked into each other's eyes—Toddy's innocent but puzzled, Mazel's now amazingly dry. Then Mazel blinked and turned quickly away. What Toddy saw in her mother's eyes she could not name but instinctively recognized. It was abandonment.

3

Greystone Orphanage

Toddy sat on the edge of the narrow bed, assessing her new situation. Her feet, now encased in itchy black woolen stockings and shod in sturdy black shoes that laced to the ankles, swung back and forth. She smoothed down the front of the blue muslin pinafore buttoned over a coarse cotton dress. Then she turned up the hem and examined the untrimmed flannel petticoat and biscuit-colored pantaloons. She had been given these in exchange for the clothes in which she had arrived. Those had all been removed by Miss Doby, the matron in charge of Greystone uniform and supplies, with a look of obvious disapproval.

Toddy gave a sigh of resignation. She had always liked the things Mazel paid Tess, the theater costumer, to cut down or make over from her own discarded blouses and skirts into outfits for Toddy. Mazel liked bright colors, patterns and flowered material, lace and ribbon trims, and so did Toddy. But it didn't really matter. She wouldn't be here long.

Toddy looked around the long room with its high windows and the double row of small iron cots. Beside each one was a chest of drawers, on which was set a white enamel washbowl and pitcher. Next to it was an unpainted wooden stool.

So this was the "orphanage" where Flo thought she shouldn't be "dumped."

Toddy was used to sudden moves, abrupt changes in living arrangements. She was not afraid of strangers nor of new places. Her mother had often left her with people she scarcely knew for periods of time varying from overnight to a week or more. Since Toddy had the curiosity of a kitten she enjoyed exploring and experiencing different environments. Her innate sense of adventure enabled her to discover something interesting wherever she found herself.

At her age, Toddy had no real sense of time. Her mother had left her before but always came back. Undoubtedly she would do so this time as well. In the meantime—Toddy gave a little bounce on the mattress but it resisted. She shrugged. It was as easy for Toddy to sleep on the rigid seat of a day coach as on a pile of theatrical costumes or in an empty trunk. She had done all three.

Luckily for her, she could adjust to this set of circumstances as easily as any other.

As she sat there absorbing her new surroundings, she heard the sound of running feet along the linoleum hall outside, the muffled sound of children's voices. Then the dormitory doors burst open and in rushed a group of girls. They halted at the sight of Toddy.

A chunky, red-headed girl, taller than the others, pushed to the front and addressed her loudly. "Hey you! You're new, ain't you!" she asked accusingly. "What's your name?"

Toddy, who always expected to be liked, smiled and got to her feet. "I'm Toddy!"

The girl walked forward, followed by the rest trooping behind her. Approaching Toddy she shoved her fat, freckled face right up into hers and said belligerently, "Think you're smart, don't you?"

The others tittered behind hands clapped to their mouths, eager to see what was going to happen next.

Toddy wasn't used to being around other children, but she recognized a bully when she met one. This girl with her squinty eyes, jutting chin, and pugnacious manner was

threatening her for some reason. Somehow Toddy knew that
the rest of her days at Greystone depended on this moment.
She remembered what she'd been taught by the Carelli
Brothers, an Italian acrobatic team who had traveled with
the troupe for a season.

"No, I don't think I'm 'specially smart, but I can show you a
trick!"

"What kind of a trick?" The girl seemed startled.

"Stand back," Toddy said pleasantly.

The girl backed up a few steps.

With that, Toddy moved from where she was standing
beside her cot out into the aisle. She took a deep breath and
then executed a series of cartwheels down the length of the
room. Over and over she went until she finished the last one
and stood up triumphantly. Hearing a unified gasp behind
her, she turned around grinning. Immediately a cluster of
little girls surrounded her. At that minute Toddy knew she
was accepted. She had defeated whatever purpose the
pudgy redhead, whose name she was told was Molly B., had
intended. And in doing so she had earned the admiration of
the others.

Just then they all heard the snap of wooden clappers and
Miss Massey, their dormitory matron, stood at the entrance.

"Come girls, time for outdoor recreation. Get your
sweaters and form a line to go out to the play yard."

From that time on Toddy's place was established within
the pecking order of Greystone Orphanage. She was a born
leader with a personality like quicksilver, sparkling and
spontaneous. She had a wonderful comedic sense, no doubt
inherited from her wandering father, the elusive Johnny
Todd, and was an effortless mimic. She could turn any situation into an adventure, delighting and entertaining the
other children.

Coming as she did from the drama of the backstage theater world where all was chaos, color and change into this one
where order, discipline and routine prevailed was a drastic

transition. However it might have been harder for her to fit in so easily had she not comforted herself with the belief that she was only a "temporary" placement.

But as the weeks and months passed, the seed of possibility that her mother might never come back to get her began to take hold. She'd received two postcards dashed off by Mazel—one, a picture of Buckingham Palace in London, "where the Queen lives" scribbled on it, the other, written on the boat train to France. There had been nothing after that. Toddy kept those two cards under her pillow, taking them out, examining them, re-reading the brief messages over and over until the edges were worn.

Then one day Molly B. confronted her in the hall.

"Is your *real* name Zephronia Victorine Todd?" she demanded.

One of the first toys Toddy ever got was a set of blocks from Flo who had taught her to spell out her name years ago. This feat had always been a source of pride for Toddy.

She drew herself up and replied, "Yes, it is, why?"

"I'll tell you why, Miss Smarty. I saw your name on the list in Miss Clinock's office. You've been transferred from 'temporary' to 'permanent.' That means you're just like all the rest of us now. An *orphan, no mother, no father, no home!*" With this Molly B. stuck out her tongue and made an awful face. Then, laughing maliciously, she ran off down the hall.

Toddy stood looking after her. A cold chill, like an icy finger, trailed down her spine. Up until now Toddy had held on to the hope that Mazel *would* show up with the big French doll and they would go "home" together to whatever shoddy boardinghouse that might be.

No one else had witnessed the scene between the two girls in the deserted hall, and Toddy told no one about it. Whatever Toddy felt she buried deep inside, and showed no visible distress. It was all hidden behind the smile, the twinkling eyes, the ready wit. Popular with the orphans and staff alike, Toddy seemed carefree and reasonably happy.

But Toddy had no real friend at Greystone until Kit Ternan arrived.

Kit was the quietest person Toddy had ever known. One day Miss Massey brought her to the classroom, and the teacher assigned her to sit with Toddy. She slipped in beside Toddy on the other side of the double school desk Toddy occupied. Toddy smiled at her new seatmate and the smile was shyly returned. Kit had shiny brown hair, neatly parted and braided into two long plaits, and large, clear gray eyes. They shared a reader and a slate to do sums until Kit was given her own supplies. When the recess bell rang, Toddy took Kit in tow, escorting her to the long tables where they picked up their mid-morning "tea" of a slice of buttered bread and a mug of watery cocoa.

Little by little Toddy's warmth and friendliness overcame Kit's initial reticence and the two became inseparable. Kit was given the cot next to Toddy's in the dormitory and after the "lights out" bell, the two whispered confidences. Toddy found out Kit had a little brother and sister who were in the Primary and Nursery sections of Greystone, and that she would be allowed to visit them on Sundays.

"But that's not often enough!" Kit mourned, wiping the tears that kept rolling out of her beautiful eyes. "I've always taken care of Gwynny. She's not used to anyone else, and I *know* she misses me terribly. And Jamie is shy. I'm worried about how he'll be getting along with other boys, 'specially if they're rough and all."

Toddy tried to comfort Kit, but not ever having had any brothers and sisters of her own, she did not really understand. Still, her sympathetic heart and natural instincts helped more than she was aware. After a few Sunday visits Kit seemed somewhat reassured that Gwynny was well cared for and Jamie was getting along surprisingly well.

Toddy lost track of the months she had been at Greystone when the other child who would become her friend and the third member of the little trio that would be jestingly referred to by the staff as "the Three Musketeers" arrived at Greystone.

Laurel Vestal caused quite a sensation among the girls in the dormitory. She looked like the French doll Toddy imagined her mother might have brought her on her return from Paris. She had rosy cheeks, round brown eyes, and dark curls that tumbled over her shoulders and reached her waist in back. She was dressed in a blue velour coat with a short scalloped cape and a matching bonnet she refused to take off. She sat, with her arms crossed determinedly, on the little stool beside her cot, her mouth trembling and tears hovering brightly in her dark eyes.

The other orphans were all watching to see how the matrons were going to deal with this dilemma. Toddy and Kit were especially anxious because the new girl's cot had been placed between their two. They could hear her sobbing at night and longed to do something. As if by mutual agreement, the third night they both crept out of their own beds and, sitting on either side of Laurel, one held her hand, while the other gently stroked her hair away from her hot, tear-wet face.

Eventually, by what means the children never knew, Laurel dressed in the Greystone uniform, entered the classroom, and took a desk not far from Toddy and Kit. At the bell for recess, both girls ran over to Laurel, took her hands, and led her out to the recreation yard.

From then on an unspoken bond was forged between the three, one that would develop into a friendship to last all their lives.

4

Meadowridge

The face of the young man leaning forward from the pulpit of Meadowridge Community Church was earnest. His eyes searched the congregation for the response he sought.

"Picture, if you will, young boys, many eight years old and younger, huddled in doorways, their clothes ragged, their feet shoeless in the freezing cold of a New England winter—or a squalid tenement flat where a sick mother lies in bed covered by a threadbare blanket while her children hover around a cold stove, hungry and bewildered by the circumstances over which they have no control. Consider the plight of three pitiful youngsters shivering in a doorway of a large industrial city abandoned by an alcoholic father—"

Matthew Scott, only recently ordained as a minister, halted and looked into the faces of the assembly of well-fed, well-dressed citizens of Meadowridge. How could they possibly understand what he was trying to convey? "God help me," he prayed silently before going on.

"If this brings a twinge of compassion or a wince of distaste or, hopefully, an urge to help alleviate some of the suffering I have described, then I plead with you now to consider what I am going to propose. The Rescuers and Providers Society, which I represent, has done a mighty work in taking some of these children off the streets and finding homes for them among the warmhearted people of the West. In the generous heartland of our great country, we have found willing families to welcome these helpless children into their loving care, giving them the affection and protection, every child's birthright, of which cruel fate has robbed them.

"In the five years the Society has been actively involved in rescuing these children, providing for them, outfitting them, sending them by train into rural communities throughout the western United States, we have hundreds of stories of children whose lives have been changed, families who have been blessed by their presence.

"I have spent two days in your beautiful town and the surrounding countryside. I have walked your shady streets, looked at your pleasant houses, well-kept yards, observed the faces of the people I have encountered. I have driven beyond the township limits into the rural areas, admired the rolling pastures with sleek cattle grazing, sheep on the hillsides, the whitewashed fences, brightly painted barns, flourishing vegetable gardens and neat farmhouses. Everywhere I have seen evidence of prosperity, contentment, absorbed the healthy wholesome atmosphere, the perfect environment for any fortunate child."

Here Matthew paused, bowed his head, as if he found it difficult to continue. Then, his voice husky with emotion, he went on.

"When I remember the places I have visited in the city—the shacks, the tenement houses, the bleak institutions where dozens of children wait in vain to be adopted—and see the great contrast to life here, I am overwhelmed. But because of it, I am encouraged, yes, bold enough to ask you who live in these bountiful circumstances—will you share what you have been given with others so much less fortunate? Will you take a child—perhaps you have room even for two children—into your homes, to raise in this healthy,

Christian atmosphere? If you can find it in your heart to make such a commitment, I can guarantee that *you* will be beneficiary as well as benefactor. God's generosity can never be surpassed.

"If any of you who have been moved by the testimonies I have recounted and feel led to offer your home to one of these hapless little ones, my wife, Anna, and I will be here—the guests of your pastor's kind hospitality—for the next few days. If you want more information, if you want to talk further with us about any aspect of such an adoption, we will be more than happy to answer all your questions.

"In closing, it is my sincere prayer that next spring when Anna and I are accompanying these children west, one of our stops will be in Meadowridge. Thank you and God bless you all."

After church, Mrs. Olivia Hale came into her house, the enormous Victorian some people in Meadowridge considered magnificent and others called a monstrosity. With its three tiers of balconies, overhanging eaves, elaborate fretwork under the peaked roof, it loomed over the town from its hilltop like a claret-colored giant.

She paused briefly before the hall mirror to remove her hat with its crepe mourning veil and to smooth her hair, untouched by more than a trace of gray. Olivia was a tall, handsome woman in her mid-fifties, dressed in a black faille dress, a black onyx brooch at its high collar, fluted ruching at the wrist of its long "leg-of-mutton" sleeves. Although she had been a widow for more than twenty years, Olivia had never put aside the traditional black. She continued to wear "widow's weeds" more out of habit and lack of interest in fashion than any morbid clinging to the past. Olivia was too strong-minded to live in the past. It was the very real present which concerned her this morning.

She remained standing there a few minutes, not to view her reflection, but because she was preoccupied with her own thoughts. The appeal made by the visiting minister this morning had been very moving, had touched a deep responding chord in Olivia's heart. But it was something she wanted to consider very carefully before she took any action.

As if agreeing with this wise decision, the woman in the glass gave an imperceptible nod of her head. The rather stern expression seemed to soften momentarily as Olivia smiled to herself, turned and went into the parlor.

Moving with the erect carriage of someone much younger, she seated herself in a sculptured mahogany armchair in the bay window. From this vantage point she looked down upon the town and the river beyond. It was because of this fine view that her late husband, Ed, had chosen this spot as the site of the mansion he wanted built soon after he struck it rich in the gold fields and they moved to Meadowridge.

At the thought of Ed, Olivia automatically turned to look at the elaborate gold-framed portrait over the black marble fireplace.

Olivia sighed. Even after all these years, she still missed the towering, raw-boned fellow with his thundering voice, his glass-shattering laugh, his insistence on wearing cowboy boots with the $400 suits he had tailored for himself in San Francisco. Granted, as the years went on, they were hand-tooled Moroccan leather ones, but none the less he must have felt the boots kept him in touch with the "old days."

Olivia smoothed the silky ribbed fabric of her skirt with one ring-encrusted hand. After all the years of following her husband from mining camp to mining camp, Ed had showered her with every luxury once he had made his fortune. He liked the showy kind, such as the huge canary diamond solitaire she wore next to the thin gold band he had placed on her finger when she had married him at sixteen. Beneath a brusque exterior, Olivia was sentimental, and she would never let Ed replace that cheap little wedding ring. Instead, he gave her more rings, brooches, pendants, earrings.

Yes, she missed him *and* their only son, Richard. Left fatherless as a ten-year-old boy, Dick had grown up with the legend of Big Ed and had spent his life trying to live up to his father's reputation, though he was nothing like him in physical build or temperament. Dick was killed breaking a new horse, thrown as he was trying to prove he was every bit the man his father had been. And right before the eyes of his fragile, young wife, Marilee.

Olivia winced as if warding off the shock of it again, as if it had happened just yesterday instead of seven years ago. Marilee had not lived long after Dick's fatal accident. Died of a broken heart, many said. Olivia did not agree. No one died of a broken heart. If so, *she* would have been dead long since. Instead, Olivia had gone on living, bringing up the delicate little girl her son and his wife had left—Helene, her adored granddaughter.

This should have made up for all the heartbreak Olivia had suffered, but there was yet another blow to be borne. It was discovered Helene had a defective heart. Ever since, Olivia had lived from day to day with the threat of losing her, too.

Although Helene was now nearly twelve, she had never been able to attend school or lead a normal child's life. Though Olivia was able to afford tutors, a nurse to care for her, it was not enough. Helene was lonely for companionship, children her own age. The problem was, no normally active child would be content to sit quietly and play lap games, or do watercolors, or read, the way Helene's precarious health required.

Again, Olivia's eyes turned to the lantern-jawed man in the oil painting, whose keen blue eyes seemed to regard her with a mixture of ironic humor and shrewd wisdom. Often in times of indecision or anxiety, Olivia found herself turning to that picture of Ed, whom the artist's masterly skill had brought so vividly to life, as if seeking in some ways the advice she had always sought from him when he was alive.

The words of the young man who had spoken at church that morning echoed in Olivia's mind.

"We plan to bring a specified number of children ranging in ages from five to ten by train next spring, making stops at the towns where folk have agreed to take these children into their homes, adopt them as their own.

"I would remind you of Christ's own admonition: 'Whoever does this to the least of these, will have done it unto me.'"

Olivia had never considered herself particularly spiritual. Oh, she was God fearing and churchgoing, but she had always been a down-to-earth, sensible sort of person. That is why what happened to her as she listened to this earnest young man's appeal was so startling. Quite unexpectedly she had felt a stinging sensation behind her eyes and a definite sharp twinge in the region of her heart. It was almost as if the Lord Himself were saying, "Here is your answer. You have room in your house and your heart for another child—a companion for Helene."

Olivia had felt quite uncomfortable. She had glanced quickly around her to see if anyone sitting near her had noticed anything strange or heard anything. But of course, she knew it was an inner voice. A gentle nudging within, a thought quietly planted but not easily dismissed. She was not given to emotional reactions or sudden demonstrations of religious zeal. However, on the way home in her elegant carriage after the church service, she realized her experience did not fade. In fact the thought grew stronger that this was something she should do.

And if I brought a child to live here—and it would have to be a girl—she would have to be a very special type, one who could adapt herself to a household centered on a young invalid. Would I be able to find such a child among those on the Orphan Train that young man and his wife are bringing out here next spring?

Some of those he described were street urchins. He had told heartrending stories of such children. No, it would never do to have a child with that kind of background come to live with Helene here. Of course, Mr. Scott explained, not all the children had been abandoned, left to live by their wits on city streets. Some were the victims of homes ravaged by incurable illness, death, or desertion by one parent. Many were from "homes such as your own," he had pointed out, where death or disaster of one kind or another had struck.

Scott and his wife were staying at Reverend Brewster's house while they were in Meadowridge. For the next few days they would be interviewing prospective adopting families, he said.

Gradually Olivia's thoughts took shape. She would write a note, outlining her requirements for a child suitable to be Helene's companion—the personality, age, interests that would be necessary in order for her to fit into this household.

Yes, she would do that right away, then arrange to have Mr. Scott and his wife come to tea. Meeting Helene would give them a better idea of what kind of child to place with her.

Having made the decision, Olivia immediately rose, went straight to her desk, took out her fine stationery with the swirled gold monogram at the top, and, dipping her pen into the inkwell, began to write.

5

Greystone Orphanage
March 1890

Anna Scott controlled a shudder as she and her husband,
Matthew, approached the tall, forbidding building behind
the black iron-spoked fence. The afternoon was gray, the sky
heavy with dark clouds. A fierce wind tossed the barren
branches of the few trees. Even though it was the last week
in March, there was not a sign of spring anywhere—not
a crocus, or a green bud, or a robin to give hope of its
coming.

Anna took Matthew's arm with one hand as they
mounted the stone steps; with the other, she held onto her
bonnet while her cloak billowed behind her like a sail.
Maybe the bleakness of the day had something to do with
her odd feeling of depression, Anna told herself.

As they waited for an answer to the doorbell, Anna gazed
at her husband adoringly. Their first year of marriage,
filled as it had been with difficulties, almost constant traveling, strange towns, new experiences, coping with the
obstacles and discouragement, had nonetheless been a fulfilling one. Their love had remained as steadfast as Matthew's determination to achieve his inspired vision.

Since the day he had come to her church and spoken of his
dream to take every homeless child, abandoned or
orphaned, to a Christian home in the rural heartland of the
country, Anna had been unwavering in her admiration,
respect and devotion for Matthew.

She still considered him the most ideal of all possible choices she might have made in a husband, and herself the most fortunate of women that he eventually returned her love and asked her to join him in his quest.

Anna knew she fell far short of the paragon such a man was entitled to in a wife, but she prayed every day to be more worthy.

His high-mindedness, lofty morals, and idealistic goals had drawn her to him with blinding fervor. Now, as all his hopes and ideals were at last coming to fruition, she stood beside him with strong confidence in his ability as he stood firm in the faith that he was doing God-ordained work.

It was her own competence she doubted, her own capabilities that seemed inadequate for the task before them.

Greystone Orphanage was the last institution they were contacting to fill the quota of children they would be escorting west. Matthew had spoken at a dozen churches in these communities willing to receive these orphans.

Anna came from a sheltered home where she had grown up an only child. She had no real experience caring for children. She had attempted teaching a Sunday school once. But with no gift for keeping a room full of lively eight- to ten-year-old boys and girls in order, she had quickly resigned as a volunteer teacher.

How on earth would she manage overseeing a train carload of orphans across the country on the transcontinental railroad? She had asked herself often, with inner trepidation. She would repeat the Scripture verse from Philippians that Matthew was fond of quoting to her whenever she expressed her doubts: "I can do all things through Christ which strengtheneth me."

Just then Matthew turned and smiled at her encouragingly as though he had been reading her thoughts. Anna smiled back, although her lips trembled a little. Then the door was opened by a gaunt-looking woman and Matthew introduced them, saying they had an appointment with Greystone's Head Matron, Miss Clinock.

The woman nodded. "I'm Miss Massey, Miss Clinock's assistant. She's expecting you. If you'll wait here in the hall, I'll tell her you've come."

As she stepped across the threshold into the shadowy hallway, another quotation flashed through Anna's mind: "All hope abandon, ye who enter here." Where had *that* come from? And why should she think of it now?

As they stood waiting they heard the tramp of dozens of little boots and Anna turned in the direction from which the sound came. Two lines of little girls were descending the wide main staircase.

When they reached the bottom, the matron in charge herded them into a single line, straightening the line with little pushes and shoves as she walked its length.

To a less sensitive, observant person than Anna, they might have all looked alike, dressed as they were in identical buff cotton dresses, blue denim pinafores, black stockings, and black high-top shoes. But for some reason, Anna's eyes were drawn to one child who was returning her look with curiosity and interest.

She had a gamin face with round blue eyes sparkling with mischief, and a turned-up nose. Dimples winked on either side of a rosy mouth. Riotous red-gold curls had escaped the tight braids into which someone had attempted to confine her hair.

There was something immensely appealing about this little girl that evoked an immediate response in Anna. Then she noticed the child directly behind her. She had an enchanting beauty that the drab institutional outfit did nothing to diminish. A cameo perfection in miniature, a Dresden doll with rosy porcelain cheeks, dark eyes, wavy dark hair that also defied the restraint of plaits.

She seemed to be daydreaming and had absentmindedly stepped out of line as the matron was passing. The woman halted and said something in a sharp tone, then took her by the shoulder and jerked her back into formation.

Anna was indignant. That was unnecessary, she thought. But even as she watched, she saw another little girl, taller, slimmer. Her shiny brown hair was neatly parted, correctly braided. She remained quietly waiting in line, not wiggling or looking around as the little impish one was doing, nor lost in her own thoughts like the other one. As Anna watched she saw her slip her hand over and pat the shoulder of the child who had been reprimanded. Then the two exchanged a smile.

Something warm seemed to coat Anna's heart at this small unnoticed act of comfort and kindness. Her interest at once focused on the comforter. For some reason these three children seemed to stand out from the rest.

As if sensing Anna's gaze, the child returned her look. Anna drew in her breath, stunned by the sweetness of expression and most of all by the child's beautiful eyes. At that moment the matron snapped her wooden clapper and the line of children began to move forward.

Anna let out her breath slowly. Even though it had lasted a mere second, something indefinable had passed between her and that sad-eyed little girl. Anna was moved to her very depths. For the first time in this entire year of talking about them, searching for homes for them, she realized that the "orphans" who were Matthew's cause, his life's purpose, and through him, now hers, were more than that—they were individuals, each different, separate, with hearts and minds and souls of their own.

Each of those little girls with whom she had had the briefest kind of encounter had their own history, their own story to tell, their own life to live.

And maybe now she, Anna Maury Scott, could be part of it. Maybe in some small way she could help them find the home they needed, the home that would nourish them, love them—

"Miss Clinock will see you now. Come in, please." Miss Massey's voice snapped Anna back to the present.

Gripped by the impact of her new insight, Anna took a seat beside Matthew in the austere office of Greystone's Head Matron. She listened as Matthew discussed the requirements for orphans to be taken on the Orphan Train.

"They must be in good health, and at least old enough to take care of themselves physically, that is, dressing, hygiene, and the necessities. They must be reasonably intelligent, capable of understanding and appreciating the opportunity they are being given."

"And how many from Greystone will you be able to handle?" Miss Clinock asked, her pen poised over a paper bearing a long list of names.

"On this trip we are limited to fifteen children from each of the four institutions with whom we have made arrangements," Matthew answered.

"Only fifteen?" Miss Clinock tapped her bottom teeth with the tip of her pen and sighed. "And so many children need homes—"

"I know," Matthew agreed with a sorrowful shake of his head. "But our resources are, alas, limited, as well. Only two railroad cars have been allotted to us—one for boys, the other for girls. Contributions to our Society are the main funding for this enterprise and we have to figure food along the way, with a contingency fund in case of any unforeseen events, any sort of emergency." He paused. "We expect to be helped out by the prospective adopting families in the towns where we will be stopping. The churches involved plan to have a kind of Orphan Train Day. They will serve a meal, give the families considering adoption and the children time to meet, get to know each other a little, talk together— talk with us. Then the children who are selected will go home with their new parents and the rest of us will get back on the train and go on to the next designated town."

Miss Clinock nodded. "It seems a sound plan. Then you *do* expect all the children to be adopted?"

"That is our fond hope, our earnest prayer," Matthew replied solemnly.

"As you may now know, Reverend Scott, Greystone is largely for the shelter of very young abandoned and orphaned children. We do not keep children after they enter their teens. At that time boys go to the Poor Boys' Home over in Milltown; most go to work in the cotton mill there until they are eighteen and on their own. The girls we divide into two classes. The brighter ones we try to find apprenticeships for in various trades, the rest go into factory work." Miss Clinock sighed, then continued, "What I'm saying is, our babies are pretty much in demand and do not stay here long. Neither do the temporaries, that is, the children who are placed here during family crises of some sort for a short time, and are usually claimed by relatives even if something has happened to their real parents." Here Miss Clinock paused significantly. "It is the older children, the ones *past* that cunning baby stage so attractive to childless couples, who are hard to place." She said with an ironic half-smile. "You know everyone wants a blue-eyed, blond, curly-headed baby girl."

Miss Clinock rose from her seat behind the desk and paced the narrow room again. "So, I suggest I pick a few of these children for you to meet, and then we can decide who are the best potential travelers to take with you on the Orphan Train." She checked the watch pinned to the lapel of her fitted brown bombazine jacket. "The children are at recreation now. It is a half-hour until their midday meal. This would be a good time to see them when they are unaware that they are being inspected or singled out in any way."

She went to the door, opened it, and motioned them to come with her. As they followed her pencil-slim figure down the corridor, Anna breathed a prayer that the three special little girls would be among the children chosen for her to "shepherd" to their new homes in the West.

6

Orphan Train En Route

At the far end of the transcontinental railway car that was now converted into a moving dormitory, Anna Scott sat reading her Bible by the wavering light of an oil lamp suspended from the rack over her head.

She was tired and found it difficult to keep her mind from wandering. They had been traveling for three weeks and Anna was feeling both physically spent and emotionally discouraged. She had never imagined the task she had so willingly taken on would prove so wearying, so mentally fatiguing.

Keeping the children occupied from early in the morning when the first one awakened until the last one settled down at night was exhausting. At first she had tried to set up some kind of routine for the day—washing up, short devotions and morning prayers, then passing out the jam and bread and apples that composed their breakfast, this followed by a semblance of some kind of lessons.

Anna had brought along a map of the United States and pinned it to the wall, showing the children where they were each day and pointing out the next stop. She had taught them a number of games to play in groups, and often she would gather them together to sing hymns as well as songs in which there was clapping or some kind of activity. Still, with all her efforts, the days were long.

One welcome diversion was the frequent stops the train made to take on food for the dining car, water, wood and coal. Then Anna would bundle the children off the train and march them along the platform for fresh air and exercise. If the stop was long enough and there was a nearby field, she would encourage a game of tag or run-sheep-run. This helped the children release some of the pent-up energy stifled by their confinement in the train.

Anna had also brought along some books and read aloud to the girls in the evenings before bedtime and evening prayers—prayers that always ended with the sincere cry of her heart, "That each child will find a loving home."

Of the thirty little girls who had accompanied her from Boston, eleven remained, with only two more towns where they were scheduled to stop, towns which had expressed interest in becoming adoptive parents to some of the children on this trainload of orphans.

But if some of these who were left were not adopted, what would she and Matthew do? In some of the towns where the original response and enthusiasm had been high, only a few people had come forward to claim their adopted children. And those mostly boys. Farm families needed extra "hands," Anna realized. But these little girls needed homes, too.

She raised her head, feeling the tension in her neck and shoulders. She had been searching through the Psalms, seeking verses from which she could find renewed encouragement and strength. But now the words on the page had begun to blur. Anna blinked her tired eyes and looked down the length of the darkened car.

At night the backs of seats were turned down and over, pillows and blankets spread upon them and made into beds. Most of the children were sound asleep. Except for the three huddled together in the far corner at the very end. Judging from the muffled sound of their whispers and giggles, *those* three were still awake.

Anna stifled a smile. Maybe she should get up, go down to them, reprimand them. But, on second thought, what harm were they doing? They didn't seem to be disturbing anyone else.

For a minute, Anna's eyes rested on the three little heads so close together, one a tousled golden mop of ringlets, the next a tangle of dark curls, the third a smooth crown of satiny brown. From the first, Anna was intrigued by this trio. Toddy, Laurel and Kit—such contrasts in every way and yet seemingly inseparable.

Anna frowned unconsciously. It puzzled her that none of the three had yet been adopted. They were certainly among the most winsome of all the girls. Yet at stop after stop, they reboarded the train with the other unselected ones, while some of the less attractive children were chosen right away.

Anna simply couldn't understand why. Just then the murmur of voices grew louder, followed by a peal of light laughter. Anna looked sharply in the direction of this burst of merriment, and knew she must act before they awakened the other children.

She made her way down the aisle between the rows of sleeping bodies, lying in every possible position, until she reached the laughing culprits.

Trying to sound stern, she whispered, "Now, you girls must settle down immediately. You will wake the others up. And tomorrow's a big day. You all need a good night's sleep," she reminded them, tucking their blankets around them.

Returning to her own place at the other end of the car, Anna's questions were still not answered. The sight of each angelic little face lingered in her mind's eye.

These three had everything any adoptive mother could want—personality, alertness, charm. Laurel was so pretty; Toddy, so quick and amusing; Kit with such sweetness, such spontaneous generosity—who would not fall in love with one of them or, for that matter, all three?

She wished she could discuss this dilemma with Matthew. But he was in the other car with the boys and there was no passageway between. Anna sighed. He probably had his hands full with problems of his own, anyway.

During all this journey, she and Matthew had had little chance to exchange more than a few words. They each were so busy with their charges, and at the train stops, dealing with the questions of the prospective parents or the merely curious.

Some of *those* asked the most outrageous questions! Anna's cheeks burned with indignation at some of the tactless people she had encountered. Some made disparaging remarks about the children right in front of them, commenting on their appearance, their size, as if children had no ears, much less *feelings!*

People said things they would never say about another adult. At least not in their hearing. And these folks were supposed to be Christians! It made Anna so furious she often had to send up a hurried prayer for forgiveness at her thoughts.

As she got ready to make herself as comfortable as possible on her own narrow car-seat bed, the same disturbing worry intruded itself. What would they do if some of the children never found a home? What would become of them? Were Matthew and she compelled to return them to the orphanage from which they came? Anna bit her lip. That was one possibility she and her husband had never discussed.

As she plaited her hair, a preview of tomorrow's scene flashed through Anna's mind. If it followed the pattern of the other towns where the Orphan Train had stopped, she knew approximately what to expect.

Looking their very best, hair neat, faces scrubbed, shoes shined, the children would come off the train and line up on the platform where the townspeople were usually awaiting their arrival.

There was always someone in charge, the minister of the hosting church, or his wife, or some members of the City Council. Matthew was the one who handled that aspect. Anna was too nervous overseeing the children, hoping no one had an urgent need to use the "necessary" or that none of the boys would start shoving or poking each other or pulling a girl's pigtail.

Even for Anna, the inspection ordeal was agonizing. She could only imagine what it must be like for the children being inspected!

She never was sure, except in the case of some of the taller, heftier-looking boys who were taken right away by a sharp-eyed farmer, why one child was chosen over another. But tomorrow, Anna determined, she was going to pay special attention to Toddy, Laurel and Kit. She would try to discern why they had not yet been selected for adoption.

Anna bunched up her pillow, curled herself on the unyielding makeshift mattress, and tried to settle herself for sleep. But sleep did not come easily. Those three little faces kept her awake.

Tomorrow she would try to move about, eavesdrop a little, listen to the comments exchanged between the couples looking over the children, try to see what they discussed among themselves. Perhaps she could figure out the riddle of why, out of all the orphans, Toddy, Laurel and Kit remained unclaimed.

Anna closed her eyes wearily. She knew she had broken all the rules outlined by Reverend Macy, the founder of the Rescuers and Providers Society, at the rally just before the Orphan Train pulled out. The cardinal rule: DO NOT ALLOW YOURSELF TO BECOME EMOTIONALLY INVOLVED WITH THE CHILDREN.

"You are there to administer Christian charity, to follow our Lord's admonition to care for the poor, the widows and orphans of this world. Keep in mind that it is your duty to see that these children are placed in good homes," he told them emphatically.

Well, she had failed, Anna sighed. A persistent idea would not go away. If, for whatever reason, no one adopted those three little girls, she and Matthew could take them!

Her own thought surprised her to full wakefulness, maybe because it was the first independent decision she had made in her entire life. She had been a dutiful daughter to her father, and for a little over a year now, a submissive wife to Matthew. How could she possibly be so positive she would make such a life-altering decision without even consulting her husband?

Anna pulled the covers over her suddenly shivering shoulders and shut her eyes determinedly. Before she drifted off, her last conscious thoughts were the words of Scripture from Matthew 6:34: "Take therefore no thought for the morrow, for the morrow shall take thought for the things of itself. Sufficient unto the day is the evil thereof."

In the morning the train chugged into the Springview station, with its engine emitting puffs of steam and the whistle giving a shrill toot. Peering out one of the car windows, Anna saw a crowd of people clustered on the depot platform, craning their necks as the train screeched to a stop and scanning the windows for a glimpse of its cargo.

Anna felt the familiar tightness in her middle, and her palms were damp as she pulled on her gloves. She looked over the children pushing into the aisles, surveying them anxiously.

"Remember be pleasant, polite and above all—smile!" she coached them. "Are we all ready? Come along then," she said, leading the way.

Toddy tugged at both Laurel's and Kit's arms, saying in a stage whisper, "Now, don't forget. Kit, *you* be sure not only to turn your foot sideways, but drag it and *limp!*" Then turning to Laurel, she instructed her, "Remember, hunch up your shoulders, one higher than the other, and twist your mouth. See? Like this." She modeled an awful grimace.

Laurel made an attempt to comply.

Toddy looked doubtful. "Try to stay behind me as though you can't walk right on your own. And I'll—how's this?" she asked, crossing her eyes.

The other two clapped hands over their mouths to suppress their giggles.

"Careful!" Toddy hissed warningly. "This has *got* to work, remember!"

With that, the three fell in at the end of the line of children following the distracted Mrs. Scott out of the train.

For the next half-hour Anna was completely involved in the business at hand, surrounded by inquisitive people with insistent questions.

As soon as they had descended from the train, they were greeted by the Mayor and his wife, who immediately tucked her arm through Anna's and led the way to the Town Hall.

"The church ladies have set out a very nice lunch, brought all their best recipes. We *knew* the poor little dears must be starving," Mrs. McLeod purred. "And *you* must be worn to a frazzle. Some refreshment is what everybody needs. Some food to restore your strength which I'm sure has been sorely tried on this long journey." She patted Anna's arm comfortingly. Not waiting for Anna's disclaimer, she continued, "No matter how good children are—they can be—well, we all know how trying little ones that age can be, don't we, my dear?"

Mrs. McLeod was an indefatigable talker and so Anna did not get in a word all the way on the walk to the Square. At the Town Hall the wives of all the members of the City Council, dressed to the nines for the occasion, were lined up to meet her.

They plied her with cake, coffee and conversation so that she had no chance to keep an eye on the children. But Matthew was there, and she sent up a silent prayer that he had everything under control as she tried to concentrate on what one of the Council ladies was telling her about her sciatica.

At least a half hour passed before a woman, who had been circling and hovering during her chats with some of the other ladies, finally cornered her. Blocking access to anyone else, she planted herself firmly in front of Anna.

Skewering Anna with a cold, stilettolike gaze she burst out furiously. "I must say I think it is reprehensible to mask this endeavor as a charitable effort beneficial to couples who have been deprived of children of their own by bringing these misfits, these cripples, these disabled urchins from the city and try to palm them off on decent folks by playing on their sympathy! We understood these orphans were healthy, strong, ready to work in our homes and fields, to be a blessing not a burden!" She drew herself up indignantly. "Did you really expect to get away with it?"

"I—I don't know what you mean—" stammered Anna. "These children *are* well, perfectly able to do any kind of house or farm work within reason."

The woman stepped aside so that Anna could see around her bulk and pointed across the room. "Then what do you call *those* three!" she demanded with a sniff.

Anna looked in the direction of the pudgy finger, and gasped.

Moving slowly with an exaggerated limp was Kit, carrying a plateful of food from the table to Toddy, who sat slumped in one of the chairs along the wall, the most horrible expression on her face and her beautiful eyes crossed. Following Kit, Laurel was playing the part of a little hunchback to the hilt.

The woman gave Anna another withering glance, and swept out of the door.

For a moment Anna looked after her helplessly, then with her mouth determinedly set, she started toward the three girls.

"Just what do you think you three are up to?" she asked, trapped between laughter and tears.

Before they could do anything but look back at her with startled, sheepish faces, Anna was beckoned by Matthew to meet a couple ready to take one of the other children.

"We'll see about *this, later!*" Anna promised the trio.

Once back on the train she confronted them. "But *why* would you do such a naughty thing?" she asked severely.

The three little girls were abject, but no one answered. "Isn't anyone going to tell me the truth?" Anna continued, studying the three downcast faces. "You all know it's sinful to tell lies, don't you? Well, you were all *acting* a lie, pretending something that was not true. That's just as bad. Why, you should get down on your knees and thank God that you're *not* crippled or deformed in any way. Why on earth would three perfectly healthy little girls want to *look* any other way?" Anna asked in frustration.

"Because we didn't want to get adopted!" Toddy burst out.

"*Not* want to be *adopted?*" exclaimed Anna. "But that's the very purpose of this whole trip! It's the reason you were selected to come on this train. You were picked out of dozens of other children at Greystone who would have given anything to come, and now you say you don't want to be adopted!"

"We don't want to be adopted *separately,* Mrs. Scott," explained Kit finally.

"We've made a pact, you see, to be *forever friends*," Laurel added. "We want to be *sure* we get adopted in the same town."

"So we wanted to wait until the *last* town," finished Toddy with satisfaction, as though now everything was understood and accepted.

"So *that's* it!" Anna sighed. At least the mystery was solved. "Who's idea was this—little charade?" She tried to look stern.

Toddy had the grace to hang her head, but not before Anna spotted that mischievous twinkle in her eyes.

"That was very, *very naughty*," Anna said solemnly, letting her words sink in. Then she turned to the other two. "But going along with it was just as naughty," she scolded. "Remember what happened in the Garden of Eden? Adam sinned as much as Eve when she yielded to the serpent's temptation to eat the forbidden fruit. Adam could have refused to eat the apple, couldn't he? So, you see, you are *all* to blame."

"There *is* only one more town, isn't there, Mrs. Scott?" Toddy asked innocently. "So we won't do that again. But we *do* want to stay together, go to the same school, play together, always be friends. And we figured that wouldn't happen unless we did something about it. We decided it was the best way to keep any one of us from being adopted at some other stop. Don't you see? We thought it was the only way to be *sure.*"

"You could have come to me, told me what you wanted to do. You could have trusted me enough to arrange it instead of—"

All three looked remorseful.

"But could you have *promised* us, Mrs. Scott?" Toddy asked.

When Anna did not answer right away, Toddy shook her head and turned up her palms in a helpless gesture. "You see, we had to be *sure* we stayed together. That's why we did it!"

7

"Meadowridge! Meadowridge! Next stop, Meadowridge!"
That call sent an involuntary shiver down Anna Scott's
spine. This was the end of the line, the last stop on the long
journey that had carried the trainload of orphans across the
country. This stop was the most important one of all. Anna
whispered a quick, silent prayer, a repeat of the same
urgent one she had sent heavenward for the last two hundred miles.

As her prayer took wing, her eyes instinctively sought out
the three little girls most on her mind. They looked like
three little angels this morning, she thought, but not without a sinking feeling in the pit of her stomach. With those
three—you just never knew!

On the surface everything seemed in order; their faces
were shiny clean, fingernails immaculate, hair neatly
braided, clothes brushed and tidy. Toddy, Laurel and Kit
were sitting demurely, hands folded in their laps waiting for
the train to come to a stop. Anna drew in her breath, subconsciously knowing she would be holding it until all three
girls were safely "placed out."

Nervously she looked out the window as the train began
to slow down. It was beautiful countryside they were traveling through—rolling hills, lush farmland, trees with the
pale green haze of budding leaves. Everywhere she looked
gave evidence of the coming of spring.

Anna felt her heart lift. Spring had always been her favorite time of year, with its promise of loveliness after the long winter. They had left Boston in a cold rain. Now they were coming to the end of their journey with the hopeful signs of budding life. It must be a good omen.

Immediately the Scripture verse from Philippians 1:6 flashed into Anna's mind: "He who has begun a good work in you will complete it." Surely God would honor His Word and all these orphans would find homes.

The train jolted to a stop and Anna, standing in the middle of the aisle, quickly steadied herself by gripping the back of one of the seats.

The children now knew the routine and got to their feet, ready to move out of the train and line up for survey. Compassion for the ordeal they were facing made Anna wince inwardly.

Hurrying to where Toddy, Laurel and Kit stood, she bent down and looked earnestly into each face. "No games this time!" she whispered.

The three nodded solemnly.

"If I may say so, Mrs. Hale, you'll live to regret it," declared Clara Hubbard with the familiarity of a longtime servant as she watched her mistress put on her hat.

"You may certainly say so, Clara, but I don't agree. I think it is the best possible thing I can do for my granddaughter. Why, you've heard her a dozen times yourself, I'm sure. Over and over. Helene has always said her dearest wish was for a little sister."

"But, ma'am, what kind of a child will you get from an Orphan Train? They drag the city streets for 'em, so I've heard. The very scum from who knows where? And you want to bring one *here*, into your home, *this* house, to live with Miss Helene, the most delicate of creatures!"

"I have outlined very explicitly the kind of child we are looking for, Clara, and I have been assured that the available children are all healthy, bright, personable," Mrs. Hale replied calmly. Then she added, "Besides Helene herself will make the final selection."

Clara folded her arms on the starched bosom of her crisp white apron and sniffed disdainfully.

"And I might add, Clara, once the child enters this house, she is to be treated as one of the family," continued Mrs. Hale, turning around from the mirror where she had been inserting hatpins into her crepe-trimmed bonnet, securing it to her upswept hairdo. Facing her housekeeper she said sternly. "You *do* understand, Clara? Do I make myself clear?"

"Yes, madam, very clear."

"And I expect you to relay my wishes to the rest of the staff." Mrs. Hale picked up her long kid gloves and started to put them on, carefully smoothing each finger as she did so. "Now, will you please go and see if Miss Tuttle has Helene ready to go with me to the train station."

The housekeeper started out, but at the door she paused and turned back for a final word, "You know, don't you, madam, that Miss Tuttle is upset about this. She don't approve of it one bit." With that Clara gave a little self-satisfied nod of her tightly braided gray head and went out.

Mrs. Hale finished buttoning her gloves thoughtfully. Outwardly composed, she had some inner doubts of her own she had not shared with her housekeeper. Was she doing the right thing bringing in a stranger to live as a companion to her frail granddaughter?

But Helene had been ecstatic when Olivia first broached the idea. Now there was no turning back. That is, unless the child proved impossible, as Clara had predicted she might! Her practical, down-to-earth housekeeper was more often right than not. But in this case, Olivia hoped to heaven she was wrong.

Muted voices in the hall alerted her to the fact that her granddaughter and her nurse were approaching. Olivia hurried to the door to meet them.

"You mustn't hurry so, Helene," Miss Tuttle was saying to the slender, dark-haired girl as they came down the curved staircase.

Attired in a blue velvet coat and matching bonnet, Helene was pale with excitement, but her big dark eyes were shining.

"Oh, Grandmother, it's really time, isn't it? I can hardly wait to see my little sister! I wish they'd sent a picture of her so I could pick her out right away. But, of course, they couldn't. They didn't know which one, but *I'll* know her right away, I *know* I will."

"Now, now, Helene!" remonstrated Miss Tuttle, patting the girl's shoulder while throwing a reproving glance at Mrs. Hale. Shaking her head so that the stiff wings of her nurse's cap fluttered, she said, "All this excitement isn't good for Helene. Do you really think she should go down to the train station with all that crowd, all that confusion?"

Olivia looked at Helene with concern.

But immediately Helene protested. "Oh, Grandmother, please! I want to go. I *have* to go!"

"I think it would be far worse for her to stay at home when she has been looking forward so much to this day." Olivia spoke directly to Miss Tuttle. Ignoring the nurse's sour expression, she said soothingly to Helene, "Of course, you're going, dear."

"Oh, thank you, Grandmother. See, Miss Tuttle, it's all right. I feel perfectly fine. And I want to be there when my little sister gets off the train!"

Clara was standing in the background, her brow furrowed in a frown. Although she and the nurse, whom she considered too high and mighty for her position, rarely agreed on anything, this time they had collaborated in their disapproval of this venture.

"Well then, Clara, tell Jepson to bring the carriage around. We want to get to the station in plenty of time before the train arrives." Olivia gave the order firmly so there would be no doubt of her intentions.

"I've got her present, Grandmother. I hope she likes it!" Helene beamed, holding up a brightly wrapped and bowed package.

"I'm sure she will." Olivia smiled fondly at the child. Because of her illness Helene was small for her age and fragile-boned. Her eyes seemed too big for the thin face that seemed almost translucent in its pallor. But her smile was radiant. A smile so like Dick's, the son she had lost so tragically, that it melted Olivia's heart to see it. If only his daughter had inherited his strength and vitality as well, she thought sadly.

So what if the excitement meant Helene would have to stay in bed for a few days after? It was well worth it to see her so happy today.

The Meadowridge Community Church ladies had outdone themselves with a showcase of the best dishes prepared by the best cooks in the congregation. Some of the recipes on hand had been prize winners at the County Fair. Platters of fried chicken, sliced ham, succulent meat loaf, bowls of coleslaw, potato salad, homemade bread and rolls still warm from the oven, cherry, apple and berry pies, walnut bundt cake, lemon pound cake and chocolate layer cake were set on long tables covered with crisp blue-checkered cloths in the church Social Hall.

This delicious sight made the children's eyes widen and their mouths water. For days at a time, their fare aboard the train was limited to what could be safely stored without fear of spoilage. The daily menu consisted mainly of crackers, jam, oatmeal cooked on the small pot-bellied stove at one end of the car, and dried apples. Sometimes Anna doled out small quantities of hard candies from her hoarded supply. But in general, the menu seemed dismally monotonous. Of course, there were times when the train made longer stops and Matthew was able to go into the town to purchase fresh milk or fruit. However, these were at long intervals.

So it was no wonder that for a few long minutes, the children stood staring, wide-eyed, at the feast spread out before them. It wasn't until one enterprising church lady stepped forward and pushed them gently into line that the boys and girls moved forward to accept plates of food dished out by other ladies standing behind the tables.

While the orphans were treated to a feast, the prospective families were seated around the rooms, watching and murmuring to each other as the children passed before them.

When Toddy was told she would be one of the children designated to go to the Orphan Train out West, she had been filled with excitement. She had packed and repacked the small cardboard suitcase each child was given with the new things issued for the trip and for which each orphan had been made to write a laboriously printed "thank you" note to the Rescuers and Providers Society.

Toddy had been at Greystone longer than either of her two best friends, Kit and Laurel, and although she had seemingly adjusted to the institution, the idea of traveling hundreds of miles by train to a new town and being adopted by a real family sounded like the greatest of adventures to her.

From the time Miss Clinock assembled the selected ones in her office to tell them what was going to happen, Toddy could talk of little else. Subconsciously, she had long ago given up hope that Mazel would ever show up and she would return to the backstage life to which she was accustomed. But neither had she ever completely accepted the fact that she was just like all the rest of the children at Greystone, an abandoned orphan. Toddy's vivid imagination kept creating fairy tales of magical "happy endings" for her future.

But, not even in her wildest dreams, had Toddy expected it to happen so easily and simply as it did.

She was sitting on one of the straight-backed chairs placed around the walls of the Meadowridge Community Church Social Hall, finishing her meal. Because her feet did not quite reach the floor, she hung her heels over the rung to steady herself as she tried to eat daintily. Balancing her plate on her knees was not an easy task—especially when she could feel observant eyes upon her as she took each bite, though Toddy had become fairly used to being watched. "They" had done it often enough, off and on the train at the various stations. Not all the times had been as nice as this one.

Glancing up from her plate, Toddy saw a girl on the other side of the room, looking at her. She was pretty, tall, slim, dressed in a blue dress, with a tucked bodice and pleated skirt. Her dark hair was drawn back from her pale face with a large bow. Her eyes seemed almost too big, but they were sparkling and she was smiling—smiling right at Toddy!

Anna had had every intention of keeping a close watch on Toddy, Laurel and Kit, trying to see that they were never farther than an arm's length away from her supervision lest they forget her stern warnings and revert to their "play-acting" to keep from being separated.

She had even half-harbored the fanciful notion that some family would be willing to adopt all three girls. Of course, this was a practical impossibility, Anna told herself, and her chief concern was that each girl *was* "placed out" in a good home. Still, she *did* want to be able to talk to the adoptive parents and tell them how important their friendship was to the little trio.

Anna glanced over to the table at the other end of the hall where Matthew and Reverend Brewster sat conferring. In front of them were all the children's papers containing their vital statistics—birth dates; natural parents' names, if known; place of birth; release forms of availability for adoption signed by one or both parents, or from the orphanage from which they'd come. After making their choices, the adoptive parents would come here to sign the adoption commitment.

Maybe she should remind Matthew of their discussion about the three before any of their papers were signed.

But before she could do so, her attention was diverted by a woman who introduced herself as Mrs. Kingsley, the Chairman of the Ladies' Guild, who immediately launched into a monologue.

"I wasn't sure whether you knew that although Meadowridge is the county seat, we have many families in outlying districts who regularly come here for church, shopping and so on. You'll be glad to know that we sent out announcements of the coming of the Orphan Train to all these areas so I feel sure people will be arriving all day with plans to take some of these poor little ones."

At this information Anna felt a stab of alarm. She had promised the girls they would live close to each other, attend the same school. If they were taken by a family outside Meadowridge, it might be too far, especially in bad weather, for them to come in to school during the winter. She *must* make sure that didn't happen. She had to speak to Matthew. Hurriedly excusing herself, Anna started over to him.

But she had taken only a few steps when she was halted by an imperious voice.

"One minute, if you please, Mrs. Scott."

Anna turned as a handsome woman, elegantly dressed in fashionable black attire, placed a gloved hand on her arm.

"I am Olivia Hale," she said. "You may remember that you and your husband came to tea at my home on your last visit to Meadowridge. I invited you to discuss my adopting a child, a girl, to be a companion to my granddaughter, Helene. At that time I outlined the requirements necessary in such a child because of the special circumstances of my granddaughter's health. I asked that with these in mind, you select a child and bring her with you on this trip for me to meet."

At her words Anna recalled the day vividly. Matthew had received a note from Mrs. Hale—ostensibly an invitation, but more like a summons—to come to the enormous hilltop home, tiered and towered, overlooking the town of Meadowridge. They had been shown into a magnificently furnished parlor where they were met by the lady, as regal as Queen Victoria herself.

They had been served tea poured from a silver pot into delicate china cups while Mrs. Hale described the type of child she wanted for a companion to her granddaughter.

Afterwards Anna and Matthew had discussed the interview.

"She doesn't want a real child!" Anna declared indignantly. "She wants a paragon of virtue, intelligence, and disposition."

"Yes, she does seem to have forgotten, if indeed she ever knew, what most children are like. No matter how obedient, demure or agreeable, they are still flesh and blood little human beings with all the natural flaws and faults we are all disposed to," Matthew replied thoughtfully. "But we can only do our best to find a child who will fit into that situation."

"It sounds impossible!"

Matthew smiled at her. "Remember, 'with God all things are possible.' We'll just pray that we will find exactly the right child for the Hales."

"I wonder what the granddaughter herself is like," mused Anna. "Given those luxurious surroundings, that doting grandmother, she's probably a pampered, spoiled brat."

Anna felt herself flush, recalling her less than charitable comment. In the busy months since that visit, Anna had almost forgotten Mrs. Hale and her specific requirements. Matthew, of course, had conscientiously written them down and put them in his files. Now as it all came back to her Anna immediately thought of one of her special three, Kit Ternan. Kit, with her sweet quiet ways, her sensitivity and spontaneous warmth would make an ideal companion for a semi-invalid. But before Anna could voice her suggestion, a dark-haired girl with shining eyes was tugging at Mrs. Hale's arm.

"Oh, Grandmother, I've found her!" she exclaimed. "My 'little sister.' She's darling. Look, Grandmother, over there! See?"

Both women turned to follow the direction of Helene's pointed finger.

To Anna's amazement, it was Toddy.

While Helene happily took Toddy by the hand and began regaling her with all the things she had planned to do once her "little sister" came to live with her, Olivia went with Mrs. Scott to fill out the adoption agreement papers.

Her concern over her granddaughter's choice must have been evident because Anna began an enthusiastic recommendation of Toddy designed to counteract any fears Mrs. Hale might have.

"Toddy is a delightful child, Mrs. Hale, cheerful and bright. I think she will be a wonderful companion for your granddaughter."

"Not too lively, do you think?" posed Mrs. Hale cautiously.

"Well, she's certainly not dull!" Anna fielded the question adroitly.

After her first surprise at the selection, the more she thought about it, Anna realized that Toddy *was* the right one. For a lonely child such as Helene, confined as she was and sentenced to a life of limited activity, Toddy would be the proverbial breath of fresh air.

Mrs. Hale pursed her lips, withholding comment. She had never yet denied Helene anything it was in her power to give her, and she wasn't about to start now.

But as she looked over the background information on this child Helene had chosen, Olivia almost faltered. She read:

NAME OF CHILD: Zephronia Victorine Todd
BIRTH DATE: June, 1882   Female, White
Hair, Blond
Eyes, Blue   Health: Excellent
MOTHER: Mazel Cooper
OCCUPATION: Dancer

LAST KNOWN ADDRESS: Rialto Theater No communication since 1886. Child transferred from "Temporary" Status to "Available for Placement"—January 1888.

FATHER: John Todd, Comedic Actor, Song & Dance—Haynes Vaudeville Troupe PRESENT WHEREABOUTS UNKNOWN

Good Heavens! Olivia rolled her eyes, then gamely took the pen and signed the adoption form. Whatever she had gotten herself into, she was determined to see it through. As the Good Book exhorted, having set her hand to the plow, she would not look back. One glance at Helene's smiling face and shining eyes was enough to convince Olivia that however it turned out, this was the only decision she could have made.

"Oh, I'm so glad you've come, Toddy! You can't imagine how I've longed for a little sister," Helene said, once they were settled in the carriage opposite Mrs. Hale. "Oh, Grandmother, isn't Toddy cunning?" Turning to Toddy, she said, "Oh, we are going to have the most wonderful times together. Just wait and see!" And she gave a little bounce of excitement.

Reacting at once to Helene's enthusiasm, Toddy clapped her hands together and gave a corresponding bounce on her side. Helene laughed and then Toddy did and soon they were both laughing merrily as if at some hilarious joke.

Mrs. Hale could not keep her own mouth from lifting in amusement at the two children's delight with each other. Well, maybe it was going to be fine after all, in spite of all Clara's dire predictions and warnings of the dark consequences of bringing a strange child into their lives. Olivia was not given to premonitions, but she had a strong feeling with the arrival of *Zephronia Victorine* that everyone in the Hale household was in for big changes.

8

The first thing Toddy saw when she entered the Hale house was a tall woman wearing a starched white apron, a stiff peaked cap, and a severe expression. She was standing by the staircase in the front hall, arms folded, her foot tapping impatiently. Before Mrs. Hale could say anything, the nurse was at Helene's side, helping her off with her coat, shaking her head.

"Helene looks very flushed, Mrs. Hale. It is my opinion she should go straight to bed and have supper on a tray. I refuse to take the responsibility if she has any more excitement this evening."

"But, I'm not a bit tired, Miss Tuttle!" Helene protested. "And I don't want to leave Toddy on her first night here. Oh, you haven't met Toddy yet, Miss Tuttle. Look, isn't she a darling? Look at her rosy cheeks, her adorable little nose. Isn't she the sweetest thing you've ever seen?"

The subject of this rhapsodic recital smiled hopefully at the nurse hovering over Helene. When the smile was not returned, in fact, was met with a cold stare, Toddy was alerted. This was someone who was not pleased by her arrival. Somewhere Toddy had learned the wisdom of knowing the enemy and in that one chilling moment she recognized hers.

Mrs. Hale looked at her granddaughter anxiously. Helene *did* have unusually high color in her cheeks. There was no use taking chances. After all, she did pay Miss Tuttle a handsome salary to take care of Helene's health. In this case, she would have to rely on her judgment.

"Oh, Grandmother!" wailed Helene. "I feel fine, really I do! Let me stay up for dinner at least! Then I'll go straight to bed. I promise." Helene turned pleading eyes on Olivia, who in turn, exchanged a glance with the frowning Miss Tuttle. She hesitated.

Then unable to resist her granddaughter's plea, Olivia gave in.

"Well, just until after we've had dinner. But then, you must go to bed. It won't do for you to be ill when Toddy has just come. There'll be plenty of time for the two of you to be together, Helene. Toddy is going to be living here from now on. You don't want to be ill tomorrow and not be able to enjoy her company, now do you?" she asked in a reasonable tone of voice.

"Oh, thank you, Grandmother. Come along, Toddy. I want to show you the playroom. When we knew you were coming, we got some toys and games and other things especially—" Helene took Toddy's hand and started upstairs.

"Slowly, Helene!" cautioned Miss Tuttle, hurrying after them. "Don't rush up those steps!" She paused at the foot to cast another reproving look at Mrs. Hale before following the girls.

Ignoring it and her own misgivings, Olivia turned away. Only time would tell if this had been a terrible mistake. Right now all she could see was the happiness in Helene's eyes. She was not going to borrow trouble.

An hour later the three of them were seated in the candle-lit dining room, at the long table covered with a creamy linen cloth and set with gleaming silver and crystal. Helene, who had not stopped chatting, took her place with the ease of familiarity, while Toddy's eyes grew large with the newness of things about her.

At Greystone they had lined up and passed along the serving counters with their plates while the meal, whatever it consisted of, was dished out to them. There were no choices, no seconds.

Here, a man in a dark jacket moved silently from the massive buffet over to the table, bringing a number of covered silver serving dishes, one at a time, first to Mrs. Hale, then to Helene. Toddy watched how they each helped themselves from the dishes he held to their left, while they would help themselves with their right hands. When he approached her with a platter of chops, she still felt unsure.

"Would you like me to serve you, miss?" he asked quietly. She nodded shyly. "Yes, please." Toddy observed as he deftly picked up a chop with silver tongs and placed one on her plate. Next time she would know how.

After that came a silver bowl with a mound of snowy potatoes, then two different kinds of vegetables. Each time, Thomas, as she heard Mrs. Hale call him, would offer her the serving dish for a few seconds, allowing her time to decide if she could manage. He never was obvious about it and, if she seemed uncertain, he then served her a portion.

Toddy was grateful for his discreet help and, when he brought around a covered dish of hot rolls, she gave him one of her best smiles. She couldn't be sure but she thought she saw one eyelid drop briefly in a wink, although his expression remained impassive. Perhaps this kind man would be someone she could count on in this strange new world she had entered.

After she ate the last bite of a creamy caramel custard and the pretty crystal dish was removed, Mrs. Hale told Thomas she would take her coffee in the parlor. At the same time, Miss Tuttle appeared at the door.

"Time for you to go up now, Helene," Mrs. Hale said in a tone that brooked no argument.

Reluctantly Helene slipped from her chair, went over to Toddy and hugged her impulsively.

"Good night, Toddy. I'll see you in the morning." At the door she paused and looked back longingly. "I'm so glad you're here!"

After Helene left Mrs. Hale rose. "Come along, Toddy, we need to get acquainted."

A cheerful fire was burning in the fireplace, the curtains drawn and the lamps with ruby glass globes on the marble-topped tables had been lighted. Mrs. Hale took a seat in one of the chairs by the fireplace and indicated Toddy should take the matching one on the other side.

"Toddy, there are a few things you must remember now that you will be living here. The first is that although Helene may seem fine to you, she has a very weak heart and she must not get overexcited. So you will have to be careful what games you suggest playing. She wants to please so very much that she sometimes extends her strength and then gets very ill. When that happens, the doctor has to be summoned and—well, I think you understand what I'm saying."

Toddy, her hands folded in her lap, nodded gravely.

"Mrs. Scott told me you were a very smart little girl, that you learned quickly. So, I'm relying on you to follow both my orders and whatever Miss Tuttle, Helene's nurse, suggests. Remember, it is for Helene's good."

"Yes, ma'am, I'll remember," Toddy replied, her round little face very serious.

"Good." Mrs. Hale seemed satisfied.

The parlor door opened and Thomas brought in a tray bearing Mrs. Hale's coffee and set it down on the table in front of her.

"Will there be anything else, ma'am?"

"Not for me, Thomas. But ask Mrs. Hubbard to come in, please." After Thomas went out, she said to Toddy, "It's been a long, tiring day for all of us, and especially for you, Toddy, so I think you should go to bed. Our housekeeper will show you to your room, which is right next to Helene's. She's probably asleep by now, so you won't disturb her, will you?"

A knock sounded on the door, and Mrs. Hale called, "Come in, Clara." A stout, gray-haired woman bustled in. She cast a curious, unsmiling look in Toddy's direction, then stood a few feet from Mrs. Hale and waited.

"Mrs. Hubbard, this is Toddy who will be staying with us, as you know. Would you kindly take her upstairs, show her where she's to sleep, and get her settled?"

"Yes, ma'am." The woman nodded, turned and walked briskly to the door. There she speared Toddy with a rapier glance. "Come along."

"Good night, Toddy, sleep well," Mrs. Hale called out as Toddy got down from the chair and followed the housekeeper out of the room.

Clara never looked back to see if anyone was behind her. She just marched up the wide staircase with Toddy hurrying to keep up. At the landing the housekeeper made a turn and went down a long corridor. At the end, she paused at a door and held it open for Toddy, who was trotting as fast as she could down the hallway.

Toddy stepped in and stood, looking around in awe. The bedroom seemed immense, partly because there was only *one* bed instead of dozens of cots. There was a dresser with a tall mirror and two plumply cushioned chairs covered in flowered material, the same as the curtains that were pulled over a curved bank of windows on one side of the room.

Toddy spotted her battered suitcase, very much the worse for wear from the cross-country train trip. It looked somehow forlorn, even if familiar, in the midst of all this luxury.

The housekeeper was turning down the crocheted coverlet on the high bed and fluffing up the ruffled pillows.

"Well, I suppose you have something to sleep in, don't you?" she asked abruptly.

Toddy started over to the suitcase. She really hated to get out the rumpled flannel nightie which she had worn so long and with no chance to launder it—particularly under the sharp eyes of the housekeeper. Everything here looked so new.

"What kind of a name is *Toddy* anyway?" Mrs. Hubbard asked sharply. "Don't you have a decent, Christian name?"

"I've just always been called Toddy." She shrugged. "But my *real* written-out name is Zephronia Victorine."

At this Mrs. Hubbard threw up her hands in a hopeless gesture.

"For mercy sakes! What can people be thinkin' of to dream up such as *that!*" Then, taking one look at the wrinkled nightgown Toddy had lifted out of the suitcase, she gave a huge sigh. "No, that will never do! You can't wear that rag of a thing into a bed that's just been made up fresh. You'll have to wear one of Helene's, even if it does swallow you." She put her hands on her hips and scrutinized Toddy. "I think you'll be needing a bath, too."

Toddy's cheeks flamed with embarrassment under Mrs. Hubbard's critical gaze.

Seeing the little girl turn red, the housekeeper hurried to take the edge off her words. After all, it wasn't the child's fault that her clothes had been packed all that long time. Land sakes, they'd traveled clear across the country, she reminded herself.

Clara Hubbard was a realist. Although she had disapproved of the plan to take in one of the children from the Orphan Train, now that it was a fact of life, she might as well make the best of it. Besides, the child seemed a spunky little tyke. There was no call to be so sharp with her.

"Wait 'till you see the bathroom in this house!" she told Toddy, beckoning her to follow as she opened the door and went out into the hall again.

Five minutes later Toddy was seated in a froth of soapy bubbles in the biggest tub she had ever seen. When Clara had shown her the bathroom, Toddy was speechless. It was every bit as big as the bedroom. Besides the gleaming bathtub with its lion's claw legs set on a platform, there was a porcelain washbowl on a pedestal and a rack beside it, laden with thick towels of every size, edged with cotton lace and embroidered with the initials *OH*. With pride Mrs. Hubbard assured her the rest of the "necessities" were the very latest in modern plumbing.

Using a huge sponge, Mrs. Hubbard scrubbed Toddy until she was pink and tingling all over, then shampooed her hair and vigorously dried it. Finally, puffing with the exertion, the housekeeper dropped the sweet-smelling, lace-trimmed nightgown over Toddy's head, and helped her climb up into the tall bed where she sank into its feathery depths.

Standing over her, Mrs. Hubbard declared, "Well, then, you're all settled. Next time, you can do for yourself, a big girl like you." She spread the quilt over Toddy, then picked up the lamp and went to the door. "So, good night to you."

She went out, taking the light with her and closed the door, leaving Toddy staring into the dark.

Toddy heard the housekeeper's firm footsteps fading as she went down the hall and then everything seemed very quiet. Too quiet. Used to sleeping in a dormitory with dozens of sounds—the sound of others breathing, turning over, coughing, muffled whispers, the squeak of bed-springs—to Toddy the deep silence seemed eerie.

For the first time in her life, Toddy was alone. And she didn't like it. She missed the comforting sense of her companions on either side. She longed to reach out her hand and feel Kit's—or Laurel's responding clasp. She wondered where each of them was tonight and if they, too, were lonely and did they miss *her* as much as she missed them?

There came a stinging rush of tears into her eyes. They rolled down her cheeks and saltily into her mouth. Much as she tried to check them, sobs began to fill her throat and she could not hold them back. She stuffed the end of the sheet into her mouth. Still they came.

But Toddy had learned early that tears never brought an end to what caused them. She turned over, burying her head in the soft, lavender-scented pillows. It would be all right, she told herself. Tomorrow she would see Helene again. Helene had promised they would be "sisters." Tomorrow would be the beginning of that "happily ever after" Toddy had always longed for.

9

Whatever Toddy had expected her life at the Hales to be, she soon discovered it was not going to be a fairy tale.

It soon became quite clear that except for Helene, her presence was resented.

Mrs. Hale, a remote figure who remained at some distance, tolerated her for Helene's sake, but the rest of the household made plain their feelings in various ways.

The day after Toddy's arrival, Helene awakened with a fever and Dr. Woodward had to be sent for. There was a great deal of rushing about up and down the halls as Miss Tuttle issued orders.

Miss Tuttle, now fully in charge, made it known in no uncertain terms what she felt had brought on Helene's fever.

Downstairs, Mrs. Hale awaited Dr. Woodward's verdict. Obviously concerned about her granddaughter, she did not even seem to see Toddy.

For the next few days everything in the Hale residence centered on Helene. Meals were served by a distracted maid named Paula in the small morning room adjoining the big dining room where they had eaten the first night. Other than that, nobody paid any particular attention to Toddy. She only caught glimpses of Mrs. Hale who seemed to pace the upstairs hall outside Helene's room most of the time. Either she wasn't eating or else having her meals served in her own suite at the other end of the hall from Helene's room where she kept an anxious vigil.

Always self-reliant, Toddy occupied herself. This was not hard to do because Helene had provided many new books and games in anticipation of her arrival. The trouble was, most of the toys and games required partners or opponents.

Toddy wandered about listlessly, wishing she knew exactly where Kit and Laurel had been "placed out." But there was so much last-minute confusion at the church social hall after Helene had claimed her that Toddy had not had a chance to find out her friends' whereabouts.

It had all happened so fast Toddy's head was spinning. The next thing she knew they had been rolling along the streets of Meadowridge in the Hale carriage up the hill to the castlelike house where Toddy would live with her new family.

The afternoon of the second day of Helene's confinement, Toddy became restless. It was a beautiful sunny day and much too nice to stay inside. Unnoticed, she slipped downstairs and out the side door into the garden.

It was every bit as big as the playground at Greystone, Toddy realized as she looked around. There were narrow gravel paths winding between colorfully blooming flower beds. Toddy recognized some of the flowers from the arrangement in the bowl in the center of the dining room table; others she had seen in vases throughout the house. She had never seen so many different kinds of flowers. She walked around, stopping to touch them gently, to bend down here and there to inhale their sweet scent.

Then she saw a man in overalls busily trimming the hedges against a spiked iron fence that rose at the outside edge of the garden. Eager for a chance to talk to someone, Toddy skipped over and greeted him cheerfully.

"Hello!"

He turned a scowling face to glance down at her and went on snipping with his wide pointed shears.

"I've come to live here," Toddy told him.

No answer.

"I came all the way 'cross the country in a train," she said next hoping to pique his interest.

Another grunt. The snippers moved without stopping.

"My name's Toddy. What's your name?"

"Ferrin," he growled.

"I'm going to be Helene's little sister," she said brightly, moving along with him as he went to the next hedge.

At this he turned and gave her a hard look. "You're one of them orphans, ain't you? Come on the train?"

"Yes!" she nodded, smiling.

"Well, wouldn't be gettin' no fancy ideas if I wuz you," he said. "Blood's thicker 'n water. Make no mistake 'bout that."

Toddy was puzzled. What did he mean? she wondered. As Ferrin moved forward, she fell into step beside him, ready to pursue his enigmatic remark. But he turned toward her, brandishing his shears.

"Now, go along with you! I'm busy. Don't have time for gabbin'. Got my work to do."

Taken aback by this abrupt dismissal, Toddy whirled around and started down the path in the opposite direction. At the far end was an elaborately fashioned gazebo with a pointed roof and latticed sides. Curious, Toddy headed for it.

What a wonderful place this would be to play in, she thought. It would make a great stage for pantomimes and little skits, if only there were someone to play with, she thought.

Just then she saw a boy's face, topped by a tousled head of tawny hair, peering over the fence at her.

"Who are you?" she gasped.

"Chris Blanchard. Who are you?"

"I'm Toddy. What are you doing there?"

"I'm climbing trees in ole Mr. Traherne's orchard. What are you doing over there?"

"I live here," she replied.

"Since when? Nobody but rich ole Mrs. Hale lives in *that* house," he retorted.

"Not any more. *I* live here and so does Helene."

"Who's Helene?"

"She's my sister. We're sisters and I do *so* live here!"

Chris seemed to be considering that fact. Then he asked, "Wanna play?"

It was just exactly what Toddy wanted to do.

"Sure!"

"Can you climb trees?" he asked doubtfully.

"Of course."

"Well, come on then."

But first Toddy had to figure a way out of the Hales' garden. She was so intent on proving that she not only could climb trees but could also scale the fence into the orchard, that it never entered her mind to ask anyone's permission to go.

It was only an hour later when she climbed back over the fence, minus her hair ribbon, with her dress dirty and sticky with resin, her stockings torn and her shoes scuffed, that she realized she was in trouble.

She and Chris had had a great time climbing one after the other of the low-hanging branches of the gnarled, twisted old trees in Traherne's apple orchard. Chris had turned out to be a jolly fellow once he saw Toddy could match his athletic prowess. He had shared with her some crumbled gingerbread he had stashed in his pocket while they exchanged vital information. They found out they were the same age and would, come September, Chris told her, both be in Miss Cady's class at Meadowridge Grammar School.

It was only at the sound of Clara Hubbard's irritated voice calling her name that Toddy hurriedly said goodbye to Chris and scrambled down from the tree and back over the fence into the garden.

There she found Mrs. Hubbard, hands on her hips, glaring at her as she slid down.

"Well, if you aren't a sight!" she declared. "We've been looking all over for you. Mrs. Hale's been that worried. She thought you'd run away or something. Not that that would worry me none. Come along. Let's get you cleaned up. Helene's feeling better and has been asking for you."

She grabbed Toddy by the arm and pulled her along toward the house. Toddy knew she was in disgrace. But the afternoon had been worth it. Chris was fun, for a boy. And Helene would like to hear all about her adventure, Toddy was sure.

"More trouble than it's worth!" mumbled Mrs. Hubbard as she swiped the dirt off Toddy's face with a damp washcloth. "And what in the world will we put on you?" she demanded irritably.

Instinctively, Toddy knew Mrs. Hubbard was a friend she needed and she looked up into the flushed, frowning face and smiled, saying sweetly, "I'm sorry."

Mrs. Hubbard felt an unexpected thaw in the icy reserve she maintained. In spite of all the extra work this child was giving, there *was* something cherubic in that uplifted face.

"Oh, well, children will be children, I suppose," she sighed resignedly. And maybe after all it would be good for Helene to have this lively little person around. "Now, you're presentable, so go along with you. Helene's been frettin' to see you."

Toddy hurried along to Helene's room where Miss Tuttle stood sentinel at the door.

"Now, you're not to tire, Helene, you understand," she said severely.

"No, ma'am," Toddy answered meekly knowing that she might have won over Mrs. Hubbard, but Miss Tuttle was still a formidable hurdle.

10

On doctor's orders Helene had to stay in bed for the remainder of the week. But Toddy was allowed to spend a good deal of time with her. She learned this privilege was at Helene's insistence and with Mrs. Hale's reluctant consent, despite the advice of Miss Tuttle.

"Now you mustn't tire Helene" was the repeated caution.

How in the world could you tire someone who was sitting up in bed on mounds of ruffled pillows propped against its curlicued headboard, playing Parcheesi? Toddy, sitting cross-legged at the foot of Helene's high, shiny brass and white enameled bed, the board game between them, pondered the question.

Helene's room was the grandest Toddy had ever seen. Carpeted in soft green with designs of large roses in pale pink, its tall windows were curtained with white dotted Swiss tied back with enormous pink taffeta bows. Wallpapered in patterns of trellised roses, the room blossomed like a garden bower. On a pink marble-topped table beside Helene's bed was a tall lamp with a beautiful glass shade with painted roses on it.

Dominating one side of the room were bookcases filled with books, more than the orphanage library! Facing these on a long table was a large globe of the world. This was where Helene had lessons when she was well. A lady came to teach her at home since she wasn't strong enough to attend regular school, she had told Toddy.

A door opened out onto a little balcony with a cushioned lounge chair for Helene to lie on and white wicker chairs and a matching table where she had lunch on warm, sunny days. The trays were brought up by Paula, the maid, who would have been pretty except for her sullen expression and a mouth in a perpetual pout.

Toddy was puzzled about Paula. She tried smiling at her every time she saw her—whether in Helene's room or when they passed on the stairs. But the maid only tossed her head and turned away, never speaking. It bothered Toddy to feel Paula didn't like her for some reason. But, then, the most important thing was that Helene *did.*

And Toddy had loved Helene right from the beginning. Who could help loving someone who thought you were adorable, who laughed at everything funny you said, and wanted to hear all about you?

For some reason Toddy wasn't sure she should tell Helene about her life before Greystone. That life had become rather vague even in her own mind in the last two years, almost like a dream, or something that had happened to someone else. The Carellis, Flo and the other dancers, even her mother, Mazel, had faded into the gray regions of memory. It was only every once in a while, mostly when she was drifting off to sleep at night, that Toddy would remember something about that life—a snatch of a song she had learned by listening to it every night from the wings, or the flash of the vivacious Donna and Doug, a "song and dance" team, who were always so nice to her.

Anyway, what Helene was mainly curious about was Greystone. She wanted to know what it was like in an orphanage, a place she had only read about in stories.

"You know, Toddy, *I'm* an orphan, too," Helene confided one day. "If it weren't for Grandmother, I would probably have been put in an orphanage just like you. My mother and father are both dead. I hardly remember either of them."

Toddy almost said that *she* wasn't *actually* an orphan, that *her* parents weren't dead. But she bit her tongue. For at Greystone she had long ago stopped saying, "My mother is coming to get me soon," especially after Molly B. had taunted her about being moved from the "temporary" to "available for placement" list in Miss Clinock's office. Toddy *knew* Mazel wasn't dead and that her father was "somewhere," though she had not the slightest idea *where.*

But Helene seemed to like the idea that they were *both* orphans. That fact seemed to bring them closer, make them more like *real* sisters. And whatever made Helene happy, Toddy began to understand, was what was important in the Hale household. As long as Helene was happy, Toddy's place was secure.

So Toddy began to regale Helene with stories about Greystone, some true, some she made up, embellished with fine dramatic flair.

"So did you have many friends there?" Helene questioned her.

"Well, I had two special ones," Toddy told her. "Kit and Laurel. They got 'placed out' here in Meadowridge, too. I guess we'll all be in the same class at school."

"Oh, do you know who took them? Where they are?" asked Helene excitedly.

"No-o-o," Toddy drawled. "I wish I did. I'd like to see them."

"Well, Grandmother can find out!" Helene exclaimed. "Then maybe we can have them over—"

"Really? That would be fun!" Toddy gave a little bounce, upsetting the Parcheesi board, and they both laughed. As they began picking up the markers, Toddy said, "You'll like Laurel and Kit, Helene. At Greystone we—" she halted, then leaning forward and lowering her voice, she asked conspiratorily, "Want me to tell you a secret?"

"Yes, of course. I *love* secrets," Helene assured her, even though she had never had one to keep before.

"You mustn't tell anyone—" Toddy began—"though, I guess it doesn't matter anymore. And Mrs. Scott found out about it anyway." Then Toddy proceeded to describe how the three of them had worked out a plan to avoid adoption until the last stop on the cross-country trip, to insure they would all three stay in the same town.

"Oh, Toddy, if you aren't the limit! The whole thing was *your* idea, wasn't it?" Helene giggled.

Toddy dimpled and nodded. "But we *had* to do it, Helene. You see at Greystone we promised each other we'd be 'forever friends' and there wasn't any other way."

As it turned out, Toddy was to see Laurel and Kit sooner than she expected. Part of the agreement when The Rescuers and Providers Society "placed out" a child in a home was the stipulation that the children would receive a Christian upbringing and regularly attend Sunday school. To Toddy's delight when Mrs. Hale left her in the Sunday school room at church the following week, the first child she saw was Laurel.

But earlier that morning there had been the first of many incidents with Miss Tuttle that subsequently would not endear her to Helene's nurse.

Since Helene was still running a low-grade fever, she would not be accompanying her grandmother and Toddy to church that Sunday. But Helene had a surprise for Toddy—a new dress and hat for her to wear, purchased in secret by Mrs. Hubbard after Toddy's arrival. Helene told Toddy to come in after her bath and finish dressing in her room before leaving for church.

Helene eagerly watched Toddy's eyes widen as she pushed aside the tissue paper in the big box, kept hidden until that moment. Almost reverently she lifted out the white serge "middy" dress, trimmed in dark blue braid, with a pleated skirt and a red scarf for the collar. The white straw "sailor" hat had long blue streamers. There were white stockings and white buttoned shoes to complete the outfit.

Standing there in her cotton camisole fastened with buttons onto ruffled bloomers, Toddy was speechless. "Oh,

Helene!" Toddy said in hushed tones as she held up the dress.

"Well, go ahead, try it on!" urged Helene, pleased at Toddy's delight.

Toddy looked at her, eyes sparkling mischievously, then jammed the straw hat on her head and went into a spontaneous little "sailor's jig." Without missing a beat, she started singing:

When I was a lad, I served a term,
As office boy to an Attorney's firm,
I cleaned the windows and I swept the floor,
And I polished up the handle of the big front door.
I polished up the handle so carefulee,
that now I am the Ruler of the Queen's Navee!"

Helene laughed and clapped her hands.

"Oh, Toddy, that's marvelous! It's from *Pinafore*, isn't it? Grandmother took me to see it when we were in San Francisco last year!"

Encouraged by her enthusiastic audience, Toddy did another verse and another until a razor-sharp voice sliced through the song, "Stop! Stop that at once, you irreverent child!"

Toddy stopped mid-jig and turned to see Miss Tuttle standing in the doorway. Her flushed face was the picture of outrage, her eyes bulged in indignation, even the starched wings of her nurse's cap bristled. "Need I remind you that this is the Sabbath? I'm shocked, positively shocked. And you, Helene. I'm appalled at you condoning such a vulgar performance. And on *Sunday* too!"

But Helene did not look in the least shocked, Miss Tuttle noticed as she bustled over to her bedside, carrying a tray with her medication on it.

"But, Miss Tuttle, it's from a Gilbert and Sullivan operetta, the Admiral's song from *Pinafore*!" Helene came to

Toddy's defense. "The composers are very famous. One writes the music; the other, the words to the songs. All their musical plays are very popular in England. Even members of the Royal Family have attended them. Isn't Toddy clever to know all the words? To be able to sing like that?"

Miss Tuttle suppressed the angry rebuttal that sprang to her lips. She might have known Helene would defend the little street urchin Mrs. Hale had brought into this house. She probably sang for pennies on city streets before she was rescued and taken to an orphanage. And that's where she should have remained, in Miss Tuttle's opinion. From the first she had heard of it, she had thought that it was a foolish risk, a mistaken act of charity bringing these children out West on the train, palming them off on gullible people, placing them in decent homes, with no thought of the effect. She had said as much to Mrs. Hubbard. She was astonished that a sensible woman like Mrs. Hale would agree to it. But, then, she would do *anything* for Helene, even something as foolhardy as this!

But *this* vulgarity was going too far! Miss Tuttle had learned about the child's background from Clara Hubbard, who had seen the adoption release papers Mrs. Hale had signed, and she had been stunned. What could you expect of someone who came from that sort of life! Her parents— *vaudeville performers!*

Yes, Miss Tuttle assured herself, when she reported *this incident,* Mrs. Hale would certainly see her mistake in allowing this child to associate with her granddaughter.

Miss Tuttle pressed her lips together primly. She poured out the thick, syrupy medication into a spoon and offered it to Helene who took it submissively. Filling a tumbler with water, she handed that to her as well. Then she turned to Toddy.

"Take your things into your own room, young lady," she said sharply, "and finish getting dressed without delay."

Miss Tuttle busied herself straightening Helene's covers, thinking all the while just what she would say to Mrs. Hale.

Behind her back the girls exchanged smiles and winks, but Toddy left.

Later, in replaying for Mrs. Hale the shocking scene in Helene's room, Miss Tuttle could not have been more disappointed at her employer's reaction. To her chagrin, Mrs. Hale had listened impassively to the recital, then passed the entire matter off as unimportant. She even seemed annoyed that Miss Tuttle had brought it to her attention.

"But—but aren't you even going to reprimand the girl?" Miss Tuttle gasped.

"Reprimand?" Mrs. Hale frowned, seeming not to understand the question.

"Punish her for breaking the Sabbath in such an outrageous way? Singing music hall songs and dancing?"

"I don't think the incident calls for any sort of punishment, Miss Tuttle. Evidently, Toddy was entertaining Helene, and Helene was enjoying it very much. So if I punished one, I must punish the other, and I have no intention of doing either."

"But, madam, aren't you concerned about the bad influence this child might have on Helene?" protested Miss Tuttle.

"I think Toddy has been a very good influence on Helene, Miss Tuttle," Mrs. Hale said coolly. "I've never seen Helene as happy or heard her laugh so much as she has since Toddy has come." A smile softened her firm mouth as she continued in an effort to placate the irate nurse. "I even think the Lord Himself might approve, Miss Tuttle. Making a sick child happy is all I see Toddy doing. She is helping Helene in ways all the doctors I've consulted, all the medicines, the care and attention she has had, have not. If I remember my Proverbs correctly, isn't there something about a 'merry heart doing good like medicine'? I believe Toddy is 'good medicine' for Helene."

Miss Tuttle retreated, but she was undaunted in her own conviction that bringing this disruptive child into her well-ordered domain was a dreadful mistake. Mrs. Hale would rue the day, Miss Tuttle was sure.

As she walked haughtily out of the parlor where she had confronted her employer with her indignant report, Miss Tuttle's thoughts were in turmoil. She had never been so humiliated. In other homes where she had done private duty nursing, her word was law. But Mrs. Hale had dismissed her as she might have an ordinary servant—as if she might have been Paula!

If the position did not pay so well, she thought, she would give notice. And, *of course,* if she weren't *absolutely* devoted to Helene. No, it was her duty to stay here and try, somehow, to combat the influence of that child.

Oblivious that she had incurred the wrath of a determined adversary, Toddy blithely entered Sunday school and found herself an immediate success. Lively, bright, and enthusiastic, Toddy was always the first to volunteer to hand out the weekly Sunday school tracts, collect papers, pick up crayons. The teacher, Glenda Harrington, who had been a little apprehensive of the addition of three of the Orphan Train children into her class, was amazed.

At the mid-point, when the class treat of milk and graham squares was served, the three girls shared information about their new homes. Kit was living on a farm just outside town, the only girl in a family of five boys, and Laurel told them that the doctor who had examined them upon their arrival had taken her home with him to be "his little girl." Toddy, of course, had the most to tell about Helene and her new life at the Hales'.

When Miss Harrington lined up the children to re-enter the church for the final hymn and benediction, Toddy noticed Chris Blanchard, her tree-climbing companion in the Traherns' orchard the week before, in the middle of the boys' line. She almost didn't recognize him in his white shirt with his unruly hair slicked down. When she smiled at him, he looked blank, then stuck out his tongue, his face turning scarlet. Toddy shrugged. Boys!

After her reunion with her friends, Toddy looked forward to Sundays. Sometimes Helene felt well enough to go to church, but she sat with her grandmother for the service because there was no class for her age group. Most often, only Toddy accompanied Mrs. Hale in the grand carriage each Sunday.

By the Fourth of July Toddy had been at the Hale home nearly six weeks. She had no idea what a big celebration this holiday was until the week before.

They were having lunch in the small, sunny breakfast room, with all the windows open to the garden letting in the soft June air, when Helene said to Mrs. Hale, "But Toddy shouldn't miss all the fun just because I can't go, Grandmother. Couldn't Paula take her to the park so she can see the parade and play some of the games? Then Toddy could stay with the Woodwards who adopted her friend Laurel. I'm *sure* they're going and I'm *sure* they wouldn't mind having Toddy. In fact, they'd probably like for Laurel to have someone to be with. Please, Grandmother!"

Toddy looked from one to the other expectantly.

"Well, the servants *do* have the day off—" said Mrs. Hale slowly. "We'll ask Paula if she would take Toddy—" She lifted the small silver bell by her plate and tinkled it gently. Paula appeared as if by magic. She dropped a little curtsy.

"Yes, madam?"

"Paula, we were wondering if you would take Toddy along with you over to the park on the Fourth of July? After the parade you can leave her with Dr. and Mrs. Woodward who will be picnicking there."

Toddy, watching Paula hopefully, thought she detected a look of dismay as the maid darted a quick glance at her. But her only outward reaction was a bob. "Of course, madam."

"Thank you, Paula. It's settled then. I'll send a note to Mrs. Woodward with you," Mrs. Hale said, picking up her spoon and returning to her fruit compote.

Helene's back was to the doorway where Paula stood so no one else saw her eyes narrow into daggers as she glared at

Toddy. It was such a cutting look that Toddy shrank back into her seat. She wished the subject had not even been brought up. She'd almost rather not go than have Paula so angry about taking her.

In the rush of excitement about the Fourth, Toddy eventually forgot that moment of fear. The children in Sunday school were full of talk of the races, games, and the concession booths at the park on the big day. And there would be firecrackers, too, and sparklers and the big display put on by the town once it got dark, with Catherine wheels and Roman candles.

Finally the day arrived and when Toddy went into Helene's room early in the morning, a slight feeling of apprehension returned. Climbing up on Helene's bed, she asked anxiously, "Are you sure you don't mind my going?" Her blue eyes were troubled.

"No, of course, not, Toddy! I *want* you to go! I've been a few times and it's lots of fun. Besides, Grandmother says you can invite Laurel and Kit to come home with you and we can all watch the big fireworks from my balcony. She's already checked with Mrs. Woodward, and Laurel can come. You're to ask Kit when you see her at the park. The family who adopted her will be there. *Nobody* in Meadowridge would miss the Fourth of July celebration."

"You're *really* sure? I don't like leaving you here all day by yourself."

"Yes! *Yes!* I'm *sure.*" Helene laughed. "Go on, get ready. Paula will want to leave early since it's her day off."

Since Toddy had never seen Paula wearing anything but her prim, blue-striped uniform and apron, she thought she looked especially pretty in a ruffled shirtwaist—a red checked skirt with a wide belt cinching her small waist— and a shiny straw hat wreathed with red poppies.

Toddy had to trot to keep up with Paula as she hurried down the stairs, out through the kitchen, along the garden path, and through the back gate. Once out of sight of the house, Paula grabbed Toddy's arm and gave her a good shake.

"Now, listen, you little pest! I'm only taking you as far as the park! I'm meeting my own friends and I'm not spoiling *my* day by havin' you tag along. You're plenty big enough to take care of yourself. And you're not to say a word about it to Miss Helene or Mrs. Hale, you understand?" she hissed. "You think you're better'n me, livin' upstairs like you were somethin' when you're nuthin'. Nuthin' at all. Just becuz Miss Helene took a fancy to you don't mean you're special, 'cause you ain't!" Her grip tightened painfully. "If anything happens to *her* you'd be out on your ear, quicker'n you can say Jack Robinson! You'd have to go beggin' like you probably did afore you come! Or worse still, be somebody's skivvy if you're lucky, peelin' spuds and havin' nuthin' to eat but the skins, and sleepin' in the cellar with rats!"

Paula's face was all red with the exertion of her vicious attack.

"So you better listen good to what I'm sayin' or you'll be sorry, you hear me?"

Toddy nodded, feeling the cruel pinch of Paula's fingers on her upper arm.

"So come on." Paula let her go, straightened her hat, which had come askew while she had been delivering her diatribe, then started down the shady sidewalk toward the park, with Toddy following behind.

The day had darkened miserably. Paula's words hung like a weighted chain around Toddy's shoulders. She knew Paula meant every word and that the maid probably was right. Toddy's future was as fragile as Helene's health.

Afterward, a shadow had fallen on the bright sunshine in which Toddy seemed to move. Although within months Paula had left the Hales' employ to marry and move away from Meadowridge, those heedless words spoken in anger etched themselves on Toddy's subconscious mind and remained there long after her childhood.

11

January 1891
Mrs. Anna Scott
c/o The Rescuers and Providers Society

Dear Mrs. Scott,

In compliance with the requirement in the provisional adoption agreement I signed for the housing, care, and welfare of the female orphan, Zephronia Victorine Todd, I herewith submit a progress report.

The above-mentioned child, called "Toddy," has in all respects adjusted well in our household. She is of cheerful disposition, obedient and eager to please. My granddaughter Helene, for whom Toddy has functioned as companion, is very fond of her. They spend many happy hours together, playing, talking and reading. Helene tells me Toddy is very bright and loves to look at travel picture books, wanting to learn about foreign countries and other peoples. She seems to absorb and retain a great deal of what she reads and can converse quite well about the things she is learning.

Although my granddaughter's delicate health requires her to be tutored at home, Toddy entered the local school in September in a combination fourth and fifth class. Her first report card at mid-term showed high grades in Elocution, Composition, Botany, weaker marks in Arithmetic and History. These, her teacher assures me, should improve as her concentration and reading skills progress.

Olivia's flowing script slowed, then paused. Her pen poised, she rested her chin upon her hand and looked out the window beyond her desk. Should she say anything about the day Toddy had come home from school, her face smudged with dirt and tears, her hair ribbons gone, her dress mud-stained and rumpled?

Mrs. Hubbard had come to Olivia in a state quite unlike her usual placid self. Looking up from her needlepoint, Olivia had asked the housekeeper for an account.

"Well, ma'am, it seems Toddy got into some trouble in school."

"What kind of trouble?" Olivia frowned.

Clara looked uncomfortable. "A fight, ma'am, on the play-ground. Her teacher has sent home a note."

"Well, then, let me see it."

Clara reached in her apron pocket and drew out a folded piece of paper, handing it to Mrs. Hale.

Olivia's eyes raced over the few lines.

"It doesn't seem all that serious. Miss Cady doesn't say whose fault it was, just that I should question Toddy about it and make it clear to her that such things as kicking and hitting are unacceptable behavior." Olivia looked up from the note. "But I'm sure Toddy knows that already. Was she hurt?"

"No ma'am, but—" Clara hesitated, "I think she gave the Blanchard boy a bloody nose."

"Bernice Blanchard's son?"

Clara nodded.

"My word!" exclaimed Mrs. Hale. "What was it all about, do you know?"

"The most I could get out of her was some of the children began taunting Toddy's friends, the two other little Orphan Train girls—well, Toddy rushed to their defense, it seems. Just plunged into whoever was doing the teasing—I don't know how the Blanchard boy got mixed up in it—"

"Very well, Clara. I'm sure it will all straighten itself out."

Mrs. Hale's pen began to move again.

"Toddy is very loyal to people she cares about," Olivia wrote.

She had almost forgotten the unpleasant scene with Bernice Blanchard, who had come storming up to the house demanding to see Olivia and had flown into a tirade.

Olivia smiled to herself somewhat grimly. It had been a "tempest in a teapot" certainly, but the underlying prejudice had to be confronted. She had made her own feelings very clear when she had scoffed at Bernice's making a fuss. But later she had made a trip to the school to talk to Miss Cady. She suggested it might be well to talk to the whole class about the virtue of charity, the importance of acceptance, fairness and kindness to one another.

Since then there seemed to have been no more trouble of that sort. At least, if there was, Toddy never mentioned it and her school life seemed to go along smoothly.

Once more Mrs. Hale began to write.

"Toddy has settled in well, has friends at school, gets along with apparent ease with everyone with whom she has contact. We feel she will continue her present progress.

"Our holidays were very pleasant. My granddaughter was excited about having a young child in the house this year, so Helene took great delight in planning many secret surprises for Toddy. She was particularly anxious to make this Christmas special since Toddy confided she had never had a 'real' Christmas. We had a tall evergreen on our property cut and brought in for the girls to decorate. They spent days making circles of gilt paper chains and strings of cranberries and popcorn to drape on the tree. Then we ordered ornaments from a mail catalog to hang, as well.

"On Christmas Eve we attended the program at the church put on by the Sunday school children, then came home to open the presents that had been placed under the tree."

Olivia stopped writing again, thinking about the scene that night.

The spicy scent of the tall cedar, heightened by the warmth of the house, filled the parlor with its fragrance. Thomas and Mrs. Hubbard had hurried to light all the candles when they heard the carriage wheels on the drive outside so that when Mrs. Hale and the girls came in, the sweeping branches of the tree were ablaze with light.

Her eyes, wide and brilliant, her mouth a round O, Toddy stood on the threshold, unable to move or speak.

"Go on, Toddy, don't you want to open your presents?" Helene urged, eager to see her reactions to all the surprises she had chosen for her "little sister."

There were wonderful books, games, pretty things to wear, and a big box pushed way under the lower boughs that Toddy opened last.

Olivia recalled the strange incident that happened next as they both watched Toddy tear away the wrappings and take off the lid of the box containing the big doll Helene had picked out for her "because, Grandmother, do you know Toddy has *never* had a real 'store-bought' doll?"

Slowly Toddy had lifted it out, exquisitely dressed with an angelic bisque face framed in long dark curls, and stared at it. Olivia exchanged a glance with Helene. This subdued reaction was not what they had expected. You would have thought a doll like that would have elicited cries of delight, that she would have been hugged and held and admired extravagantly. Instead, Toddy's face was expressionless and after a while she laid the doll gently back in its box, then turned to a colorful picture book about Holland.

Later, when Olivia had gone into Helene's bedroom to say good night, Helene registered her disappointment.

"I thought Toddy would adore the doll, Grandmother," she said, puzzled.

"Maybe we were mistaken, dear. Perhaps Toddy is too old for dolls."

It was a mystery to both of them. Neither could guess that at the sight of the beautiful doll, a phantom had crossed Toddy's heart. A scene flashed into her mind—that small painted face, with its pointed chin and huge dark-lashed eyes, brought a hurting memory painfully alive. The long-gone mother, the unfulfilled promise, and Mazel's parting words—"I'll bring you something nice back from Europe when I come, maybe a big French doll with real hair. You'd like that, wouldn't you?"

Toddy never played with the doll. It sat stiffly propped against the pillows of the window seat in her room, a silent reminder of a past growing dimmer but a hurt never healed.

January 1892
Mrs. Anna Scott
c/o The Rescuers and Providers Society

Dear Mrs. Scott,

Toddy has been with us now for nearly two years and we are very well pleased with her progress, as I hope you will be.

She was promoted to the Fifth Grade, with A's and B's in all subjects, and is reported by her teacher, Miss Millicent Cady, to be attentive in class, diligent in studies, prompt with her homework. She is particularly fond of reciting and does well with oral reports and compositions.

Her disposition is consistently pleasant, her table and other manners much improved, and her overall demeanor is continually growing in refinement.

She is helpful and considerate in many ways around the house, not only in regard to Helene, my granddaughter, when she is unwell, but also is constantly finding ways she can be of assistance to me. She is generous and seems to find great pleasure in helping others.

As you know I had some reservations about taking Toddy as Helene's companion at first because she seemed altogether too lively and vivacious to be content in a life of a household necessarily centered on a semi-invalid child. But with each passing day I become more convinced we did find the "right home for the right child" as you and Mr. Scott said was your goal.

Sincerely,
Olivia Hale

January 1893
Mrs. Anna Scott
c/o The Rescuers and Providers Society

Dear Mrs. Scott,
It is hard to believe that another year has passed and that I am again sending you the required annual report on Toddy. She is so much a part of our household now that it is difficult to remember when she was not here. As my granddaughter remarked not too long ago, "Grandmother, wasn't our life boring before Toddy came?"

Indeed, I do not know what my granddaughter's life would be like now without the companionship of this child. Her life, I am much afraid, would have been not only boring but without much joy and very lonely. Deprived as she has been of the natural childhood environment of school, companions her own age, and the normal diversions and activities of a healthy girl, Toddy has been a real godsend to Helene. She brings her vibrant health, vivacious personality, her many activities into the sickroom to share with Helene. Even our doctor has remarked on the beneficial effect this has had on his patient.

By the above, I would not lead you to believe that Toddy's life is absolutely subverted to that of Helene's

invalidism. Toddy has her own friends, regular outdoor exercise (this winter she learned to ice-skate and
has gone sledding with her school friends), and is
active in all sorts of events in both school and church. I
just wanted you to know that her devotion to Helene is
remarkable and I believe they really do consider each
other "sisters."

Again, I must commend you and your husband for
the marvelous work you continue to do in finding
homes for these unfortunate children who, through no
fault of their own, are left homeless. It is my sincere
hope that other families who open their homes to one of
these will be as satisfied as we have been.

Cordially,
Olivia Hale

January 1894
Mrs. Anna Scott
c/o The Rescuers and Providers Society

Dear Mrs. Scott,

I hope your trip to the Holy Land this fall was both
edifying and enjoyable. Both the girls enjoyed the postcards you sent them and talked of nothing else for days
but that one day, when Toddy was finished school and if
Helene's health permitted, they, too, might make such
a pilgrimage.

Speaking of Helene's health, we have both good and
bad reports to make. She was feeling strong enough
this summer for me to take the girls for a few weeks
stay at the seashore, hoping the mild climate and brac-
ing ocean air would be beneficial. It did so seem and for
weeks after our return, she seemed much stronger.

Unfortunately in the beginning of winter, she
caught a bad cold which developed into pleurisy, and
we were all quite anxious about her recovery. I must

tell you, Toddy was a devoted nurse to her during her illness (provoking the very vocal complaints of the obsequious Miss Tuttle, I must add with some amusement). However, Helene seemed to quite prefer Toddy's ministrations to the aforementioned, which makes me wonder if perhaps Toddy has a talent in that direction and if we should encourage her to take training when she completes her high school education.

She also did a very nice recitation at the school Christmas program this year. She is growing into a very pretty young woman, delicate-boned, graceful and with a spritely charm.

From all this, you will gather we are a very content household and continue daily to be grateful to your society for placing Toddy with us. Enclosed you will find a check for a donation that will show my gratitude for the fine work you are doing in bringing the Orphan Trains west.

> With all good wishes to you and
> your husband, I am,
> Olivia Hale

12

"Grandmother, I want to give Toddy a birthday party," Helene began. "You see, she's never had one. Not ever. And she'll be thirteen and that's a very important age, don't you think? I mean, once you're into your teens, no one considers you a little girl anymore. It's a special birthday and I want to make it special for Toddy."

May sunshine flowed in through the windows of the dining room where Olivia and Helene were having breakfast alone, since Toddy had already left for school.

"I'd like it to be a surprise party. We could keep everything secret until the last minute. What do you think? Please say yes, Grandmother."

Mrs. Hale carefully buttered her toast before replying. Could it actually be *five* years since Toddy had come to live with them? Good heavens, how quickly the time had passed, she thought, giving an imperceptible shake of her head.

Helene, watching her grandmother closely, mistook that as a sign her request was being refused. Disappointed, she tried again. "I promise I won't overdo and Clara will help me. Won't you change your mind, Grandmother?"

"Change my mind?" Mrs. Hale exclaimed. Then a hint of a smile softened her expression as she realized Helene had mistakenly anticipated a negative answer. "No! Indeed I'll not change it! I think giving Toddy a party is a splendid idea."

Helene blinked, then grinned in understanding. "Oh, thank you, Grandmother! I can't wait to see Toddy's face when we all yell 'Surprise.'"

Helene had already planned the party in her mind and she quickly enlisted the housekeeper's help to bring it to reality. There were consultations with Cook to concoct the perfect menu. It would be a luncheon served in the garden, for the early June weather was sure to be pleasant. There would be chicken salad, and tiny sandwiches, a fruit mold, lemonade and a marvelous cake—Toddy's favorite, an elaborate German chocolate, which was also the cook's specialty.

No effort was spared to keep the whole thing a secret. Helene designed and painted lovely watercolor invitations to send out to six of Toddy's friends, which, of course, included Laurel and Kit. Along with the time and day, there was a strict admonition to keep the party a secret. It was to be a complete surprise for Toddy.

Busy with all the events of the last week of school, Toddy, usually so aware of everything going on around her, was preoccupied. She did not seem to notice conversations that came to an abrupt halt at her approach or stopped completely when she entered a room. Concentrating on the poem she was to recite in the closing program, Toddy, uncharacteristically, was oblivious to everything else.

On the morning of the party there was a conspiracy of silence in the Hale household. No one was to mention Toddy's birthday. At breakfast, Helene asked Toddy if she would go downtown and do a few errands for her. Toddy readily agreed. Helene told her there was a handiwork project she wanted to start, and Toddy was given a long list of miscellaneous items she needed. It was a list guaranteed to keep Toddy occupied and away from the house for at least an hour or two.

Meanwhile, the balloons would be blown up and strung around the gazebo where the party table and chairs would be set up and decorated, and the brightly wrapped birthday presents piled nearby. Her unexpected guests would arrive and be hidden in the garden until it was time to spring the surprise on Toddy.

Clara was to watch for Toddy and then alert everyone to quiet down and stay hidden until she sent Toddy out to the garden on some pretext. Then they could all jump from their hiding places and shout "Surprise! Happy Birthday!"

Helene's face was flushed and Mrs. Hale glanced anxiously at her as she fussed over the table, moving the centerpiece of fragrant roses, smoothing the pink tablecloth, or straightening one of the place cards in the small porcelain flower holders that were to be party "favors" for each guest to take home.

Miss Tuttle had complained several times during the weeks of planning that Helene was doing too much, getting too excited. Being hostess for this lively group of girls, she maintained, was dangerous for someone of such fragile health. But Mrs. Hale had put aside her own concern and withstood the nurse's protests.

"Let her enjoy herself, Miss Tuttle," she said firmly. "Helene doesn't get many chances like this. If she has to stay in bed tomorrow—well, so be it. I don't want this event spoiled for her by gloomy predictions that will only make her nervous."

Olivia hoped she wouldn't regret her directive. All her life Helene had had to listen to this sort of cautionary advice and walk on eggshells while everyone around her held her breath. Planning this party for Toddy had given Helene enormous pleasure, and Olivia was determined it wasn't going to be ruined for her.

Everything went according to plan and Toddy arrived home, a little breathless from hurrying, a little concerned because she had not been able to find all the items on Helene's list. Helene, of course, had made sure of that by adding some supplies which would almost certainly be unavailable.

When Toddy stopped to explain to Mrs. Hubbard why it had taken her so long and how she had not been able to find some of the things Helene wanted, Mrs. Hubbard shuttled her out to the garden, saying Helene wanted to see her the minute she got home.

As soon as Toddy stepped outside, she was greeted by shrieks of "Surprise!" and "Happy Birthday." Toddy's face was Helene's reward.

Mrs. Hale stood at the parlor window which overlooked the garden, watching the fun and festivity. At a sudden burst of laughter, she smiled. What a good time they were having. Helene had been right. It was a wonderful idea to give Toddy a surprise party for her thirteenth birthday.

My, how the years go, she sighed. If Toddy was thirteen, the meant Helene was nearly eighteen—an age to which she had not been expected to live. Mrs. Hale breathed a prayer of thanksgiving. Helene seemed so much stronger. Surely Toddy's coming had given her the will to live. At least she was more *alive,* happier since Toddy had become her "little sister."

"Excuse me, madam." Clara's voice interrupted Olivia's thoughts. She turned to see her housekeeper standing in the doorway, a strange expression on her face.

"Yes, what is it, Clara?"

"There's—well, ma'am, there's a *person* at the front who *insists* on seeing you."

"A *person?*" Olivia frowned. "What do you mean? What kind of person?"

Clara darted a quick look over her shoulder and started to say something more, but before she could do so, she was pushed aside by a gaudily dressed woman who walked past her and into the parlor.

"Mrs. Hale?"

Olivia glanced questioningly at Clara then back at this stranger who had addressed her in a husky voice. At first, she was most aware of the hat the creature was wearing—a plumed affair that looked as though it weighted down her head. Under its brim emerged masses of curls that could only be described as orange. Her outfit was cut in the latest style, but the material was cheap, the workmanship shoddy. She carried a parasol that she tapped as she set it down in front of her.

She was young, in her early thirties Olivia guessed, pretty in a coarse sort of way. Her features were nice enough, but her complexion was obviously heightened by a liberal use of cosmetics. She had a theatrical look, a flamboyance in both dress and manner that unconsciously repelled Olivia.

"You *are* Mrs. Olivia Hale?" the woman repeated.

"Yes," Olivia replied coldly and was about to ask, "And who are you?" when the woman placed both hands on the handle of the parasol, leaned forward on it and announced, "I'm Mazel Todd, Mrs. Hale, and I've come to get my daughter."

These startling words, spoken in an exaggerated imitation of an upper-class English accent, sent a chill racing through Olivia's body. She felt every muscle in her body stiffen as she stared back at the woman.

To gain time, she let her gaze sweep from the quivering feathers on the astonishing hat down to the pointed toes of the high-heeled boots. All the time her mind was racing; she tried to gather her wits about her enough to absorb what the woman had said and deal with this unexpected, but dreadful turn of events.

The eyes of the two women were locked. It was Mazel who blinked first and glanced away. She had expected something, anything rather than this stony silence. She shifted her feet, then twisted the long, sleazy silk gloves she was carrying and fiddled with her beaded purse as she glanced around.

She did not miss a thing worth taking note of—the polished mahogany furniture, the crystal candlesticks on the mantelpiece with their glittering prisms, the marble-top tables and velvet upholstery. Her survey seemed to stiffen her posture.

"Is she here? My little girl, Toddy?"

Mrs. Hale gestured to one of the fan-backed armchairs.

"Won't you sit down, Mrs.—Todd."

Mazel hesitated a second then minced across the deep-piled carpet to the chair Mrs. Hale indicated. As she passed, Olivia thought she detected, in addition to a heavy scent of perfume, a whiff of something suspiciously alcoholic.

With a swish of her skirt, Mazel perched on the edge of the chair.

All Olivia's instincts tensed for battle. She felt certain this sudden, unexpected appearance meant trouble. What kind Olivia wasn't sure but, like an experienced soldier, she braced herself for combat.

She waited for the woman to speak, but Mazel was preoccupied, her eyes roaming greedily around, appraising everything. Olivia was forced to open the conversation.

"May I inquire how you happened to come here, Mrs. Todd?" Olivia asked. "And what is the purpose of your visit?"

"I told you. I come for my kid, that's what!" Mazel retorted, immediately on the defensive, her affected accent gone.

"But, Toddy lives *here* now. I adopted her, Mrs. Todd. I signed papers from the Rescuers and Providers Society who brought the children from Greystone Orphanage west by train for placement."

Mazel's face flushed.

"Them people had no right to do that. I didn't give them no permission for her to be adopted!"

"Surely, you understood when you left her at Greystone that children left over six months are made available for adoption?"

"I don't remember any such thing," Mazel snapped. "How did I know our troupe would get another engagement to tour the provinces in England? Then after that we went all over the Continent. We was billed as headliners in theaters in Germany and Austria. We had posters in five different languages sayin' we'd played before the crowned heads of Europe, we did." She preened herself, then added, "But I never expected to be gone this long."

"You've just returned from a—European—engagement, then?" Olivia asked.

Mazel's flush deepened. "Well, no, not *just*. I mean, we got back but we went on the road again right away and—"

"You must have checked with Greystone as soon as you returned to the States to see about Toddy, didn't you?"

Mazel shifted uneasily. "Well, not right away. I knew, I mean, I *assumed* she was safe and well took care of there and—" Mazel opened her purse and with a flourish pulled out a hanky dripping with lace, and dabbed her eyes. "And then when I come to get my baby girl, they told me she was gone!"

"*Seven years later?*" Olivia's voice emphasized the irony of this statement as she raised skeptical eyebrows.

Defiant, Mazel lifted her chin. She put the handkerchief away and glared at Olivia.

Olivia ignored the look and pressed on.

"I understand Toddy was only six when she was brought to Greystone. Didn't it occur to you that she *might* be put up for placement if you didn't come back for her within six months? You *had* to have signed release forms with that stipulation when you left her at Greystone in the first place," Olivia persisted.

"I don't recall signin' no such thing!"

"You *did* sign such a paper though, Mrs. Todd. I *have* such a paper with your signature on it," Olivia replied evenly.

"I don't believe it! Where?"

"In my safe deposit box at the bank. Along with the other papers I myself signed."

Mazel dropped her eyes, started to fidget with the chain on her purse, knotting it, then unknotting it.

"How did you find out where Toddy was?" persisted Mrs. Hale.

"I run into an old friend who knew about the Orphan Trains. They keep records, you know."

"But Greystone is clear across the country, in Massachusetts. You mean to say you traveled all this way to get Toddy? Where do you live, Mrs. Todd? Where is the home you're going to give Toddy located?"

Under the rouge Mazel's face reddened again. "What do you mean?"

"Just what I asked. If you propose to take Toddy away from this comfortable home, where do you plan to live? Where is she to go to school? She's very bright, you know. In another year she'll start high school." Mrs. Hale's voice was very matter-of-fact.

Mazel looked flustered. When she didn't reply right away, Olivia followed up with another question.

"How did you happen to come here to Meadowridge, Mrs. Todd? It isn't exactly on the main road from Boston." A definite tinge of sarcasm was evident in Olivia's tone. Observing Mazel's discomfiture, Olivia pressed her advantage, her words clipped and sharp. "Do you want to hear what I believe is the truth, Mrs. Todd? I think somehow your...*profession* brought you into the vicinity. And somehow, I'm not quite sure how, you found yourself near where you learned your child had been placed. But—" here Olivia paused significantly—"I don't think you had any intention of coming to take Toddy until you learned who had adopted her...and saw this house."

Mazel's eyes widened. She looked startled, then a little frightened. Olivia knew she had called the woman's bluff. Somewhere in the back of her mind, she remembered seeing an ad in the newspaper about a dance troupe being part of the midway entertainment at the County Fair at Minersville, the next town over. That was *it!* After having found out where Toddy had been sent, Mazel must have known she was close enough to check it out. A few pertinent questions would have given her the address of the Hale mansion, plus the information that Olivia Hale was the wealthiest woman in town.

Trusting her intuition, Olivia prodded. "I think your curiosity brought you here, Mrs. Todd. And maybe a little greed. I think somehow you've done some investigating and discovered Toddy is my granddaughter's companion and very important to her. I believe you thought if you could come here and threaten to take her away, I would offer you some financial compensation for not doing so."

"Why, why—" Mazel sputtered. "That's insulting!"

"I believe it's true," Olivia declared quietly. "But, I also feel children should be with their natural parents whenever that is possible. And since you have come such a long way, and gone to so much trouble to find her—you must now be able to provide for her adequately." Olivia watched Mazel shrewdly, noticing her instant agitation. "I think we should let Toddy decide for herself."

"But, but—" began Mazel.

"She is outside in the garden with her friends. They're having a party. You know, *of course*, what day it is?" Olivia's eyes held hers in an unwavering gaze.

Mazel's mouth twitched in a nervous smile. "Oh, sure, I come by the school and seen it was closed. It's the start of summer vacation, right?"

Olivia did not bother to reply. Inwardly outraged that the woman didn't even remember it was her own child's birthday, she asked, "Shall I call Toddy in now, let her choose?"

Mazel jumped up. "Oh, I don't want to take her away from her friends." She paled under the garish makeup. Her hands fluttered, wringing the handkerchief. "Goodness knows if the kid would even remember me...it's been so long—" Her voice trailed away weakly as if she knew she had trapped herself by her own words.

"*Hoist with her own petar,*" Mrs. Hale quoted to herself with grim satisfaction.

"So, Mrs. Todd, what do you propose to do now?" Olivia rose to her feet also.

"Well, I didn't mean to upset everybody." She shrugged, saying uneasily, "You're right. I don't have a proper home for a kid—a growin' young girl, I mean. We're tourin' all over the state, doin' the Fairs and then we're on to 'Frisco. California, you see. The company don't pay for families to travel with the dancers—I mean, it wouldn't be no life for a kid," she floundered.

"It's up to you, Mrs. Todd. Do you want to see Toddy? Take her with you?"

Mazel was panic-stricken. Her plans had collapsed. She was caught by this steely-eyed woman like a hooked fish on a line. Mentally, she flogged the friend who had egged her on to come here once she found out Toddy had been "placed out" with the wealthy Olivia Hale. She wished she'd never bothered that woman at the Rescuers and Providers Society with her story, putting on that act about being so shocked to find Toddy gone, so that the woman had broken the rules and given Mazel the Hale address, happy at the prospect of mother and daughter being reunited. They were both wrong.

Shamefaced, Mazel mumbled, "I guess—I want to do what's best for her—the kid—for Toddy."

"Then, let us agree on it." Olivia unclenched the hands she had unconsciously been gripping so tightly in her lap during this interview. She walked over to her desk. "If you will sign a written statement that you will not try to contact me or Toddy in any way until she is eighteen, I shall write a check to cover all your expenses in coming here." She slid a piece of her expensive monogrammed stationery onto the blotter, picked up her pen, dipped it in the inkwell. Her quick, firm handwriting quickly covered the page with a few strong, clear sentences; then she beckoned Mazel over.

After Mazel had signed it, Olivia sat down and wrote out a check, folded it and handed it to Mazel, who hastily slipped it into her purse as if Olivia might snatch it back.

"Good afternoon then, Mrs. Todd." Rising and moving to the parlor door, Olivia held it open. Mazel scurried out without glancing at her hostess.

The same stern-faced, gray-haired woman who had let her in the house earlier was standing just outside the door in the hall and, without a word, opened the front door for her to exit.

On the front porch Mazel took out the check, unfolded it and gasped. The sum was far more than she had ever expected! Maybe she should have been a little tougher, prolonged the suspense, made the old lady dig a little deeper.

Just then she heard the sound of girlish voices, a peal of laughter from around the side of the house. Mazel's curiosity got the better of her, and she went down the porch steps and walked around the house, her French heels teetering in the velvety soft grass. A high ornamental fence enclosed a formal garden. Mazel moved closer, peeking through the railings.

In the white-latticed gazebo she could see about a half-dozen young girls, dressed in pastel-colored dresses, gathered around a table, beautifully decorated with pink streamers and flowers, and piled high with brightly wrapped presents. They all seemed to be laughing and talking at the same time.

Which one was Toddy? Mazel wondered, pressing her face closer holding on to the iron posts. There was an older girl, slender, fragile-looking, the only one whose hair was worn up, who seemed to be in charge of things. Then there was another smaller one, with flyaway reddish-gold hair, moving like quicksilver. There was something about that one—

Johnny Todd! That same lightening grace, those dancing steps! That's *her!* Mazel's grip on the railings tightened. Something unfamiliar was squeezing her chest, making it hard to breathe.

Then Mazel shrugged and turned away. The kid had a good life. Why should she feel guilty? She'd probably done her a favor leaving her at Greystone.

In the parlor Olivia sank slowly into the sofa. She was trembling, and her heart was beating erratically. She was far too old for this kind of tension. What a brazen piece that woman was. Thank God, she'd been able to read her mind, to see through her trickery. Thank God, she had the money. If she hadn't, would Mazel have carried it off? Taken Toddy with her, introduced her to the shoddy, backstage life she herself was living? As pretty and talented as Toddy was, an unscrupulous stage manager might see the possibilities in her—

Olivia closed her eyes, drew a suddenly shaky hand across her brow, and took a deep breath.

A discreet knock on the door was followed by Clara herself, bringing a small tray.

"I thought you could do with a spot of tea, ma'am," she said, putting it down on the table in front of Mrs. Hale.

The two women exchanged a wordless look. It was enough.

Then Clara stepped back, folded her arms, and with a nod toward the windows said, "The girls are havin' the time of their lives. And if I may say so, ma'am, sendin' that woman packin' is probably the best birthday present Toddy's ever had!"

13

The Class of 1900

The afternoon sun was sending long shadows across the grass as the four tennis players, having finished their set, prepared to go home. Tying the strings on her racket cover, Toddy shook back her hair impatiently. Her face was flushed from the exercise, and a few new golden freckles spattered her pert nose.

Beside her, Chris pulled a white, V-necked, cable-stitch sweater over his dark, tousled head.

Laurel and Dan, on the other side of the court, were talking in low tones when Toddy called to them. "Coming, you two?"

Dan picked up both their rackets. "Coming."

They joined Toddy and Chris at the gate of the tennis court and the four of them walked across the wide expanse of lawn in front of Meadowridge High.

"Has anyone done the final book report yet?" Toddy asked.

Chris moaned. "Ugh, don't mention it. *Ivanhoe!* So dull."

"Dull?" echoed Laurel. "I thought it was wonderful, so romantic!"

"Then maybe you can help me write a two-thousand-word theme on it," suggested Chris, looking hopeful. "I keep getting the characters mixed up, can't keep track of what's going on."

"Chris! Do your own work!" Toddy reproached him. "Why do you always expect other people to rescue you?"

"*Rescue*? You mean like a gallant knight rescuing the fair damsel from the tower of the wicked king?" he retorted, striking a dramatic pose with one arm held against his forehead.

"No! I didn't mean *that*! Not unless you consider yourself a damsel in distress!" she retorted. "But you do act like a young prince sometimes! I've seen you trying to wheedle someone into doing something for you that you're too lazy to do yourself—for example, make yourself read something you don't particularly like."

"Well, what's wrong with getting some help from a friend? If Laurel enjoys *Ivanhoe*, maybe she'd like to tell me about it and then I can write my report from *her* report!" argued Chris.

"It's not right! It would be better to turn in a report telling *why* you *didn't* like *Ivanhoe* than give a second-hand version of someone else's report," she explained as if talking to a two-year-old.

"And get an 'F'? When everyone knows Mrs. Harrison *adores* Sir Walter Scott and everything he writes?" countered Chris.

"At least he knows who wrote *Ivanhoe*," Dan intervened, laughing.

"Thanks, my friend," Chris said. "See, Dan knows you're falsely accusing me of dishonorable motives."

"You men! You always stick together!" declared Toddy.

"Why not? You girls certainly do. Toddy, Laurel and Kit—the invincible, inseparable trio—"

"You're deliberately changing the subject," Toddy said severely. "We were talking about how you always expect special treatment. Like royalty! The Prince of Hemlock Hill." She made an exaggerated sweeping bow. "What is your highness's pleasure? How can we serve you, O Prince?"

"*You* should talk! It's the Hale house that looks like a castle, not my humble abode, even if it is on Hemlock Hill," Chris snapped back.

Dan and Laurel exchanged glances. They were used to the way Toddy and Chris baited each other.

"But I'm only a lowly servant, not the Crown Prince of the royal house of Blanchard!" jeered Toddy, her blue eyes twinkling.

Though he knew she was teasing, Chris colored under his tan, and Toddy, realizing she might have gone a little too far, eyed him warily. Then, as he made a snatch for her hair ribbon, she dodged and started to run. Chris took off after her.

Even though he was a natural athlete, Toddy was small and light and very fast. She whisked through the iron gate of the Hale's impressive Victorian home and shut it. Breathless and laughing, she leaned over the gate as he came panting up on the other side.

"Tortoise!" she teased.

"Don't you ever let up?" he scowled.

"Not when you're such an easy target!"

A worried expression crossed Chris's handsome boyish face and he asked, "Toddy, you don't really think I'm—well, all you said, do you?"

She put her head to one side as if studying him intently.

"Well, only a little—" The dimples on either side of her rosy mouth winked. "You know you wouldn't *object* if Laurel, or better still, *Kit*, would write your book report for you, now be honest, would you?"

"Come on!" Chris was derisive. "Even *you* might be tempted to have *Kit* write something for you!"

"I do my *own* work! I might not be the best student, but I respect *integrity*, even if it means getting a low grade."

Chris looked skeptical. "Toddy—" he began.

"Oh, well—" she pursed her lips in contemplation. "I'll admit it would be *tempting*—Everyone knows Kit's the writer in the class. But that's not the point!"

"Now, take back the rest of what you said," Chris demanded.

"I don't remember what I said—"

"You know the part I mean, about my being the 'Prince of Hemlock Hill,'" Chris insisted.

"Oh, *that!*"

"Yes, *that!*"

"I must have hit a nerve, if you're so upset about it!" Toddy taunted.

"Come on, Toddy."

"But, *that* part *is* true, Chris. You know it is. Your mother spoils you silly!"

Chris knew there was *some* truth to that and decided not to deny it. Instead, he changed the subject. "Did I tell you my father is taking me up to the University the week after graduation? There's some kind of alumni weekend, a father-son sort of thing. He wants to introduce me to the right people up there in case I don't get an athletic scholarship or in case my grades aren't acceptable."

"Oh, you'll get in, Chris, no question." Although she didn't say so, Toddy felt sure Mr. Blanchard had pulled enough strings to ensure his son's acceptance into the University he was so proud to have graduated from himself. He'd do it, no matter what it took—a sizable donation to the building fund or even a new building! Or preferably a gymnasium or basketball court where Chris could star.

"I don't know exactly how I feel about going to the University when it comes right down to it," Chris said slowly. "I don't like the idea of going so far from Meadowridge, for one thing. I mean, I guess it will be interesting and the sports stuff will be fun, but—" Chris stopped mid-sentence. The words he was fumbling to say left him—escaped in his sudden realization of how pretty Toddy was.

Funny, he'd never noticed before. She's always been, well—just *Toddy*. Now he gave her a sidelong appraisal. In the slant of the setting sun, her red-gold hair flamed to life, curling fetchingly about her pixyish face. The lithe, neat figure fairly burst with energy. But it was her eyes that held him—sparkling, always hinting of mischief and what was that French phrase? *joie de vivre!* He grinned. Wouldn't she be impressed to know he could come up with *that?*

"What's the matter?" Toddy prodded. "Are you afraid of being homesick?"

"No! It's not that," Chris said indignantly, coming out of his reverie. "It's just that it will be a long way to come—I mean, I'll miss seeing you, Toddy."

Toddy seemed pleasantly surprised, but her tone was amused. "They let you out for holidays and good behavior, don't they?"

"Doggone it, Toddy, aren't you ever serious?" Chris said, losing his temper. He leaned over the gate and yanked off her hair ribbon. She made a futile grab for it but Chris was already backing away.

"So long! See you tomorrow!" he called over his shoulder, and trotted down the street toward Hemlock Hill.

"I'll get you for this, Chris Blanchard, see if I don't!" Toddy shouted after him. But all she heard was laughter as he turned the corner.

She shook back her hair, now tumbling all around her shoulders in a riot of ringlets and started up the path to the house. She just reached the bottom step when the front door opened and Mrs. Hubbard, the housekeeper, stood there, glaring.

"What gets into you, I'd like to know? Carrying on like a regular hoyden with that Blanchard boy right out in front of the house! And look at you, hair every whichaway, shirt-waist coming out of your skirt! Tsk, tsk!" Clara Hubbard shook her head in despair. "Come along inside. Miss Helene's been wondering about you, said she was supposed to help you study for your history exam tomorrow!"

"I almost forgot, sorry!" Toddy murmured as she skipped past the disapproving bulk of the housekeeper and sprinted up the wide staircase, calling as she went, "I'm coming, Helene. Sorry I'm late!"

Nearing the top of Hemlock Hill, Chris slowed to a trot as the large, gray house his mother always referred to as "our Queen Anne" came into view. Chris winced. Maybe Toddy was right. Sometimes his mother *did* put on airs. It made him squirm to think of it.

Maybe it was just because she was proud of being the wife of the president of Meadowridge Bank, the *only* bank in town. But that didn't make them "royalty" or make *him* a "prince"!

He halted and looked at Toddy's hair ribbon still in his hand. Rolling it up, he jammed it into the pocket of his tennis flannels and walked slowly toward home.

Chris wished his mother wasn't always pushing him to ask other girls out, accept invitations to parties given by people he didn't care anything about. He didn't want to be with anyone but Toddy. Compared to her, other girls seemed so ordinary.

Well, he would be taking Toddy to the Class Picnic and the Awards Banquet and most certainly to the dance on graduation night! No matter what his mother said!

14

The sunlight on Toddy's hair fired it with dancing sparks of red and gold. Though tied back with a broad, dark blue ribbon, clusters of ringlets had managed to escape and curled in tight tendrils over her forehead and around her ears.

Chris, gazing at her across the table at the Senior Class Picnic, thought she looked especially nifty today in her trim blue-checked shirtwaist and darker blue chambray shirt, her tiny waist nipped in with a wide belt.

They had all lunched heartily on cold fried chicken, potato salad, several kinds of homemade pies and cakes, as well as fresh-cut watermelon at three of the long rustic tables pushed into a U-shape for more conviviality.

The small class of seniors who had grown close during the past four years were a congenial group. There was a great deal of boisterous laughter, good-natured teasing and jokes during the meal. When they finished there was still the rest of the afternoon ahead, and they began to break up into smaller groups to wander along the winding paths of the big park.

Chris suggested to Toddy that they walk up to the bluff overlooking the river, and she invited Laurel and Dan to come along.

Much to Toddy's irritation, Chris continued an argument that had been interrupted by lunch.

"But I don't see why I can't take you to the Awards Banquet, Toddy."

"I've already told you, Chris. Helene and Mrs. Hale are coming and I'll be with them."

"But the seniors are going to have their own table. Doesn't your family know you'll be sitting with your class?"

"Of course, they know *that*, Chris. And I'll see you there and sit with you then. But Helene is so excited about all the graduation events, and I do so want her to feel a part of everything I'm doing."

"But being with your class is important. It will be the last time we'll all be together as a class. Can't Helene understand that?" he persisted.

"How *could* she, Chris? Helene's never had a chance to go to a real school, be a part of a real class. I'm just trying to give her the feeling that this is her graduation, too. It means so much to her, don't you see that?"

"Well, what about afterwards? You know Mother wants to give our class a party after the Banquet. You can go with me to that, can't you?"

"Oh, Chris, I don't know. I'm not sure."

"What do you mean 'not sure'?" Chris sounded shocked.

"I think, I mean, I'm almost sure, Mrs. Hale has planned some kind of surprise for me after the Awards—" Toddy felt guilty at Chris's crestfallen expression.

"I don't believe this!" he exclaimed. "I told you about this party weeks ago! There just won't be any party if you're not there. Why would I even want to have a party if you aren't coming! It was Mother's idea anyway. I'll just call it off," he declared.

"Oh, you can't do that, Chris!" protested Toddy. "Your mother would be so upset, and she'd be furious at me for being the cause of it."

"Then promise you'll work it out with Mrs. Hale and Helene," he said stubbornly.

"How am I supposed to do that? Ask them if they are planning a surprise for me? I can't do that."

"Hey, you two. Stop arguing!" called Dan from the top of the hill. "It's too nice a day for quarreling."

Toddy grinned. "He's right. Come on, let's go down to the river," she said and held out her hand.

Chris, still angry, hesitated for a second, but Toddy was smiling at him appealingly. And in this mood, Toddy was hard to resist. He could never stay mad at her long. With a sigh, Chris gave in, took her hand and together they started down the path to the river.

Toddy balanced herself delicately as she hopped from rock to rock along the edge of the river. Chris followed with longer, surer strides. For the moment they had ended their verbal sparring and were simply enjoying the easy companionship they had known since they were both children. All of a sudden Toddy, one foot poised behind the other, seemed to wobble precariously.

"Whoops!" she cried and Chris reached out, putting both his hands around her waist to steady her. He held her until she regained her footing. She paused, then stuck one foot out tentatively to the next rock.

"I'm all right, now. You can let go!" she told him.

Chris's hands remained a split second longer, then released her. She ran ahead with a few light steps. Making it to the strip of sand, she turned and smiled as he came alongside her.

There's something different about Chris, Toddy thought. *Wonder what it is.* She looked at him more closely. He was tall and tan, with the most amazing blue eyes. And he had that lopsided grin revealing teeth, straight and white and square. Her heart did a queer little flutter.

Why? What had come over her? She'd known Chris forever, or almost forever, at least since she had come to live in Meadowridge nearly ten years ago. He was the first person her own age she had met. They had climbed trees together, had gone through school together. Except for Kit and Laurel, Toddy had always thought of Chris as her closest friend. So why this new unsettling feeling, this new awareness of him?

Toddy found her mind hurtling back through the years, seeing them like the picture cards in Helene's steriopticon set, remembering Chris as the teasing tormentor of grammar school days, when he had been afraid to acknowledge their friendship in front of his jeering boyfriends at school, tweaking her hair ribbons, chasing her on the playground. But when they reached high school, a different pattern emerged.

Chris soon became the most popular boy at Meadowridge High. A handsome six feet, with a powerful athletic build, easygoing and likable, he was a champion runner and the star of the basketball team. All the girls admired him, secretly longed for his attention. Wary of his new popularity, Toddy had kept her distance when they entered the new school. But at the beginning of their junior year, it was Toddy Chris began to seek out.

At first Toddy wondered about this new grown-up Chris, wondered if his looks were all he had going for him and if he had become dull as paint and conceited to boot. But she soon discovered under the aloof facade the little-boy "pal" still existed. After that they were friends again and any social activity that required a partner usually found them together.

Not that Toddy had no other choice. Vivacious and outgoing, Toddy, too, was popular. The same personality skills that Toddy had perfected to win acceptance and affection within the Hale household were applied with other people as well. If she was cheerful and friendly to everyone, she expected everyone to like her in return. If she ever suspected her popularity earned her detractors, who made snide remarks behind her back, Toddy pretended she did not know. She had learned long ago, the hard way, that to survive there were some things you had to overlook. One thing she knew for sure, she would never do anything to jeopardize her hard-won place with the Hales.

She and Chris walked slowly now along the riverbank, under the graceful swaying branches of the willows. There seemed to be an almost sleepy haze over everything—the afternoon sunlight dappling the water, making it glitter as it flowed over the rocks and swirled into the eddies.

How many times had they walked together like this? Yet this day had a different, indescribable quality, as though it were detached somehow from all the rest of the days they had ever been together. They weren't even arguing about anything, or teasing each other.

Then Chris took her hand, and Toddy looked up into those blue eyes. They stopped walking, as if startled by the contact of palm against palm. The unspoken words between them remained unsaid. It was as if neither wanted to spoil this strangely special moment.

Toddy felt a gathering tension she could not name or explain. She withdrew her hand and moved a little ahead to gather some of the wildflowers—Queen Anne's lace and purple lupin—making a little nosegay.

"I'll take these home to Helene," she said. Helene rarely had a day like this to enjoy.

"Wildflowers don't last long," Chris remarked.

"She'll enjoy them this evening anyway," Toddy replied, thinking days like this didn't last either. The breeze off the river was turning cool and the afternoon was nearly over. "I guess we'd better go back to the others," she suggested and with her hands full of flowers, Chris couldn't hold one hand as they clambered back up the hill to the high meadow.

15

As Toddy arrived for the Awards Banquet with Helene and Mrs. Hale, she saw that the high school gymnasium had been turned into a banquet hall. Tables had been set up all around the room, with one T-shaped one in the middle reserved for Mr. Henson, the principal, and such dignitaries as Mayor Thompson, the County Superintendent of Schools.

The table for the Senior Class extended from the head table and was decorated in the class colors. It was draped with twisted streamers of green and gold crepe paper, with great bunches of yellow daffodils, centered in wreaths of green leaves and flanked by tall gold candles, set at intervals down its length. Marking each senior's place was a rosette of gold and green satin ribbon with CLASS OF 1900 in sparkly gold letters to pin on a coat lapel or the shoulder of a dress.

Toddy waved to a few of her friends, then escorted Helene and Mrs. Hale, regal in black lace and pearls, to one of the tables reserved for the families of the graduates. Helene, who had rested all afternoon so she would be able to attend, wore a lovely apricot taffeta dress that lent color to her pale face and skillfully disguised her frail form.

As Toddy seated them with the parents of one of her classmates, she said regretfully to Helene, "I wish I could sit with you, tell you who everyone is, but the seniors all have to be together."

"Of course, Toddy. I understand. You go on and be with your friends," Helene reassured her. "Grandmother and I will be fine."

Toddy wasn't too sure when she left and looked back over her shoulder to see the chatty Mrs. Burroughs animatedly introducing herself to Mrs. Hale. Well, maybe it would do her good to mix with other people more—at least for one night. She kept herself too isolated up in the house on the hill. And Helene, of course, was too cloistered. Toddy wished there was something she could do to bring Helene into a more normal flow of activity. But everyone in the household was always so concerned about Helene's health that it was impossible to overcome all the objections to some of the outings Toddy suggested. Sometimes she felt frustrated trying. She *did* invite her own friends often and Helene always seemed to enjoy them.

Toddy wondered if all the fuss over her heart condition didn't make Helene too conscious of it. If they would just let her *do* something sometime without all the planning and preparation, the insistence on rest before and after, and having Dr. Woodward come at the least little flutter or fever. Was Helene *really* that fragile?

When Toddy reached the Senior Table and was greeted enthusiastically by her fellow classmates, her troubling thoughts about Helene disappeared. Chris had saved a place for her, with Laurel and Kit sitting opposite. For the moment she lost herself in lively conversation.

A chicken dinner was followed by fresh peach ice cream and little cakes iced in green and gold frosting. Then Mr. Henson rose, tapped on his water glass with his fork, and gradually the hum of conversation subsided until it was only a murmur before quieting completely.

"Ladies and gentlemen, parents, friends, and our honored guests, the Class of 1900!" Mr. Henson smiled with benevolence—an attitude with which he had not *always* regarded those particular young men and women. "Tonight we are here to honor several students with special awards which they have earned by outstanding work, talent, or skill. But before we begin our award ceremony, we have a treat in store—a musical rendition by one of our own. Many of you have enjoyed hearing her in the church choir or on other occasions. We now present Laurel Woodward."

Only Toddy and Kit noticed the sudden rush of color into Laurel's face at this introduction. "Laurel *Woodward*." They had all discussed the problem many times when the three of them were alone together.

In spite of the fact that the Woodwards had legally adopted her, Laurel had stubbornly insisted on retaining her birth name, Laurel Vestal, and used it on all her copybooks and school papers until Miss Cady had taken her aside the day she was promoted out of the eighth grade.

"Laurel, next year you will be entering high school, and I suggest you begin using the name 'Laurel Woodward.' You know Dr. and Mrs. Woodward have officially changed your name to theirs. I think it hurts them when you don't use it."

So Laurel had given in. But somehow she still resented being forced to do so. In her own heart and mind she was *still* Laurel Vestal.

Laurel's voice rose sweetly—each note clear and true. When she finished, the room was hushed. Then slowly the clapping began and went on and on, even after Laurel returned to her place at the table, shaking all over.

Toddy whispered, "I think they expect an encore."

But Laurel just shook her head and finally the applause died away.

Then Mr. Henson was making another announcement. "And now we'll proceed with the presentation of the Awards. First, for his outstanding athletic ability in both Track and Basketball, the winner of four letters and the trophy for County Athlete of the Year, our own Chris Blanchard."

Toddy joined in the wild clapping as Chris, red-faced, went up to receive the engraved loving cup. He mumbled

"Thank you." Then, clutching the trophy, he ambled back to the table, sank into his seat, and glanced at Toddy for approval.

Several other awards were announced. Dan won the Science Prize and Kit, the award for English Composition. Toddy's heart swelled with pride to see her two friends receiving tribute for work well done.

But when her own name was announced for the best dramatic performance of the year, Toddy could hardly believe her ears.

She had loved the role of Portia in *The Merchant of Venice*, loved being part of the production, even memorizing her lines and the rehearsals. The night the play was given, she had donned her costume as though it belonged to her and moved out onto the stage with a minimum of stomach butterflies.

Although she had joined the Drama Club her freshman year in high school, this year was the first Toddy had had the courage to try out for a part. Before, she had just volunteered to paint scenery, sell advertising for the program, help with costumes, or usher on opening night.

Toddy could not explain her reluctance, even to herself. There had seemed some inner denial of how desperately she wanted to get up on the stage and perform. In a way, the excitement she felt, the relish of applause, seemed somehow unworthy, as if it were a vice rather than a virtue.

Or maybe, it was something far deeper. The last nine years had been so far removed from her early gypsy life of the vaudeville theater, that sometimes Toddy had the feeling it had never happened.

Several times, however, she had overheard Miss Tuttle's comment to Mrs. Hubbard when discussing some minor infraction. "Blood will tell," she had said with a knowing look.

Had these years of affluence and respectability, living with the Hales, erased her true identity? Or was she, after all, still the child of a chorus girl and a roving song and dance man?

Yes, in a way, Toddy had felt there was something shameful about wanting to be in the play, loving doing it so much. But now she was being rewarded for it. Somehow Toddy got to her feet and managed to get up to the platform and make a nice little acceptance speech.

Olivia Hale, listening to Toddy expressing her thrill at winning the Drama Award, realized she was nervously pleating her napkin in her lap.

Zephronia Victorine Todd was now known as Toddy Hale. Only a few Meadowridge people remembered how she had arrived on the Orphan Train nearly ten years ago.

Olivia glanced at Helene, who was clapping her thin hands delightedly. She too was recalling the night they had attended the play together and heard Toddy say those memorable lines: "The quality of mercy is not strain'd, It droppeth as the gentle rain from heaven." Olivia herself could not remember ever being more moved by an acting performance.

Was Toddy a born actress? Would she leave someday, drawn by some inner compulsion to her parents' precarious profession? Those two irresponsible people who had abandoned her? Would "blood tell," after all?

And what would happen to Helene if Toddy followed this illusion, this dream Toddy herself might not yet recognize? Again, Olivia looked over at her granddaughter. Helene's delicate face was flushed. She looked so fragile tonight that it frightened Olivia.

At least she had been able to give Helene her heart's desire, a "little sister," whom she adored, she comforted herself. But was it right to expect Toddy to remain with Helene forever? Olivia recalled Dr. Woodward's comments a few years ago, "If Helene continues to receive the tender, loving care you are able to provide for her, if there is no stress or sudden shock, she could possibly live for many years. To be truthful, given the condition of her heart, I am gratified that she has survived this long."

Olivia was convinced having Toddy in their home had been a strong reason for Helene's continued well-being. But what if Toddy left? And she herself could not live forever. What would become of Helene then?

At the next table sat the Blanchards. Bernice Blanchard's eyes were not on the recipient of the Drama Award so much as they were fixed speculatively on her son. It was plain to see that Chris could hardly contain his proud reaction to Toddy's triumph.

Bernice felt a mixture of irritation and concern. Why, oh why had her dear boy—such a catch—so stubbornly set his sights on that little nobody from nowhere? Chris, Bernice was positive, could have any girl in town. Why, there was a steady stream of invitations to parties, picnics, outings of all kinds from far more suitable girls, daughters of some of the best families in Meadowridge.

Not that Olivia Hale wasn't considered at the very top of Meadowridge society *if* she cared to participate in any of the social events. Now, if it had been *Olivia's granddaughter* Chris was interested in, that would be a different story! But, Helene, poor thing! Well, there was no use wasting time on the unavailable.

With narrowed eyes Bernice observed Toddy, looking undeniably charming in a white muslin dress embroidered all over with tiny daisies, and a wide, green sash spanning her tiny waist, her red-gold curls swirled up in a becoming style.

Well, thank goodness, in the fall Chris would be going away to the University and meeting lots of pretty girls. Bernice pursed her mouth petulantly. Perhaps in a few months in a new place with lots of new activities, Chris would get over his silly infatuation for Toddy.

Of course, Bernice sighed, there was still the long summer to get him safely through. And anything could happen in a summer!

16

Bright June sunlight poured in through the open windows of Toddy's bedroom, the breeze sending the ruffled curtains billowing like sails. She was putting the finishing touches on her hair when Helene tapped on the door, then stuck her head in.

"Need any help?" she asked.

"Oh, yes, Helene, will you please? The buttons on my right cuff! I can't seem to manage them with my left hand. Or maybe I'm just too nervous," she said with a little giggle.

"*You* nervous, Toddy. You who won the best actress award? Nothing to be nervous about. All you have to do is go up when they call your name and get your diploma!"

"That's just it. I can play Portia or somebody else. I'm not so sure when I'm being myself."

"You'll do fine, don't worry. And Grandmother and I will be there to give you moral support and clap our hands off when you stand up."

Toddy held out her arm for Helene to fasten the tiny pearl buttons.

"You look lovely, Toddy," Helene told her. "That dress is perfect."

Toddy twirled around, sending the white dotted Swiss skirt flaring.

118

Another tap came at the bedroom door at this point, and both girls turned as Mrs. Hale, carrying a small package bowed with silver ribbon, came in.

"Are you nearly ready, Toddy? I thought the graduates were supposed to be at school a half hour before the program starts. But then promptness was never your forte, was it." She spoke with a severity that seemed surprising on such a special day. "I do think you should learn to be on time from now on."

Toddy looked appropriately repentant. She knew tardiness was one of her besetting sins. It seemed that no matter how early she started to get ready to go somewhere, things got hectic at the last and she usually dashed out a few minutes behind schedule, leaving her drawers half opened and chaos in her wake.

"Yes ma'am, I'll try," said Toddy with suitable humility. Why was Helene smiling, she wondered? And Mrs. Hale's mouth was twitching.

"Maybe this will help." Olivia offered her the daintily wrapped package.

Toddy looked at her in surprise. Her pretty dress and white kid slippers with French heels were, she imagined, her graduation presents. Now something more?

"Well, go ahead, Toddy, open it!" urged Helene.

Toddy pulled the ribbons and paper to reveal a tiny leather box. Lifting its lid she saw an exquisite gold oval watch on a narrow, braided gold chain suspended from a delicate fleur-de-lis of gold and blue enamel.

"Do you like it?" Helene asked eagerly as Toddy stared speechlessly. "Here, let me pin it on for you."

"Oh, it's beautiful! Thank you! Thank you so much!" Her face was at once all smiles.

"Well, the jeweler set it for you, Toddy. So there's no excuse for you to be late to your own graduation—or anything else in the future!" said Mrs. Hale as she swept out of the room, a twinkle in her eye.

"Helene, I know you picked this out for me! It's the nicest thing I've ever had. Thank you!" She hugged Helene.

"Look out, Toddy. I'll wrinkle you!"

"I don't mind these kinds of wrinkles!" Toddy declared.

"They're love wrinkles!" She laughed and Helene joined in.

"Oh, Toddy, I love you! What did we ever do without you?" sighed Helene.

Olivia Hale sat in one of the rows reserved for the parents and family of the graduates, with Helene beside her. One face stood out among all the eager young faces on the stage—a piquant, smiling face alert with intelligence.

"Zephronia Victorine Todd" would be written in fine calligraphy on her diploma. Olivia felt that familiar, vaguely disturbing sensation she had whenever she thought of those legal papers lying in her desk drawer. The adoption papers she had had drawn up after that shocking visit from Mazel Todd five years ago, but had never signed. Why not?

Helene had wanted her to legally adopt Toddy right away, but for some reason Mrs. Hale had put it off. She kept telling herself she wanted to see how things would work out. But before she had had her lawyer prepare the adoption document, that dreadful woman had arrived on her doorstep. Remembering that day, Toddy's thirteenth birthday, Olivia shuddered.

Well, she had paid the woman off, but would she be back? The payment was not that large, and there was no guarantee she would not come back for more. All she had agreed to do was stay away until Toddy was eighteen. Well, Toddy had just turned eighteen.

Olivia also felt guilty that she had never told Toddy about her mother's visit, but she had not wanted to "rock the boat," as the saying went. She especially did not want to upset Helene, who loved Toddy like her own flesh and blood. Well, this was hardly the time to bring it up, Olivia thought.

She glanced at Helene sitting beside her. The chiseled profile seemed even sharper. Had she lost more weight? Olivia felt a little stirring of alarm, and she moved uneasily in her seat.

Perhaps they ought to go somewhere this summer, all three of them. Take Helene somewhere that would be a pleasant change of climate and scene. It could be a kind of graduation present for Toddy, too.

Yes, that might be the wise thing to do. Close the house and go. Then if that woman got any ideas about coming back into Toddy's life, making demands—they'd be far away.

Where would they go? Europe? Yes, that would be educational for both the girls. And they could make it a leisurely journey, no hurrying from country to country, city to city. Why, there was no reason to hurry. They could take months traveling, even a year—

They could even visit some of those health spas the Continent was so famous for, the ones in Austria and Switzerland. It might be exactly the thing for Helene.

Olivia settled back in her seat as that attractive, nice-looking young fellow came up to the podium. What was his name? Olivia referred to her program, ah, Daniel Brooke, Salutatorian. His was the welcoming address. She folded her hands in her lap, her expression composed. She would start making plans tomorrow for their trip. The girls would be delighted, she felt sure.

But Helene, ever sensitive to Toddy's desires, expressed and unexpressed, made a tactful suggestion. "I think, though she would never say so, that Toddy would really prefer to spend this summer at home, Grandmother. Some of her friends will be leaving in the fall and I'm sure she would like to be with them as much as possible."

So Olivia's plans were postponed, and in June the summer seemed to stretch endlessly before them. The freedom from the routine of school, classes, and homework was welcomed by casual students like Toddy and Chris. There were weeks of unbroken sunny days to enjoy, mornings of tennis or bicycling out to the river to picnic and swim. Afternoons were spent playing croquet or badminton on someone's lawn, sipping lemonade under shady trees. The soft summer evenings offered twilight band concerts in the park, ice cream socials at the Community Hall, strolling home after the Sunday Youth Meeting at the church, gathering on porches or in parlors, around pianos singing.

It wasn't until after the Fourth of July that they realized that the time was fast approaching when many of the young people in their crowd would be going their separate ways.

Kit, of course, had been working full-time at the Library, as had Dan at Groves Pharmacy, both squirreling away what they earned to help with their college expenses. But even they had joined the others in the leisurely enjoyment of their last real summer together.

Then something happened that changed at least three of them.

The first Sunday in August, at the end of the church service, Reverend Brewster announced the arrival of a visiting evangelist who would conduct a Revival in Meadowridge. The Revival would begin on Wednesday and there would be meetings each evening for the rest of the week.

"Come prepared to receive a blessing," exhorted Reverend Brewster. "Don't let anything keep you home from these divine appointments."

Chris, who was waiting outside of church for Toddy, complained, "Wouldn't you know it would be the same week as the Carnival?"

Toddy looked shocked. "Shame on you, Chris Blanchard! Didn't you hear anything Reverend Brewster said? Not to let anything keep you from attending?"

Chris tried to look ashamed. "Then *you're* planning to go?" he asked.

"Of course!"

Chris glanced in the direction of Mrs. Hale and Helene who had walked on and were already seated in the open barouche, ready to drive home.

"I only meant—I mean, I was just going to see if you'd like to go to the Carnival with me," he said defensively. "It opens tomorrow. That's before the Revival even begins. They're already setting up over at the town park."

"I'll have to ask," she told him. "And if Mrs. Hale says I may, *and if* I decide to go, you have to promise to come to the Revival meetings," she said with satisfaction.

"I'll tell you all about the Carnival when I get home, Helene!" Toddy promised as she poked her head in the door of Helene's room the following evening. Helene, who was propped up in bed reading, put down her book and smiled.

"Have fun, Toddy. I'll see you later."

With a wave of her hand, Toddy flew down the stairs where an impatient Chris was trying to converse with Mrs. Hale.

"Have a good time, you two," she told them as they went out the door.

Chris tucked Toddy's hand through his arm as they started down the street. Over the tops of trees they could see the lights from the Carnival illuminating the lavender evening sky. The sound of the tinny calliope music from the merry-go-round swirled through the air, beckoning them with its own distinctive charm.

Hearing it, a strange little tingle of excitement quivered through Toddy, as if something familiar was triggered within her.

Approaching the entrance to the park, they experienced the smell of canvas and sawdust mingled with the sticky sweetness of cotton candy, the rich greasy aroma of popcorn, the strong odors of caravans and horses belonging to the performers tethered near the tents.

Chris held Toddy's hand as they meandered down the midway through the concession booths selling all kinds of garish wares, the barkers hoarsely enticing customers to "take a chance," "try your luck," "win your sweetheart a prize, mister."

They stopped at one so Chris could throw a few balls at a target, and astounded a chagrined concessionaire when he hit all three dead center. When the man tried to persuade Chris to try for another round, Toddy pulled him away, laughing at the man's sour expression as he parted grudgingly with Chris's "prize"—a gaudily painted plaster bulldog.

"Let's ride the Ferris wheel," Chris suggested and handed over a strip of tickets to the rough-looking operator with a cigarette dangling from one end of his mouth. He raised the safety bar and Toddy and Chris settled themselves in the flimsy seat. A minute later they were thrust swiftly back and upward into the night sky. Toddy gave a small cry of alarm and Chris put his arm protectively around the back of the seat. At the top, the Ferris wheel stopped with a jolt and they swung precariously, suspended over Meadowridge.

"Oh, my!" exclaimed Toddy with a nervous giggle.

"Scared?" Chris teased, purposely rocking their chair.

"Chris, don't!" she cried, clutching his arm.

He laughed indulgently.

"Don't worry. You're perfectly safe...with *me*." His arm dropped down on her shoulder and he leaned a little closer. "Toddy," he said tentatively. "Toddy, would you wear my class pin if I gave it to you before I leave for the University?"

Her heart jumped. Her sudden lightheadedness, she knew, had nothing to do with the dizzying height. Toddy did not answer for a minute.

"I don't know if that's a good idea, Chris," she replied at last. "You're going to be meeting lots of girls at college. Giving me your pin to wear is kind of... well, serious."

"Please, Toddy, I want you to have it. Going away isn't going to make any difference to me. I don't care how many pretty girls I meet." Chris stopped, then stammered. "You know, I—I love you, don't you?"

Just then the Ferris wheel started again with a jerk and they were whirled down and around again, leaving Toddy quite breathless. There was another quick spin and then they were brought to an abrupt stop, the safety bar was raised, and their ride was over.

"Think about it, won't you, Toddy?" Chris pleaded as they started walking toward the midway again.

As they passed one gaily striped tent three women dressed in orange, red and bright blue tinsel-trimmed dresses and wearing matching plumed hats came prancing out on a narrow stage, whirling their feather boas, while a thin, mustachioed man in a loud "Dapper Dan" yellow and green plaid suit and derby hat played the crowd.

"Come one, come all, ladies and gen'lmen, to see the Toast of Paree, the beauteous Trenton Threesome, rivaling the famed Flora Dora girls of the Zeigfield Follies, they've danced before the Crowned Heads of Europe! You ain't seen nothin' till you see these tootsie-wootsies do their Spanish fandango! Jest fifty cents a head, folks. You can see what the continental nobility had to pay a fortune to view! Step right up, folks! Get your tickets right here!"

While they stopped to listen to his spiel, an icy finger trailed down Toddy's spine. Rooted to the spot, her eyes were riveted to the painted faces of the three dancers mincing on high-heeled boots across the stage, flouncing the ruffles of their fringed skirts to the music blaring from the brass funnel of a Gramophone inside the tent.

Her stomach lurched sickeningly and, loosening her hand from Chris's, she turned and walked rapidly away toward the exit from the Carnival.

"Hey, Toddy, wait up!" Chris called after her. She heard him running behind her. "What's the matter?" he demanded, when he caught up with her.

"I've just had enough, that's all," she replied. "I want to go home now." The hot, choking sensation gripping her throat made it hard to draw a breath.

"Well, sure, Toddy." Puzzled but compliant, Chris fell into step beside her.

They walked back along the quiet, residential streets, the music of the Carnival slowly fading into the distance. At the Hales' gate, they halted.

"Was it anything I said, Toddy?" Chris asked worriedly.

Toddy shook her head. "No, I'm just tired, I guess."

"You *did* have a good time though, didn't you?"

"Oh, yes, Chris. Thanks for taking me," she replied quickly.

"And Toddy, you will think about what I asked you, won't you—about my pin?"

"Yes, sure, Chris. But I better go in now."

Chris leaned forward. "May I kiss you good night?"

Toddy hesitated. Then, remembering they had kissed often since Graduation Night, how could she refuse now?

Silently she lifted her face as he bent down to her. Their lips met in a kiss that was sweetly innocent and affectionate.

"I *do* love you, Toddy," Chris said huskily.

"I know," she answered softly, then, "Good night, Chris."

He stood there watching her slim figure in the white dress as she disappeared onto the darkened veranda and through the lighted front door.

On the other side of the door, Toddy stood for a minute trying to compose herself before going up to Helene's room to report on her evening with Chris.

What had come over her at the dancers' booth? It was as though she had suddenly been jerked backward into a half-forgotten world. For a moment she had been terrified. Afraid she would be pulled back into a vortex that would suck her into its depths.

It had been only the blink of an eye actually, but in that brief span of time, she had felt something strong and primal that left her shaken. For that split second she had the illusion that the carnival was more real than her life with the Hales. Did memory have its own truth?

An involuntary shudder swept over her. Toddy shook her head as if to clear it. Then she heard Mrs. Hale's voice.

"Is that you, Toddy? Helene's waiting up for you. Go up and see her so that she can get settled for the night, that's a good girl."

"Yes ma'am, I'm going," Toddy replied. She walked slowly over to the stairway, and stood a moment longer, her hand grasping the newel post. Then straightening her shoulders, she went upstairs.

17

"What are you reading?" Toddy asked Helene as she curled up at the end of her bed.

Helene held up the book.

"It's about Florence Nightingale, the heroine of the Crimean War. She revolutionized nursing and saved hundreds of wounded soldiers' lives by applying the things she had learned at a German nursing school—simple things like cleanliness, things no one seemed to have thought of before," Helene told her. "And she heard God speaking to her, Toddy, telling her what to do."

Toddy sat up straighter, at once intrigued.

"You mean she *actually* heard God's voice? What did it sound like?"

"Well, not as you and I are talking now, but in a very clear way, an inner *knowing*. She was directed to do things, things no one had ever done to take care of the wounded, the sick and dying," Helene explained. "She was truly inspired, she believed, and so was able to be strong and courageous. Would you like to read it? I'm sleepy now so you can take it with you, if you like."

An hour later Toddy was still reading, enthralled by the story of the "Lady With the Lamp." Florence Nightingale was given that name by the soldiers who welcomed the sight of her shadow as she made the rounds at night, moving among their cots, holding her lamp aloft to bring comfort and healing.

Finally, unable to keep her eyes open any longer, Toddy yawned, slid down into the pillows and reluctantly closed the book. She blew out her lamp, but she did not go to sleep right away.

How wonderful to be able to really help the sick and suffering, Toddy thought. And most wonderful of all to know that God had called you to do just that.

Florence Nightingale had started schools in England to train young women to become nurses, Toddy had read. Now there were schools in the United States patterned on her ideas. What a worthwhile way to spend one's life.

She wondered if Miss Tuttle, her old enemy and adversary, had trained in such a school. But Miss Tuttle was no longer around to ask. She had retired a few years ago, gone to live with a sister in Seattle, and had never been replaced. Actually Helene was so much better these days that she did not really need a nurse in attendance.

What if I became a nurse? Toddy thought as she drifted off. Would it be possible? Then if Helene should ever need one, I would be here to take care of her. Maybe she would ask Mrs. Hale, Toddy decided. But first, she would pray about it. Maybe God would tell her what to do, just as He had Florence Nightingale.

The first evening of the Revival Toddy arrived at church with Laurel, and when Kit came in with Miss Cady, all of them sat together in the same pew. So impressed were they by the persuasive preaching of the dynamic Brother Roger Holmes that all three friends were in attendance every night thereafter.

On Friday night the tall, lanky evangelist, attired in a shabby coat and flowing tie, took his place in the pulpit.

After the opening prayer, he lifted his great, shaggy head from its bowed position and holding up a few sheets of paper, dramatically tore them into pieces.

"Friends, tonight I am throwing away my prepared sermon notes. I feel led of the Holy Spirit to speak from my heart and from the guidance I feel I've been given." He clasped his hands and bowed his head again for a few minutes. The church was so still that no one seemed to be breathing.

When he raised his head again, he leafed through his worn Bible for another minute before beginning to speak.

"I feel directed to take my text tonight from the Old Testament, Exodus 4, Verse 2: 'What is that in thine hand?'—the question the Lord asked Moses." He allowed his words to hang in the quiet for a moment before continuing, "And Moses looked down at what he perceived as a mere shepherd's stick and replied, 'A rod.'

"To Moses it was a simple, ordinary, everyday object, of little value and certainly of no earthly power. It was not a sword or a lance or a weapon with which Moses could force Pharaoh to release the Hebrew people from their bondage in Egypt. Furthermore, Moses considered himself inadequate for the job—the heroic task of delivering the Jews from captivity. But with God's almighty power, that rod became the miraculous instrument parting the Red Sea so they could escape. Subsequently, it also sent the waters rushing down upon the Egyptian Army in hot pursuit." Brother Holmes paused, his eyes roving over the congregation searchingly.

"Isn't that what we do also? Look at what we have in our hands, and whine and complain and wonder what we can do with it?" Another pause. "Friends, *whatever* your particular rod, God expects you to *use* it. So I want you to look tonight at *your* rod, at the enormous possibilities within the gifts God has given *you*.

"We each possess very precious gifts which may seem small or commonplace to us, but dedicated to God's will, they can change our lives and the lives of those around us for the better, if we will only take the time to recognize them, dedicate them to God's use."

Brother Holmes leaned forward over the pulpit.

"Power often lies hidden in the obvious," he continued earnestly. "Let us prayerfully look at what lies in our hands and pray to God to show us what He wants us to do with it."

After he finished, there was a hush. His sermon seemed to have had a profound effect on his listeners. No one moved or stirred until Miss Palmtry bustled up to the organ and struck the first few chords of the closing hymn, "Lead Kindly Light."

Slowly the congregation began to file out of the pews, flow into the aisles, and make their way out of the church. There was an absence of the usual greetings and cordial chatter as the people dispersed quietly into the night.

A group of young men, who had remained seated in the back of the church and were the first to leave when the dismissal was given, stood just outside the church steps. Chris detached himself from the group as the girls came out and made his way over to Toddy.

"Can I walk you home?"

"Not tonight, Chris. Kit and I are spending the night at Laurel's."

Disappointed, Chris said, "Oh, well, all right. See you tomorrow then."

The three girls linked arms and started out of the churchyard as the strains of the last hymn floating on the summer air merged with the soft chirpings of crickets outside and the low whinnying of the row of horses tied to the fence around the church.

As if by some unspoken signal, all three began singing the words of the beloved old songs as they walked:

All praise to Thee, my God, This night,
For all the blessings of the light!
Keep me, O keep me, King of kings,
Beneath thine own almighty wings.
O may my soul on Thee repose,
And with sweet sleep mine eyelids close;
Sleep that may me more vigorous make
To serve my God when I awake.

Come unto Me, when shadows darkly gather!
When the sad heart is weary and distressed,
Seeking for comfort from your heavenly Father,
Come unto me and I will give you rest.

The evening air was fresh, cool, delicately scented with fragrance from all the summer gardens they passed. Coming through the Woodwards' gate and entering the shadowy garden, the three felt a new closeness, bonded by a shared faith, an unspoken petition: *What, O Lord, is my "rod" and what do You wish me to do with it?*

18

"I'm ready to leave now, Mrs. Hale."

Olivia looked up from the evening paper and saw Toddy standing in the doorway of the parlor.

"Oh, yes, the Blanchard dinner party, isn't it?"

"Yes, ma'am," she replied. "New Year's Eve."

"So it is. Well, I suppose it will be a fine affair."

Toddy stood there a moment longer as if waiting for something. She touched her hair tentatively. "Do I look all right?"

Olivia knew the girl was begging for reassurance. Actually, with her golden-red hair swept up, Toddy looked astonishingly grown-up and pretty. The amusing little pixie had become a real beauty. No wonder the Blanchard boy was smitten with her. Toddy kept gazing at her anxiously, waiting. But Olivia did not believe in lavish compliments; they made a person vain.

So, all she did was nod. "Yes, indeed, you look very nice, Toddy."

Toddy smiled and her eyes danced. Lifting her skirt gracefully, she made a slow pirouette. The velvet bodice of the gown was royal blue; the shirred puffed sleeves and skirt consisted of a pale blue taffeta elaborately flocked in darker blue velvet.

"Thank you! And thank you for this beautiful dress. I do want to look special tonight because all Chris's relatives will be there. I'm a *little* terrified!" she confessed.

A smile tugged at Olivia's mouth. Only Toddy would attempt to describe her feelings so paradoxically.

"How was Helene feeling when you came down?" Olivia asked.

Momentarily Toddy's smile faded. "She *said* she was better. She was resting and thought she would go to sleep soon—" Toddy paused, then asked anxiously, "Do you think I should stay? Not go tonight?"

"No, of course not, child. Helene would be upset if she thought you were missing a party on her account! Mrs. Hubbard is here and surely the two of us can keep an eye on things. I'll go up in a while and see if Helene wants me to read to her until she falls asleep."

Just then the sound of the front doorbell being twisted vigorously echoed through the downstairs. Toddy twirled around and peeked into the hall.

"There's Chris now, come to pick me up!" she exclaimed, starting out of the room.

Impulsively Olivia called to her. "Toddy, just a minute. Come here, please."

Immediately Toddy turned and walked over to stand by Mrs. Hale's chair.

"Yes?"

Lowering her voice, Olivia said, "Don't let Bernice Blanchard intimidate you. She'll try, you know. Just remember, you know which fork to use, and you're charming and considerate. So just be yourself."

Toddy's eyes widened curiously. Mrs. Hale had never said anything like that to her before. She was about to respond when Clara Hubbard appeared in the doorway with Chris, splendid in his evening clothes.

Toddy turned and met Chris's admiring glance.

"Evening, Mrs. Hale," he said politely, but his eyes were on Toddy.

"Good evening, Chris. Have you enjoyed your holidays?"

"Yes, thank you, ma'am." Chris flushed. He was always uncomfortable around the formidable Olivia Hale.

"And how are your studies coming along?"

"Fine thank you, ma'am, that is, except for Trig—Trigonometry and—" he halted, flustered, his face reddening.

"I suppose you've been busy with sports?" Mrs. Hale suggested.

"Well, yes, ma'am, as a matter of fact—"

"And when do you have to return to the University?"

Chris looked gloomy. "Day after tomorrow, I'm afraid."

And none too soon, thought Olivia, not missing Toddy's adoring gaze on him.

Chris shifted uneasily, glanced at Toddy, then said hesitantly, "I guess we better be going. Mother said dinner is going to be served promptly at seven."

"Yes, indeed, you'd best be off then."

"Well, good night, Mrs. Hale," Chris said, obviously eager to go, adding as an afterthought, "And a very Happy New Year."

Olivia smiled wryly. "Thank you, Chris. The same to you."

Watching them leave—the tall, dark-haired boy and the petite, radiant girl—she frowned. Ever since Chris had arrived home for his Christmas vacation, the two of them had spent nearly every day and practically every evening together—ice-skating, sledding, even gift shopping! She hoped they hadn't any foolish ideas. They were both too young. She dismissed the immediate reminder that she herself had eloped at sixteen with a rough-hewn young man of whom her parents disapproved. In fact, they had never forgiven her for doing so.

Compressing her mouth in a straight line, Olivia's brow furrowed. If they had only been able to leave for Europe in September as she had planned. She had hoped to be away from Meadowridge when Chris came home for the holidays. Their passports had arrived, the girls' wardrobes were assembled and the tickets purchased. Then Helene had had a bad spell and Dr. Woodward had advised against traveling. The summer had been unusually hot, and the heat had apparently taken its toll on her delicate heart.

Their departure was delayed indefinitely. Then, since Olivia was cautioned about an Atlantic crossing in winter, she had postponed their leaving until spring. That is how they happened to still be in Meadowridge when young Blanchard came home from college.

Olivia thought of the day he arrived. One might have thought he had rushed to the house straight from the railroad station, the way he had come bounding up the steps, scarf flying, coattails flapping!

Olivia gave the newspaper a sharp snap. Well, he'd be gone in a few days and things should settle back to normal without Toddy flitting about like a nervous butterfly, dashing in and out, skates dangling over her shoulder, searching for misplaced mittens, rosy-cheeked and starry-eyed. Olivia sighed, as much in regret that her granddaughter could not share such youthful pleasures as in fear of the potential danger of losing Toddy to love.

Toddy and Chris walked from the Hales' house up the hill, their boots crunching in the packed snow, their breath sending frosty plumes into the dark as they talked. They could see the Blanchards' house in the distance, every window alight, sending out rectangles of color onto the crusted snow.

Just as they started up the steps to the veranda encircling the lower story, Chris pulled Toddy gently back toward him.

Tilting her chin with one hand, he put the other into his coat pocket and pulled out a spray of mistletoe.

"See? I'm always prepared," he said mischievously, holding it over her head. "An early Happy New Year, Toddy!" He leaned down and touched her lips with his. His kiss was warm and sweet in the cold.

"Happy New Year, Chris," she whispered.

He hugged her, pulling her hard against him. "I hate to think of leaving you—"

Toddy felt her heart pound. His vacation had been so special. They had hardly had a disagreement, an argument. It had been such a wonderful Christmas. But now it was almost over.

"I'll miss you, too."

"I've a good mind to tell Ma and my father that I'm not going back to the University—" Chris began. "If my father weren't so keen on it—"

"Oh, Chris, you must go back!" Toddy cried in alarm. She drew back and looked up at him. "If you don't, they'll blame *me!*"

At that moment the front door opened and a beam of light enveloped them, and they saw Mrs. Blanchard standing in the doorway.

"Well, for heaven's sake, there you are!" she exclaimed. "We were wondering what was keeping you." She shivered exaggeratedly. "Come in! It's freezing out there. I was just going to send Hugh out to sprinkle some more sand on the path and steps so people wouldn't slip. Hurry, don't let all that cold air into the house, Chris!" She sounded annoyed.

Chris squeezed Toddy's hand in apology and they hurried up the steps and into the house.

Entering the spacious hall, Toddy saw that the whole house was still festively decorated for the holidays. Boughs of evergreens looped with shiny red ribbon adorned the staircase, and the air was spicy with the scent of pine.

Chris helped Toddy off with her coat, then told her to sit down while he knelt to unfasten the gaiters she wore to protect her blue satin slippers. She unwound the crocheted "fascinator" from her head, then craned her neck to admire the beautifully trimmed tree, an eight-foot tall cedar at the foot of the stairs. Gilt garlands glittered in the light from dozens of tiny candles. Glistening balls reflected their sparkle, while brightly painted tin birds nested in the sweeping branches.

"I'll go put these in the cloak room and be right back," Chris told her and disappeared, leaving her alone with Mrs. Blanchard.

Toddy felt the nervous tightening in her stomach. It always heppened when she met Chris's mother. Trying to overcome it, she said, "Everything looks lovely, Mrs. Blanchard," she remarked politely.

"Thank you, Toddy. Everyone says I *do* have a certain talent for making things look attractive." Mrs. Blanchard forced a smile which Toddy tried to return with a spontaneous one of her own, but her lips felt stiff.

A small pause then Mrs. Blanchard said, "I'm really surprised you came tonight, Toddy. I heard Helene was far from well." Unmistakably an implied criticism. A definite insinuation that Toddy's place was at Helene's bedside.

"Oh, she's feeling much better, Mrs. Blanchard. Mrs. Hale thinks she overdid at Christmas. Helene adores the holidays and buying gifts and planning surprises for everyone. She loves it all and—"

"You should be very grateful to be in such a lenient household," Mrs. Blanchard cut in coldly. "Sad to say, not all *you orphans* were so fortunate, like that poor—what's her name?—the girl who made the speech at Graduation—"

"Kit Ternan," Toddy supplied between clenched teeth, her fingernails biting into her fisted hands. *Surely* Mrs.

Blanchard *must* remember Kit—the first female valedictorian Meadowridge High School ever had!

"Yes, that poor thing in that awful dress! Imagine living out at the Hansens' all these years. *You* could have landed there or in some equally terrible place. You should thank your lucky stars, Toddy."

"Why should Toddy thank her lucky stars, Ma?" Chris was back, all smiles and glowing happiness.

Mrs. Blanchard looked embarrassed and passed off his question with a shrill little laugh. "Oh, nothing, son. Just girl talk. Now why don't you take Toddy into the parlor and introduce her to your aunts and uncles and cousins? Then have some punch."

"Good idea,"Chris agreed heartily and held out his hand to Toddy who took it gratefully. "Come on, Toddy."

Mrs. Blanchard smiled benignly at her son and although Toddy was included, its warmth seemed to evaporate by the time it reached her. Inwardly, Toddy was seething. Chris's mother was either unspeakably rude or completely insensitive. Toddy was included to think it was intended, because she never lost an opportunity to remind Toddy she was an orphan. It was obvious that Mrs. Blanchard was making a very decided point, that Toddy was set apart from the rest of Meadowridge, unacceptable, an outsider forever. How she must hate the idea of Chris being involved with "an Orphan Train rider."

"Did I tell you how smashing you look tonight, Toddy?" Chris whispered as they stood on the threshold of the parlor. Toddy looked up at him with a rush of gratitude. Who cared what anyone else thought of her, when someone as good-looking and nice as Chris thought she hung the moon?

Dutifully Chris took her around the room, introducing her. The middle-aged uncles were all red-cheeked, balding and jovial, and greeted Toddy with pleasant heartiness.

Uncle Jim teased that he did not realize Chris had such good taste, Uncle Cliff gave a friendly wink, while Uncle Murray merely slapped him on the back and grinned.

The aunties were a different cup of tea altogether. They looked remarkably like their sister Bernice. All were plump, with elaborately coiffed hair, wearing a quantity of jewelry and with speculative eyes. Toddy could tell right away that Chris was a favorite nephew and they were sizing her up as to whether she was the right girl for him.

Toddy was appropriately respectful and polite but genuinely relieved when the introductions were over and Chris steered her into the adjoining "second parlor" that had temporarily been turned into a convivial center for the younger members of the clan.

Here she was welcomed as a delightful addition to the gathering. The male cousins clustered around her immediately. Chris's cousin Tom lost no time trying to monopolize her while Roger and Hart circled, waiting for their chance to impress. The four little girl cousins were adorable, much younger than the others, and were happy to watch the "goings on" while each took a turn viewing the stereopticon until dinner was announced.

Toddy was always at her best with people her own age, where her wit and vivacity were a plus. Chris, proud of the good impression she had made on his cousins, manifested not an iota of jealousy.

The dining room looked like a holiday picture. On the embroidered white linen and lace cloth stood two silver candelabra with tall red tapers; in the middle, a centerpiece composed of white carnations ringed in holly, bright with red berries on a footed silver compote. At each place was a small, red-ribboned favor. The red china, edged in gold, was flanked with a formidable array of silver flatware, reminding Toddy of Mrs. Hale's ironic remark: "You know which fork to use—"

As Chris held out her chair, Toddy mentally gritted her teeth, determined to do her upbringing proud.

She took her seat, unfolded her napkin, and looked on either side of her, then down the table to where Mrs. Blanchard simpered, basking in the effusive compliments of her sisters. "Don't let Bernice Blanchard intimidate you. She'll try," Mrs. Hale had said.

Don't worry, I won't, I promise you, Toddy resolved. A small spark of independence flared into flame. She was sorry Chris's mother did not like her, did not approve of her, but she refused to let it spoil her evening. On one side of her was Chris's gallant cousin Hart, and on the other side, his charming little cousin Amelia. Chris himself was smiling at her from across the table.

Annie, the Blanchards' regular maid, almost unrecognizable in a fancy new uniform, was serving the lavish meal with the help of a hired girl. Course followed delicious course—clear soup, salad, white fish, roast lamb, five vegetables, pudding, pecan pie, glazed fruit, marzipan and mints. Mrs. Blanchard had certainly outdone herself in this holiday menu.

But even under her watchful eye, Toddy did not make a single faux pas. Working from the outside in, she even made use of the ivory-handled fruit knife and finger bowls with casual grace.

Knowing she had done well, Toddy was pleased and a little proud of herself—something she was to remember later in the evening. It was in this happy frame of mind, filled with delicious food, flattered by all the attention she had received, that Toddy enthusiastically agreed when the children begged her to join them in a game of hide-and-seek.

After the meal, the gentlemen remained at the table for their brandy and cigars, and the ladies moved to the parlor to chat. So the young folk had the rest of the house in which to play. They counted out who was "It" and then scattered, everyone looking for a good place to hide.

As Toddy stood uncertainly, not knowing which way to go, Chris pointed to the huge blue china vase holding peacock feathers that stood in the hallway outside the parlor door. He was taking the steps two at a time to the landing where a large teakwood Japanese screen would make a great hiding place.

Taking her cue from him, Toddy hurried over and slid behind the vase and, gathering her skirt about her, wedged herself against the wall. Gradually the sounds of running feet and muffled giggles subsided and she guessed everyone had safely hidden themselves. As she crouched there, fragments of the ladies' conversation floated out from the half-closed parlor door.

"I thought his being away would lessen the attachment," a voice complained.

"Well, it's been *my* experience that opposition only increases the attraction," said another.

"I definitely agree," someone declared. "You know the old saying, 'Forbidden fruit tastes sweetest!' "

"She's got quite a few airs for someone with no background!"

"But she's a pretty little thing for all that."

"That may well be, Ethel, but surely you can understand how I feel?" That was Mrs. Blanchard speaking.

Suddenly Toddy realized *she* was the topic under discussion. Chris's mother and his aunts were talking about *her*! She felt her face burn while the rest of her turned icy with resentment. Her ears tingled and she put both hands over them, unwilling to hear any more. Shifting her position, ready to move and find another hiding place, she saw Roger who was "It" move across the hall. If he spotted her and called out, the ladies would surely know she had eavesdropped on their conversation.

So she stayed put until Roger passed, heading in the opposite direction. Then very quietly she slipped out from behind the vase and crept up the stairs to join Chris behind the Japanese screen.

He grabbed her hand. "Hey, this is cozy!"

"I have to go home," she said crossly, tugging her hand away.

"Home? Right *now*?" He was surprised. "Why? Aren't you having a good time? We don't have to play with the kids all evening, you know."

Toddy shook her head. "No, I mean, yes. It's not the game, Chris. And I like your cousins. It's just that—" she hesitated unable to think of an excuse. Then she improvised. "I'd like to get home in time to tell Helene good night; she hasn't been feeling well and—"

Chris gave a heavy sigh. "Helene! It's always Helene, Toddy."

"Well, she's my sister and—" Toddy stopped cold. *Was she?* Did Helene *really* consider her a sister? Or was Toddy just *hoping* that she did? The full weight of the things Mrs. Blanchard had said to her earlier and what she had overheard was beginning to reach into that sensitive, vulnerable part of her. All her old insecurity surfaced and unconsciously she shuddered. Tears rushed into her eyes and she turned away quickly so Chris couldn't see them. But he knew he had said something wrong. He touched her arm.

"I'm sorry, Toddy," he said gently. "I didn't mean to offend you. I just—look, if you want to go home, we'll go, right now! As soon as Roger finds us—all right? Don't be mad."

Toddy forced a smile and whispered back, "I'm not mad. Honest. It's just that Helene never gets to go to parties or out very much, and she loves to hear all about everything I do. If she's still awake when I get back—Don't you see, I can share everything that happened with her?"

Well, not *everything,* Toddy amended mentally.

"Sure, Toddy, I understand." He leaned toward her and kissed her lightly, "Did I tell you I think you're the sweetest, most generous—"

Toddy rolled her eyes. "Oh, come on, Chris!"

It was hard for Toddy to face Mrs. Blanchard, tell her she had enjoyed the lovely evening as she said good night. Mrs. Blanchard smiled automatically, but her eyes were as cold as the night outside.

She gazed dotingly on Chris and wagged her finger. "Now Chris, hurry back after you take Toddy home. Uncle Jim wants to have a man-to-man talk with you about college, and they're leaving early in the morning, remember." Then she eyed Toddy with clear intent. "You won't keep him, will you, Toddy? And do wish Mrs. Hale a Happy New Year for me, won't you?"

As they went down the steps and out the gate, Chris took one of Toddy's hands and put it with his into the deep pocket of his coat. The touch of his palm against hers was comforting, but Toddy's heart still stung painfully from the cruel words she had overheard.

"What a night," Chris said, looking up at the sky, a vast dark canopy sprinkled with hundreds of sparkling stars. He squeezed Toddy's hand. "I'm glad you wanted to leave early. We'll get to say Happy New Year to each other alone."

Toddy didn't answer. Her throat was sore with distress. The cutting conversation had hurt. Like a hangnail or a stone bruise, it was there, no matter how she tried to dismiss it.

To Mrs. Blanchard, she would always be one of those "Orphan Train" waifs—unsuitable, unacceptable, unworthy of her son. Nothing Toddy could say or do or become would change that. Loving Chris, his loving her, made no difference. They would never overcome his mother's objections.

"Toddy—" Chris stopped under a lamppost and put his hands on her shoulders, slowly turning her around to the light so he could see her face. "Ma was right about Uncle Jim's wanting to talk to me," he began, his voice intense as he went on, "But it isn't about college. I already broached the subject to *him* earlier, but we haven't had a chance to be alone yet. Too many people, too many relatives around." Chris went on with mounting excitement. "What I *really* wanted to talk to Uncle Jim about was...going to work for him. You see, he has a construction firm in Brookhaven, a town about fifty miles from here. You know I've always liked working with my hands and being out of doors! I hate the thought of working in a bank, like my father. Ma only likes the idea because it's a kind of prestigious job." He hesitated. "So, what do you think? If he'd let me go to work for him, I'd quit college after this semester, and then—and then, Toddy, I could support a wife—I mean, Toddy, you *know* how much I love you—there's never been anyone else but you. Would you marry me?"

Stunned, Toddy stared back at Chris. "But, Chris, your parents would never agree to that!"

His handsome face grew stubborn.

"I don't want to go back to the University. I don't want to wait three more years." His hands gripped her shoulders tightly. "I'm afraid something will happen. I'm afraid I'll lose you."

A dozen conflicting thoughts rushed into Toddy's mind. There was no doubt of the love she saw in Chris's eyes, heard in his voice, felt in his touch, his kiss. The three months he had been gone she had missed him more than she thought possible. These two weeks he'd been home for the holidays had been heaven.

For a moment a wonderful fantasy unfolded, a fairy tale come true. She and Chris, childhood friends, high-school sweethearts, meant for each other, destined for happiness. What else did they need but each other?

A home of her own, something Toddy had always longed for, someone to love her, someone she could love and cherish and care for, and like her favorite storybook endings, live with "happily ever after." Could that really happen for her and Chris? He was saying it could, was telling her it was possible.

"Well, what do you say, Toddy? Will you? You *do* love me, don't you?"

Toddy shivered suddenly.

Quickly Chris put his arm around her, drew her close so that her cheek was against the rough tweed of his coat.

"You don't need to answer that. I know you do. And we'll work it out. Come on, you're getting cold. I'll get you home. Then, tonight, I'll talk to Uncle Jim. I'll get him to talk to my folks, convince them that it's what I want to do—"

The temperature had dropped and now the sidewalks were crusted over with a thin layer of ice. Chris's arm was around Toddy as they hurried along. The air was so cold it was almost hard to draw a deep breath. As they rounded the corner and started up the hill toward the Hales' house, Toddy stopped short. She clutched Chris's arm.

"Oh, Chris, look!" she gasped. "That's Dr. Woodward's buggy in front of the house! Helene must be worse! O dear Lord!" And Toddy broke away from Chris and started to run.

Toddy huddled on the top step of the stairway, a few feet from Helene's bedroom door. Shivering, she crossed her arms, hugging herself as she rocked back and forth.

"Oh, please dear God, help Helene, help her get well!" Toddy prayed desperately.

Ever since she had rushed into the house a few hours ago and had seen Clara Hubbard's red-rimmed eyes, Toddy had been locked in misery. In a few words, Clara told her what had happened. Sometime in the middle of the evening Helene had begun to have trouble breathing. Gradually the spell grew worse and Mrs. Hale summoned Dr. Woodward. Shortly after he arrived, Helene had had a heart seizure.

"Thank God, the doctor was here!" mumbled Clara, sniffling, holding a crumpled handkerchief to her mouth.

All the blood in Toddy's body seemed to turn to ice water. Her teeth began to chatter and she had to clench them to stop. Deep shuddering waves of panic threatened to engulf her. Only by sheer willpower was she able to prevent breaking into sobs. Helene had had "spells" before, but nothing like this. Hovering outside the closed door, Toddy had heard her rasping gasps for breath. Toddy bit her lip, fighting back the choking sobs. "Please, God, please!" she begged, the rest of her prayers wordless.

She knew it was not right to bargain with God, but that night as she cried out to Him, Toddy's plea repeated itself endlessly. "If You'll just let Helene get well, I'll be so good. I'll not pose in front of the mirror, or try to be witty or make fun of Miss Tuttle or imitate people! I'll not show off or anything, Lord. Please! I'll devote my whole life to Helene, if You'll just make her well now."

Unorthodox as her prayers were, they were straight from her aching heart. Helene was her *sister*, no matter what anyone else said! Of all the people in her life, Toddy knew Helene was the only one who loved her just as she was! If she lost Helene, how empty the world would be.

From out of the past came the jeering voice of Paula, the housemaid, long gone to wherever departing housemaids go. Still, her spiteful words echoed clear and loud in Toddy's memory. "If anything happens to Miss Helene, mark my words, you'd be out on your ear, quick as a wink!" Toddy had pretended not to care, but the warning had left deep scars in her soul.

Remembering them now, Toddy felt herself shrink back into that former state of insecurity. What *would* happen to *her* if Helene—Toddy hugged her arms about herself. She wouldn't even think about it. Nothing was going to happen to Helene. Please, God!

Just then Helene's door opened and Dr. Woodward stepped out into the hall, followed by Mrs. Hale. Toddy scrambled up from where she sat, stepped back into the shadows.

"Well, she's passed this crisis," Dr. Woodward said. "She'll probably sleep for a few hours. But she's not to be left alone. Someone should be at her bedside in case her breathing becomes labored again—"

"Was this—*serious?*" Mrs. Hale asked. "I mean, more than a complication of the cold she caught coming home from the Christmas church service?"

"In Helene's state of health, *anything* can be serious," Dr. Woodward replied.

"I wish we could have gotten away sooner!" fretted Mrs. Hale. "I had hoped to spend the winter in Italy, hoped the warm Mediterranean climate would—" she halted. "You know I was planning to take the girls to Europe in March, Dr. Woodward. Should I wait until spring?"

There was a long pause, and Toddy held her breath.

Then Dr. Woodward sighed. "My dear Mrs. Hale, I don't think *when* you go makes a great deal of difference."

"Do you mean—do you think the trip would be too much for Helene?"

"What I'm trying to say in the kindest way, Mrs. Hale, is that it doesn't matter whether she goes to Europe or stays in Meadowridge. Helene is only twenty-three, but she has the heart of a person three times her age, and it is wearing out. I have to tell you Helene may have only a year or less to live."

Toddy was not sure whether it was Mrs. Hale's moan or her own she heard. She brought her hands to her mouth, the knuckles pressing hard against her lips.

A year! One year, twelve months. Helene had only a year to live! Dr. Woodward's pronouncement repeated itself endlessly in Toddy's brain.

Gone were all those fantasies of running away with Chris, of the two of them living in a little cottage somewhere together, running hand-in-hand forever through fields of daisies. It was a dream. A childish dream to be put away with all other childish things.

If Helene only had a year, Toddy would devote herself totally to making it the best, the happiest year she had ever known. Whatever it took, whatever she had to give up, that's what she would do!

19

Germany
Winter 1902

In the mirrored elegance of the dining room at the German hotel, Olivia Hale sipped her after-dinner coffee, her expression thoughtful as she observed the two girls sitting opposite her at the table. Toddy and Helene were at one of their favorite games—the theme being to imagine the life stories of their fellow diners, providing them with fantasy backgrounds, purposes and destinies. Most of the time they played it with sly subtlety and yet it was usually accompanied by suppressed giggles and, occasionally, unrepressed hilarity. Since most of the other guests at the luxurious hotel neither spoke nor understood English, the game was fairly free from detection by their "victims."

Olivia was glad the two girls could find some relief in this innocent pastime since otherwise their sojourn in Munich would have been completely without pleasure for Helene and probably tediously boring for Toddy. They were here for Helene to be examined by a famous German specialist at the recommendation of her Swiss doctor.

Ironically, his diagnosis had supported that of Dr. Lee Woodward in Meadowridge. So all Olivia's desperate search for a cure or more optimistic prognosis for Helene's condition had been futile. All the traveling, the consultations, the clinics and the enthusiastic endorsements for this treatment or that had all, in the end, proven fruitless.

Unconsciously Olivia sighed, observing her two companions. While Toddy's complexion glowed and her hair had a healthy sheen as a result of their weeks in Switzerland, Helene, by comparison, looked frailer, paler, her dark eyes larger in her thin face.

Olivia felt a stab of resentment. Why? Why *Helene*? What good was all her money, enabling her to take her granddaughter anywhere on the globe, seek the finest doctors known, if it could not bring health and well-being to this dear girl?

Suddenly Olivia felt weary. She was tired of traveling, tired of foreign countries, alien ways, people speaking languages she could not understand. She was tired of consulting her phrase book in order to accomplish the most ordinary task. She longed for the simplicity of life back in Meadowridge. She wanted to be in her own comfortable house, eating food without strange names. She wanted to sleep in her own bed. Olivia wanted to go home.

Just then there was a burst of lighthearted laughter from across the table and Helene buried her mouth in her napkin while Toddy reached for a glass of water as though choking.

Irrepressible youth! No matter what she had been through as far as examinations, unpalatable medicine, exhausting treatments, Helene had maintained her zest for life, her sense of humor, her sweet disposition. And, of course, Toddy was the source of much of it.

At this moment, their waiter approached, his erect bearing that of a Prussian officer. With a stiff bow, he asked in almost unintelligible guttural English: "Vill der be anysing else, Modam?"

"I think not," Olivia replied and signed the check he presented on a small silver tray. Rising from her chair, she asked, "Ready, girls?"

Toddy and Helene exchanged a glance.

"We thought we might wait in the salon for a while, Grandmother, to listen to the music and watch the dancing," Helene replied, her eyes twinkling.

Olivia's mouth twisted in a smile. She knew it was an excuse to continue their naughty game. She had heard them laughingly discuss the stiff formal atmosphere of the hotel, its middle-aged, overweight guests, all of whom behaved like royalty. She knew they found the social scene in the stodgy hotel ludicrous.

Well, she couldn't blame them if they found it a source of amusement. There certainly had not been much in the way of entertainment for young people during their stay here. Especially for Toddy, so full of life and energy. Not that she ever complained. She seemed completely devoted to Helene, only wanting to be with her. She even accompanied her to her doctor's appointments, spending hours in waiting rooms. Then afterwards, when Helene was fatigued from her ordeal, Toddy would remain in her room, reading aloud to her until she fell asleep. No real sisters could have been closer. Thank God for Toddy, Olivia thought.

Toddy and Helene soon tired of the game since the dancers were few and completely impassive, oblivious to the music and their partners. They soon followed Olivia up to the suite they had occupied since their arrival in Germany.

"I'll go say good night to Grandmother, then I'll be in," Helene told Toddy when they got off the elevator.

Toddy was sitting up in bed braiding her hair when Helene came in about a half-hour later.

Helene looked pensive as she sat at the foot of the bed and watched Toddy for a few minutes silently.

"Anything the matter?" Toddy asked.

"I think Grandmother wants to go home, Toddy."

"To Meadowridge? But I thought she meant to go back to France, to Paris."

"She did, at first, but now she says she's anxious to get back to the States, to get settled in her own home again. I think she feels we've been gone long enough." Helene's eyes were troubled. "The *real* reason, I think, is what she's *not* saying, Toddy. She's discouraged, disappointed that the European doctors she was told so much about can't fix my heart!" Helene gave a little shrug. "But then nobody could do that! Dr. Lee warned her before we left not to be too optimistic. I overheard them talking—"

Something cold clutched Toddy's heart. She hoped Helene had not overheard that ominous prediction.

"So, then we'll be leaving to go back...soon?"

"That's what we were talking about. I told her I wanted to discuss it with you. Because, you see, Toddy, I have an idea." Helene paused, then leaned over and took Toddy's hand in both her own.

"Toddy, I've always wanted to spend Christmas in Austria. You know there seems something very special about that country to me. It was the place where my favorite Christmas carol, 'Silent Night,' was composed in a little village not far from Salzburg." She took a big breath. "What would you think of letting Grandmother go ahead to London and arrange for our passage home while we—you and I— stay on another few weeks and celebrate Christmas in Austria?"

"What would your grandmother say to that?" Toddy asked cautiously.

"I'm sure she'd be agreeable if you are." Helene smiled. "It's not as though we were children anymore. You're twenty and I'm almost twenty-five and after all it *is* 1902! We're living in the Twentieth Century, not the Dark Ages!"

So it was decided that Mrs. Hale would go to England by herself. There, from the comfort of her suite at the Claridge Hotel, she would make arrangements for the return trip to the States. When the girls joined her there at the first of the year, they would be able to enjoy some theater and shopping and sightseeing in London before their sailing date.

It was with much excitement and an elevated sense of independence that the two boarded the train in Munich for Salzburg and from there to travel to the Alpine valley of Badgastein, a renowned health resort. For centuries it had been a popular resort for vacationing kings, emperors, maharajahs, statesmen, Europeans listed in the Almanach de Gotha, as well as world-famous artists, such as Wagner.

The deciding factor in Mrs. Hale's concession to Helene's request was that she would also be getting the restorative benefits of this notable spa.

But as the two young women got off the train at the station and saw the picturesque Austrian village, they could not have been more delighted at its endless possibilities for a holiday.

Floating through the clear, crystal air was the sound of Viennese music, provided by a band attired in colorful Tyrolean costume. The winding streets were thronged with tourists and townspeople alike, all dressed in traditional costumes—the men in embroidered vests, lederhosen, and ribboned knee socks; the women in tight velvet basques and swinging flowered skirts, accompanied by cherubic, rosy-cheeked children looking like miniature replicas of their parents. The shop windows were bright with all sorts of intriguing gifts, and the streets were gaily decorated for the season.

"It looks exactly like one of those toy villages people set up under their Christmas trees, doesn't it?" exclaimed Helene, squeezing Toddy's arm.

The hotel had sent its horse-drawn sleigh to take them up the snowy hill to the rambling, rustic brown chalet surrounded by green-black evergreens. Perched on a cliff, it commanded a magnificent view of a waterfall and bridge so ethereally beautiful that Toddy was reminded of an Impressionistic painting.

The chalet had a fairy-tale look with its carved and fancifully painted eaves, sharply contrasting to the formal German hotel with its' stiff, uniformed staff. Inside, there were no marble pillars or potted palms, but a roaring fire blazing in the wide stone fireplace, and comfortable furniture. Everyone was friendly and smiling, the atmosphere warm and welcoming.

A bellhop, fresh-faced as a choirboy, took Toddy and Helene up a broad staircase to their adjoining rooms. Each one opened out onto its own little balcony. The furnishings were simple—a glossy wood floor, white walls, a handsome, hand-painted Austrian armoire, an alcoved bed, covered with a white eiderdown quilt and piles of feather pillows into which one sank luxuriously.

Helene was given her spa schedule which sounded interesting and not stringently therapeutic. In each room there was a map of the hotel grounds, indicating the pathways for walks, punctuated by directions to coffee shops as rewards at the ends of the routes.

"This will be a wonderful vacation!" declared Helene, looking happier than Toddy had seen her in weeks. A dart of hope sprang up in Toddy. Maybe this more relaxed environment was just what Helene needed.

So began a fortnight of serene days filled with interesting new experiences and happy events. Helene's mornings were taken up with her prescribed treatment, followed by an hour's rest. Then Toddy met her for lunch—sometimes in the hotel's outdoor restaurant, where, incredibly warm and comfortable, they sat in bright sunshine while surrounded by snow-covered hills glistening like gems. Afternoons they spent strolling the various walks and exploring the fascinating shops in town, ending up in one of the coffee shops to sip café mocha, topped with swirls of whipped cream, and to listen to Viennese waltzes from the bandstand in the center of town.

"It's all so magical!" Toddy sighed ecstatically.

"It's a long way from Meadowridge, isn't it?" laughed Helene.

At that moment Toddy noticed a passing group of young men in lederhosen and jaunty Tyrolean hats. Strangely, something about one of them reminded her of Chris Blanchard. For one brief moment Toddy felt a sharp twinge of regret. It came and went in an instant. It was all for the best, she told herself. After all, it was she who had broken off their romance, given him his freedom to find someone else. There was no room in her life now for romantic plans.

Later, when Toddy remembered these weeks she and Helene had spent together in Badgastein, it would seem an endless stream of happy days—each one a wonderful gift to be opened and enjoyed.

As Christmas drew near, they became very secretive, going their separate ways on afternoon shopping excursions as each planned surprises for the other. Spending Christmas so far from home took on a very special meaning to both of them.

Two days before Christmas Eve there was a parade through the middle of town with the arrival of "St. Nicholas," the Austrian version of Santa Claus, dressed regally in a red velvet cape trimmed with ermine. The jolly "saint" passed out delicious chocolate candies and exquisite marzipan, an almond-based confection, in the shapes of fruit. People lined the streets to cheer him and shout as he passed by, calling back the greeting, *"Froehliche Weinachten."*

Their arms full of mysterious purchases, the girls hurried back to the hotel on foot in the early darkness amidst white curtains of softly falling snow. Helene squeezed Toddy's arm as they entered the chalet.

"Oh look, Toddy, how beautiful!"

Inside, in the center of the lobby, stood a Christmas tree in sparkling splendor, its shining star nearly touching the vaulted ceiling. Decorated with beautiful ornaments—angels, birds, flowers, painted balls, draped with gilt garlands, hung with silvery tinsel—the tree gleamed with dozens of tiny candles.

"Oh, isn't it all perfect, Toddy?" sighed Helene happily.

But when they got to their rooms and dumped their packages, Toddy thought Helene looked pale and drained. Toddy insisted they order room service to bring their supper up so she could get into bed and rest.

When Helene protested, Toddy reminded her, "Remember there's to be a party for the hotel guests tomorrow, and you don't want to be worn out and miss it."

But Helene did miss it. Too weak to get up the next morning, she sent down word to the hotel doctor that she could not come for her usual appointment, and he dropped by later to check her condition. Toddy blamed herself for crowding too much into these days before Christmas, and promised herself that from now on she would make sure to slow down the pace of their activities. Helene, as cheerful as ever, reassured Toddy that *she* had overdone and only needed to rest a bit.

Still feeling too weak to attend the gala party Christmas Eve in the lobby, Helene insisted Toddy go. Reluctantly she complied, but did not stay long and came back upstairs shortly, bringing the gift that had been placed on the tree for Helene, along with eggnog and all sorts of cookies and other goodies so they could have their own Christmas party.

When they heard the church bells ringing, they bundled up and went out on the balcony to watch the procession of townspeople in their traditional folk costumes walking by on their way to attend Midnight Mass. To Helene's joy, they were singing her favorite carol in German, *"Stille Nacht, Heilige Nacht."*

"Oh, Toddy, this *has* to be my happiest Christmas ever—" she sighed.

Awakened on Christmas morning by the maid bringing her breakfast, Toddy was alarmed to find a note from the hotel doctor asking her to come to his office. As soon as she was dressed, after peeking into Helene's room and seeing she was still asleep, Toddy went straight downstairs.

The doctor wasted no words. "Your sister's condition is deteriorating," he told her gravely. "The treatments we have suggested are only a palliative, giving her temporary relief, but we cannot stop the progress of her disease."

Toddy felt a cold tide of fear wash over her.

"Miss Hale is living on borrowed time. Every day is a miracle."

Toddy's hands clenched in her lap. "What do you suggest we do?"

Dr. Ludwig shook his head and stroked his well-trimmed beard thoughtfully for a moment. "I cannot advise travel, it would be dangerous, but you two young ladies are alone and very far from home—" he paused significantly. "I think you should notify Miss Helene's grandmother—"

Toddy left the doctor's office as if in a trance. Instead of returning to her room where Helene would hear her come in and call to her, Toddy went outside and blindly turned onto one of the trails that wound through the snow-drifted woods. Unthinking, she took the one marked the Empress Elizabeth Walk, named after the mother of the tragic Crown Prince Rudolf who had died mysteriously at the Royal Hunting Lodge. It was said that it was along this path the heartbroken mother often walked, mourning her only son.

Toddy's own heart was near breaking. The vague anxiety she had always felt about Helene descended like a leaden weight. All the hopeful signs she had looked for with this change of scene she now realized were mostly her own wishful thinking. The snow-sparkled scenery about her dimmed as tears flooded her eyes.

Helene's time was nearly up, her days numbered. The fear the Hale household had lived with but never spoke of openly, was about to come upon them. Did Helene realize it, too?

Why? Oh, why must Helene be taken away from her? Bitter sobs rushed up into Toddy's throat, and she halted on the path. Leaning her arm against a tree, she put her head upon it and wept.

At length, she straightened up. The tears had not eased the pain, but they had strengthened her spirit.

"If we only have this time, it will be the best of all possible times," Toddy resolved. She wiped her eyes, blew her nose and, turning, walked back to the hotel. Helene was asleep when she looked in on her, so Toddy had a chance to compose herself before Helene awakened. By then, Toddy was her old merry self, regaling Helene with droll imitations of the porter, the desk clerk and any number of characters she had observed or drew from her own fertile imagination. If Toddy had ever doubted her acting ability, she could no longer deny it now.

Hard as she tried to keep up a brave front, when Helene awakened she looked up suddenly and saw Toddy gazing at her with wistful eyes.

Helene reached out and covered Toddy's hand with her own thin one, saying tenderly, "Toddy, dear, don't be sad, please. I know, and it's all right. I've known for a long time. I'm not in any pain physically or too unhappy about the fact that I won't get well."

"But you *must* get well, Helene!" Toddy said fiercely while tears streamed down her cheeks. "We'll go somewhere else, find another doctor. I won't accept it! I'll keep praying and—"

"Don't distress yourself for my sake," Helene said softly. "Let's enjoy what we have. Now, this day, this very minute."

Toddy slipped out of her chair, knelt beside Helene, holding onto her hand, her head against Helene's knee.

"I can't lose you, Helene," she sobbed. "There must be something we can do!"

Helene smoothed Toddy's unruly curls. "Toddy, would it help to know *you* have made all the difference in my life? Dear little sister, without you my life would have been so drab, so lonely—"

In spite of trying to be brave, Helene began to cry also and for a while the two girls clung to each other helplessly, their tears mingling.

They talked for a long time, sharing all the deep things in their hearts, agreeing to make the best of the time they had together. Then, noticing Helene's pallor, Toddy insisted she not talk anymore, just rest.

As it turned out, their time together was shorter than they had guessed.

The next morning Helene was too weak and ill to get up, and Toddy sent for the doctor.

Toddy refused to leave her and that afternoon as she sat by her bedside, Helene slipped quietly away. When the doctor came again, Toddy was still holding her hand.

Numbed by her grief, Toddy walked outside into the fading daylight. Directionless, overwhelmed by the enormity of her loss, she continued through the village, crossed over the little arched bridge at the end of the street, and found herself in the churchyard of a small Baroque chapel. She pushed open the doors and walked inside. Only a flickering lamp near the altar illuminated the interior; there was a quietness within that comforted Toddy as she advanced up the short aisle to the wooden kneelers in front of a small altar.

She lowered herself and knelt, feeling the peace of the place wrap around her like a cloak. All the questions she had had about Helene's being taken from her rose, demanding answers. But all that came into her mind were the remembered Scripture verses: "Be still and know that I am God....My thoughts are not your thoughts, nor are my ways your ways."

Toddy did not know how long she knelt there, but as she got to her feet and started out of the chapel, she saw a wall plaque on which was lettered in the artistic German script: *"Auf Wiedersehen."*

In English she knew that meant "Farewell. Goodbye. Until we meet again."

Softly Toddy whispered, *"Auf Wiedersehen,* dear Helene."

20

It was to a devastated Mrs. Hale Toddy returned when she reached London. Although they had both known for some time that Helene's life hung by a thread, the realization that she was dead was difficult for both of them to absorb.

Mrs. Hale seemed unable to think or act in her normal efficient manner, so it was Toddy who took charge of making their reservations and the arrangements for Helene's body to accompany them on the long, sad journey home.

While they awaited their departure date, the gray drab English winter weather did nothing to lift the sense of depression which weighed so heavily on both of them. They missed Helene as much when they were together as when each was alone. Soon Toddy realized her presence was a poignant reminder to Mrs. Hale of the granddaughter she had lost, and began to keep to herself.

The earliest possible sailing date was three weeks after her arrival in London and in the long days that followed, Toddy had much time to think about the past, ponder the present, and worry about the future.

On the solitary walks she took along the strange city streets and through its parks, under skies gray with fog, Toddy's heart was heavy, her thoughts troubled. Out of the past rushed that old fear, the voices taunting, "If anything happens to Helene—"

Now something *had* happened to Helene. Now that she was gone, what was to become of Toddy?

The bitterness of her first grief had dulled somewhat. Not for anything would Toddy wish Helene back to the wasting pain of her illness. Helene had gone sweetly, quietly, had not suffered at the last. With all her ardent faith Toddy *knew* Helene was at peace, joyful, healed. It was just that nothing or no one could fill that void created by Helene's passing. The whole world seemed empty now that that one dear face was missing.

At length, it was time for them to board their ship. Almost immediately Mrs. Hale retired to her own cabin and kept to it for most of the week's voyage. On this crossing, Toddy was not a part of the group of young people laughing, playing shuffleboard and deck tennis, dancing late into the night in the social lounge. She remained apart, except at mealtimes, when she sat at her assigned table and bravely tried to carry on pleasant conversation with the other passengers. The rest of the time she walked the deck, or sat bundled in her deck chair looking out at the sea that brought her, day by day, closer and closer to the time of decision.

She went over and over in her mind what she should do. The open book in her lap lay unread as she stared out into space, trying to see into her own future. Once back in Meadowridge, Mrs. Hale would not need her. She was a strong woman who had already survived other tragedies. Toddy felt she could not expect to remain part of the Hale household now that the reason she had been brought there was gone.

She must do something useful with her life. With dismay, she realized that she had never had long-term goals. Not like Kit, who wanted to write, nor did she have a glorious singing voice like Laurel. She had been in love with Chris and thought they would marry. Then that dream had been put aside when she decided to devote herself to Helene until—

She had sent Chris away, and she did not regret that, although there was still a bruised spot in her heart when she thought of him. She had done the right, the fair thing, and by now Chris probably had found someone else to make him happy. She wasn't going to look back at what might have been.

But now, with Helene gone, Toddy wanted *her* life to count for something.

Two days out of New York, Toddy paced the deck deep in thought. At one point she halted to lean against the rail. Thoughts of Helene were very strong.

Oh, Helene, if you were only here to advise me, to help me, to tell me what I should do. Toddy sighed in despair.

She could imagine Helene whispering, "Pray about it, Toddy, dear," and she felt a certain lifting of her spirit.

Of course, that's what she *should* have been doing all along! But Toddy had found it hard to pray since Helene's death. She would begin and then her thoughts would drift, remembering snatches of conversations, some of the experiences they had shared, the people they had met on their travels. What started out as prayers often became melancholy reminiscences.

But as she stood there, the wind tugging at her hat and veil, Toddy did pray. The words of a Psalm, came to mind: "Show me Thy ways, O Lord, teach me Thy paths. Lead me in Thy truth and teach me, For Thou art the God of my salvation." It was almost as if she had been guided to pray from Scripture, but she added her own postscript, "Lord, You know me. My good points and bad ones, my abilities and my weaknesses. You know my heart. Lead me in the direction You would have me go, give me a purpose in life."

The last night on shipboard before their scheduled docking the next morning, Mrs. Hale called Toddy into her stateroom.

"Toddy, there are some things we need to talk about," she began. "I've been thinking of a memorial service for Helene when we get back to Meadowridge and I want you to choose an inscription for a headstone that would be appropriate for her. You were closer to her than anyone, Toddy, so you would know what she would like best—"

Toddy felt a lump rising in her throat that made it difficult for her to reply. The request made Helene's death heartbreakingly real.

"Yes, I'll think about it," she promised.

"And there's something else, Toddy, I've meant to speak to you about before, but now is as good a time as any. Now that Helene is gone, you must begin to think of your own future. You know how much Helene loved you, Toddy. What you may not know is that she was independently wealthy. She inherited a great deal of money from her father, my son." She halted again. "I could explain all the legalities, but what matters is that Helene had a long talk with me when you graduated from high school. Helene always knew that her life hung by a fragile thread and insisted on making out a will before we left for Europe. You, Toddy, are her chief beneficiary."

Toddy looked uncomprehendingly at Mrs. Hale.

"Yes, you heard me correctly. She left most of her estate to you," she said as if anticipating Toddy's disbelief. "She wanted you to be free and independent as she was. The difference is that you have the health to travel, to accomplish your goals. I am, of course, the guardian of the trust fund she had set up for you. Until you are twenty-one, my signature will be required on any expenditures or withdrawals you make, my approval necessary for any investment." Mrs. Hale regarded Toddy sharply. "Do you understand what this means?"

Toddy nodded. "I think so."

"If you want to go to college, or return to Europe or pursue a career—We need to talk to Mr. Blanchard at the bank about your funds and how you choose to spend them."

Up until that moment Toddy's decision had not been definite. Suddenly Toddy felt what must be God's will for her life.

Her voice sounded surprisingly strong, even to herself. "I think I *have* decided, Mrs. Hale. I believe I would like to be a nurse, to enter nurses' training."

Mrs. Hale nodded her head slowly, as if considering the idea.

"A splendid idea, Toddy. You'll make a fine nurse. You're intelligent, compassionate, energetic. Your personality is steady and cheerful. Yes, Helene would be pleased."

21

1903–1904

The rising bell shrilled down the hall, echoing into every cubicle of the probationers' dormitory in the Nurses' Training School, Good Samaritan Hospital.

Toddy moaned, pulled the blanket up over her head, burying her face in her pillow. Only a faint gray light seeped in through the high windows on this winter-dark morning. She squeezed her eyes shut more tightly. Could she possibly sneak ten more minutes of sleep?

All around her Toddy heard familiar sounds coming from her awakening fellow student nurses—similar protesting groans, creaking bedsprings, opening drawers, swishing water being poured into washbowls.

Five-thirty! Only twenty minutes to get up, put on her pink muslin uniform, button on the starched white pinafore, pull on and garter the black cotton stockings, lace up and tie the sensible black duty shoes. Then wash her face, brush her unruly curls, twist her hair into the severe topknot and secure it with pins, fling the dark blue, red-lined cape around her shoulders and run downstairs and across the quadrangle to the chapel for morning prayers. After that, over to the hospital dining room, bolt a breakfast of oatmeal and coffee, and report to duty on the ward by seven sharp.

Upon signing in and checking for any special assignments in the Head Nurse's duty book, there would not be a minute Toddy could call her own for the next twelve hours. First, sweep and mop the ward floor, scrub every unoccupied bed with disinfectant and change the sheets. Then, while the Third Year students bathed the patients and prepared them for the day, six-month probationers such as Toddy set up breakfast trays. While the patients were eating or being fed, "probies" were sent down to the basement to pick up coal for their ward and carry the loaded scuttles back upstairs for the stove at the end of each corridor. Next the water pitchers for each patient's bedside table must be filled and distributed.

At nine, the staff doctors made rounds, accompanied by the ward nurse and followed by the student nurses who took notes while the charts were checked and any new diagnosis was made or new medication prescribed. The students were well advised to pay close attention since they would later be quizzed on the chart sessions. At ten, they were due in class in the school building. Two hours later, back to the wards for lunch tray distribution.

A half-hour break followed, giving little time to eat their own lunch and review any lessons before afternoon classes which lasted until three. Back on the wards at four where, supervised by the Third-Year students, they gave back rubs, refilled water pitchers, freshened the patients and readied them for Visitors Hours, and worked in the linen room, folding and sorting.

At five, dinner trays were brought up from the kitchen. Again, probies distributed and collected them. Six was their own dinner hour, followed by a half-hour recreation period before they were to report back to their wards to help get patients settled for the night.

At nine, when they returned to the Nurses Home and their own "cubes," there were still tomorrow's lessons to be studied, papers to write, chart notes to be reviewed. At ten, when the "Lights Out" bell rang, Toddy usually could barely hold her eyes open.

She had never imagined nurses' training would be so rigorous. Most of her classmates were hearty farm girls from the Midwest, used to hard chores at home and not delicate boned like Toddy. But what she lacked in physical strength, Toddy made up in enthusiasm and energy and a fierce determination to succeed in her chosen vocation. She had a real empathy for the patients and most enjoyed caring for them.

The discipline was harsh. It was the purpose of the school to weed out early the young women who would not make good nurses. The requirements for graduation, the solemn "capping" ceremony, awarding the symbol of each young woman's success, were stringent. Not only was a thorough knowledge of anatomy, physiology, chemistry, and pharmacology demanded, but the understanding of the procedure of prescribed treatment as well as its application.

There were, however, subtler, other infinitely more important aspects of the would-be nurses' personalities that were carefully noted, observed, marked by their teachers, their supervisors, and the doctors they attended. Did this person have the necessary skills, the patience, the reassuring presence, the serenity in a crisis to instill in the sick or injured patient the confidence that he was being cared for in the best and most effective manner?

The first weeks she was at Good Samaritan, Toddy was not even sure she would make it through her six-month probationary period. Sometimes, dragging up to her cubicle after a seemingly endless day, she would throw herself across her cot, fatigued, frustrated, filled with the gnawing uncertainty that perhaps she had made a dreadful mistake. Maybe she was not cut out to be a nurse.

In spite of doubts, reinforced by Miss Pryor's often cutting reprimands, Toddy got through her probationary period, and traded her pink uniform for the blue-striped one with its high, stiff collar and white-bibbed apron of the Student Nurse. When particularly discouraged or worn out, she would strengthen her resolve by repeating the reassuring verse from Philippians: "Being confident of this very thing, that he which hath begun a good work in you will complete it." She had come here believing it was God's will for her life, and she would trust Him to see her through.

But if she thought those first months were hard she had a further eye-opening when she entered into the second half of her training.

Everything was more intense and demanding—the studies, the ward work, the constant supervision by relentlessly exacting superiors. Every nine weeks the student nurses were assigned to different wards under different head nurses. Each one, with different expectations and different requirements, took getting used to. While students were expected to make these adjustments, they were at the same time learning new skills, sharpening their observation abilities, noticing and charting changes in patients, and following directions, all the while trying to be cheerful, prompt, and attentive.

One afternoon Toddy was taking a well-deserved break in her dormitory room before going on the second half of her shift, when one of the probies stuck her head in the door and announced she had a visitor in the guest parlor. Puzzled, Toddy got up from where she was curled on her cot, straightened her hair, smoothed her apron and went downstairs.

"Hello, Toddy," a familiar voice greeted her as she came in the parlor door.

Toddy blinked her eyes. To her surprise it was Bernice Blanchard, Chris's mother, sitting primly in one of the parlor chairs.

"Mrs. Blanchard!" she gasped. "How—how nice to see you."

"Well, Toddy, you look well." Mrs. Blanchard's eyes took in every inch. "You are probably wondering why I'm here. Well, Mr. Blanchard had to attend a Banking Conference in St. Louis and I decided it was too good an opportunity to miss, so I came with him. I saw your—" she halted a second, then said, "I saw *Mrs. Hale* at church last Sunday and she told me you were at Good Samaritan. It was so very close and Mr. Blanchard had meetings to attend today, so I thought I'd just come over and pay you a little visit. That way, I could give Olivia a report on how you are getting along—" She paused, her eyes narrowing in her plump, pink face.

"Oh, I'm just fine, thank you, Mrs. Blanchard," Toddy replied, still having some difficulty adjusting to the fact that Chris's mother had made a special trip to see her.

Mrs. Blanchard shifted her position slightly and settled her fur neckpiece a little before continuing.

"I'm very glad to hear that and to know that you are doing something useful with your life. One cannot expect handouts forever and I am sure it's a great burden removed from Olivia to have you on your own, especially now that dear Helene is gone."

At this, Toddy felt a rush of indignation. She checked the angry rebuttal that sprang to her lips. Hands clenched hotly behind her back, she managed to control an outburst. Surely this wasn't the reason Mrs. Blanchard had come? To go out of her way to be insulting?

Mrs. Blanchard moved uneasily. Toddy unconsciously braced herself as the woman cleared her throat.

"I *do* hope you will take this in the spirit intended, Toddy," she began tentatively, "but I did feel you ought to know Chris is back from South America. Poor dear, he looked dreadful when he returned home, so thin and sallow. He had a terrible bout with malaria while he was down there—anyway, he is much improved and has decided to go back to the University to get his engineering degree."

Pausing for breath, Mrs. Blanchard twisted the chain of her beaded handbag. "Of course, he had run off to those awful jungles after you so heartlessly...well, we needn't go into that, I suppose. But, I wanted you to understand that I feel—*we* feel, his father and I—that he is finally on the right track after his...disappointing setback. And...I hope...I do *sincerely* hope you will not try to contact him or to pick up any of the old destructive threads of your relationship with our son." Mrs. Blanchard's chins trembled in the fervor of her appeal. "What's past is past—Chris has a fine future ahead of him and I—*we*—feel any attempt on your part to—"

Toddy could not stand it a minute longer. She got to her feet and spoke in a voice she willed not to shake.

"Please, Mrs. Blanchard, there is no point in your saying any more. I understand you completely. Let me set your mind at ease. I have no intention of contacting Chris. As far as I'm concerned, he doesn't even know where I am, unless you've told him." Toddy swallowed hard. "I'm glad to hear he's doing well and that he's happy. Chris will always mean a great deal to me, but as far as attempting to disrupt his plans or his life—"

"Well, I wouldn't have put it so bluntly—" stammered Mrs. Blanchard, perhaps realizing she had gone too far.

"No? Well, how would you have put it, Mrs. Blanchard? You made yourself quite clear," Toddy replied coolly. Then checking her watch pinned to her apron, she said, "you will have to excuse me. I go on duty in ten minutes. Goodbye, Mrs. Blanchard, you may tell Mr. Blanchard you accomplished your mission."

Then Toddy turned and with all the dignity she could muster, she left the parlor and started up the stairs. But when she reached the landing the scalding tears spilled down her cheeks.

What Mrs. Blanchard said had hurt. But maybe she was right. About Mrs. Hale, about Chris.

"What's past is past." Chris was part of Toddy's past in Meadowridge. Now, more than ever, Toddy understood fully what she had always known. The Blanchards did not approve of her for their son. They never had accepted her they never would. Any hope Toddy might have entertained about a future with Chris must be put away forever.

Yes, Mrs. Blanchard had achieved her end in coming. From now on, Toddy would banish everything else from her mind but her nurses' training.

22

1905–1906

Well into her second year Toddy found an almost immovable object on her way toward gaining her nursing certificate in the form of Miss Mabel Pryor, the supervisor of Student Nurses.

As they entered into this second year of training, the student nurses worked in pairs in the wards. Toddy was teamed with Helga Swenson, a sturdy, rosy-cheeked girl with flaxen braids from a Minnesota farm family. For all her robust appearance, Helga was terrified most of the time. She was afraid of Miss Pryor and all the head nurses, scared speechless around the doctors, nervous with the patients.

To offset her partner's paralyzing tension, Toddy joked, teased, did imitations of some of the more pompous members of the medical staff, particularly the overly important interns and residents.

One day when they were making beds together, one on each side, Toddy was at her most hilarious and Helga was giggling as they precisely turned neat corners and pulled the sheets tautly. Suddenly Miss Pryor's acid voice cracked behind them.

"There will be no levity on my ward, young ladies. Is that understood?"

Helga turned red then white and began shaking. Toddy immediately tried to straighten her face as they both chorused, "Yes, ma'am."

But as Miss Pryor turned and walked stiffly away, Toddy dissolved into helpless laughter and Helga pressed both hands against her mouth, her plump shoulders shaking with suppressed merriment.

Ever after that, at every opportunity, Toddy would come up to Helga and whisper sternly, "No levity!" and that was enough to send the poor girl into spasms of uncontrollable giggles.

Perhaps it was this ability not only to make others laugh but to laugh at herself that saw Toddy through some of the really hard and often sad times during her training.

Because she was naturally outgoing and friendly, Toddy was at her best with the patients. She seemed able to establish an instant rapport with them as she gave them a bath, brought food trays, or delivered medication. She always had a smile, a cheery greeting and listened to their complaints or worries with sympathetic attentiveness.

This was especially true with one patient, Mrs. Agnes O'Malley, an elderly woman who had been admitted for surgery. Because she was tiny and frail, the doctors wanted her to gain weight and strength before undergoing a scheduled operation.

During the time Toddy cared for her, she and Mrs. O'Malley formed a special relationship. The little lady was as optimistic and pleasant as Toddy, and they hit it off right away. The only thing she worried about while she was in the hospital, she confided to Toddy, was her two cats, her canary and her rosebushes.

"Mrs. Sutton, my neighbor, is taking care of Dickie, my bird, but the cats—you know they are such creatures of habit!" she said. "They like things to be the same. Eat out of the same little bowls in the same place in my kitchen by the stove, and they like their cream a little warm—you know how 'tis?"

Toddy nodded as she gently smoothed the sheets and turned the pillowcase.

"And pretty soon my rosebushes will need pruning and who's to see to that?"

As the day for Mrs. O'Malley's surgery drew near, she fretted more. "I do hope as soon as my operation's over the doctors will let me go home pretty quick. I don't like to be away from my little family any longer than necessary. They depend on me so."

From chatting with Mrs. O'Malley every day, Toddy got a mental picture of her small cosy house, of the two cats and the bright yellow canary in its cage in the window of her snug little kitchen, "singing his tiny heart out" as Mrs. O'Malley was fond of remarking. It was Toddy who prepared her when the day of her surgery came, and it was she who walked alongside the guerney, holding her hand as they wheeled her down the corridor to the operating room.

"I'll be here when you wake up, Mrs. O'Malley," she promised the old lady as she left her at the door of OR.

But when Toddy came back on duty, she noticed Mrs. O'Malley's bed had been stripped. Hurrying over to the rack of charts, Toddy pulled Mrs. O'Malley's and found it marked PATIENT DECEASED. A sob escaped Toddy and she put her head down on the counter and wept.

Fingers pressed hard into her shoulder and a sharp voice hissed into her ear, "Miss Todd, come into my office at once." Hastily Toddy straightened up, replaced the chart, and followed the rigid figure of the head nurse into her office. There Miss Pryor confronted her severely.

"Miss Todd, the cardinal rule of nursing is not to become emotionally involved with the patients. You give them the best care you are capable of, but you do not let yourself be drawn into their personal lives. If you do, you will fail as a nurse, fail the very patients who need you. Is that clearly understood? Now get back on the ward, there is work to be done."

Toddy bit back angry words, checked the indignant tears. What about Mrs. O'Malley's poor little kitties? Her bird?

Her roses? What would become of her things? She was alone in the world, she had told Toddy, after years of working as a housekeeper to a family in San Francisco. She had bought her little house with her savings when she retired.

Now, Toddy was supposed to forget all about her?

During the next few months Toddy was tried to the very limits. No one saw the enormous effort it took for her to accept correction, reprimand, a misunderstood explanation, a mistaken or unwarranted scolding from a head matron. No one ever saw the tears wept into her pillow late at night, the overwhelming feeling of exhaustion, of desperate longing to escape the inflexible routine.

She had packed Helene's worn New Testament in her trunk when she left to come away to Nursing School and nightly Toddy sought the solace and strength she needed. She missed Helene's soft voice reading aloud as she used to, but the remarkable thing, it seemed to Toddy, was how often the verse or Scripture she turned to was exactly the right one for that moment of need. It was almost as if Helene had become her guardian angel watching over her, caring for her during those long months.

And then, at the end of the year of training, Toddy had a long-overdue opportunity to rest, to spend two weeks in Meadowridge. Because she had wanted to be sure Toddy could be there, Mrs. Hale had waited until this time to plan a special event.

In her will, Helene had left money for a very specific project, one that had occupied her grandmother for the past year and a half—a bequest for a Children's Room to be added to the Meadowridge Library. The dedication was to take place during Toddy's vacation.

Helene had been very specific about the addition. "It should have lots of windows so it is full of sunlight," she had stated. "And there should be low shelves filled with books so that the children can reach them, little round tables and

177

small chairs so they can sit down and look at the books to decide which ones they want to take home."

The bequest was so like Helene, Toddy thought, a perfect "memorial" to a young woman who had loved books and reading and who had, herself, always been a child at heart.

As Toddy boarded the train in St. Louis to make the trip to Meadowridge, she was strongly reminded of the "Orphan Train" that had first taken her to Meadowridge and into the Hale home. Thoughts of the bleak days at Greystone, of her friends Laurel and Kit, of Mrs. Scott and that long, "scary" trip over the mountains and along the prairies, carrying them to an unknown destiny were vivid.

Along with the memories came the childhood doubts and uncertainties she had usually managed to mask behind activity and hard work and a bright smile. Still, lurking in her heart of hearts was the question, *Is there any place I really belong?*

Almost before she was ready, Toddy heard the conductor calling out the next stop.

"Meadowridge! Next stop, Meadowridge!"

She had not sent word of the exact time of her arrival, so there was no one to meet her at the station. It was better this way, actually, for Toddy had a sense of melancholy as she remembered the last time she had stood on this platform. Helene had been with her then. They had been leaving for their grand tour to Europe and were full of hopes and plans. Now, she was back here alone.

She left her suitcase to be delivered to the house later, and taking only one small valise, began walking along the familiar streets from the train station, then turned up the hill toward the Hale house.

At the gate she paused, struggling with her emotions, imagining Helene's face at an upstairs window, waving to her as she had done so often. Toddy stood there, her hand on the latch for a moment, before she pushed it open and started up the walk to the veranda.

But before she reached the first step, the front door opened and Mrs. Hale came out. She held out both arms and Toddy dropped her valise and ran up the steps and into Olivia's embrace.

"Oh, Toddy, I'm so glad you're here!" Olivia's voice broke. "Welcome home, my dear girl."

Toddy leaned her head on Olivia's shoulder, sobbing, knowing for the first time in her life, without any doubt, that she had come home at last.

The day of the dedication was very warm. The noon ceremony was to take place in the main library at the doorway into the Children's Room. In attendance were the Mayor, members of the City Council, the ministers from all four Meadowridge churches, each to give a short invocation or benediction. Following the speeches and the ribbon cutting, the ladies belonging to the local "Friends of the Library" were to hold a reception out on the side yard and lawn of the library. The event had been given front-page coverage in the *Meadowridge Monitor* and many more townspeople than held library cards came thronging in to witness the proceedings.

As the sun outside climbed into its midday position, the crowded library grew very hot. By the time all the speeches were given, many were anxious to get out into the cooler air and quench their thirst with the gallons of lemonade provided by the Refreshment Committee.

People immediately surrounded Mrs. Hale to shake her hand and to add their personal appreciation for this wonderful gift to the community left by her granddaughter. The first crush of well-wishers seemed to startle Olivia a little and as she took a few steps back, Toddy stepped protectively to her side. One of the ladies quickly organized a more orderly receiving line for people to express their thanks.

Looking down the line Toddy saw, to her dismay, Bernice Blanchard! Toddy had not seen Chris's mother since that fatal day at Good Samaritan. Still, she was bound to run into the woman sometime during her stay in Meadowridge and she tensed, trying to prepare herself for what could not help but be an uncomfortable encounter. Fervently praying that by the time Mrs. Blanchard reached her, she would be able to handle it graciously, Toddy attempted to focus only on the next person in line.

Despite her distraction Toddy heard Mrs. Hale saying something quite astonishing.

"Have you met my *other* granddaughter, Toddy?" Mrs. Hale was saying.

Toddy wasn't even sure that she had heard correctly until Mrs. Hale repeated the same phrase several times in the course of the next few introductions. It was particularly gratifying that she said it clearly to the couple right in front of Mrs. Blanchard, and Toddy could not help deriving some secret satisfaction in seeing Mrs. B's reaction. She seemed quite flushed and flustered as she reached them.

"A lovely occasion, Olivia," Mrs. Blanchard mumbled, holding out a limp hand as Mrs. Hale acknowledged her comment and passed her on toward Toddy.

But at that very moment, Mrs. Blanchard's face became very red then just as quickly blanched. Her eyes rolled back and she began to slump, her knees buckling, until she fell onto the grass.

There was a gasp from the bystanders who stood staring dumbly down at the prone figure as if struck into stone statues. Toddy sprang into action.

"Get back, everyone, give her air!" she said in a commanding tone.

In a moment, she was kneeling beside Mrs. Blanchard, loosening the buttons on the side of her high lace collar, freeing her throat. Then slipping one arm under her shoulders, she raised the woman slightly and with her other free hand she removed the stiff, straw picture hat.

"Someone, soak some napkins with ice water and bring them to me," Toddy ordered and someone scurried to obey.

Mrs. Blanchard's hair had come out of its pins and fell forward over her face. Toddy held her firmly as she unhooked the tight sash around Mrs. Blanchard's plump waist. As some dripping napkins were thrust at her, Toddy snapped, "Squeeze out the water." When this was done, she took one and pressed it against the back of Mrs. Blanchard's bare neck. The other she held against the woman's forehead.

In the meantime, others recognizing Toddy was in charge had managed to keep the people back, leaving a wide ring of gawkers around the stricken woman so that air could circulate.

Soon, a low moan escaped from Mrs. Blanchard's pale lips and her eyelids began to flutter slightly. At the same time, someone came pushing through the crowd. It was a perspiring Mr. Blanchard, wiping his bald head in agitation. Evidently some one had run over to the bank to tell him his wife had collapsed.

As soon as she saw her husband, Bernice began to whimper. He bent over her.

"It's all right, old dearie. I'm here now. We'll get you home. You're going to be fine—" his voice trailed off anxiously and he looked over at Toddy for reassurance.

"I'll come with you," she said firmly.

With her help, Mr. Blanchard got his wife to her feet and as she leaned against him, Toddy went to support her on the other side. Together they walked her slowly inside the library.

The crowd made a path for Dr. Woodward who had attended the dedication and ceremony. He had sent someone for his medical bag and was hurrying to assist them.

"Good work." He nodded to Toddy as he and Mr. Blanchard helped Bernice to sit down.

"I'll go get the buggy, my dear," Mr. Blanchard told her.

For the first time that anyone could remember, Mrs. Blanchard failed to instruct her husband in how to do whatever it was he planned to do. She sat there weakly, propped up in the chair, looking wan and pale. She made no protest as Toddy kept the folded damp napkin pressed against the back of her neck, the other on her forehead.

By the time Mr. Blanchard was back, Dr. Woodward assured them both that Bernice had not suffered a heart attack but had simply been overcome by the heat, the sun and the excitement. She would be fine after a day's rest in bed, drinking plenty of liquids.

"I suggest, however, that Toddy go up to the house with you," he said.

Mr. Blanchard looked grateful at the suggestion.

At the Blanchard's house a frightened Annie came upstairs with them and scurried ahead to turn down Bernice's bed. Toddy helped her get Bernice into her nightgown and into bed.

Before she closed her eyes wearily, Bernice reached out and took Toddy's hand in her clammy one.

"Thank you, dear," she whispered weakly. "No matter what Lee Woodward says, I know you saved my life."

Toddy did not argue. She knew, of course, that Dr. Woodward's diagnosis of a slight sunstroke was correct. But what was important was that the animosity she had always felt from Bernice Blanchard had disappeared. In today's incident Toddy had found an unexpected place to belong—in the heart of Chris's mother.

23

Then almost before it seemed possible, the three years had come to an end, and it was time for the State examinations. Now was the ultimate test of whether Toddy would qualify to reach her goal. The exams would cover everything she was supposed to have assimilated, would test her intelligence, her memory, the daily practice of the nursing skills she had acquired.

The three days of exams, two a day, morning and afternoon, left Toddy drained. The third day Toddy and some of the classmates with whom she had struggled and worked and shared in such close companionship throughout their training, went out for dinner to a favorite Italian restaurant to celebrate. Or at least try to forget for a few hours that the State Examiners were deciding their combined fates.

A week later when the news circulated throughout the school that the exam grades were posted, Toddy was among the first scrambling down the steps into the front hall to search the list on the bulletin board for her name. She did not have to look long or far. ZEPHRONIA VICTORINE TODD was at the top of the graduating class.

Graduation date was scheduled and invitations to family and friends sent out. Mrs. Hale was coming.

Unlike many of her fellow nurses who had applied to hospitals near their hometowns, Toddy had not thought much further than Graduation Day itself. So she was surprised when Miss Pryor called her into her office and encouraged her to apply for a position right there at Good Samaritan.

"All your teachers and supervisors have given you excellent recommendations, Todd. You have the combination of nursing skills and the right attitude to make an outstanding nurse. I have watched your progress carefully and have noted that you have conquered your original tendencies to be too personally concerned with your patients. Nurses deal with life and death every day and unless you want to be broken by it, you must discipline yourself and cultivate the needed professionalism to withstand the emotional strain."

Toddy was both pleased and gratified by her supervisor's compliment. Still, Toddy was unsure. She felt she needed a stronger leading before she made a commitment about her future. Besides there was something still in her own mind she needed to settle.

Leaving Miss Pryor's office, Toddy went into the chapel and sat there quietly. Late afternoon sunlight streamed through the stained-glass window over the altar, illuminating the picture of the Good Samaritan tending the wounds of the injured traveler. Underneath was the inscription: "...Inasmuch as ye have done it unto one of the least of these my brethren, ye have done it unto me" (Matthew 25:40).

Where would the Lord have her serve? Toddy asked herself. How could she find guidance for where to go to best use her nursing skills, these years of training? In time, God would show her the way. She could trust Him for that.

As she came out of the chapel, she met two of her friends just coming in.

One of them smiled and whispered, "You've got company waiting for you in the parlor, Toddy."

She wondered if Mrs. Hale had arrived early for graduation. Toddy had made reservations for her in one of the nicest hotels in town, but had not expected her until the next afternoon. She hurried to the visitor's parlor. At the doorway she stopped short.

Instead of Mrs. Hale, a tall young man rose to his feet at her entrance.

"Chris!" Toddy gasped.

"Hello, Toddy."

It had been almost four years and as Toddy's eyes widened in astonishment, she saw how much he had changed. The lanky leanness of boyhood had become a broad-shouldered manliness, the boyishly handsome features now strongly molded in a deeply tanned face.

"Oh, Chris, how wonderful to see you!" exclaimed Toddy, holding out both hands to him. "How did you know I was here?"

Chris put down the bouquet of pink and white carnations he was holding to take Toddy's extended hands in a tight grip.

"My mother!" He grinned. "When I got home last fall, she told me all about how you'd saved her life!"

"Nonsense! I didn't, of course." Toddy smiled. "But I'm so glad to see you. Please sit down." She gestured to a chair. "There's so much to catch up on, so much I want to know about you, Chris."

"Well, I went back to the University and got my degree and was back in Meadowridge for a few weeks before starting a new job in Arizona. I went by to see Mrs. Hale and she told me all about you—says you're graduating at the top of your class. Congratulations, Toddy. I'm proud of you." Then he looked at her and, grinning his old boyish grin, asked, "May I come to your graduation?"

Toddy felt her heart turn over.

"Of course you may! Chris, I can hardly believe you're really here!"

"Well, I wasn't sure you'd see me." Grinning, he ducked his head in a familiar shy gesture. Then, he said, "Mrs. Hale's been traveling every time I've been home, it seems, the house closed. I didn't even hear about Helene until—" he halted, then said sympathetically, "I'm so sorry, Toddy, I know how much she meant to you."

"Yes, thank you, Chris," Toddy replied. "Actually that's why I'm in nursing. I want to spend my life helping other people like Helene—" she halted, blushing. "I hope that doesn't sound pretentious, for goodness sake!" She rolled her eyes.

Chris reached over and covered her hand with his big, rough one.

"Not at all. It sounds like the Toddy I know, impulsive, generous—" He paused a moment before adding, "It sounds like the Toddy I *love*."

Toddy looked into the eyes regarding her with such tenderness and drew in her breath.

"I *do* love you, Toddy, you know that, don't you? I always have and I always will." Chris rushed on, "The main reason I came up here to see you now is because I wanted to tell you that. I've not changed about that. I never will. There's never been anyone else for me, Toddy."

"Oh, Chris, don't say any more. Not now. Not yet."

"Then *when*, Toddy? Will there be a time you'll listen to what I have to say, what's been in my heart all these years?"

She nodded. "Yes, Chris, perhaps. But not right now. I have tomorrow to think about and —"

"After tomorrow?" he persisted.

Toddy got to her feet, holding the bouquet like a shield in front of her. "Chris, I have to go. There's a Graduation rehearsal in twenty minutes." He rose too, towering over her.

"All right, Toddy. I can wait. I've waited this long." He smiled ruefully. "I'll see you tomorrow then."

"Yes, Chris, tomorrow," Toddy promised.

The organ music of the Processional reverberated into the arched nave of the hospital chapel as the twenty nursing students marched in solemnly and took their places in the two front pews.

The distinguished looking Chief-of-Staff, Dr. Willoughby, stood at the podium with Miss Pryor at his side. As each young women's name was called, she mounted the altar steps and received her rolled and ribboned certificate. Miss Pryor pinned her RN pin onto the collar of her stiffly starched new white uniform. There was, as they say, hardly a dry eye among those attending the ceremony.

When Toddy's turn came, Olivia Hale unashamedly wiped her eyes, watching as the petite, slim figure in white, the newly earned fluted organdy cap perched on her shining red-gold hair, accepted her hard-earned reward.

After Dr. Willoughby congratulated them, Miss Pryor took her place at the podium and spoke directly to the new nurses.

"Perhaps only those of us who have come along the same path can fully appreciate and understand what your cap, pin and certificate mean. *I do know* and it is with heartfelt sincerity that I commend each of you on this important day of your lives.

"What you have shown and will continue to show in this vocation you have chosen is a deep respect for life. We here at Good Samaritan have tried to instill in you that respect.

"What does it mean? It means that every life has value, no matter how new, no matter how old, no matter how rich, no matter how poor. It means that every human being is treated with dignity, no matter how sick, no matter how weak, no matter how wretched, no matter how lost.

"It means that every person is a gift from God, no matter what religion, no matter what color, no matter what age, no matter what nationality.

"This is our creed, our calling. We have tried to pass this on to you young women as you start your nursing careers, so that you might give to the world this same devotion, that your lives may be lived for the honor and glory of God."

When the benediction was pronounced, Toddy rose with the first row of nurses and moved out into the aisle for the Recessional. Through eyes misted with happy tears, she searched out one face among all the others in the crowded sanctuary.

There at the back as she passed. Chris! He had come, and suddenly their future seemed possible.

24

1908

Spring came to Meadowridge late but then seemed to explode. Blossoming orchards scented the air with rare perfume, every garden gone crazy with color. The May of which poets rhapsodized became reality.

On just such a morning in the second week of May, up on the hill at the Hales', the household was stirring early, busy with preparations for the noon wedding.

It was a wedding that no one had been sure would ever take place. Certainly not Bernice Blanchard, who was at the moment trying to decide between two hats most appropriate for the "mother of the groom," albeit a reluctant one. She had thought her opposition and their long separation would have broken the strong link between the two young people.

For that matter, Olivia Hale had had her own reservations about the match. Surely these two strong personalities would continue to clash as they had in childhood, with foolish quarrels, disagreements and disputes. Their backgrounds and experiences had given them different perspectives, formed new attitudes. Could basic incompatibility of temperament and character be bridged as adults?

Toddy herself, not denying the strong mutual attraction she and Chris had always been aware of since high school, recognized some of the problems of their relationship. She had not been as easily convinced as Chris that they were "meant for each other."

She pored over the Scriptures she had learned to search out for life's big decisions, studying any reference to choosing a mate or marrying. The one that concerned her was from the third chapter of Amos: "Can two walk together except they be agreed?" Were she and Chris enough alike to spend the rest of their lives together? Or on the other hand, too much alike? Impulsive, quick-tempered, strong-willed?

When Chris persisted, Toddy begged for more time.

But in the two years since graduating from nurse's training, much had happened to draw them closer, to help them understand each other better, to recognize the other's good qualities, accept the differences, share each other's hopes and dreams. Most of all to learn to love each other in a new and deeper way that was both binding and freeing.

At Mrs. Hale's suggestion Toddy had come back with her to Meadowridge. She had found it difficult not to burst into tears when Mrs. Hale extended the invitation. She was wanted! She belonged! And when she arrived, Clara was there to greet her, too. "Welcome home, Toddy!"

Chris left reluctantly for his job in Arizona, but persisted in his suit by letter and as many frequent trips to Meadowridge as he could manage.

Observing Mrs. Hale, into her seventies now, Toddy saw that she was slowing down. Her eyesight was failing and, when fall came, Toddy was loath to leave her. So when Dr. Woodward offered her a job as his office nurse three days a week, Toddy accepted. She also registered herself to be on call if needed at the new Community Hospital.

It had been a good year, a worthwhile, productive year. More and more Toddy felt her special place in Olivia's heart becoming firmly established. It was a place which belonged to no one else, a place she had earned. She knew she had found her niche in nursing as well, and she felt at peace that she was doing God's will for her life.

Then Chris came to tell her he had been put in charge of the entire project in Arizona, beginning the first of the year, and he wanted Toddy to come back with him. She knew she could delay her answer no longer and went to Mrs. Hale, sharing all her own thoughts, her feelings, her questions.

Mrs. Hale leaned forward and took Toddy's face in both her hands. "My dear girl, you have given me so much. I could never repay you for all the happiness you have brought into my life and, of course, Helene's. Now it is your time. Go with a free heart and mind. A fine young man loves you. Take the life he is offering you and be grateful for such a love. You have my blessing."

So on this beautiful May morning Toddy finished her final packing. After the ceremony she and Chris would leave for Arizona, going straight to the train station from the reception Mrs. Blanchard insisted on giving them.

Toddy was both calm and excited. The only shadow on this lovely day was that Helene was not here to share it with her. In the garden, as Toddy gathered lilacs, pink tulips, grape hyacinths and lily of the valley for her wedding bouquet, Helene was much in her thoughts. Helene had loved flowers and these were among her favorites.

Toddy had not wanted a big, elaborate wedding and had stood quietly determined against all Mrs. Blanchard's pleas about the "social obligations" she and Chris's father needed to fulfill.

"It's *our* wedding, Mrs. Blanchard," Toddy reminded her firmly. "And we just want the people *we* love and care about to celebrate with us when we marry."

Chris, too, was adamant and so Bernice gave in with a sigh of resignation.

But as she sat beside her husband, wearing the elegant chapeau she had finally decided upon, in the Meadowridge

Church filled with Toddy and Chris's high-school friends, Bernice had to admit that the ceremony was perfect. The bridegroom, of course, was quite the handsomest and even the bride, in her simple cream boucle traveling suit, lace blouse and biscuit straw hat, looked dainty and attractive.

As Toddy left the church on Chris's arm, she whispered, "Before we leave for the reception, there is something I want to do."

Hand in hand they walked together up the hill to the church cemetery. Inside, Toddy quickly found what she was looking for—a headstone engraved:

HELENE ELIZABETH HALE
1879–1902

Beneath the inscription Toddy herself had chosen, "The Redeemed of the Lamb," was a favorite verse of Scripture: "And God shall wipe away all tears from their eyes; and there shall be no more death, neither sorrow, nor crying, neither shall there be any more pain..." (Revelation 21:4).

Chris thoughtfully took a few steps back, leaving Toddy standing alone in quiet contemplation beside Helene's grave.

Then she knelt and placed her bridal bouquet at the headstone. As she did so, she felt a release of the one sad little corner of her heart that had so deeply missed her beloved sister this day. After a few more minutes, Toddy rose and held out her hand to Chris.

He came forward tucked Toddy's small hand into his arm and together they strode out through the gate and into the new life they had waited so long to begin together.

QUEST FOR LASTING LOVE

JANE PEART

Fleming H. Revell
A Division of Baker Book House Co
Grand Rapids, Michigan 49516

Scripture quotations in this volume are from the King James
Version of the Bible.

ISBN 0-8007-5372-0

Copyright © 1990 by Jane Peart
Published by Fleming H. Revell
a division of Baker Book House Company
P.O. Box 6287, Grand Rapids, MI 49516-6287

Printed in the United States of America

QUEST FOR LASTING LOVE

1

Boston
December 1888

Something dreadful was about to happen. Laurel just knew it. Mama had seemed strange all morning. In fact, Mama had not seemed like herself for weeks. Watching her mother move slowly about the small rooms they rented upstairs in Mrs. Campbell's big, dark house, Laurel was newly alarmed.

For weeks now, even when she was playing tea party with her dolls, Laurel often felt her mother gazing at her. When Laurel looked up, she would see a sad expression on the beautiful face, and the dark, violet-shadowed eyes would be glistening with tears.

Frightened, Laurel would ask, "Why are you crying, Mama?"

Then her mother would quickly gather Laurel up into her arms and hold her, saying, "Nothing, my darling. Everything will be all right, you'll see."

But things were not all right, Laurel knew, and day by day she could feel that little knot in her chest grow tighter. Something was wrong.

Her mother gave piano lessons on Tuesday and Thursday afternoons, and Laurel always played quietly in a corner of the room while the students fumbled through their scales and the simple pieces they never seemed to get quite right. Usually after the last pupil left, her mother would sit at the piano and play lovely, rippling melodies, filling the room with harmony. A welcome relief after two hours of missed keys and sour notes.

Lately, however, when the lessons were over, her mother closed the piano lid with a deep sigh. Then, pale and exhausted, she would lie down on the narrow sofa, one arm flung over her eyes. Laurel would come over and sit on the cushions behind her and gently stroke her forehead.

"What would I do without my little nurse?" her mother would say with a weary smile.

Sometimes she drifted into a shallow slumber, waking with a start, two bright spots of color in a face otherwise drawn and white.

"Oh, my, Laurel, our supper will have to be fashionably late this evening."

At mealtimes they pretended that the simple fare of bread, tea with milk, and a piece of fruit for Laurel was a sumptuous affair fit for royalty. Her mother would be Queen Lily and Laurel would be Princess Laura Elaine, which was her *real* "christened" name, after her two grandmothers.

Laurel did not know her grandmothers. Her mother told her that they both lived "a long way off," but someday she would meet them.

"Someday, when all is forgiven—" her mother would murmur when Laurel asked when. Laurel did not understand. But she was so happy with the life they had together, she did not trouble herself with wondering about much else.

But more and more, things had been disturbingly different. She had awakened in the night several times to the sound of her mother's weeping— weeping that would often turn into a frightening paroxysm of coughing. Stiff with anxiety, Laurel, in her own small bed, would hug her doll Miranda. Hearing her mother get up, she would awaken to see her throw a shawl over her long, drifting nightgown and huddle in the chair by the window, trying to smother her hoarse racking cough.

It was one afternoon soon after a particularly bad night when the coughing had lasted a long time that her mother had left Laurel with Mrs. Campbell to go to the doctor.

Laurel liked staying with Mrs. Campbell, who was fat and jolly and cooked for the boarders who lived in her other rooms. She was usually in her large cheerful kitchen where she always seemed to be stirring something and where all sorts of wonderful things simmered on the stove, filling the air with delicious odors.

She pushed a little stool over for Laurel to stand on beside her at the big, square, scrubbed pine table and let her help roll out the biscuit dough. Then she showed her how to take a small glass tumbler, dip it into flour, and cut out the round shapes to be put on the baking sheet and placed in the oven of the big, black iron stove.

They were thus happily occupied when Laurel's mother returned. Mrs. Campbell took one look at her and pulled out her oak rocker for her to sit. Then she filled her blue kettle with water from the kitchen pump and placed it on the stove to boil.

"There now, rest a bit and I'll have a nice cup of tea for you in a minute. You look that worn out, Lillian." Then in a lowered voice and with a furtive glance at the child, she asked, "Is it bad, then?"

Laurel's mother leaned her head against the high, fan-shaped back of the chair and nodded wordlessly. Laurel wiped her floury hands on the large apron Mrs. Campbell had tied around her, got down from the stool, walked over and climbed up into her mother's lap. Her mother nestled her close, resting her chin upon Laurel's soft dark curls, and answered Mrs. Campbell's question.

"Yes, Mrs. Campbell, very bad, indeed, I'm afraid. I shall have to make plans—" Her voice drifted away weakly.

"If there's anything I can do to help—"

There was something in Mrs. Campbell's response that made Laurel cuddle even closer to her mother, winding her little arms around her mother's waist, breathing in the sweet, violet scent of her. She felt an inner trembling. That dark thing she had felt hovering over them crept nearer.

Before she was even fully awake, Laurel heard the steady pattering of rain against the windows and felt her mother's hand gently stroking her hair.

"Come, darling, you must get up."

As Laurel sat up, sleepily rubbing her eyes, she saw that it was still dark outside.

"Is it nighttime?" she asked, watching her mother's slender figure moving about in the lamplight, setting the table for breakfast.

"No, precious, it is very early in the morning. But we both have to go somewhere, and I am fixing a special breakfast for us. Cocoa for you and the last of the coffee for me."

Even though her mother was being especially cheerful and gay, Laurel felt that queasy sensation stirring deep inside. Was this the day the dark unknown thing was going to happen?

The feeling was so strong Laurel could not really relish the surprise treat of sticky buns or the creamy hot cocoa.

But it wasn't until her mother had brushed her hair for an extra long time, carefully winding each curl around her fingers then tying them in bunches with velvet ribbons on both sides of her head, that she told Laurel what it was.

"You know, darling, Mama has not been feeling too well lately and the doctors tell me I must have a long rest if I want to get strong and healthy again. So, I have to go away to a place in the mountains where they can take care of me and help me get better. And you are going to stay at a nice place with a lot of other little girls and boys whose mamas are sick or away—" Here her voice broke and she hugged Laurel to her. Laurel felt the wetness of tears on her mother's soft cheek and she clung to her in sudden panic.

"But I don't want to go anywhere without you, Mama!"

"I know, my darling, but it will only be for a little while. I will come as soon as I can and get you and we will be together again. I promise!"

In stunned disbelief Laurel watched her mother pack a small valise with all her neatly ironed clothes—the dresses with the embroidered yokes, the pinafores, the white cotton chemises, panties, ruffled petticoats trimmed with crocheted edging, all handmade so lovingly for Laurel.

Then Lillian took off the gold chain and locket she always wore from around her own neck and fastened it around Laurel's.

"I want you to wear this until I come for you, Laurel." She pointed out the intertwined swirled letters on the heart-shaped front. "See these? They spell out our initials. The L.M. stands for Lillian Maynard—my maiden name—and the P.V. is for your father—Paul Vestal. It's important for you to remember that, Laurel," she said. "Your father gave me this before we were married, since he couldn't afford an engagement ring. But I always loved it." Then she opened the locket to show the pictures inside. One was of Lillian herself when she was a young girl with her dark hair falling in curls around her shoulders; the other picture, of a handsome, dark-eyed young man. "This is your precious papa, Laurel."

Laurel could not remember her father. He had been killed in a tragic accident, knocked down by a team of runaway horses when he was crossing the street on his way home one snowy evening when Laurel was just a baby.

"Now, remember, Laurel, don't take this off for any reason, until I come."

After that her mother buttoned her into her velour coat with the scalloped cape that she had fashioned for her only the month before. After she tied Laurel's satin bonnet strings under her chin, she kissed her on both cheeks. Then, hand in hand, they went quietly down the stairs of the sleeping house and out into the dark, rainy morning. At the street corner they found a cab and sad-looking horse, its driver bundled into a muffler, his chin on his chest, a battered stovepipe hat slipping forward on his brow.

Lillian squeezed Laurel's hand and said with a hint of the old gaiety in her voice, "This is going to be quite an adventure, darling. As long as we have to go, we're going in style."

"Where to, lady?" The driver roused himself with a jerk.

"Greystone," Lillian told him as she helped Laurel mount the high, rickety steps into the cab.

"You mean the County Orphanage?" he barked.

"Yes," Lillian said and this time her voice quavered.

Inside, she put her arm around Laurel, drawing her close. The ancient gig swayed and jolted over the cobblestone streets through the dreary morning drizzle, jogging slowly up a steep hill. All the while, Laurel felt the chill creep in through the cracks of the old vehicle, into her very bones, and she shivered, leaning into her mother. They did not speak on the way, just clung to each other.

Finally the cab jerked to a stop in front of a stone fortress-like building.

The driver opened the roof flap and hollered down. "Greystone!"

Laurel's mother grasped her hand tightly and, after getting down herself, lifted Laurel down. Then she said to the cabbie. "Wait, please. I need to ride to the train depot."

Still holding Laurel by the hand, she mounted the steps. At the massive, double door, Lillian gave the metal doorbell a twist. Her mother was holding Laurel's hand so tightly it hurt her fingers, but even so she did not want to let go.

Finally the door was opened by a tall woman. She seemed to loom over them, making Laurel's mother seem smaller, more fragile than ever.

"Yes?" She regarded them with narrowed eyes, waiting for Laurel's mother to speak.

When it came, her voice seemed thin and faint. "I'm Lillian Vestal, I've come to....This is my little daughter—"

"Ah, yes, Mrs. Vestal. We were expecting you." The woman stretched out her hand toward Laurel, who drew back. Then she spoke crisply to Laurel's mother. "It is best you leave now, ma'am. The children are at prayers and will be going into breakfast. There will be less of a fuss if you say goodbye here."

Laurel's hand clutched her mother's convulsively. She felt the sick rise of nausea into her throat. "No, no," she tried to say, but the words wouldn't come out.

Her mother bent to hug her, whispering, "You must be a brave, good girl, my darling. I will be back soon. Very soon."

"Come along, child." The voice in the doorway was firm.

Lillian pried Laurel's hands from around her neck, murmuring soothing words as Laurel felt herself being pulled out of her mother's embrace. She heard a smothered sob and turned to reach out again for her, but Lillian had already started down the steps.

At last she heard her own scream shrill through the air. "Mama! Mama! Come back!"

At that moment Laurel was picked up bodily and thrust through the door. When she heard it slam behind her, she wriggled out of the confining arms that held her, flung herself sobbing against the thick impenetrable door, and pounded her tiny fists against it.

2

Greystone Orphanage

All her life Laurel would remember the bewildering change from her life with her mother to that at Greystone. Numbed with shock, she moved like a little sleepwalker, unconscious of the stares of the other children, the worried frowns of the orphanage staff. Unresponsive, she allowed herself to be placed in line for meals, but barely touched her food. Eyes lowered, she did not respond to friendly overtures, merely nodded yes or no if asked a direct question.

Only her big, dark eyes reflected the pain caused by the abrupt transfer from the small, warm, sheltered world she had shared with her adored mother to the large, impersonal institutional life of Greystone.

For the first two days Laurel was at Greystone, she got up in the morning at the rising bell like everyone else. Then she dressed, put on her coat and bonnet, went down the main stairway and planted herself on the bottom step, her arms folded across her chest, her mouth set stubbornly.

"My mother is coming for me," she stated flatly and shook her head at any request to come away. Miss Clinock wisely rejected the use of any disciplinary action on the part of the other matrons or having Laurel physically removed from her post.

On the third day, however, the Head Matron herself approached Laurel.

"Laurel, your mother left you with us while she is in the sanatorium getting well," Miss Clinock intoned. "But until then, she expects you to try to be happy here with the other children, to be obedient and do as you are told. Now, come along, Laurel," she said firmly and held out her hand. "You want us to give your mother a good report of you when she *does* come, don't you? You wouldn't want us to have to tell her you had been a naughty girl who wouldn't mind, would you?"

Tears turned Laurel's eyes into glistening coals. She didn't want Mama to be disappointed in her. Slowly she got up, lifting her chin bravely, but refusing to take Miss Clinock's outstretched hand.

"Come along, then, there's a good girl," the woman said and led the way upstairs to the third floor dormitory.

Rows of small iron cots lined the long room. Beside each bed was a small chest, on which was an enamel pitcher and washbowl. Next to that a wooden stool. As Miss Clinock entered with Laurel, two dozen heads turned and all the little girls momentarily stopped tidying their cubicles.

"Get on with your duties, children," Miss Clinock spoke crisply. Her eyes roved around the room, then spotted the one narrow cot left unmade, its blankets tossed back, the pillow rumpled. "Come along, Laurel," she said and made straight for that one.

"Kit," Miss Clinock addressed a girl with smooth brown braids, who was pulling up the covers of her own cot next to Laurel's. "Will you please show Laurel how to make her bed and put her clothes neatly away?"

The girl turned around, glancing at Laurel with a shy smile. "Yes, ma'am."

"Every morning before prayers and breakfast, Laurel, your bed is to be made, your nightclothes put away." Miss Clinock spoke directly to Laurel. "Starting today, you will wear the Greystone uniform like the rest of the girls in Third."

"But my *mother* made *my* clothes! She wants me to wear these," protested Laurel, her lower lip beginning to tremble.

"We will put the things your mother made for you away carefully, Laurel, so that they will be ready for you when she comes. But while you are at Greystone, you will wear what the other girls wear," Miss Clinock said decisively.

Then she told Kit, "After things are put right here, Kit, take Laurel to Mrs. Weems in the Sewing Room to get a uniform." With that directive, the Head Matron left.

Laurel plumped down on the end of her cot, chin thrust out, arms folded again. She felt a gentle tug on the bed-clothes underneath her as Kit began pulling them straight.

"Come on, I'll show you how. It's really easy," she said in a low voice.

A tear rolled slowly down Laurel's cheek. She didn't uncross her arms to free a hand to brush it away. Then she felt Kit's arm go around her shoulder. "I know how you feel," Kit whispered. "I felt the same way when I first came here. But you get used to it, honest."

"I'm not going to stay here," Laurel said as if trying to convince herself. "I don't have to. My mother is coming for me. *Soon!*" She squeezed both eyes shut tight, letting the tears flow unchecked.

"So is *mine!*" piped up a cheerful voice and Laurel opened her eyes to see a smiling little face with a tip-tilted nose pushed right up to hers, round blue eyes staring at her inquisitively. "Any day now." She reinforced her statement with a little nod and bounce as she popped herself down on the bed beside Laurel.

"And so is my *da*," chimed in Kit, adding her declaration to theirs. "At least, as soon as he gets a job."

The three looked at one another appraisingly. In that moment of mutual affirmation, some kind of bond was forged. As yet it had not been tested, but the foundation for friendship was laid. Each of them, in her desperate bid to believe that she was different from the other children at

Greystone, found hope alive in at least two other hearts. By associating with the other two who also were determined to cling to that hope, her own was bolstered.

No three little girls could have been more different in appearance, personality or disposition, yet they became inseparable as the weeks turned into months and their status as "temporaries" inevitably changed.

If it had not been for the other two, Laurel would have found it even harder to adjust to Greystone. The overall drabness of the routine, the cheerless halls, the grinding daily routine of life was brightened a little for her by the companionship of Toddy and Kit.

The three sat at the same table at mealtimes, sought each other out during recreation. Kit was protective, shielding Laurel from some of the older children who were prone to bully the younger, shyer ones. Toddy, though small, was spunky and with her gift for mimicry often turned a potentially ugly playground incident into a comedy with herself as the clown.

During the weeks that followed, Toddy, Laurel and Kit grew closer. It was at night, when the lamps had been taken away, and she lay in her narrow little bed alone that Laurel felt most keenly the reality of her situation. Would her mama never come? she asked herself over and over, fingering the delicate chain of the locket she never removed from her neck. This anxious question would start the tears and the choked sobs. It was then the friendship of the three counted most.

Their cots were side by side in the vast dormitory and, when any one of the three was suddenly gripped by a terrible longing for comfort, her little hand would grope between the cots to find the others' extended in silent understanding.

Their ages varied by a matter of a year, but when tested, it was found they were at the same grade level. Kit, the eldest of the trio, had already had a year of schooling and had kept up her reading skills by reading to her little brother Jamie. Laurel's mother had taught her at home and Toddy, though the youngest of the three, had learned to read from playbills and theater posters, sheet music and railroad schedules.

Separately they had suffered the most traumatic experience in life. Together they helped each other survive by reassuring themselves and each other that soon their parent would come to get them, take them away from Greystone.

After the first long week, Laurel received a letter from her mother. A note, actually. Lily had written:

> My darling little girl,
> This can be only a few lines. They want me to rest and don't allow me to write more than this. I am getting better every day. Soon we'll be together again. Don't forget to be a good girl and say your prayers every day, especially for your loving mother.

Enclosed was a picture postcard with the words SARANAC LAKE SANATORIUM identifying a low, rambling rustic building surrounded by pine trees with porches all along the front. Lillian had drawn a tiny arrow to one of them, printing above it, "This is where I sit out in the sun and fresh air every day."

Laurel looked at the picture, trying to imagine her mother on the small porch. Then she put the letter and picture under her pillow. She unfolded it and read it so many times it became creased and worn around the edges.

Every week Laurel laboriously printed a letter to her mother with her version of daisies, her mother's favorite flower, drawn carefully down the border and on the flap of the envelope. Then she gave it to Miss Massey to address and mail.

Laurel never forgot the day that Miss Massey took her by the hand and led her into Miss Clinock's office.

"Sit down, Laurel, I have something to tell you," the Head Matron said. In her hands were two envelopes which Laurel immediately recognized from the daisies on them—the same daisies she always drew on her letters to Mama.

However, there was something else printed in bold black letters across the front. She could not make it out, so Miss Clinock held up the letter so Laurel could see. Slowly Laurel spelled out D-E-C-E-A-S-E-D. DECEASED.

"Do you know what this word means, Laurel?" Miss Clinock asked kindly.

Laurel shook her head but her heart began a drumbeat that felt as if her chest were exploding. "No, ma'am," she replied in a hoarse whisper.

"It means, Laurel, that your mother is dead."

Dead! Dead? Laurel did not know what *dead* was! Mrs. Campbell's old cat had died, she remembered, and once she had heard Mrs. Campbell tell a visiting neighbor while pointing a thumb at Laurel, "The child's father is dead." But Mama had always told her her Papa was in Heaven with the angels. Did that mean—

Laurel could neither move nor speak. She simply sat there, glued to the straight chair opposite Miss Clinock's desk.

"Are you all right, Laurel?" prompted the Head Matron. "Do you understand what I just told you?"

Suddenly everything got very bright and hot. The room tilted crazily and the pictures on the walls swayed. Laurel saw Miss Clinock rise from behind the desk and start toward her, but her approaching figure began to blur and wobble.

A roaring started in Laurel's ears, getting louder and louder as she felt herself pitch forward, plunging into a whirling black hole. The next thing she knew she was lying down, with both Miss Clinock's and Miss Massey's worried faces leaning over her. One of them propped her up.

"Here, Laurel, sip this," Miss Massey said, holding a glass of water to her lips.

Laurel never remembered too much about the next few days. Somehow they passed in a kind of gray fog. Toddy and Kit were always nearby, but it was as if she were alone. Other people were only vague images to her, while, awake or sleeping, she seemed to see her mother's face everywhere.

She was never sure when the realization actually took hold that her mother was gone forever. Lillian would never come so that they could go home together. In fact, Laurel had no home to go to—except Greystone. She had become just like all the other children. An orphan.

When Laurel was told she was among the children from Greystone who would be traveling west on the Orphan Train, her first reaction was fear of the unknown. But as soon as she knew Kit and Toddy would be going, too, it was all right. Toddy's excitement was contagious and soon Laurel was looking forward to the day when they would meet Reverend and Mrs. Scott, representatives of the Christian Rescuers and Providers Society, and their escorts on the trip west.

The children were given small cardboard suitcases in which to pack their few belongings to take with them on the long trip to their new lives in the Midwest.

To her dismay Laurel discovered she had outgrown all the lovely, handmade smocked and embroidered clothes her mother had made for her. So she had to accept the small wardrobe given to each girl for the journey. The garments were serviceable, if plain—a warm merino dress of dark blue, two cotton pinafores, one to wear and one to keep clean for the stops in the rural towns where the adoptions would take place, two changes of underwear, chemises, pantaloons, two petticoats, three pairs of cotton stockings, and a flannel nightgown. All the girls were issued a warm coat and bonnet and a new pair of high-top black boots with two sets of laces. All these were purchased from contributions made to the Rescuers and Providers Society by interested donors.

But as she packed, Laurel slipped into her suitcase one of the finely tucked and lace-edged camisoles her mother had made. Even if it didn't fit, it had come from beloved hands. Besides her locket, it was the only thing Laurel had left of her life before Greystone.

3

Meadowridge

On a glorious spring Sunday Dr. Leland Woodward drove his small black buggy into the cleared area between the Community Church and Ryan's pasture. He sat for a minute, the reins slack in his hands, listening to the voices floating out from inside the white frame building.

Smiling, he hummed along with them. "Blessed assurance, Jesus is mine! Oh, what a foretaste of Glory Divine—" It was one of his favorite hymns.

He knew he was late arriving for the eleven o'clock service, but he'd had to go home first to bathe, shave and change. He had been out most of the night delivering the Storms' new baby. But he didn't feel tired. In fact, he was exhilarated. Helping bring a new life into the world always gave him a boost that lasted for days. That is, if there weren't complications.

And everything had gone splendidly this time. Irma Storm was a healthy young woman who'd had no problems giving birth to a fine baby boy. Her husband Tom was a happy man. That made four sons for the Storms. Good for a farmer. In the next few years, Tom would have his own crew of harvesters come haying time! Leland chuckled. Children—that's what life was all about really. Suddenly the expression on his lean, handsome face saddened and unconsciously he sighed.

He ran his hand through his thick, prematurely gray hair, then reached for his hat on the seat beside him, put it on, gave the brim a snap, and got down from the buggy, his movements agile for a man nearing forty. Leland tethered his mare to a nearby tree, close enough to the fence so she could reach over and nibble some of the long meadow grass.

Mounting the church steps, he walked inside. One of the ushers saw him and greeted him. Leland dismissed with a gesture the offer of assistance to show him to a seat, but took the hymnal he was handed, then stood for a moment at the back looking around.

He and Ava used to have a regular pew they sat in every Sunday, but that was when—Leland checked another sigh. Ava didn't attend church with him nowadays. Hadn't for nearly two years. Folks seemed to understand and yet maybe he should insist. Maybe it would help. Even seeing the children filing out for Sunday school before the sermon might jolt her from her malaise. But nothing really seemed to help.

His eyes made a quick search for an empty spot. It was better to sit near the door. That way, if anyone should need to send for him during the service, he could slip out without disturbing the congregation or start any buzzing speculation among them as to who might have taken sick or had an accident. Or been shot!

Leland suppressed a wry smile. When he had first arrived here right out of Medical School, Meadowridge was only a mere twenty years away from its roots as a raw mining town. Often he'd had to patch up the rowdies who had gotten into some Saturday night fiasco or other, and a few times some fellow got "trigger happy." Mostly ended up shooting his own foot. But that was a long time ago. Things had settled down quite a bit since then. When the women and children came, schools and churches and houses were built. Decent family folk wanted a decent town to live in, and farming became more popular and productive than searching for gold in the hills that rimmed the pretty valley.

Leland saw a seat at the end of the row in one of the last pews and moved toward it with his light, springy step. Everyone occupying that bench shifted over one to make room for him, nodding and smiling a greeting. The town's only doctor was well liked.

The last of the opening hymns sung, there was a general murmuring of voices, rustling skirts, and shuffling of Sunday-shined shoes, as the congregation settled in for one of Reverend Brewster's sermons. Leland sat back, folded his arms, ready to be instructed, inspired or exhorted. He was in a for a surprise, however because the Reverend was even now announcing a guest speaker.

"Mr. Matthew Scott of the Christian Rescuers and Providers Society is here with a message today that I think will have special meaning for all of us. Living as we do in this beautiful, peaceful valley, surrounded by rolling hills, bordered by a river that gives us our pure water, abundant fish, refreshment and recreation, sheltered in our comfortable homes, lacking nothing in the way of food or clothing, we are apt to forget there are people in this world so unfortunate as to be without any of these necessities." Reverend Brewster paused significantly.

There was an uneasy stirring, glances exchanged among the parishioners as if wondering what their pastor had in store for them.

"I am not speaking only of grown men and women, but of innocent little children as well—abandoned, some of them left to fend for themselves on the streets of a great city—like New York or Boston. Ah, but I shall let Mr. Scott, who knows these sad stories better than I, tell you from his eyewitness experience of this deplorable situation. Mr. Scott, I turn the pulpit over to you."

A tall, thin young man stepped up to the lectern. He had tousled, rusty-brown hair, wore wire-rimmed glasses, and his scrawny neck rose out of a stiff, high collar that seemed too big for it. He looked like a timid, bookish college student.

But when he began to speak, his voice was rich and full and he spoke with an earnest fervor and dramatic depth.

There was not a dry eye in the crowd when Mr. Scott had finished. There were the sounds of sniffles, throats being cleared, and noses being blown throughout the church building. Mr. Scott took off his glasses and wiped his own eyes before he made a last statement.

"I feel sure this appeal has not gone unheard in this community. I know the plight of these children I have described has touched some of you. If that is the case, perhaps you will then be led to open your homes to one or possibly two of these abandoned and orphaned children, to share your warm hearth, your affection, your good examples of Christian charity.

"The Christian Rescuers and Providers Society is dedicated to placing the right child in the right home. We do have certain requirements for the welfare of the child, and to help the adoptive family. Our main goal is to provide these poor lost children with Christian homes in which to be nurtured, trained up in the way they should go, to become God-fearing, law-abiding, self-supporting human beings. The alternative that awaits such children, it grieves me to mention, may be a life lived on the streets, forced into crime and degradation at an early age with the inevitable result—incarceration in one of our nation's prisons. Need I say more? I feel sure your generous hearts will respond. Anyone who may be interested in talking with me further, please see me after the service. I will remain as long as there are questions."

Leland swallowed hard. He had felt an increasing stricture in his throat as Scott had spoken. In spite of his outwardly impersonal professional manner, Leland Woodward had a tender heart that was easily touched, and he had been greatly moved by this talk.

He rarely showed his emotions, however. Even in the great tragedy of his life, the death of his little daughter from diphtheria at the age of seven, he had maintained a stoic composure. It was his grief-stricken wife to whom the sympathy had flowed. Perhaps feeling that a doctor was accustomed to dealing with death, people assumed he could cope with Dorie's death. Many homes had been ravaged by the terrible epidemic that had swept through Meadowridge at that time. They did not know Leland tortured himself that he might be to blame for his little girl's death. Had he somehow brought the infection home to his own child? No one could comfort him for no one knew the depth of his sorrow, his self-scourging, his guilt.

So many came to mourn with Ava. And one by one they had come away shaking their heads. "Her heart is broken. She'll never get over it."

Leland wondered if she ever would. It had been nearly two years since they had lost their only child. Now Ava scarcely ever left the house. She never came to church, saw friends, involved herself in any of her old activities, the things she used to enjoy.

Leland knew his wife was in what was clinically called "melancholia," a depression so deep nothing seemed to be able to lift the dark cloud of sorrow from her.

She had kept Dorie's room untouched. The child's dolls, toys, playthings and books remained as though she might come running in from school at any minute.

Leland knew it was unhealthy. Everything should be put away, given away, swept out of sight. It only aggravated his wife's condition, kept her moored in the same desperate state of inconsolable sadness. But he, though a man of medicine who brought healing to others, was helpless to help the one he loved so dearly.

Leland saw the line of church members forming to meet Mr. Scott. They were clustering around him, asking questions, finding out more about the Orphan Train that would be coming west and would be making a stop in Meadowridge.

He hesitated, turning his broad-brimmed gray felt hat in his hands thoughtfully. Better not to act precipitously. Certainly, he would have to talk to Ava first.

Was it too late to reach her? He missed desperately the sound of a child's voice, laughter in the house, of running feet on the stairs. Would Ava consent, could she accept another child into her life, one who needed her?

He thought of the charming girl he had married—her laughing hazel eyes, her sparkling smile and happy nature. Was it possible she could be that way again? Maybe a child could bring it all back.

Was it worth suggesting? Worth bringing all the old wounding memories to the surface? Then he thought of the darkened room where his wife spent most of her days, staring out the window, or wandering into the bedroom with the white wicker furniture, the dollhouse and bookshelves of fairy tales that had belonged to the little girl who was gone.

It couldn't go on. Something would change. Ava would break—Leland shuddered unconsciously. No, he had to do something, take some action before it was too late. Ava could slip over the brink, and he would have lost not only his daughter but his beloved wife as well.

He would wait until just before the Orphan Train was due to come before he pressed for a decision. In the meantime he would gently persuade her to start thinking about it. Ava loved children. She was made to be a mother. Unfortunately nature had made it impossible for her to bear another child physically—but in her heart? Surely that gentle, caring heart was able to love another child.

In the meantime he would sincerely seek God's will in the matter. Leland had always asked the good Lord for guidance and direction in his life. And so far, he had never failed to get it.

4

Laurel saw her face reflected in the train window as if in a mirror. She stared out into the darkness as the Orphan Train sped across the prairie through the night.

With her finger she began to spell out her name on the gritty surface of the windowsill. "LAUREL VESTAL."

As she wrote, she formed the words silently with her tongue: "My name is Laurel Vestal." The metallic clickety-clack of the train wheels along the steel rails seemed to repeat them. *Laurel Vestal, Laurel Vestal, Laurel Vestal.*

Laurel moved, shifting her position on the hard coach seat. Her head felt hot and she leaned it against the cool glass of the window. Her throat was scratchy, too. Noticing she looked slightly feverish, Mrs. Scott had made up two of the seats into a bed earlier than usual so Laurel could lie down.

"You'll feel better in the morning," Mrs. Scott said, tucking the blanket around Laurel's shoulder. "We can't have you sick when we get to Meadowridge, now can we? Who would want to take a sick little girl home with them?"

Even though Mrs. Scott had spoken teasingly, it worried Laurel. Who, indeed, would want to take her home anyway? Because it was the first time Laurel had not been surrounded by other children for weeks, she allowed her secret fears to emerge. It was the secret fear of all the children on the Orphan Train, really, although nobody talked about it. What if nobody wanted her? No family adopted her?

Laurel closed her eyes and wished—the old wish, the one that never came true. She tried to wish herself back to the little flat on the top floor of Mrs. Campbell's house, tried to hear her mother playing on the piano, tried to recall the melodies of her favorite pieces—"Annie Laurie" or "The Robin's Return"—feel that warm, sweet security of her mother's presence again.

She sighed, a sigh that came from deep inside. If only she had Miranda to cuddle. Why hadn't she remembered to carry her doll with her that last morning when she and her mother had left the apartment?

Laurel blinked, trying not to cry. Her mother had said there would be lots of toys to play with where she was going. But at Greystone the toys had to be shared with everyone, and there were never enough to go around. Besides, none of the dolls could replace her beautiful Miranda. Most of them were worn, battered, the wigs gone, the paint chipped off their faces.

Unconsciously Laurel's hand moved to her neck, fingering the chain and locket that held her mother's and father's pictures. She had promised Mama she would never take it off. At least "until I come to get you." Recalling her mother's words, Laurel felt angry.

Why had her mother not told her the truth? About Greystone? About how sick she was and that she might die? Now, Laurel could not halt the tears. They rolled down one by one and, as she brushed them away, they made sooty streaks on her cheeks.

What had become of all their things? Her books, her doll's bed, the little china tea set that had belonged to Mama herself when *she* was a little girl? The piano and the painting her father had done that hung over it, the one of the lighthouse at Cape Cod? When they hadn't come back, had Mrs. Campbell taken everything up to her attic?

Once Laurel had gone there with Mrs. Campbell when she had lugged up some big boxes that some tenant had left behind. Laurel remembered Mrs. Campbell saying, "You just never know when a person may show up again. And as long as I've got the room, why not? Poor Mr. Lonergan might have had a spell of bad luck, or been hit over the head and lost his memory or something, who can tell?"

Mrs. Campbell was an avid reader of the kind of newspaper that printed the dramatic catastrophes of life in lurid detail. Laurel had a vivid picture of the woman, sitting in her kitchen rocker with the newspaper spread open, clucking her tongue and shaking her head as she read out loud some of the headlines of the stories printed on its pages: "Excursion Boat Capsizes, All on Board Perish," or "Fire Ravages Building, Frenzied Tenants Leap to Their Death."

Mrs. Campbell had probably packed all their belongings neatly and carried them up to her attic. That thought gave Laurel a little comfort.

Just then the mournful sound of the train whistle hooted shrilly as they approached a crossing. Laurel huddled further into the skimpy blanket and pressed her face against the window, peering out eagerly. Laurel liked it when the train slowed a little going through a small town and she could see lights like little yellow squares in the houses they passed. They looked so inviting, so cozy. She tried to imagine who lived there, what kind of family, how many children, what they were doing. Maybe a mother knitting, a father smoking a pipe, children playing on the floor, maybe a baby in a cradle nearby. She would try to imagine what it would be like to be inside—safe, happy, secure.

The familiar longing gripped her heart, bringing on that uncomfortable, choking sensation, a kind of emptiness, that started in the pit of her stomach and spread slowly through the rest of her.

Behind her, Laurel could hear the other children's voices as they finished up a game they were playing. Above all the others, Toddy's voice taking the lead, giving orders. She was glad Toddy was her friend, and Kit. It was Toddy who had come up with the plan of how the three of them could stay together, be adopted in the same town at least. At first, Laurel thought her idea was wrong, like telling lies. But then Toddy had explained it was just like being in a play! And it was the only way they could be *sure* they wouldn't be separated. Of course, Mrs. Scott had scolded them when she discovered what Toddy had coached them to do—Kit, dragging her leg as if she were crippled; Toddy, crossing her eyes and twisting her face into the most awful grimace, and Laurel, hunching one shoulder higher than the other as she walked.

Even though they had gotten into trouble for doing it, Laurel was glad it had worked. There was only one more stop on the trip. Meadowridge. Here they would all find homes. Here, in the same town where they could go to school together and see each other often. That was important. Without Toddy and Kit, Laurel didn't know what she would do.

Unconsciously, Laurel shuddered. She dreaded having all those grown-ups staring at her at every train stop. Trying *not* to get adopted had been bad, but now that she wanted to be adopted, it was even scarier.

The day after tomorrow, they would be in Meadowridge. Mrs. Scott had shown them where it was on the map she had pinned up on the wall. She said it was about the pleasantest town she had ever seen, that she would like to live there herself instead of in Pennsylvania where she and Mr. Scott lived.

Laurel's eyes began to feel heavy. She was sleepy. She pushed the lumpy pillow under her head and closed her eyes. No matter what, even if it *was* scary, it was better being on the Orphan Train on its way to Meadowridge and being adopted—than staying at Greystone and being an *orphan!*

5

"Just to make sure no one's coming down with some contagious disease with which a whole family could be infected," Dr. Woodward had volunteered to give each of the Orphan Train children a brief physical checkup before he or she was "placed out" in one of the adoptive homes. Reverend Brewster, on the advice of Mr. Scott, had suggested it might be a good idea.

On the morning of the Orphan Train's arrival, Leland stopped at the door of his wife's darkened sitting room, and stood there for a moment frowning. Then, striving to sound cheerful, he spoke. "It's a beautiful day, my dear. Why do you have the shutters closed and the curtains drawn? Let me open them, let in some of that lovely sunshine," he urged and started to move toward the windows.

"No, please, Lee," she protested, raising a fragile hand. "I have a slight headache. The glare bothers my eyes."

Leland halted then went over to the chaise lounge where Ava Woodward lay. He lifted her thin wrist in his fingers, automatically feeling for her pulse. He placed his other hand on her forehead but it felt cool to his touch.

"Do you think you'll feel better later? Well enough to accompany me to the train station? The Orphan Train is due in at one o'clock."

"Oh, no, Lee, I couldn't." Ava shook her head.

"But the child—don't you want to help me choose?" he persisted gently.

"No—" she murmured. "It was your decision—"

Leland checked a quick spurt of irritation. "But we discussed it thoroughly, my dear, and you agreed."

"Because you wanted it so, Leland." Ava sighed deeply. "You can be very persuasive."

Leland felt his fists clench. "Ava, if you had any doubts about this, you should have expressed them when I first brought up the subject, not wait until *now*...the very day the children are coming."

Her fingers picked at the fringe of the shawl wrapped around her frail shoulders. She did not meet his pleading eyes.

"I've had the room made ready," she said meekly.

But your heart, is it ready? Leland asked mentally, gazing down at his wife.

She raised her head and, seeing his beseeching look, reached for his hand. "Be patient with me, Lee. It will take time—"

"It's been two years, my dear. It's time we got on with our lives." He paused. "A child is what this house needs now. You said so yourself—"

"I know, Lee. I thought I was ready. But, now, I don't know—" her voice wavered uncertainly.

Leland tried to control his impatience. He took out his watch and consulted it.

"I have to make house calls. I'll be back by noon. Please, dear, make the effort to come with me to the train. It would mean a great deal to me. And to the child."

He leaned down and kissed her on her cheek, then left the room and the house in an agony of indecision. Maybe it had been a mistake to talk Ava into taking one of the Orphan Train children. Perhaps a terrible mistake.

But down deep, Leland didn't think so. He felt it was the right thing. At any rate he was committed now. He had written the Rescuers and Providers Society that he and his wife would take a child into their home. He had stipulated a boy. A boy, he felt, would be easier for Ava than a little girl. It would be too hard for her to accept another little girl... after Dorie.

Like most men, Leland Woodward had always wanted a son. Dreamed of having one. A lad everyone would call "Doc's boy," to ride along in the buggy with him when he made house calls. He planned to get him interested early in science, buy him a microscope, send him to one of the best medical colleges, and then when he got his degree, he could go into practice with his father.

Leland had adored his little daughter, but still had longed for a son. When it was definite Ava and he would never have another child of their own, Leland had put away his dreams of a son to follow in his footsteps. But now that possibility had arisen once more. An adopted boy he could bring up as he would have his own son. It could all still happen.

In spite of Ava's resistance, Leland felt fairly sure that once the boy was in their home, she would come around. Yes, Leland reassured himself, he had made the right decision.

At twenty minutes before one o'clock, Leland arrived at the Meadowridge Church Social Hall—alone. When he had returned home after making house calls, Ava was still lying on the chaise, now with a cologne-dampened cloth over her eyes. She felt too indisposed to go with him, she whispered. Knowing it was useless, he had not argued.

But while he arranged his makeshift office, adjusting the window blind for more light, filling a glass tumbler with wooden tongue depressors, Leland's mind was troubled. Suppose Ava really did not want a child. Evidently she had made herself ill over the prospect. What should he do now? He supposed another home could be found for the boy. He had not signed anything legal; he could explain to the Scotts—

Leland had no more time to consider the problem because the door of the Social Hall opened and there was a rush of voices as a crowd of people entered. Soon he was busy peering down little throats, checking ears, listening to the thrumming of dozens of healthy little hearts.

As one child after the other filed into this temporary medical facility, Leland felt that old yearning for a child grow stronger. Each child whose clear eyes he looked into, each pink tongue he depressed, each pair of lungs he pronounced sound intensified his desire to take one home with him.

Leland had always had a wonderful way with children. He could calm their fears with affectionate teasing, dry their tears with a fond tweaking of a nose, always holding out the jar of hard candies he kept alongside for a small hand to dip into when the examination was over.

"Next!" he called out to one of the church ladies who was standing in the doorway ushering in the next small "patient."

Leland finished the paperwork on the last patient before he looked up to greet the newcomer. When he did so, he stared right into the eyes of the prettiest little girl he had seen that day. At the same time it was with a stab of recognition. It was uncanny. This child could have been Ava at the same age!

Tendrils of dark hair curled around a rosy face and fell in lustrous curls onto her shoulders. Long-lashed brown eyes regarded him steadily, a tiny tentative, smile tugging at the rosebud mouth.

Leland held out both hands. "Well, little lady, come in. Don't be afraid. I won't hurt you. What is your name?" he asked.

"Laurel," she replied, approaching him slowly. She didn't seem afraid but had a sort of touching dignity.

Poor little tyke, Leland thought. A long journey, now this.

He proceeded with the examination, allowing Laurel to hold the tongue depressor before he looked down her throat, let her listen to *his* chest, hear *his* heart beat, then place the stethoscope on her own while he listened.

All the while he spoke to her gently, all thoughts of the boy he had planned to take home with him slowly vanishing from Leland's mind. If God had blessed him and Ava with another little girl of their own, she couldn't have looked more like this child. The longer he talked to her, the more he gazed into her sweet little face, saw her smile, heard her laugh at his silly jokes, the more convinced Leland became that this was the child he was meant to have. And the conviction grew within him that this child would bring with her the blessing he had prayed for, to his wife, to their marriage, to their home. With her, God would restore the joy that had been missing so long.

Had he not asked God for direction? This strong inner drawing toward this little girl *must* be His sign. How else was he to know God's will but in the very human feelings he was experiencing?

He leaned forward and took both Laurel's little hands in his.

"Would you like to come home with me, Laurel, be my little girl? We have a big back yard with trees and a swing. And there's even a pond with goldfish swimming in it. I think you would like it."

Laurel looked into the strong face searching hers for an answer. Behind his glasses, kindly blue eyes twinkled. She felt the warmth reach out from him to enfold her.

"Well, Laurel, what do you say?"

"Yes." She nodded solemnly.

Leland felt his heart leap. Suddenly his glasses misted and he took out his handkerchief to wipe them. Then, clearing his throat, he said, "Come on, then, let's make it official."

Leland made short work of the red tape. Having completed all the necessary papers with his usual dispatch, he was getting ready to leave when he saw the Hansens.

He hesitated for a minute, wondering whether to speak to them or not. Although their farm was a good distance from

Meadowridge Township, he had delivered all five of their children. The last two had been difficult births for Mrs. Hansen, a case of too many, too close together and not much time to recover before the next pregnancy. He'd warned her to be careful, to let up on some of the heavier chores for a while.

"Those big fellows of yours are old enough and strong enough to take on some of the load, aren't they?" he had asked her.

She had nodded meekly, but said nothing. Her husband had been present. Maybe that was it. Was Cora Hansen afraid of her husband?

Dr. Woodward turned away without greeting them. He didn't much like Jess Hansen. Seemed an insensitive, uncaring sort.

Just then Reverend Brewster spoke and Leland turned to answer him. When he looked again, he saw Jess Hansen with a little girl following him. At the door she turned to wave at Laurel, who waved back.

Leland lifted Laurel up into the buggy, placing the small suitcase on the floor in front of her so she could put her feet on it. Then he went around, got in beside her, smiled down at her as he picked up the reins.

"Well, Laurel, we're off. We're going home."

Home! The word made Laurel feel strange, excited but at the same time a little afraid. She had not allowed herself to think "home" or say the word for months. Home meant the cozy, little rooms on the top of Mrs. Campbell's house. She had missed it so much, and Mama—Laurel felt the old sadness sweep over her and she resolutely set her jaw and looked out around her.

Dr. Leland's horse trotted along a pleasant, curving street lined with shade trees. Neat houses were set back from the road, with pretty gardens behind picket fences. Then they slowed to a halt, and the horse stopped in front of a white frame house without Dr. Woodward even saying "Whoa!"

Laurel glanced at it curiously. It had lace curtains at the dark green shuttered windows, and baskets of pink geraniums swung along the railings at the top of the deep porch. It looked like a nice house, a friendly house, Laurel thought as Dr. Woodward helped her down, took her hand and led her up the steps and into the house.

"Are you hungry, Laurel? Would you like something to eat?" he asked.

Laurel shook her head and said politely, "No, thank you."

Thinking she might be refusing out of shyness, Leland suggested, "Well, I am, and thirsty, too. I'll tell you what. We'll go into the kitchen and see if Ella, our cook, has some lemonade and maybe some cookies. Then we'll go upstairs so you can meet my wife. Come on," he said, and Leland took Laurel's hand again and led her into the sunny spotless kitchen.

A half hour later, Ella Mason, the cook, hands on her hips, raised her eyebrows and looked at Jenny Appleton, the hired girl who came three days a week to clean.

"Well, what do you think of this?"

It was more a declaration than a question, so Jenny shrugged.

"What the missus will say is what I'm wonderin'." Ella gave a shake of her head.

"Well—" Jenny ventured, but Ella went on as if talking to herself and did not notice.

Ella got out the vegetables she was preparing to scrub and shook one of the carrots to emphasize her words. "She'd agreed to a boy, you know."

"Girls aren't so messy or noisy either, for that matter," Jenny declared, thinking of her own mother's brood of six and the bedlam Jen went home to each evening.

Ella rolled out dough for a pie on the cutting board.

"She's never got over it, you see. The little girl dyin' like that." Ella shook her head. "Don't know as if she can take to another one. It would be like she was trying to replace Dorie, don't you know?"

Jenny leaned against the counter listening. She had only worked for the Woodwards this past year. But of course the whole town knew about their tragedy.

"I say, either way, it's a good thing," Ella went on. "This house has been gloomy too long. A child will make a difference, boy *or* girl."

"That's for sure." Jenny nodded. "When I first come here to work, it was so quiet it near gave me the creeps. I used to say to Ma when I'd go home in the evenin' that I didn't even mind the noise there so much after being here all day. I told her—"

But Ella wasn't interested in whatever Jenny had told her mother. A seraphic expression suddenly crossed her plump, rosy-cheeked face. "I think I'll make a custard pudding for tonight. Children like something smooth and sweet, you know." She paused, then remarked thoughtfully, "She's a pretty little thing, ain't she?"

Ella opened a cabinet, took out a big bowl, got down the basket of fresh eggs, and began cracking them one by one into it.

Jen realized the discussion was over for now. Ella was too busy with her recipe to talk.

Jenny went to the broom closet and got out the carpet sweeper. She'd just do the rugs in the hall downstairs and see if she could hear anything to report back to Ella when the doctor took the little Orphan Train girl upstairs to meet the mistress.

Jenny felt sorry for Mrs. Woodward, although she did not know her very well. She was a pretty, dark-haired lady, even if she was too thin and had such mournful eyes. She spoke in a soft voice and gave very few directions about the housework Jenny was to do, but spent most of her time in her upstairs sitting room.

One afternoon Jenny had ventured up with a note from Dr. Woodward, delivered by a hospital messenger. The note said he had an emergency and would be late coming home for dinner. The note could have gone straight to Ella, Jen found out. In fact, after she'd read it, Mrs. Woodward had folded it and asked Jenny to take it down to the kitchen.

But it was *where* Jenny had found Mrs. Woodward that had been so strange and sad. She had knocked at the sitting room door which was always closed. When there was no answer, Jenny had inched it slowly open. But Mrs. Woodward wasn't in there.

Thinking she might have one of her sick headaches—and might be lying down, Jenny tiptoed down the hall to the bedroom. But the door was ajar and she was not in there either.

Then Jenny had heard the sound of sobbing. It came from directly across the hall. Turning, Jenny could see through the half-open door leading into a spacious, airy room flooded with sunlight. It was a room that she had never been asked to clean or dust, a child's room, belonging to a little girl, from the looks of it. And there sitting on the floor by the window seat was Mrs. Woodward, in front of a big dollhouse, holding a teddy bear in her lap.

Jenny stood there frozen, the note in her hand, not knowing whether to go or stay. Just then Mrs. Woodward had turned her head and seen her. For a few seconds neither of them moved nor spoke. Then Mrs. Woodward got to her feet and came over to the door. "What is it, Jenny?" she asked quietly.

Jenny could see that her pale cheeks were wet with tears. Embarrassed, she had stuttered out about the boy from the hospital and handed Mrs. Woodward the note.

Later, back in the kitchen, Jenny related what she had seen to Ella.

"Oh, my, don't I know?" Ella clucked her tongue. "She didn't want a thing in that room touched after Dorie died. With my own ears, I've heard the doctor beg her many times, 'Ava, please,' he'd say, 'you're just making it harder on yourself,' and she'd say, so pitiful, 'Lee, I can't, it would be like losing her forever. It's all I have left.'"

Remembering that incident and the conversation with Ella afterwards, Jenny unconsciously shook her head.

Would this Orphan Train girl *really* make a difference? Or would it just make things worse?

Leland left Laurel sitting on the porch swing when he went upstairs to tell Ava what he had done. He found her still lying on her chaise in her sitting room. He told her as quietly and quickly as he could.

Ava Woodward stared at her husband with an expression of grieved betrayal.

"Oh, Lee, how could you? Bringing a little girl into this house...she could never take Dorie's place!"

"She's not intended to take Dorie's place. No one could do that. She'll make her own place here. Give her time. Give yourself time, a chance to know her," he entreated.

Ava shook her head, tears glistening in her dark eyes as she looked at him in disbelief.

"You said you were getting a boy and I agreed to that. I understood what a boy would mean to you." She clasped her thin hands together, held them to her chin in a pleading gesture. "You know how I longed to give you a son of your own." Ava closed her eyes, recalling the months, the years, her hopes had risen only to be dashed. "But this...you're asking too much of me, Leland."

"Darling, I would never knowingly do anything to hurt you." He took a step toward her, but she held up her hand to ward him off, turning her head away from him as he leaned forward to kiss her.

The silence that followed stretched interminably between them. She did not move to stop him as he went to the door, stood there for a full minute. Then she heard the door close quietly behind him as he left the room.

6

The few days after Laurel arrived at the Woodwards had been the longest Ava could remember. After her first startled reaction to the fact that, instead of a boy orphan of about ten or twelve, Leland had brought home a little girl nearly the same age as the child they had lost, Ava had maintained a cold, hurt silence.

It seemed an unspeakable breach of understanding on his part, an inexplicable lack of empathy for Leland who was usually so considerate, so kind. It had created a chasm between them, wider and more dangerous than any difficulty or difference they had ever faced in their fifteen-year marriage.

Ava had not come downstairs for breakfast since Dorie died because she could not sleep at night unless she took the sleeping draughts Leland meted out to her sparingly. Since Laurel's coming, she stayed in bed until she heard Leland leave the house to go on his house calls every morning. Then Ava shut herself up in her sitting room. She refused to allow herself to wonder what the little girl did with herself. It was, after all, Lee's responsibility, she told herself, and she assumed he had made arrangements for Jenny to look out for the child.

She and Leland had had the worst argument of their entire marriage the night he had brought the little girl here. They had both said things they knew they would regret later. But the hurtful words had been said and still hung between them tensely.

Leland had slept on the couch in his office, as he often did when Ava was unwell, and had been uncomfortably sleepless and troubled. He spent a good deal of the night praying that Ava would relent, would come around and accept Laurel, who had to be the dearest little girl in the world.

The third morning, Ava rose and stood at her door, listening to Leland speaking to someone downstairs. The child? Hearing the front door close, Ava lifted shaking hands to her throbbing temples. She had awakened with all the frightful warning signals. She knew the signs—the shooting flashes of light zigzagging before her eyes, the dizziness, the tension in her stomach, the clamminess of her palms— all signaling the onset of a sick headache.

She should have known! Getting so upset always brought on one of her migraines.

She pressed her fingers over her eyes for a minute. Dear God, what was she to do? She dearly loved her husband, had always tried to comply with his wishes. And she wanted him to be happy, wanted to live up to his expectations of her, but *this* she simply could not do!

Ava had prayed about accepting a boy. At length, she had seemed to have peace about it, even though she knew it would be difficult, at least at first. But a boy was so different in every way from a girl that there would have been no reminders of her own little daughter. A girl nearly the same age as Dorie would have been if she had lived? Well, that was simply too much to ask of her!

Ava walked over to the window overlooking the garden. Pushing the curtain aside, she looked down and saw Leland, hand in hand with the little girl, walking along the flagstone path to the back gate leading out to the stable.

Leland was going on his house calls this time of day, Ava knew. She watched as Leland bent down, one hand gently stroking the child's long, dark curls as he talked to her. Then he kissed her cheek and went through the gate. The little girl jumped on the bottom ledge, leaning over the top and waving her hand. For a few minutes the child stayed there, swinging back and forth on the open gate. Then as the sounds of Leland's horse's hoofs and buggy wheels died away, she got down, turned and started walking back through the garden.

There was something pathetic about the droop of her shoulders, the way her feet lagged, an air of loneliness about the small figure in the drab denim dress and pinafore. In spite of herself, Ava's heart was touched.

Suddenly the stabbing pain in her head made Ava sway slightly. She grabbed onto the nearby chair to steady herself, then staggering with vertigo, she stumbled over to her chaise lounge and lowered herself onto it.

If she could only sleep for a few hours, the headache might go away or at least diminish. She prayed for oblivion, to block out not only the physical pain, but the pain of her heart's distress. She prayed to be released from her feeling of guilt and failure. She prayed to be free of the sting of Leland's accusation that she was shutting out a child who needed caring parents, a home.

Laurel sat on the bottom step of the polished staircase. The house was hushed. There was not a sound anywhere. Not the rattle of pans or the noise of any activity coming from the kitchen, for this was Ella's afternoon off. No murmur of voices or of doors opening and closing, people coming and going from the doctor's office at the side of the house. Dr. Woodward kept office hours only three mornings a week. The other days he went to see sick people in their homes. Today he would be gone all afternoon, he had told Laurel when he left.

Laurel sighed. She was lonely. She was glad to be in this lovely big house with Dr. Woodward. But she missed her two friends, Kit and Toddy. Dr. Woodward had promised she could have them over to play in a few weeks.

That was a long time to wait. Laurel sighed again. But Dr. Woodward said his wife had not been well and until she felt better it would be best not to have other children here.

Laurel had only seen Mrs. Woodward briefly. She was a very pretty lady, but when Dr. Woodward took Laurel in to meet her that first evening, she looked very pale and had only murmured a few words. Then Dr. Woodward sent Laurel out to the hall, telling her to wait for him there. She had stood uncertainly just outside the sitting room door, not knowing what else to do. And that was when she heard Mrs. Woodward say, "Lee, why in the world did you bring that child here?"

Remembering, a sad little ache pressed against Laurel's chest. Mrs. Woodward did not want her. So what was going to happen to her? Would she be "placed out" somewhere else? Just thinking about it gave her that scary feeling again.

But Dr. Woodward was so nice. He seemed to like having her here, and everyone else was so kind. Ella, the cook, was jolly and Jenny, who came three times a week, was always friendly and ready to chat.

But today Jenny hadn't come and the house seemed big and empty. What could she do all afternoon? Laurel wondered. There was nothing much for a girl to play with here. Funny, but the room Dr. Woodward had said was hers that first night held lots of things a *boy* might like! There were books about Indians, a building game, and a set of toy soldiers. But Laurel would have liked something like paper dolls to cut out, or jackstraws or a book of fairy tales.

She sighed again and took out her locket, pressed the place on the back that snapped it open, and looked long and lovingly at the pictures in the two ovals. Laurel still missed her mother. But their life together at Mrs. Campbell's was getting dimmer and dimmer. Of course, she didn't want to forget, but there had been so many new experiences since then. Still, she always looked at the pictures and kissed the photos of her parents every night before going to bed.

Sometimes she lay in bed, reliving some of the things she and Mama used to do together. Certain things they did every week, like taking the rent money down to Mrs. Campbell.

Laurel remembered how Mama would carefully count out the exact amount, taking it from the tin box where she put the money her students paid for their music lessons and placing it in the envelope marked RENT. There were other envelopes marked FOOD, TITHE, CLOTHING MATE-RIAL, even one marked FUN. That was the one Laurel liked best, because out of that came the rare cups of ice cream they bought at the stand in the park after a trip to the Zoo, or a new piece of music for Mama to learn, then teach to her piano students. Sometimes FUN meant an excursion downtown. Taking a horse-car was always an adventure, and then those special trips to the Art Museum. There, Mama would show her the big paintings in gold frames that hung in room after room in a vast building.

"Your father was an artist, Laurel," Mama would say, her eyes very bright.

"Did he paint these?" Laurel once asked, pointing.

"No, he had to sell most of his work. Although some of the ones I thought were his best ones didn't sell. If he had lived, I believe he would have been famous," her mother told her, then added, "but I've kept them all packed away except for that one we have over the piano."

Laurel thought of that painting now. It was of a lighthouse on a cliff overlooking the ocean. The sun in the picture was very strong, casting sharp shadows on the white building and on the beach below and the sparkling blue water. It was a happy painting, one that made Laurel feel good inside when she looked at it.

"That was painted the summer we spent at Truro," Mama had told her. "You were hardly more than a baby, Laurel, but I used to take you down to the beach with me and take off your little shoes and stockings and let you put your feet in the sand. We'd sit under a big umbrella and sometimes your father would sketch us, or set up his portable easel and paint. Oh, darling, I wish you could remember!" Mama would say, looking sad.

Now, as she thought of those times, Laurel's feeling of aloneness sharpened along with an intense longing for her mother. Laurel crossed her arms and hugged herself, rocking back and forth slightly.

Time hung motionless. It would be ages before Dr. Woodward returned. Aimlessly, Laurel began to count the rungs of the stair railings on each step. Humming a little tune she recalled her mother's music students practicing over and over, she moved up slowly from step to step.

Finally, she reached the top of the stairway. Now what could she do to pass the time until Dr. Woodward came home and took her for a buggy ride as he had promised?

Laurel pulled herself to her feet, holding onto the banister. Feeling the satiny surface, she was strongly tempted to mount it and slide backwards down its smooth length. She fought the temptation for a full moment. Resisting it, she decided to go and look over the books in her room once more to see if any of them had interesting pictures. If so, she could take one outside and sit in the porch swing and look at them while she waited for Dr. Woodward to come home.

She started down the hallway toward her room when, passing a half-opened door, she halted. She had passed this room a dozen or more times before, but the door had always been closed. Now it stood open so Laurel could look inside.

Curious, Laurel moved closer and peered in. Nobody was there but it had a waiting look, as though expecting someone to come at any minute. A little girl? For surely this room was intended for a little girl, Laurel thought, inching closer.

Sun poured in through crisp, white ruffled curtains onto the flowered chintz cushions of the window seat, gilding the blond curls of a big doll seated in a small wicker chair by a low table all set with little dishes. Under the window were shelves full of toys, games, and books.

Drawn irresistibly forward, Laurel pushed open the door and stepped inside, looking around her with wide-eyed wonder.

Walking very slowly, as if in a dream, Laurel went to the middle of the room and pivoted, gazing from the scrolled white iron bed, with its ruffled coverlet, piled high with dolls and stuffed animals, to a tiny red rocking chair decorated with painted flowers in one corner next to a large, peaked-roofed dollhouse.

What a wonderful, wonderful room!

Laurel tiptoed over to the dollhouse and knelt down in front of it, gazing into the tiny rooms. There was a parlor, a bedroom, a little nursery with a canopied bassinet in which a tiny china doll nestled. There was even a kitchen, with wee little pots and pans! Laurel put out her hand to move one of the dollhouse occupants that had fallen out of a winged chair next to the fireplace, complete with brass andirons.

But just as she did, a voice from behind her ordered sharply, "Don't touch that!"

Startled, Laurel jerked around, dropping the little figure. Mrs. Woodward was standing in the doorway. Masses of dark hair tumbled wildly around her shoulders and her eyes were fiery coals.

"What are you doing in here?" she demanded furiously.

Laurel was so frightened she burst into tears.

A lavender dusk had fallen over the garden as Leland came through the gate, went up the back porch steps and into the house. There were no lamps lighted yet and Dr. Woodward set down his medical bag and stood for a few minutes, sorting through the mail left on the hall table.

Then he lifted his head in a listening attitude. From somewhere in the house, he heard the sound of soft singing—a familiar, low, sweet melody that struck a reminiscent chord deep within him. He had not heard it in a very long time. And where and when, he could not think.

He went to the bottom of the staircase and, out of long habit, started to call up that he was home. Then he thought better of it, and instead, climbed the stairway, hoping against hope that Ava might be feeling better. Their problem weighed heavily upon him. Nothing was worth this estrangement. The little girl would have to go. He must find a good home for her, a place where she would be welcomed, where she would be loved as she deserved to be loved.

When he reached the landing the sound of singing became clearer. Puzzled, he moved along the hall toward his wife's sitting room.

At the door he paused. What he saw made his heart leap. Stunned, he stood there unmoving.

The room was in shadows. Only a soft, violet light filtering through the filmy curtains illuminated Ava's profile. She was seated in her rocker, holding Laurel in her lap, gently rocking her. The child's head rested on Ava's shoulder as if it belonged there.

When Ava saw Leland's figure silhouetted in the doorframe, she put her index finger to her smiling lips warningly.

It was then he remembered the song Ava was singing. It was the lullabye with which she used to rock Dorie to sleep.

Later that night, as Leland cradled his wife in his arms, long after they had both put Laurel to bed, she wept quietly. "Oh, Lee, to think I frightened that dear little thing, scared her into tears! I'm so ashamed. I have been so selfish, Lee, so self-absorbed, so wrapped up in my own feelings I haven't thought of anyone else's. Can you ever forgive me?"

"There's nothing to forgive, my darling," he murmured, smoothing back her hair from her forehead, tangling his fingers in its silky waves. "I love you and all I ever wanted was your happiness."

"We *will* be happy again, Lee. I feel it, I know it! And I promise you this will be a home for Laurel to be happy in, too!"

7

The Fourth of July in Meadowridge was celebrated with enthusiastic fervor—parades, picnics, political speeches, patriotic pantomimes held at the town park, with a lavish fireworks display after dark.

The whole community entered into the festive occasion. Main Street was decorated with red, white and blue bunting banners, and each storefront displayed its own American flag. At Tanner's Field, where a softball game between the town's two rival teams would be played in the afternoon, the bleachers were festooned with streamers and balloons.

By eleven o'clock families carrying wicker baskets, laden with special holiday food, began to arrive at the city park looking for the ideal spot to picnic. In the white-latticed gazebo in the center, the Meadowridge Town Band, attired in their gold-braided, bright red jackets buttoned in shiny brass, were tuning up their instruments for the music they would be providing throughout the day.

Ava brushed Laurel's dark curls and then tied them with a dark blue satin ribbon in a flat bow.

"There now, turn around so I can see how you look."

Obediently Laurel swung away from the mirror, holding out her skirt for Ava's approval. She was wearing a blue and white striped chambray dress with a square white eyelet lace collar threaded with narrow red ribbon.

"Just perfect," Ava declared with satisfaction. "Perfect for the Fourth of July and for this beautiful summer day." She patted Laurel's cheek. "You'll be the prettiest little girl at the picnic."

"All ready to go?" asked Dr. Woodward, coming to the door of Laurel's bedroom. He looked at them both admiringly. "What a lucky man I am to be escorting two such lovely ladies."

"You *could* be slightly prejudiced, you know, Lee," Ava chided him playfully. "But isn't Laurel a picture?"

"I see two pictures," declared Dr. Woodward, beaming. "If there were going to be a beauty contest today, you would both win hands down."

"Will there be a contest?" asked Laurel.

Dr. Woodward chuckled. "Well, maybe not for beauty, but there'll be plenty of contests—potato sack races, best pie contests, watermelon eating contests—more contests than you can shake a stick at!"

Laurel giggled. Dr. Lee, as she had begun to call him, was always saying funny things like that. Who would shake a stick at a contest?

"Come on, let's get going," he urged. "You can already hear the band music from the park. We don't want to miss anything."

"Just wait until I put on my hat," Ava pleaded gaily, thrusting a long, pearl-headed pin into the band of white roses circling the crown of her straw hat. "There, we're ready!" she said with satisfaction, giving Laurel's hair ribbon a final flip.

Leland held out his arm to his wife, reached his other hand to Laurel, and the three of them went downstairs and out to the buggy. Laurel loved riding in the buggy, especially when all three of them rode together. That wasn't often because Dr. Lee needed it most of the time for his work. Today he had fastened the canvas top back so that she could feel the sun on her head and back as they trotted down the street on the way to the park.

Looking up she saw Dr. Lee, smiling over her head at Mrs. Woodward who smiled back at him. That gave Laurel a nice warm feeling in her tummy. Things at the Woodwards' had become very pleasant. The three of them spent many happy hours together. Ever since that awful time Mrs. Woodward had frightened her in Dorie's room, things had changed.

Dr. Lee had explained to Laurel about Dorie so that she understood.

"You see, Laurel, we lost our little girl just as you lost your parents. And now, we can all help each other. You'll be our little girl and we'll be your parents."

Laurel had nodded. But, unconsciously, she felt for the heart-shaped locket under her dress, as if to remind herself that no one could *ever* take the place of her *real* parents.

Dr. Woodward maneuvered his buggy between the other vehicles, buggies, wagons and gigs that were lined in zigzag rows, horses hitched to the rail fence that surrounded the park. Then he assisted Ava out, lifted Laurel down, and removed the covered picnic basket Ella had packed for them.

"Where would you like to settle, my dear?" he asked Ava. "I see there are still some empty tables near that cluster of oak trees."

Before she had a chance to answer him, a shrill voice called, "Ava! Ava Woodward, wait a minute!"

They all turned in time to see a plump, blonde woman, holding onto her hat with one hand, while with the other she was pulling along a tousle-headed boy. Laurel recognized him as the same obnoxious boy in her Sunday school class who thought it funny to pull her curls when he stood behind her.

When she reached them, the woman said breathlessly, "Oh, Ava, my dear, it is *so* good to see you!"

Laurel felt Ava stiffen as if to ward off an unwelcome embrace. The other woman ignored this rebuff and went right on talking. "We have *all* missed *you* so. I cannot *begin* to tell you how my heart has gone out to you all these months in your sorrow. We thought, at least... *some people* thought you would *never* get over it and—"

"Thank you, Bernice, I appreciate that. I'd like you to meet our Laurel," she said, interrupting the sticky flow of words. "Laurel, this is Mrs. Blanchard and her son, Christopher."

At this, Mrs. Blanchard lowered her voice significantly as though Laurel were deaf and said, "When I heard you and Dr. Woodward were taking in one of those waifs, Ava, I couldn't believe it! After all you've been through to take such a chance—Why, you can't tell what kind of background they come from. I've heard most of them have lived by their wits on city streets—"

"I think you're mistaken, Bernice," Ava cut in coldly. "If you'll excuse us, Doctor is beckoning us. We must go and get our table—" Ava took Laurel's hand tightly in hers and left the woman standing there with her mouth open.

Later, Laurel overheard Ava repeating the conversation to Dr. Woodward. This time her icily polite tone of voice changed. She was obviously very angry.

Dr. Woodward tried to calm her down. "Bernice Blanchard!" he scoffed. "Everyone knows what a rattle-brain she is, speaks before she thinks, likes to hear herself talk. Don't give it another thought, my dear."

"But if she'd say a thing like that to my face, what is she saying behind my back?" demanded Ava.

"What difference does it make, darling? We know the truth. Don't let it spoil things for you."

"I just don't want her spiteful remarks to make things difficult for Laurel as she's growing up in this town. Or for any of the other Orphan Train children," Ava said.

"Put it out of your mind. It isn't that important."

"I don't know, Lee. After all, Bernice is the town banker's wife. She has a lot of influence." Ava sounded doubtful.

"It's too nice a day to worry about something like that. Remember, 'This is the day the Lord hath made, let us rejoice and be glad in it'!" the doctor said, patting his wife's hand reassuringly.

Dr. Lee often quoted the Bible, Laurel had begun to notice.

Sometimes it was his way of ending a discussion, she realized, but it was a nice way. Otherwise, Mrs. Woodward went on and on, fretting about something.

But on this lovely summer day there did not seem to be anything that could disturb anyone for long. There was not a single cloud in the sky. The sun was warm, but there was a breeze gently fanning the leaves overhead. It was, as Dr. Lee kept saying, "a grand and glorious Fourth."

Ava seated herself comfortably at a picnic table, her parasol protecting her from the sun. Lee stood, surveying the holiday activities underway, nodding and returning the greetings of many who passed on their way to their own picnic spots. Of course, as the town doctor, Lee was known by nearly everybody in Meadowridge. Ava was aware of a few curious looks and unconsciously put a protective arm about the child.

Then all of a sudden Laurel, pointing toward a small child across the park leaped down off the bench, and called happily. "There's Toddy! Oh, can we ask her to have lunch with us? Toddy! Toddy, over here!" she shouted, waving her arms.

The two girls were so happy to see each other, they flung their arms around each other and jumped up and down. Ava and Dr. Woodward smilingly watched the reunion. When they found that Toddy had been left on her own by the Hales' maid, they immediately invited her to join them.

The girls chattered excitedly, so fast that their words tumbled out, overlapping the other's. Ava watched them fondly remarking to Lee, "The dear little things. How much they must have to talk about. Laurel says nothing about her life before the Orphan Train, but I'm sure there are sad memories for all the children."

"Well, they look happy enough now," Dr. Woodward commented.

"Yes, I know, but—"

Leland took Ava's hand, raised it to his lips, and kissed it. "Better not to dwell on the sad part, my dear. Laurel has a brand new life with us now. Children soon forget the past."

"I suppose you're right," Ava said, but her eyes lingered on the two little girls, their heads close together.

A few minutes later they were diverted by the arrival of the Hansen family. This would not ordinarily have attracted the Woodwards' attention except for the fact that both Toddy and Laurel scrambled to their feet and hand in hand ran toward another little girl who had come with the Hansens. Ava saw that she was taller than the other two, with smooth brown braids. To Ava's shocked surprise, however, she was still wearing the drab dress and pinafore assigned by the orphanage!

Soon, Laurel came running over to ask if Kit could eat lunch with them, too.

"Of course," Ava smiled. A minute later Laurel returned with a disappointed face, saying Mrs. Hansen needed Kit to help serve their lunch.

"Well, perhaps she can come over later for lemonade and cake," suggested Ava, wondering why the Hansen woman couldn't see that the three little orphans needed this time to be together. Mrs. Hale had already rendered an invitation through Toddy for Laurel to come watch the fireworks display from their upstairs balcony. *She* certainly understood.

Kit, a sweet, shy child did come over later, and seeing the trio so happy together encouraged Ava to do something. She decided she would speak to Mrs. Hansen herself about allowing Kit to come, offering to drive Kit home to their farm afterward.

So, when one of the Hansens' boys came over to get Kit after she had only been with the other two a half hour, Ava walked over to where the Hansens were picnicking, and introducing herself, made her plea.

But Ava's persuasion failed to work on Mrs. Hansen who shook her head.

"No, Kit has to come with the rest of us," she said firmly.

"But the children are so looking forward to it. Surely you wouldn't want to deprive Kit of a chance to be with her friends after such a long separation—" Ava protested.

But Mrs. Hansen raised her chin defensively and her mouth was set in a stubborn line. "Kit has chores to do before it gets dark, Miz Woodward. We're gettin' set to leave now" was her reply.

Ava saw that no extension of her considerable charm would work on the woman, so she sighed and turned to leave. Seeing Kit's expression, she impulsively took the child's face in both hands. Leaning down, she kissed her cheek. "There'll be another time, Kit, I promise. We'll plan to have you come visit Laurel very soon."

Later she fumed to Lee. "What a shame, disappointing Kit like that. How can people be so insensitive?"

"She's a different kind of person from you, Ava, doesn't see things the same way."

"But to treat a child like that—"

"None of the Hansen children seem abused to me, my dear, and Kit looked fine," Leland said in an attempt to placate his wife. But he kept to himself his own concern that had sprung up the day he saw that Jess Hansen was taking Kit home with him. The child looked too delicate for heavy farm chores...but then, what could they do about it?

Ava bit her lower lip in frustration. She had seen something in Kit's eyes that haunted her. No matter what, she was going to do something to help the child.

8

One afternoon in early September, Leland looked in the door of Ava's sitting room. Every surface and space was covered with all sorts of fabric in a melee of color and pattern.

Glancing up, Ava saw him and motioned him into the room.

"What's all this? A circus?" he asked in amazement.

Laurel, who was sitting in a pile of jumbled cloth, giggled as she always did at Dr. Woodward's jokes.

Ava gave him a distracted glance and held up a length of material she was examining. "No, silly, we're choosing material for Laurel's school clothes. Mrs. Danby is coming tomorrow and it's going to be a week of selecting patterns, cutting and fitting and pinning. You are going to be completely surrounded by sewing women!"

"A circus! I was right." Dr. Woodward struck his head in mock horror. "Maybe I'd better take the week off and go fishing."

"Nothing of the kind, Lee. We need your opinion on some of these outfits," Ava said, pretending to be stern. "You have excellent taste."

"Mrs. Danby doesn't think so!" he declared. "The last time she was here for a week of sewing, she glared at me every time I ventured near. I think she thought I was going to perform surgery on her precious sewing machine."

At this, Laurel rolled over in a fit of giggles.

Dr. Woodward raised his eyebrows. "At least, someone appreciates me."

"I appreciate you, too, Lee. Didn't I just say as much?" Ava said. Then holding up a colorful swatch, she asked, "What do you think of this?"

He came over and took the piece and draped it about Ava's head and shoulders, then stepped back to admire her.

"Lovely! Pink is *your* color. I've always loved you in it," he said. "The first time I ever saw you you were wearing pink."

Ava smiled at him indulgently. "Actually, it was a dusty rose dress I was wearing—and *this* is coral."

"Whatever it was, you were ravishing in it," he said in a gentle, teasing voice, and leaned over to kiss her uplifted face.

For a moment they looked at each other, then at Laurel and both of them smiled, holding out their arms to her. She scrambled over the mountain of material and was drawn into the circle of their embrace.

"I'd better get out of here and let you ladies get on with whatever it is you're doing," Dr. Woodward said and started toward the door.

Ava, preoccupied with her choices once more, was holding up the rosy material to Laurel. "This will be such a becoming color for you. We'll have Mrs. Danby make it up into a little suit with a short jacket and lace collar. Oh, it will be perfect! And you will be the prettiest little girl in the whole school!"

Hearing Ava's happy chatter, Leland paused at the doorway, turning to see his wife give Laurel an impulsive hug. It gladdened his heart to see her so happy. She was completely absorbed in readying the child's wardrobe for school. It was her nature, he knew, to throw herself into a project. Yes, whatever it was—joy or grief—Ava was apt to plunge right into it!

As he made his way slowly down the stairs, he felt the vague stirring of uneasiness. As a doctor, Leland knew the danger of that kind of intensity, the extremes of emotional highs and lows to which his wife was prone. Now Laurel had become the focus of Ava's concentrated time, attention, devotion.

But wasn't this new interest in life, this enthusiastic acceptance of Laurel exactly what he had hoped would happen? Why, then had a tiny seed of fear planted itself within him and taken uneasy root there?

Mrs. Danby, the town's best seamstress, arrived on the dot of eight o'clock the next morning and took possession of the upstairs spare room. There she and Ava made the final decisions about patterns, materials and trimmings. Soon her big sewing scissors were slashed authoritatively into the cloth with a sureness that would have unnerved anyone lacking her expertise.

Laurel stood patiently while Mrs. Danby, a tape measure around her neck and her mouth full of straight pins, knelt on the floor draping, tucking, hemming, all the while with tight-lipped murmurs and grunts and little pushes, indicating which way she wanted Laurel to turn.

The result of all this week-long activity was a complete new wardrobe for Laurel. Besides four new school dresses, there was a Sunday-best outfit and blouses, jumpers, skirts, and jackets, as well as new camisoles, petticoats, and bloomers.

On the first morning of school, Laurel was late coming down to breakfast and Dr. Woodward sent Jenny upstairs to see what was delaying her.

When Jenny walked into her room, Laurel was still in her petticoat, staring into the open armoire filled with her new clothes.

"My land, Laurel, you'll have all the other girls green with envy!" remarked Jenny in awe, thinking her own little sisters and brothers were lucky to have a couple of hand-me-downs and a new pair of sturdy boots to start school. "So what are you planning to wear?"

Laurel turned a stricken face to Jenny. "I don't *know*—"

There had never been any choice at Greystone and before that, Mama had always laid out her clothes for her to put on in the morning.

"Didn't Mrs. Woodward say what you were to wear?" Jenny asked.

Laurel shook her head.

"Well, come on then, I'll help you. You mustn't be late the first day of school now. What would your teacher say if you come in like the ten o'clock scholar in the nursery rhyme?" Jenny bustled over to the armoire, studied its contents with a slight shake of her head, then pulled out a bright blue dress trimmed with darker blue braid. She held it up for Laurel's approval. "How about this? Here, then, let me help you."

Jenny slipped it over Laurel's head, guided her arms into the sleeves, and proceeded to button the dozen small buttons in the back. When she got to the top, Laurel's chain caught and Jenny fumbled to untangle it. As she struggled unsuccessfully to free the chain or to get the button into the opening, she said, "I'd better unfasten this clasp, Laurel."

"No!" exclaimed Laurel sharply, jerking away from Jenny both hands on her neck, holding the chain.

Startled, Jenny stared at her. "Whatever is the matter? I was just—"

"I can't ever take this chain off! Not ever!" Laurel shook her head vehemently.

"I meant just until I got the top button done." Jenny explained, puzzled by Laurel's reaction. When she saw the child's eyes fill with tears, she thought, *Why she's afraid! Probably about going to school the first day.* But Laurel's next words surprised her.

"I can't take this off, Jenny, because Mama told me not to."

"But Mrs. Woodward would understand that we—"

"I don't mean *her! She's* not my *mama*," Laurel said in a low voice. With that, she took a step closer to Jenny, pulled the chain out and held up the small, heart-shaped locket. Opening it, she held it up for Jenny to see the pictures inside. *"This* is my *real* mama, and this is my *real* father."

Jenny studied the faces of the lovely, dark-eyed young woman, the handsome, serious young man, then Laurel's small, anxious one. Her thoughts were mixed. She thought of her mistress whose whole life had changed since the coming of this little girl, and of Dr. Woodward who already adored her. What would they think if they had seen the quick, possessive way Laurel had challenged the idea that either of them were her *real* mother or father?

"I'm sorry, Jenny," Laurel said quietly. "I didn't mean to yell at you."

"All right, dearie, never mind. Turn around now, and I'll do the buttons carefully so as not to catch the chain again. We'll have to hurry now. Dr. Lee is waitin' to drive you over to school."

Jenny was in the kitchen with Ella when the doctor drove off with Laurel sitting beside him in the buggy, both of them waving to Ava who stood on the porch waving her handkerchief as they left.

Unconsciously Jenny shook her head. People were already saying the Woodwards were spoiling their "little orphan." Not that Jenny agreed. She had never seen a child spoiled by too much love or caring. What bothered her now was whether Laurel would ever be able to love them back enough.

It was a strange situation, Jenny thought to herself as she began her dusting. There was still that closed door upstairs that had belonged to the Woodward's *real* daughter, Dorie. Just as there was that locket where Laurel kept her *real* parents.

Laurel's heart was hammering as she entered Meadowridge Grammar School's fenced schoolyard, filled with boisterous children. Her hand tightened on the handle of her lunch pail, and she felt her mouth go dry when she tried to swallow. The distance from the gate over to the school building looked so far, and if she made it over there, how would she ever find the right classroom?

At the moment she was about to panic, Laurel heard someone calling her name. Turning, she was grateful to see Toddy, red-gold curls flying, running toward her across the crowded playground.

"Laurel!" Toddy came up to her smiling and breathless, holding out her hand to clasp Laurel's. "I'm so glad to see you! Let's wait here and see if Kit comes," she suggested.

At once Laurel sighed with relief. When Kit came, everything really would be all right. The three of them would be together again.

9

Christmas 1894

The Christmas program put on by the schoolchildren in the church social hall was a great success. Everyone said so, parents congratulating Miss Cady and complimenting each other on performances of their offspring. Ava, basking in the many comments on Laurel's solo of "O Holy Night," clutched Leland's arm excitedly and whispered, "Lee, we must see that Laurel has singing lessons! Her voice is surely a God-given gift."

Unaware of the plans for her future already spinning forward in Ava's mind, Laurel found Kit and Toddy and the three of them settled together in one corner to enjoy the refreshments and compare notes about the coming holiday week.

"I'm so thankful I didn't miss a line of your poem, Kit!" Toddy gave an exaggerated sigh of relief as she forked up a large bite of applesauce cake.

"You read it so well, Toddy. You made it sound much better than I thought it was when I wrote it," Kit told her. "And Laurel, you didn't seem a bit nervous doing your song."

"I *was*, though. I thought my voice sounded shaky on the first few notes," confessed Laurel, glad that it was over.

"No school for ten whole days! And if it keeps on snowing, we can go sledding!" Toddy said with a little bounce.

"I don't have a sled," Laurel said.

"Well, you'll probably get one for Christmas." Toddy nodded her head confidently. "Bob Pennifold's father...you know, he runs Pennifold's Hardware Store...and he said a lot of folks have put in orders for sleds to give their children for presents."

"Oh, well, maybe," agreed Laurel, brightening.

Kit did not say anything. She knew there would be no such things as sleds for Christmas at the Hansens' farm.

Soon people began searching for their wraps and boots as they prepared to leave. Ava called Laurel over, handed her the new white sheared rabbit fur tam and muff. The set was "an early Christmas present," Ava had told her when she had given it to her that evening.

Toddy made both girls promise they would come over the first day after Christmas to see the Hales' tree. Its tip touched the ceiling of the parlor, she told them, and was decorated with ornaments Mrs. Hale had ordered from a store in San Francisco. Just then, Helene and Mrs. Hale called to her and Toddy went off to join them. Kit left to say goodnight to Miss Cady and Laurel, tucking her hands into her muff, walked out with the Woodwards.

Coming out into the cold, starry night from the warmth of the church social hall, the air rang with cheerful voices calling out "Merry Christmas!" as people found their buggies and wagons, and gathered their children for the ride home.

Dr. Woodward helped Ava and Laurel into theirs and tucked a warm rug over their knees. Snow was still falling gently, slowly covering the rooftops of houses and lawns along the way home, muting the sound of the horse's hoofs and buggy wheels on the snow-softened road.

"Tired, darling?" Ava asked, putting her arm around Laurel's shoulder and drawing her close.

Laurel nodded, but she really wasn't as tired as she was preoccupied with her own thoughts. The Woodwards had set up their tree in the parlor on Sunday when Dr. Woodward was home and could help. He mostly supervised Laurel's and Ava's hanging of the ornaments and then finally climbed up the ladder to place the glittery star at the top.

Before they left for the Christmas program that evening Laurel noticed some brightly wrapped packages had already been placed underneath the tree. Laurel had been busy for weeks making her presents—an embroidered glove case for Ava and four finely hemmed linen handkerchiefs for Leland with his initials satin-stitched in the corner. They lay, prettily wrapped and hidden in her bottom drawer. She had been wondering how to get them under the tree without anyone seeing her. As soon as they got home the opportunity presented itself.

"Would you like a cup of cocoa, Laurel?" Ava asked her as they came into the house. "I'm going to make some. I got quite chilled on the drive home."

"No, thank you. I had the hot spiced cider after the program. I think I'll go get ready for bed," Laurel replied and she kissed Ava good night and went upstairs.

What luck! she thought. She would wait until they were both safely in the kitchen having cocoa, then she would slip downstairs and put her gifts under the tree.

Ava was still standing at the bottom of the stairs, lost in thought, when Leland came in the door after taking care of his horse. He came up behind her and put his arms around her waist, leaning his cold cheek against hers for a minute.

"Oh, Leland! Laurel is such a treasure. We are so blessed." Ava sighed happily.

"I couldn't agree more, my dear."

"And with the voice of an angel."

"She sang very nicely indeed."

"Nicely? Is that all you have to say about it?"

"Well, I'm no music critic."

"You don't have to be to recognize talent like that."

"Didn't I hear you say something about making some hot cocoa?" Leland asked mildly.

"Yes, but don't change the subject." Ava removed her hat and veil, placed them on the hall table while Leland helped her off with her fur-collared cape. "We must see that Laurel's voice is properly trained." Eyeing her reflection in the hall mirror, she patted her hair absentmindedly then turned around with a small frown. "Whom should I ask about a voice teacher for her, do you suppose? Mr. Fordyce, the music teacher at the high school?"

"I'm sure I have no idea." Leland shook his head. "There's plenty of time for that."

"No, not really, Lee. It is important to start early, I've read. See that she doesn't acquire any bad habits, doesn't strain her vocal cords, learns to breathe correctly, that sort of thing."

"Laurel's only twelve, darling," Lee protested gently.

"It's soon enough. It may even be a little late!"

"Well, that may be so, my dear."

"I'm sure I'm right about the necessity of nurturing a natural gift like hers."

"Well, nothing has to be decided tonight," Leland murmured.

"You think I'm being silly, don't you?" Ava accused.

"No, not silly, my dear. Maybe just overestimating Laurel's talent *and* her desire. Maybe Laurel won't even be interested in developing her voice. Maybe, she'd rather do something else entirely."

"But it's up to us as *parents* to guide her in what's best for her. We have a responsibility to see that Laurel appreciates her gift and does whatever is necessary to cultivate it." Ava's tone became higher, more intense. "You must not have heard all the comments I heard tonight about Laurel's singing. Everyone was so complimentary, marveling at the quality of her voice." She faced him, eyes flashing. "She *has* a gift, Leland, and I intend to see that she doesn't waste it!"

"Fine, my dear," Leland said soothingly, seeing how excited his wife was becoming. "Come along, how about the cocoa you promised?" and Leland took her hand, leading her toward the kitchen at the back of the house.

Unknown to either of them, Laurel, standing at the top of the staircase, her packages in her arms, had heard their conversation.

As their voices faded away, her hand went unconsciously to the delicate chain she always wore and she fingered the heart-shaped locket. The familiar sadness swept over her. Mama had seemed very close to her tonight, especially when she was singing.

Ever since she was a very little girl, Laurel had known all the Christmas carols. She could recall clearly sitting beside Mama at the piano while she played and sang all the lovely old songs, and Laurel had sung along with her.

Christmas was always a special time in that small apartment at the top of Mrs. Campbell's house, even though they had only a tiny tree set on the table and a few little gifts. It was special because Mama made it so. Laurel closed her eyes and she could almost see it all again—the candles' glow, the sound of the piano, Mama's beautiful smile, her graceful hands moving over the keys—

Laurel loved to sing, knew that when she sang she felt a soaring sensation, as if a part of herself left and became one with the song, with the music. She remembered Mama saying, "Why Laurel, you sound just like a little lark!"

When she sang it was always for her—for Mama.

10

The Class of 1900

Laurel stood at the hall mirror retying the bow at the collar of her pink shirtwaist when Dr. Woodward came downstairs and stopped behind her.

"Good morning, my dear, you look as fresh as a daisy," he complimented her. "All ready for the Senior Picnic, are you?"

"Yes, Papa Lee." Laurel whirled around to greet him. "I'm waiting for Dan. He'll be here in a few minutes. We'll walk over to school and meet the rest of the class. There will be hay wagons to take us out to Riverview Park for the picnic."

"That sounds like fun." Dr. Woodward smiled. "Well, I have office hours this morning, so I'd better get out there. Have a good time."

"We will, Papa, thanks," Laurel assured him, offering her soft cheek for his kiss.

Leland went out the side door, stopped in the garden to pick a rosebud from one of his wife's prized bushes to put in the lapel of his tan linen jacket, then proceeded to his small office at the back of the house.

At three months past fifty, Leland was still handsome, with well-defined features and a pleasant smile. There was more silver in his thick wavy hair now, but with his erect, lean build, he had the appearance of a much younger man.

A few minutes later, standing at his office window, he watched Laurel and Dan Brooks go out the front gate together. Fondly, his eyes followed Laurel's graceful figure and the lanky one of the tall boy at her side as they turned in the direction of Meadowridge High School.

He was pleased that Laurel was going to their class picnic with Dan. He liked the young fellow. Of all the boys whose bicycles had cluttered up the front walk since Laurel was about fifteen, or who had parked themselves on the front porch, bringing valentines or flowers, boxes of candy and Christmas gifts, Dan was Leland's favorite.

If he had had a son of his own, Leland would have wanted one like Dan. The boy was courteous, intelligent, dependable. He could carry on a decent conversation with an adult, which was more than Leland could say for half of those who had stood tongue-tied and awkwardly ill at ease in the Woodwards' hallway, waiting for Laurel to come down and rescue them.

Leland only hoped Laurel had the good sense to recognize Dan's good qualities and appreciate them. Maybe in a few years things would develop between them and become more than a friendship. Of course, they were still very young, plenty of time to think of the future.

Just then looking up at Dan, Laurel's head tilted sideways, and Leland could see her enchanting profile—the small sweet nose, the slender neck above the ruffled edge of her high-necked blouse. Just this week, in anticipation of her official entry into young womanhood via graduation, Laurel had begun pinning up her dark, wavy hair. It made her look very grown up.

Unconsciously, Leland sighed. Was it possible it had been ten years since as a seven-year-old child, Laurel had come into their home?

"Lee, still alone? No patients yet?"

Ava's voice interrupted his thoughts and Leland turned to see her face peering around the office door.

"Yes, I mean, no—I'm alone, no patients. Come in, darling," Leland invited.

Ava slipped in, closing the door quietly behind her.

Looking at her, Leland was struck, as he always was, that she seemed to grow lovelier with each passing year. Her figure was still girlishly slim, the dark hair still untouched by a single strand of gray, her skin pale and smooth, translucent as fine porcelain. Of course, since Laurel had come into their lives, they both seemed rejuvenated.

At the moment, however, a small anxious frown cast two vertical lines between Ava's dark, winged brows. Her expression alerted him that something was troubling her. A tiny twinge of concern stirred, tightening his chest. Ava tended to get upset about small, unimportant things. What was it now?

Leland went over to her, took both her hands in his, and was startled to feel they were icy.

"What is it, Ava, what's wrong?"

"Did you see Laurel?" she asked.

"Yes, right before she left. She looked charming, as usual."

"Yes, that pale pink blouse is so becoming—" Ava said with a distracted air, then rushed on. "Did you see her leave with *that* boy?"

"With Dan? Yes, of course, why?"

"*Why*? That's why I'm so upset. He's taken her to every single graduation event. *That's* what upsets me. He's totally unsuitable."

"Unsuitable?" Leland repeated in surprise. "How do you mean *unsuitable*? I think he's a capital young chap. What do you mean?"

"His *family*, Leland, *that's* what I mean."

"There's nothing wrong with the family, as far as I know. His grandmother and aunts are patients of mine. They're members of the church. They're fine ladies. I don't know what you're talking about."

"I *know* he lives with *them*, Leland, and everything looks very respectable, but—" Ava lowered her voice. "His mother lives in Chicago and his father, well, no one seems to know much about him. But the *brother, Dan's uncle, is Ned Morris—*" Ava broke off in dismay. "Surely, you know he runs a pool hall on the other side of town."

Leland started to laugh. Shaking his head he protested, "But, darling, what's that got to do with Dan? He lives with Mrs. Morris over on Elm Street—"

"Leland, you're purposely trying not to understand." Ava sounded exasperated. "I just don't want Laurel associating with that sort of person."

It was Leland's turn to be irritated. "Laurel isn't associating with Dan's uncle, my dear, so I don't see the problem."

Ava hesitated a moment before answering.

"The boy is obviously in love with Laurel. Doesn't *that* disturb you?"

"In love? At *their* age?" Leland scoffed. "They aren't even out of high school yet."

"They will be in a week, must I remind you, and then—"

"Ava, my dear, you're borrowing trouble. Besides, Dan told me he has applied to medical school. He's got long years of study ahead. He hasn't time to be serious about anything but getting his education. I *know* what that's like. It will be a long time before he can think about anything else."

Ava seemed somewhat appeased. "I just don't want him getting any ideas about Laurel," she went on. "You know how she is. I'm afraid he might convince her to make some kind of promise about the future—"

"Be sensible, Ava. You must be imagining things. I haven't noticed Laurel treating Dan in any special way. No more than any of the other young men who've come calling. Laurel doesn't even see as much of him as she does her girl friends, Toddy and Kit. I believe you're worrying unnecessarily. Besides, I don't think Laurel would keep anything as important as being in love from *us*."

"I suppose you're right, Leland," Ava sighed. "You usually are!"

Leland put his arms around her, held her. "Sweetheart, you must not fret about things that may never be! Remember the Scripture, 'Sufficient unto the day,' " he said soothingly. "Now, why don't you find something better to do than worry about two youngsters who have nothing on their minds but having a wonderful day at a picnic?"

"Laurel, I love you," Dan whispered.

"Oh, Dan, I wish you wouldn't say that," Laurel protested softly.

"But, it's true. You must know it, Laurel. Why can't I say it?"

After the delicious picnic prepared by the mothers of the Junior Class and served by rising Meadowridge Seniors, most of the "honorees" had paired off and left the picnic area, to roam along the wooded paths through the park or to follow the trail down to the river.

Dan and Laurel had climbed up the hillside to the meadow overlooking the river and had settled under the shade of a gnarled, ancient oak. The afternoon seemed to stretch endlessly under a lapis lazuli sky. The hum of insects among the wildflowers in the tall grass floated on sweet-scented summer air. The sun was a drowsy warmth. For a while Dan lay on his stomach, gazing at Laurel, wondering if she had any idea what a picture she made. What was she thinking about?

Laurel leaned her head back against the tree, feeling the roughness of its bark through the thin material of her blouse and camisole.

With eyes half-closed, Laurel could see Dan, his head turned so that his clear-cut profile was outlined against the cloudless blue background of the sky. Her mind drifted aimlessly and she began to mentally rehearse the lyrics of the song she was to sing at the Honors Banquet.

It was then that Dan had raised himself to a sitting position, reached for her hand, brought it to his lips and kissed the tips of her fingers.

When he declared, "I love you, Laurel," she tried to pull her hand away, but Dan held it fast.

"Why is it wrong for me to say what I've felt all these months...for years actually. I guess it's just *this* year I realized what it's going to be like when I go away to medical school next fall and won't be able to see you every day."

Laurel met his earnest, brown eyes and felt her own heart respond to what he was saying, but at the same time she was afraid. She knew "Mother" did not like Dan and she felt torn between her two loyalties, not knowing how to explain one to the other without betraying either of them.

"What I want to know, Laurel, is do you care for me?" Dan's voice was intense, pleading. "I mean *really* care, more than just a friend, more than anyone else...enough to wait ...until I finish my training, become a doctor? I know that's a long time, an awful lot to ask. But, Laurel, I don't know how I can go off next fall, leave Meadowridge and not know that you—that you—"

"Oh, Dan, I *do* care, but I don't think you should talk like this. We're both...well, we're just getting out of high school. We have our whole lives ahead of us. Don't you think it's too early for us to make plans, or promises?"

"Don't you ever daydream about the future, Laurel? Wonder what it will be like to make our own decisions, our own choices?"

"Of course, I do—" began Laurel, then stopped short. Of course, she daydreamed but she had never shared those daydreams with anyone. Laurel had always had a "secret life" filled with dreams and plans about the future. But, mostly, she lived in the present, drifting from day to day, trying to please everyone, trying to make "Mother" and Papa Lee happy, proud of her.

Like with her music. "Mother" was always so interested in the new songs Mr. Fordyce gave her to learn, so thrilled every time Laurel was asked to perform. Ava always had Laurel sing for her Sewing Circle when it met at the Woodwards' but "Mother" never guessed how nervous it made Laurel to sing for an audience, how much it cost her to meet those expectations.

And now Dan was pressuring her, wanting her to make a commitment to him. Gently, Laurel withdrew her hand.

"Dan, it's too soon for us to make any promises. Can't you be satisfied to know I *do* care very much about you? Isn't that enough for now?"

Dan sighed heavily. "I guess it will *have* to be."

He got to his feet, walked over to the cliff, bent down and picked up some small stones and stood tossing them down into the river below. Laurel looked over at his tall figure, the shoulders drooping slightly with disappointment. Then she leaned back against the tree again and closed her eyes.

Sometimes she wished she could go away somewhere where no one expected anything of her at all. She let her mind wander back to that old fantasy, the one kept locked in her heart all these years, the story she used to tell herself at night when she was lying in bed not quite ready to go to sleep.

It was then she planned how, when she grew up and finished school, she would go back to Boston and find Mrs. Campbell's old house. She would ring the doorbell and Mrs. Campbell would come to the door. Seeing her, her old landlady would throw up her hands and say, "Why, land's sake, if it isn't Laurel Vestal, all grown up!" Then she would take Laurel upstairs to their old apartment unlock the door, and Laurel would walk inside and everything would be just the same as the last time she had seen it.

Laurel would go through it, room by room, remembering—the upright piano with the candleholders on either side of the music rack with her father's painting of the lighthouse hanging over it, her mother's rocker over by the window with the little footstool where Laurel used to sit. In the bedroom, Laurel would picture the trundle bed they pulled out from under her Mama's high poster, and in the corner the table with the lamp and the books—

Sometimes, at this point, Laurel would fall asleep. But the next night and the night after that, she would begin her journey again. The longer she was with the Woodwards, the less she had done that. But today it all came back to her as clearly and vividly as ever.

It was not that Laurel was unhappy. Her life at the Woodwards could not have been happier or more pleasant. It would have been hard to find a more loving, caring atmosphere for a child to grow up in.

But all through the years, Laurel had clung to her memories like a drowning person clutching at a straw, as if by letting go, she would drift down the stream, be swept into the rushing current, and lose something vital. Lose her other life, that life with Mama that filled her with such sweet longing and sadness.

Why could she not let it go? Was it because it had taken her so long to accept that her mama had really died? For weeks she had refused to believe it. Mama had promised she would come back—

Or couse, eventually, the reality had penetrated. Still, buried deep in her child's heart was the determination that one day she would go back and find that lost part of herself.

"Come on, Laurel. Everyone's starting back. They're loading up the wagons to go back into town!"

"Wake up, Laurel!"

Toddy's voice broke into Laurel's thoughts, and she opened her eyes, blinking into the sunshine. Toddy and Chris Blanchard were standing over her.

"We just came up from the river," Toddy said, holding up her white cotton stockings and shoes. "We went wading!" Then, pointing to the hem of her bedraggled skirt, she made a face. "Miss Klitgard will look daggers at me! So very *unladylike*, Miss Hale!" she declared, mimicking one of their teacher-chaperones for the picnic.

It was such an exact imitation they all laughed.

Joining in, Dan held out his hands to Laurel and pulled her to her feet. "Time to go!" Then, hand in hand, they walked back down the hill to the picnic area where the wagons for the ride back to town were loading.

As the three wagons, drawn by plodding farm horses and filled with young people singing at the top of their voices, lumbered into the school yard, passers-by on Elm Street smiled nostalgically, recalling their own bygone youth.

In one last exuberant burst of song, the strains of the school song echoed through the early evening air: "Forever we'll remember thee, Meadowridge High, we'll faithful be!" and ended with riotous laughter and clapping hands.

Dan jumped down from the end of the wagon and held up his arms to Laurel, who placed her hands on his shoulders. Lifting her down, he held her a moment longer than necessary. "I'll walk you home," he whispered.

"Oh, you don't need to, Dan. It's still light. Besides, don't you have to get to work?" Laurel asked, knowing Dan had a job at the pharmacy three nights a week.

"I have time," he assured her planning to skip supper in order to make it to his job by six.

"You're sure?" Laurel sounded doubtful.

"Yes," Dan told her, drawing her hand through his arm as they started out of the school yard.

Toddy and Chris, heading toward the Hale house, called and waved as they went in the other direction.

"I *can* take you to the Honors Banquet tomorrow night, can't I, Laurel?" Dan asked on the way home.

Laurel hesitated. "I don't know, Dan. Papa Lee and Mother plan to attend and I think they expect me to go with them."

He frowned. "Well, I realize parents will be there, Laurel, but our whole class will have its own table and—"

"Maybe I'd just better wait and see—" Her voice trailed off uncertainly.

Dan knew better than to persist, but his jaw tightened.

They said nothing more until they reached the Woodwards' white picket fence. Dan opened the gate for her and they went through into the back garden, fragrant now with June roses.

"About the Banquet, Laurel—" he began.

"I told you I'd have to see, Dan," Laurel reminded him gently.

Dan did not want to argue about it. Anything to do with Laurel's parents' wishes always presented a problem. He'd run into that barrier often enough before.

"I know, but I'd just like to know—"

"I understand. But if Mother and Papa Lee want me—" Laurel sighed softly. It was so hard to explain to anyone, even Dan, how easily Mother's feelings were hurt.

Just then they heard the squeak of the screen door opening and Mrs. Woodward came out onto the back porch, a slim figure in a filmy white dress. She walked to the edge of the steps, peering into the gathering lavender dusk.

"Oh, there you are, Laurel darling!" she called. "I was getting worried. It's nearly five-thirty. I thought you'd be home way before now. I was afraid there might have been an accident...those narrow country roads and those top-heavy wagons—"

Laurel moved quickly away from Dan and took a few steps forward so Ava could see her.

"No, Mother, everything's fine! Nothing happened! I'm sorry you were worried."

"Oh, well, as long as you're home safe!" Mrs. Woodward sounded relieved. "Come along, I'll run a nice tub for you. You must be tired after such a long day."

"I'll be there in just a minute. Dan's here. He walked me home."

"Hello, Mrs. Woodward." Dan stepped into Mrs. Woodward's line of vision.

"Oh, hello, Dan." There was a definite coolness in Ava's voice.

Laurel winced inwardly. Why did Mother always ignore Dan unless he made it a point to force her to see him, speak to him? He had never mentioned this to her, but it was so obvious, it hurt Laurel for him.

"Well, come along, Laurel, or your bath water will get cold." Mrs. Woodward disappeared into the house.

"I'll have to go in." Laurel turned to Dan. "It was such a nice day. Thanks for seeing me home." As she put her foot on the first step of the porch, Dan caught her hand and held it.

They stood for a long minute in the soft twilight, looking at each other. Laurel drew in her breath. She saw something in Dan's eyes that both stirred and frightened her.

Withdrawing her hand, she said breathlessly, "Good night, Dan," and ran lightly up the steps and into the house.

11

On the afternoon of the Honors Banquet, Laurel walked over to the high school for her final rehearsal of the songs she was to sing that night and at the graduation ceremony.

This last week of the school year, the building was nearly empty. A few students were sitting in the sunshine looking at the yearbook when Laurel went up the steps and inside. As she walked down the deserted corridor, she heard the sound of a trumpet solo being played haltingly. She opened the door to the Music Room and quietly took a seat at the back. The boy with the trumpet struggled on valiantly until Mr. Fordyce spoke to him.

"That's enough for today, Billy. You need some practice, young fellow. Guess we've had too much baseball weather lately, eh?" He tousled the youngster's hair affectionately. "But I expect you to know that piece by heart next week."

"Yes, sir," the boy mumbled getting to his feet. There was much scuffling and clatter as he packed his instrument in its carrying case and hurried out into what was left of the beautiful afternoon.

Then Mr. Fordyce looked over, acknowledged Laurel's presence, and beckoned her forward while he took his place at the piano. Mr. Fordyce had given Laurel private lessons for years, and she considered him a friend.

"All right now, Laurel, let's begin with scales before we go into your numbers."

Laurel adjusted the music stand, placed her music sheets on it and, when Mr. Fordyce struck the first note, she took a deep breath and began.

Less than an hour later, Mr. Fordyce stopped playing and announced, "There, that's it. I think we're through for today. You can over-rehearse, you know."

Laurel was surprised. Usually Mr. Fordyce made many corrective comments, made her go over and over her pieces. Now he stood up, gathered his music, shut the lid over the keyboard.

"Then, it sounded all right?" she asked doubtfully.

"It was fine, Laurel. You'll do splendidly, I'm sure."

Laurel hesitated, there was something in the way he spoke that vaguely troubled her. She stood by the piano uncertainly. She felt there was something he was *not* saying that was more important than what he had said.

"Mr. Fordyce?"

"Yes, Laurel,"

"Did I do something wrong?"

"No, not at all, Laurel. Everything was fine, on pitch, on key. Be sure and rest your voice for the next few hours. Drink some hot lemonade before the performance."

"There's nothing else you wanted to say to me?" she persisted.

Mr. Fordyce continued busily stacking music sheets, then he turned toward her, his face thoughtful. "I guess, I was just wondering what your plans are for after graduation."

"I'm not sure—" she said.

Mr. Fordyce opened his briefcase and began stuffing the music sheets inside. When he looked up again, his face was serious, his eyes grave as he regarded her.

"No plans, eh? What about your voice?"

"I do want to continue my lessons through the summer—" she told him, smiling tentatively. "That is, if you—"

"Laurel! I didn't mean just this summer!" He sounded irritated "You *have* a voice, you know. Don't you care about

it? I know dozens of others who would die for what you have."
He sighed heavily. "Laurel, I've taught you all I can. I can't
do any more to help you develop your voice. There's so much
you still need to know, to learn. But you can't do it here in
Meadowridge. There's no one here who has what you need."

Laurel stared at him.

Again Mr. Fordyce sounded annoyed.

"But you have to *know* that, not have me *tell* you. You have
to *want* it for yourself. Some things cannot be taught. For a
singer there has to be something inside that tells her she
has to go on, that she will *die* if she cannot learn everything
there is to learn, to seek to be the best she can be with the
talent she's been given." He stopped, shook his head. "If you
don't have that desire, Laurel, well, what more can I say?"

"But where could I go? Who could I find to teach me?"

"You'd have to go somewhere like Chicago or Boston
where there is a music conservatory, where there are
teachers who can give you what you need—" He paused
again. "Haven't you even discussed the possibility with
your parents? Surely, they could afford to send you. Your
mother has always been so supportive of your singing—"

"No. I guess we just assumed I'd go on taking lessons from
you, that I would sing in the choir, or for social occasions—"
Her voice faltered. For some reason Laurel felt apologetic,
confused, and something else she could not quite name.

"You mean singing for your friends' weddings, some-
body's funeral service, for the Ladies Aid Guild meetings?"
Mr. Fordyce's tone was sarcastic. He shook his head again.
"Forgive me, Laurel. I've seen so much wasted talent I think
I've become—" He stopped, head down, as if deep in thought.
Then he raised his head and looked straight at Laurel.

"Well, Laurel, I think, after graduation, you should sit
down with Dr. and Mrs. Woodward and discuss this seriously. In fact, if you like I'll come and talk to them. Suggest a
school or teacher."

QUEST FOR LASTING LOVE

Laurel twisted her hands nervously. "Maybe—yes, I suppose...I don't really know, Mr. Fordyce. I'll have to think about it."

"Yes, I hope you will do that." Mr. Fordyce seemed weary. Then he attempted a lighter tone, "And, Laurel, don't worry about tonight. You'll do just fine. Enjoy the next few days. High school graduation is very special. There's time enough to think of the future."

"Thank you, Mr. Fordyce," Laurel murmured and, picking up her music, left.

Outside, she felt disoriented. She started walking but not in the direction of home. Instead, she turned and headed for the town park. There she found a bench near the duck pond and sat down. She realized she was trembling.

She tried to remember everything Mr. Fordyce had said, but what kept repeating itself over and over in her head were the words, "You would have to go to Chicago or *Boston* where there is a music conservatory, teachers." Was this the sign she'd been praying for? If she could go to *Boston*, then perhaps she could trace her real parents, find out about Mama's death, where she was buried, what had happened to all their things. The hope Laurel had carried for so long, hidden in her heart, burst into new life! Maybe this was the way being opened for her.

Her singing had been so much a part of her life that she had never considered it as separate from herself, as something to be developed, cared for, polished, like a rare instrument. She had sung all her life, as a little child alongside her dear mama at the piano; after coming to Meadowridge, at school and at church. Later she had sung in the choir.

It was Mother who insisted on her having lessons with Mr. Fordyce. But what Mr. Fordyce was suggesting was something different entirely. He was talking about her studying voice seriously, devoting her life to singing.

Laurel knew that something strange and wonderful happened to her when she sang. She felt a lifting, soaring sensation that carried her far beyond the room, the people, the faces of the listening audience or congregation. It was a feeling she never experienced in any other way.

Is that what Mr. Fordyce was trying to get her to express? To speak of that inner joy she felt while she was singing? Or had he meant more than that?

Yes, Laurel was sure Mr. Fordyce was looking for something else in her answer today. He was trying to see if she had that necessary desire, testing her to see if it was strong enough to make the choice of a life of total dedication.

Laurel realized that now was the time of decision. Would it be wrong to use her voice as a means to pursuing her real desire? If the Woodwards would finance her musical education in *Boston*—

Unconsciously, Laurel fingered the locket she still wore around her neck. She thought of that long-ago promise she had made to herself that, just yesterday, at the picnic, had come back to her so vividly.

Of course, Laurel knew it was foolish to suppose anything was still there. Even Mrs. Campbell might be gone. But maybe she could find out something about her father, his family, the Vestals.

Would it be deceitful to combine studying voice, which should please Mother especially, while she pursued her long-cherished dream of solving the mystery surrounding her own background?

Laurel tried imagining the discussion with Papa Lee and Mother, Mr. Fordyce had suggested. What would they say? Would they let her go?

It was too much to think about now. There was the banquet tonight, Baccalaureate service the following day, then graduation and the Graduation Dance to look forward to— Laurel rose and started walking slowly home.

She wouldn't say anything about this yet. Not tell anyone, not even Dan. There was plenty of time. The whole summer before anything would really have to be decided.

12

The evening of graduation day, Dan walked over from Elm Street to the Woodwards' house to escort Laurel to their class party. He carried with him a small corsage of sweetheart roses for her.

Before ringing the doorbell, he adjusted his tie, ran a nervous finger around the inside of the unaccustomed high, stiff shirt collar, and straightened his new navy blue jacket.

To his dismay it was Mrs. Woodward, not Laurel, who answered the door.

"Good evening, Dan," she greeted him. "How nice you look!" She smiled but there was the usual wariness in her eyes. "Do come in. You're a little early, aren't you? Laurel is not quite ready yet, which doesn't really matter, because we have to wait for Dr. Woodward. He was called out on an emergency, but he should be along soon. He wanted to see Laurel before you left for the party."

Dan tried to swallow his disappointment. All day he had been looking forward to this evening, the chance to be alone with Laurel. The early part of the day had been chaotic, with the graduation ceremony, the long program of speeches in the hot auditorium, and afterwards family and friends crowding around. The picture-taking session had dragged on endlessly. He had hardly seen Laurel.

But tonight was different. Tonight was *their* night. As graduates, they were almost adults by most standards.

Tonight was their exclusive party. Even though it would be well chaperoned by teachers and some parents, Dan planned to manage having Laurel to himself for once—at least, that's what he had hoped.

"Come along, out to the side porch and have a glass of iced tea," invited Mrs. Woodward, leading the way across the parlor out through the glass doors onto the side porch.

Its white wicker furniture gleamed in the gathering twilight; the plump flowered cretonne cushions were crisp and new. On a round table in the center was a tray holding tall glasses and a crystal pitcher filled with amber liquid, aswim with lemon slices and mint leaves.

Everything at the Woodwards' was always so perfect, thought Dan, not shabby, mended and drab like his grandmother's house. All the rooms in the house on Elm Street, except for the parlor which was rarely used, needed paint, new wallpaper, new curtains, rugs or furniture. It was a very old house; it smelled old, looked old, felt old. His grandmother had been very young when her father had built it. She had been married from there, moved back into it after she was left a young widow with three little girls. Dan's mother was the only one of them who had married and left home; his two maiden aunts still lived there.

Dan was thinking about his mother when Mrs. Woodward's voice interposed, "I suppose your family is mighty proud of you, Dan. Being the class salutatorian is quite an honor."

"Yes, ma'am, it is," replied Dan, still standing awkwardly, holding Laurel's corsage, not knowing exactly where to sit.

Mrs. Woodward, occupied with pouring the tea, turned to hand him a glass when she saw his problem. "Would you like me to take the flowers up to Laurel, or would you rather just set them aside for now, and give them to her yourself?" she asked.

"Well—" he hesitated.

With a barely perceptible sigh she put the glass back on the tray and held out her hands for the corsage. "Here, we can just set them down over here. They're very pretty, Dan, but the color—I'm not sure with Laurel's dress—" her voice trailed off doubtfully. Then she added, "Well, I'm sure it won't matter, she'll appreciate them anyway." Mrs. Woodward shrugged slightly as though it were not important.

Dan felt his face grow hot. Why hadn't he thought to ask Laurel the color of her dress? All he'd thought of was how much she loved roses, and the pale yellow ones with a blush of coral seemed so right for her. But now he was unsure.

Dan tensed. Why had Mrs. Woodward had to say anything? Why did she have to spoil his pleasure? Make him feel uncertain? He felt a raw resentment rise up within him. But then, to be fair, she didn't know he had splurged his hard-earned money to buy them, or how long he'd stayed at the florist shop deciding which ones to get.

Mrs. Woodward picked up the filled glass again and, placing a small embroidered napkin under it, held it out to him.

Dan took it and backed up toward the chair behind him and sat down, balancing the glass carefully. He glanced cautiously in Mrs. Woodward's direction as she gracefully seated herself opposite him.

"And what are your plans now that you've graduated, Dan?" Her soft voice somehow accentuated his discomfort. He wished Laurel would come. He had never spent much time with Mrs. Woodward, and he always felt uncomfortable around the lady, even in these brief times. He cleared his throat.

"Well, I'll be working full-time for Mr. Groves at the Pharmacy for the summer, then in the fall I'll be going to college—"

"Oh, and where will that be?"

"I'll be going back to Ohio—"

"Ohio? Why is that?"

"Well, it's near my father's folks and—"

"Your father?" There was a hint of surprise in Ava's voice.

Dan's mouth felt dry. He didn't want to have to go into a long explanation about the family. It was all so complicated. All his relationships were. Even his own questions about them had never been satisfactorily answered. All he really knew was that for reasons he had never been told, his parents had lived apart since he was a little boy. His father had been in the Army and died in Cuba during the Spanish-American War. Since he was nine, Dan had lived in Meadowridge with Grandmother Morris, his aunts Sue and Vera, while his mother worked as a milliner in a big city department store.

"Yes, I'll be attending the State College and I can spend weekends with them. They have a farm, I can help out—"

Dan took a gulp of tea and felt a piece of ice lodge in the back of his throat. He worked it forward to keep from choking.

"I see," Mrs. Woodward said in a tone that implied she did not see at all.

He glanced over at her, looking cool and serene in a light flowered dress with a wide bertha collar edged in deep lace, dark hair swept back from a pale, aristocratic face.

Dan had a momentary mental picture of his mother meeting Ava Woodward. It was hard to imagine. They were so different. His mother had had a hard life, so his aunts were often fond of saying. An image of her came to Dan—the thin face, anxious eyes, her brow puckered in a perpetually worried frown. Yes, he guessed she had a lot of things to worry about, a woman struggling alone to work and support a child. And she had done that. Regularly every month a money order came to Dan's grandmother, and every fall she had sent money for his new school clothes. As Dan had "shot up like the proverbial weed," as Grandma Morris complained, the cost of his clothing went up, too. That was the reason his mother hadn't been able to afford the train fare to visit the last few years. Dan had not seen her in over a year until she had arrived for his graduation.

They had been awkward with each other after so long a time apart. They seemed to have little to say to each other. She was going to stay until the end of the week and then would be leaving again. He had felt guilty leaving her tonight. Not knowing about the long-planned graduation party, she had thought they would have a little family get-together. Even Uncle Ned was coming.

Thinking of his uncle, Dan felt self-conscious. He knew Mrs. Woodward did not approve of him, or at least of what he did. But if it weren't for Uncle Ned, many things would have been impossible for Dan. He might have even had to drop out of school at the eighth grade as so many of the fellows did to help out at home. And Uncle Ned had promised to help him with college and medical school expenses.

Just then, to Dan's immense relief, the screen door opened and Dr. Woodward came out onto the porch, saying jovially, "Well, here I am, my dear. Hello there, Dan."

Dan got to his feet as the doctor extended his hand and in doing so spilled some of his tea. Neither Dr. or Mrs. Woodward seemed to notice, and Dan quickly brushed it off his new white flannel trousers, hoping it wouldn't stain.

Desperately, he wished Laurel would hurry and come.

Upstairs, Laurel slid a filigreed silver comb, one of her graduation gifts, into her swirl of lustrous dark hair, then took a step back from the mirror to judge the effect.

"How does that look, Jenny?" she asked.

Jenny, standing alongside, waiting to help Laurel into her evening gown, nodded approvingly, "Lovely! Land sakes, Laurel, but you do look growed up, with your hair up and all."

"I'm supposed to look grown up, Jenny! I'm eighteen and finished school!" Laurel laughed, the high, sweet laugh that always reminded people of wind chimes.

"Don't seem any time since I was helping you get dressed to go to Toddy's surprise birthday party!" Jenny shook her head in disbelief.

That afternoon, as Jenny and Ella sat proudly with the Woodwards at the graduation ceremony, watching Laurel march up to receive her diploma, they had both remarked that it seemed only yesterday since Laurel was a little girl.

"Well, let's get your dress on now," Jenny suggested. "You know Dan's come, don't you?"

"Yes," Laurel said and slipped her arms into the dress Jenny was holding, then turned around so that Jenny could button the tiny satin-covered buttons down the back.

"My but this *is* a pretty dress!" Jenny nodded appreciatively as the silk voile fell in ruffled tiers over the taffeta underskirt. The delicate blue-violet material set off Laurel's coloring—her peach-bloom complexion, her dark eyes and hair. Its exquisitely embroidered bodice traced the graceful line of her shoulders, the tucked bandeau, her small waist. "You do look a picture."

Even allowing that Jenny was hopelessly prejudiced in her favor, Laurel knew the dress was flatteringly becoming. And it *was* a very grown-up dress!

"You're wearing this, aren't you?" Jenny picked up the necklace of seed pearls and tiny amethysts from the top of the dressing table.

She saw Laurel hesitate a second. Her hand went to the chain and locket she never took off before she answered.

"I suppose Mother will wonder if I don't—" she sighed, then she tucked the locket under her dress into her chemise leaving the thin chain barely visible, and turned so that Jenny could clasp the pearl necklace around her neck.

Then Jenny handed her a small beaded purse, in which was a scented handkerchief, a small brush, some extra hairpins, a slim silver container for rice powder, a tiny vial of eau de fleur cologne, and her gloves.

"Oh, Jenny, thanks!" Laurel exclaimed. "Thanks for everything and for the lovely present, too!"

Jenny had given Laurel a scrapbook with gold printed letters on the front "Schoolday Memories."

"I thought it would be a nice thing for your keepsakes," Jenny said, pleased that Laurel seemed to like it as much as several of the expensive graduation gifts the Woodwards had given her.

"Oh, it will be just right for all my mementos...like this!" Laurel dangled the small tassled dance card before putting it in her evening bag, too. "Thank you, Jenny. Good night!"

Laurel gave her a hug, then pirouetted across the room to the doorway, waved and went along the hall and down the stairway.

"Good night! Have a good time, Laurel!" Jenny called after her.

For some reason Jenny shivered. She didn't know why on such a balmy June evening! A strange, unwanted thought crossed Jenny's mind. What will happen to Laurel now? She did not like the cold, shuddery feeling that passed over her, and she quickly set about picking up some of Laurel's discarded clothes, hanging them up in her armoire, and then turning down her bed.

The walk from the Woodwards' to Meadowridge High had been all too short for Dan who had wanted to delay sharing Laurel as long as possible. As they strolled through the soft summer evening, he had been newly aware of everything about her—the sweet smell of her freshly washed hair, the delicate violet scent of her, the rustle of her gown. He had not wanted their time alone together to end.

But it did, just as they reached the school steps. Chris Blanchard, with Toddy coming from the other direction, greeted them. The girls immediately began to chatter, admiring each other's gowns and flowers and exchanging news about graduation gifts. Then the four of them went into the building together.

Japanese lanterns, strung from the ceiling rafters, shed mellow rosy-golden light, transforming the school auditorium. Lively music was playing and couples were already on the dance floor. Standing at the threshold the foursome was at once surrounded by their classmates, everyone in high spirits with a new sense of freedom since being graduated that afternoon.

"There's Kit!" exclaimed Toddy, waving her over to join them.

Kit, Laurel thought, had never looked so lovely. She had changed from the atrocious dress she had worn for graduation into an elegantly simple lace-trimmed blouse and slightly flared white skirt. White roses were tucked into the braided coil of her dark hair and her smooth, olive complexion was faintly flushed. Her smile was radiant and she seemed happier and more carefree than Laurel had ever seen her. And why not? She had given a superb valedictory speech and been awarded a scholarship to Merrivale Teachers College. It couldn't have happened to a nicer person, Laurel thought fondly.

Everyone clustered around Kit to congratulate her, and she laughed and accepted it all with a new sparkle.

Just then the band blared a fanfare. Mr. Dean, the athletic coach, was on the stage and held up his hand to quiet the hum of conversation to make an announcement.

"Ladies and Gentlemen...you noticed that *since this afternoon*, I am not addressing you as *boys and girls!*" he joked. This comment received a general laugh and a spatter of applause. He smiled and continued. "Now, you have been together as a class for four years and probably think you know each other pretty well, but, how often have you *really* talked to a member of your class who wasn't a *special* friend? Well, tonight we thought we'd give you a last chance to meet and talk to someone you might have wanted to for a long time, and were too shy, too busy or too scared to talk to before!" He held up a large box decorated in their class colors of green and gold. "In here on slips of paper are names of famous people, but separated into first name and last name. Each of you will have to find the matching part. And when you do, you and your match will have five minutes to ask questions and find out something about that person you didn't know, and vice versa!"

A buzz of comments and laughter followed this as everyone lined up to draw a slip of paper from the box.

Inwardly, Dan groaned. If this was going to be a night of party games...when all he wanted to do was to be with Laurel—

But when he found that the person who completed the name he had drawn—"Robin"—was Toddy, holding a slip of paper on which was written "Hood," his heart lifted in relief.

"Not fair!" she pretended to pout. "We know each other too well." She glanced around. "Shall we trade with someone else."

"Not on your life! There are lots of things I don't know about you and I mean to find out!" Dan teased. This was great! With Toddy he could relax, not have to search his mind for questions or make small talk with some girl who was practically a stranger. Dan had always been so busy with his after-school job and his studies that he had not had time to do much socializing. Actually, the only girls in his class he knew other than Laurel to speak to were Laurel's two best friends, Kit and Toddy.

"Well, then, come on," Toddy laughed, "and I'll tell you all the deep, dark secrets of my life." They found two chairs on the edge of the dance floor and sat down. "Now, I'll ask you the question everybody's been asking me most of the day. What are you going to do now that you've graduated, Dan?"

"But you know that, don't you? I'm going away to college in the fall, and then on to medical school. That is—"

"I think that is wonderful, Dan! Most of the boys don't think past college if that—" She sighed. "Take Chris—"

"*You* take him, Toddy!" Dan laughed. "It's *you* he wants."

"That's just it. Just what I'm talking about, Dan. We should all have plans, ambitions and dreams beyond Meadowridge."

"Doesn't Chris?"

"He's going to the same college his father did, then he'll come home and go into the family business."

"Are you sure? You may be selling Chris short, Toddy."

"Maybe. Maybe college will change him."

"It's bound to. College changes everyone."

Toddy's pretty face looked serious. "I wish—"

"What do you wish, Toddy?"

"Oh, nothing," she said, giving her head a little toss. "Now it's your turn to ask me something you don't know about me."

"Did you read the Class Prophecy?" Dan asked.

"Of course, why?"

"Well, was it true? Are you going to become a famous actress?"

For a minute Toddy looked startled, then she seemed to shudder slightly. "Oh, no!"

"But you won the Drama Prize at the Awards Banquet for playing Portia in *A Merchant of Venice.'*"

"Well, that's all it was, playing—I want to do something much more worthwhile than *that!*" she declared.

A whistle blew. "Time's up!" shouted Mr. Dean. "Did you get to know one of your classmates better?" A loud "Yeah!" came forth. "Good!" the coach beamed. "Now, we're going to have some music. Enjoy the rest of the evening!"

Chris came to claim Toddy for the first dance. Dan went in search of Laurel, only to find to his chagrin that she had already been wisked onto the dance floor.

Not wanting to dance with anyone else, Dan was forced to stand on the sidelines, watching until the set was over. When the third dance ended, he began weaving his way through the dancers over to her when another announcement was made.

"Ladies and gentlemen, the next dance is a 'Paul Jones.' Ladies make a circle and gentlemen form a circle around them, moving counterclockwise to the music. When it stops, whoever you're standing opposite is your partner for the next set."

"Come on, let's get into the circle!" said Toddy, grabbing both Laurel's and Kit's hands.

The music started and the two circles began to move. Some of the guys, trying to guess when the band was going to stop playing and wanting to be opposite a favorite partner, would either quicken or slow their pace accordingly. Laurel saw that Dan was one of those. He was trying to keep his eye on her position. But when the music finally stopped, he was standing right in front of Kit.

Amused, Laurel glanced at her friend, then caught her breath. She had never realized before how beautiful Kit was. There was both delicacy and strength in her fine features. Her luminous gray eyes lighted up and a smile trembled on her sweetly curved mouth as she held out her hand to Dan.

For a moment Kit's face was unmasked. And then Laurel saw something more, something she wasn't intended to see. Kit was in love with Dan!

13

Then summer was over. The maple trees along the street began turning gold. The Virginia creeper clinging to the sides of the house blushed crimson. In the mornings, thin frost glistened on the lawn and mist rose, blurring the sharpness of the blue line of hills surrounding Meadowridge.

Soon, like leaves scattering in the wind, everyone would be going away, each to a different destination, a whole new life—Toddy to Europe with Helene and Mrs. Hale; Kit, for her first year at Merrivale College. Chris Blanchard had already left for the University and Dan had gone off to college. Only Laurel was left behind.

Returning home one September afternoon and hearing in the distance a train whistle at the Meadowridge crossing, Laurel paused to listen. It had such a melancholy sound, as wistful as her own thoughts.

She sighed, unlatched the gate, and walked up the path and into the house. For the first time the place was depressing. The home that had always seemed so warm and welcoming now seemed somehow cold and hostile. In just a little over a week, everything had changed—ever since she had brought up the subject of going away to a Music Conservatory to continue her vocal studies.

Laurel had avoided Mr. Fordyce all summer, hoping not to run into him on the street or at church, afraid he would press her for a decision. Realizing she had been putting it off, and apprehensive of the outcome, she had gathered her courage and first broached it with Papa Lee. She had gone around to his office at the back of the house early one morning before any patients were due.

She recalled every detail of that scene now with a little shudder.

"Dismiss it from your mind" had been Dr. Woodward's first shocked reaction. "A young lady your age traveling across the country by herself? It's out of the question."

Laurel bit her tongue, ready to remind him that she had taken that same long trip years ago as a child. She had carefully rehearsed all the reasons he ought to give her permission to go, backing them up with Mr. Fordyce's supportive comments. She thought she had met every objection he might raise, but she had not been prepared for this unexpectedly abrupt refusal.

In a voice that shook she pleaded, "Will you at least think about it, Papa Lee, discuss it with Mother?"

"Discuss what with me?" a voice behind her asked, and Laurel turned to see Ava standing in the office doorway, her arms filled with purple asters she was bringing from her garden for Leland's waiting room.

The scene that followed was worse than Laurel could have imagined. Ava's reaction was immediate and volatile. Her face turned pale, her eyes dark and wild with alarm.

"But you can't possibly go so far and alone! No, I won't hear of it!" she protested. "Leland, talk to her!"

Laurel looked helplessly at Dr. Woodward. The face that had always beheld her with such indulgent love was now grave, the eyes usually twinkling with affection and fondness now seemed unfathomable.

"But, Mother, *you* were the one who wanted me to study voice in the first place. It was *you* who said I had a gift I should develop. I would never have even thought of it if you hadn't encouraged me, had Mr. Fordyce give me lessons—" Laurel turned a bewildered gaze on Ava.

"But I never dreamed it would take you away from me—from *us!*" she said indignantly. Then changing her tactics, she added, "I still believe you have a gift and I want you to go on with your lessons, of course."

"But Mr. Fordyce says he's taught me all he can. He says I *need* further training elsewhere—at a Music Conservatory—if I'm to learn what I must learn—"

"To do what? To become a professional singer? To go on the stage?" Ava flung out her hands in a helpless gesture. "I never heard of such nonsense. What is Milton Fordyce thinking of to put such ideas into a young girl's head?"

"Papa—" Laurel began, but Dr. Woodward held up his hand warningly.

"I don't think we should discuss this further right now. I have patients coming in a few minutes and we all need to calm down," he said soothingly. "Ava, my dear, there is no use upsetting yourself. Nothing will be decided or settled right away. When we are all more composed, we can talk about this reasonably."

But they had not talked it over calmly or reasonably. They had not talked it over at all. Laurel waited for one of them to reopen the discussion, but nothing was ever said. It was as though the whole subject had never been mentioned.

Everything went on as before, and yet everything had changed subtly. Laurel felt both of them watching her, not angrily but with disappointment and bewilderment. She sensed they felt they had somehow failed to make her happy since she wanted to leave them.

In turn, she felt guilty and ashamed, knowing they must think her unappreciative, ungrateful. Ava's face became strained. A sad, anxious expression gave it a pinched look. Laurel struggled with her conscience. Her deep desire had always been to please, but something new began to assert itself. Did she not have a right to explore the person she was apart from these dear adoptive parents? And if they had not believed in her talent why had they encouraged her? It was all so dismaying and disturbing.

Dreams do not die easily, however, and Mr. Fordyce had fueled Laurel's hope. The memory of Kit's graduation speech strengthened her. "To thine own self be true." Laurel must be true to herself, she thought. She could not continue living the safe, sheltered life others wanted for her. Her own true identity demanded to be free. Whether that would be through her voice or whatever might be waiting for her in Boston, she knew she must pursue it.

She was torn between loyalty to her secret goal and loving sympathy for the Woodwards, and decided not to spoil the holidays by bringing up the subject of leaving until after the New Year.

So Laurel plunged herself into the church choir's Christmas performance of Handel's *Messiah,* so that much of her time was taken up by rehearsals. Willingly taking on Ava's Christmas list, she kept herself busy with shopping and wrapping presents. In the kitchen she helped Ella and Jenny with the holiday baking.

Sometimes she felt like a puppet, with someone else pulling the strings, making her move and get up in the morning. Too often there were purple shadows of sleeplessness under her eyes, their lids swollen by tears shed at night. What was to become of her? she daily asked herself. Was she wrong? Was leaving selfish? Desperately Laurel prayed for guidance: "Show me Thy way, Lord, that I might find favor with Thee."

Dan wrote he could not come home for Christmas; he couldn't afford the train fare. Lost in her own dilemma, the uncertainty about her future, Dan seemed very far away.

The days before Christmas seemed outwardly serene, peaceful, but within Laurel, a fire storm raged.

The performance of the *Messiah* was hailed by everyone who attended as the finest program Meadowridge Community Church choir had ever presented. Afterwards there was a reception in the festively decorated social hall. It was the custom to hang small gilt-paper cornucopias on the church Christmas tree. Inside each cornucopia was a slip of paper bearing a Scripture verse. These were considered each person's special Bible message for the coming year.

When Laurel opened hers, she read: "Be strong and of good courage; be not afraid, neither be thou dismayed; for the Lord, thy God is with thee whithersoever thou goest" (Joshua 1:9). It seemed a confirmation, and Laurel took it as such. Her conviction grew that she *must* go.

The New Year came and a week later Laurel gathered up her courage and went into Dr. Woodward's office. The sun was streaming in through the windows of the small L-shaped office, a fire going in the Franklin stove took the chill off the January morning. Its warmth accentuated the combined smells of old leather from the shelves of medical books, the Jonathan apples in the bowl he kept on his desk to reward small patients, and the spicy pine scent of the crackling wood.

At Laurel's entrance, Dr. Woodward looked up with pleasure, but that look slowly faded into alarm as she stammered out her reason for coming.

In a voice that shook slightly Laurel told him she had written the Music Conservatory in Boston for an application, and that Mr. Fordyce had given her names of a few well-known teachers she could contact and now she was determined to go.

He took a long time responding. He turned and gazed out the window for an interminable minute, his hands under his chin, his fingers pressed together forming an arch. When he looked back around at Laurel, his eyes were full of concern.

"Do you have any idea what this will do to your mother?" he asked solemnly.

Laurel felt her heart accelerate frantically. Steeling herself for the attack on her emotions that would follow, Laurel begged, "Papa Lee, I *have* to go. Please don't make it any harder than it's going to be!"

But it had been hard, the hardest thing Laurel had ever done in her life. The last thing she had ever wanted to do was hurt these two dear people.

When all possible arguments against her going failed, the Woodwards retreated into injured silence. Laurel hardened her heart self-protectively, knowing if she did not she would be trapped by pity. Even if she came back, she had to go now. Didn't they see that?

The night before her departure, while packing in her bedroom, she heard Ava's muffled sobs. Overcome with compassion, she almost ran down the hall to her adoptive mother's room. She wished there were some way to comfort her. But she knew the only comfort Ava would accept would be compliance. Knowing she could not give that, Laurel put her face in her hands and wept.

She had meant to bring only happiness to these two who had given her so much. Instead, she was causing them grief and distress.

Morning came at last. A gray, wet mist cloaked the barren trees outside her bedroom window. Her train departed at seven. She knew Ava would not come down to say goodbye, or see her off. Laurel dressed and carried her suitcase and small valise downstairs. She stood in the front hall, straining to hear some movement upstairs that might indicate that either Ava or Dr. Woodward were up, that perhaps they might relent and give her their blessing before she left.

Laurel stood in front of the hall mirror, as she had so many other happier times, to put on her hat. As she did, she saw an envelope propped against the vase. In Dr. Woodward's bold scribble was her name. She picked it up and opened it. Inside were five crisp twenty-dollar bills and two fifty-dollar bills. But there was no note.

Laurel pressed her lips together tightly. The night before, he had kissed her cheek and said "Good night, my dear" as usual. At least there had been no last-minute request that she change her mind. Ava had nursed a migraine in her room all day. It was no more than Laurel expected.

Her heart was heavy with all that was unspoken between them.

A minute later she saw Jenny's reflection in the mirror behind her as she came from the kitchen and stood in the archway of the dining room.

Slowly Laurel turned around. Jenny sniffed and wiped her eyes with a balled handkerchief. Laurel felt a rush of affection for Jenny, who had been her confidante, her comforter, her exhorter, her friend. Spontaneously the hired girl opened her arms and Laurel went into them. She could feel Jenny's shoulders shaking with suppressed sobs.

"I'll be back. Don't cry!" Laurel whispered, patting her.

"Your cab's out front." Jenny sniffled, pushing Laurel away gently. Her plump chin was trembling as she looked at her with red-rimmed eyes and in spite of her brimming tears, nodded approvingly. "I must say, you do look very smart and grown up, Laurel."

Laurel walked over to the foot of the stairway and stood there a minute, looking up. Should she go back upstairs, knock at Mother's door, say all the things that were in her heart to say? She glanced over at Jenny who met the look with a sorrowful shake of her head.

Laurel sighed. Jenny was right. It would just make things worse. She picked up her coat, put it on, straightened the brim of her hat. Walking resolutely to the front door, she blew Jenny a kiss, picked up her bags, and went out into the mist-veiled morning.

She closed the door behind her and its click took on symbolic significance. She knew she was leaving something precious and yet something from which she had to flee, or it might cripple her forever.

At the station, Laurel waited impatiently. Now that she had come this far, she wanted no further delay. She was tense with apprehension, the nervous anticipation of all that lay ahead.

The platform was deserted. Laurel saw no one she knew. No other passengers from Meadowridge seemed to be boarding the early train. Except for the clerk in the office, no one was around.

Finally the train rounded the bend and came to a stop with the screech of steel brakes on the rails, steam hissing from its engine. No one else boarded, and only mailbags were exchanged from one of the boxcars farther down the line.

The whistle blew shrilly. Heart pounding, Laurel moved toward the train. At the entrance to the coach, she turned to take a last look around. She remembered the first time she had seen the rolling Meadowridge hills when she had stepped off the Orphan Train onto this same platform years before. When would she see it all again?

"All aboard, miss," the conductor said, coming up beside her and offering his hand to assist her up the high steps into the train.

Entering the car, she saw it was nearly empty except for a few sleeping passengers. She found an unoccupied seat and put her valise in the rack above, then sat down on the scratchy red upholstery. She was taking off her hat when she heard the chug of the engine and felt the train begin to move. As it lurched forward, Laurel pressed her face against the window, looking back to watch until the yellow station house was out of sight.

14

Boston! She was here at last! Laurel thought to herself peering eagerly out the window of the hired hack. She had followed Mr. Fordyce's instructions to take one from the train station and go straight to the rooming house near the Music Conservatory.

Until now Boston had been only a name in a history book. A name associated with the Boston Tea Party and the poem she had memorized in school about Paul Revere's ride to Lexington to warn of the British coming. Now, here she was in the heart of the great historic city called "the Hub of the Universe" and "the Cradle of Liberty."

As she looked first to the right and then to the left, she was filled with excitement. The city was alive with people and activities, a long distance from Meadowridge's sleepy, small-town atmosphere. It bustled with noise and movement. Here things happened, here anything seemed possible.

Of course, she could not remember much about Boston from the days she had lived here with her mother as a little girl. Children are only aware of their immediate surroundings, and Laurel's memories of that time were centered on her life with Mama in the cozy upstairs flat of Mrs. Campbell's house.

The streets were winding and rather narrow, lined with tall brick buildings of imposing architecture. The heart of the city was a jumble of businesses, banks and churches. Trolleys sped right down the middle of the street, vying for space with wagons loaded with produce and elegant buggies. And right in the center was a huge park where people strolled and children played.

Laurel had given the cab driver the address of the rooming house run by a distant relative of a former college classmate of Mr. Fordyce.

"I'm sure it's not luxurious, but it's clean, comfortable, and conveniently near the Conservatory," he had told her. "The rates are very reasonable and that's important since there are always unforeseen expenses once you're a student, and everything adds up."

Everything he had told her about the boardinghouse was true. What Mr. Fordyce hadn't told Laurel, she soon found out for herself. Mrs. Sombey, the landlady, was insatiably curious. Laurel felt she was being interviewed for a position instead of renting a room, and only managed to escape by saying she had to go right over to the Music Conservatory. Eager to begin her adventure, she covered the few short blocks quickly.

Laurel's heart sounded like a percussion instrument to her as she stood looking up at the Music Conservatory building. Her first instinct was to turn and run. How dare she think herself ready to brave such a prestigious institution, present herself as a candidate for admission as a student here?

Well, she had come this far and she was not going to turn back now. She reminded herself of all that her decision had cost her emotionally, to say nothing of the Woodwards. Fortifying herself with her own version of the Scripture verse that speaks of setting one's "hand to the plow," Laurel started up the stone steps and opened the door into the entrance lobby.

Once inside, a cacophony of sounds greeted her ears. Assorted music floated through the transoms of a dozen practice rooms, merging into an unplanned symphony. Woodwinds, violins, cellos, piano and French horns, all blended in an exciting, if not perfectly harmonic, whole. From somewhere she heard a soprano vocalizing the scales and echoing down the hall came an a cappella chorus of male and female voices.

Proceeding timidly, Laurel followed a sign with an arrow directing her to the Administration Office. In a burst of laughter a group of chattering young people, carrying portfolios and music sheets, came rushing down the main steps. Laurel moved against the wall to let them go by, thinking soon she would be one of them. A thrill of nervous excitement rippled through Laurel. She *was* actually here! Here, where others like herself had come to take that step into serious musical training.

Mr. Fordyce's oft-repeated admonition to all his students rang in her ears as clearly as the sound of a flute being practiced in one of the rooms: "A career in music is one of the most difficult professions in which to achieve success. It takes more than talent and interest. To attain even a minimum, one must be absolutely dedicated, be convinced that music is the most important thing in life."

Laurel felt something tighten within her. Was that *her* feeling about music? To be truthful, she knew it was only means to an end. But she would honestly try not to waste this opportunity. If she were accepted, she would do her best. That she could promise.

An hour later Laurel's initial excitement had drained away. She held in her hand a sheaf of forms that must be completed before she could apply for her first interview for admission to the Conservatory. Telling herself she was just tired from the long train trip and that things would look brighter once she was settled, she went back to the rooming house and unpacked. At least, she was here in Boston, her plans underway. It would all work out, Laurel assured herself. But a week later she encountered a more discouraging setback.

At the Music Conservatory, Laurel was shocked to find that she would have to audition before she could qualify for admission, and the audition list was long. Perhaps she should have applied long before leaving Meadowridge to insure a place on the list for next fall's classes. After applying for an audition, she would be given a date and time to appear before a board of the faculty. Then it was a matter of waiting to find out if she was accepted as a student.

Laurel's heart sank. She had never imagined it would be so difficult. She was sure even Mr. Fordyce was not aware it would take this long. In the meantime, what was she to do?

As Laurel left the Admissions Office, she encountered another young woman checking the bulletin board on which the audition list was posted.

"I know just how you feel," the girl said. "I applied the first time last spring. If you have a coach—preferably, one of the teachers here—your chances are better."

"A coach?"

"Yes, someone to keep you on your mark so that when you do get to audition, you're at peak."

"But, I don't know anyone—" Laurel began, feeling even more discouraged. "How does one find a coach?"

"Well, I was lucky that my violin teacher is a recognized coach. Do you live in Boston?"

"I just came. I mean, I've only been here a short time."

The girl frowned. "You mean you don't know anyone locally who could help you?"

Laurel shook her head.

"Then I'd advise you to check at the office. They should have a list of teachers willing to coach." The girl made a wry face. "It's expensive though. They charge by the hour and they want their money first. You know how it is with musicians, always broke! But it's worth it...at least, I *hope* it's worth it."

With that, the girl picked up her violin case, wished her luck, and left. Laurel stared at the long list of names and scheduled audition dates. It was discouraging but not hopeless, Laurel told herself.

Following the advice the other student had given her, Laurel checked at the office for a list of coaches. Everything the girl had said was confirmed. The list of available coaches was much shorter than the list of hopeful applicants for auditions, the hourly price of lessons daunting.

Downhearted, Laurel left the cavernous hall outside the administration office, pushed open the door to go out of the building, and found it was raining very hard outside.

One thing she had learned since arriving in Boston midwinter was that the weather was as uncertain as her future now looked. Luckily she had taken an umbrella with her when she started out that morning.

Buttoning the top of her coat, she shifted her music portfolio more securely under one arm, then opened her umbrella and, using it as a shield against the driving rain, she started down the steps.

Preoccupied with her new set of problems and trying to hold the umbrella steady against the gusty wind, Laurel did not see the figure hurrying up the Conservatory steps heading directly toward her until their two umbrellas collided with a jarring thrust, halting them both.

"Oh, sorry!" a male voice said just as Laurel exclaimed, "Excuse me!"

As she righted her umbrella, Laurel saw a tall, young man in a caped coat, also carrying a portfolio. For a moment they inspected each other. Then he lowered his umbrella to tip his hat. At that moment the wind whipped the hat out of his hand and sent it whirling down the steps, depositing it in a puddle at the bottom of the steps.

"Oh, my!" cried Laurel in dismay.

But the young man only laughed. As he started after it, he called back over his shoulder, "No problem!"

Laurel hurried to the bottom of the steps, where he was retrieving the hat, shaking the water from its brim.

"I'm dreadfully sorry. I wasn't looking where I was going!" Laurel apologized. "Is it ruined?"

"No harm done," he assured her. "It will dry out." He replaced the top hat at a rakish angle and grinned. "Beastly day, isn't it?"

What an attractive man! Hatless, his thick hair had sprung into a tangle of dark curls, Laurel observed. His eyes, too, were dark and crinkled in the corners, as if he found much to laugh about. How wonderful to take life as it came, she thought, the mishaps as well as the lucky moments.

"Well, I must be off, or I'll be late!" he said and went bounding up the steps and into the building.

Laurel stood there a minute longer, staring after him. His easy laughter reminded her of Toddy, who had always helped her see the bright side. She suddenly missed her old friends more than ever. Both Toddy and Kit had always been there for her when things went wrong. And things seemed to be going very wrong for her right now.

Sighing, she moved on in the direction of her boarding-house. Maybe she should have reported to the Conservatory the minute she arrived, found out about the possible delay of enrolling as a student. But there was something Laurel had wanted to do first.

Finding Mrs. Campbell's house had been a priority. Mama had made Laurel memorize her address in the unlikely event she should ever get lost, and Laurel had never forgotten it. But when she got there, she discovered that the whole row of old frame houses on the street she remembered had been destroyed by fire several years before, and a warehouse had been erected in their place.

The neighborhood itself looked run-down, not at all as she remembered it. Of course, she had only been a child then, and it was possible that nostalgia had distorted the facts.

Although this was a disappointing setback, her hoped-for source of information gone, Laurel was still determined to pursue her search for her real family.

All this had meant countless, time-consuming hours, and long, usually fruitless excursions. The days of February, spent in the musty archives of the courthouse slipped away. Here, Laurel had pored over old records, checking out hunches and hints that led nowhere.

Finally one day in the County Records office, much to her joy, Laurel found the marriage license issued to Lillian

Maynard of Back Bay, and Paul Vestal. Shortly afterward she also found her father's death recorded, though no place of burial was given. And Laurel made the rounds of several cemeteries, looking for his grave, all to no avail.

But the most traumatic trip of all was the one she took out to Greystone Orphanage. She went by trolley, having to transfer twice, then walked up a long steep hill. Her heart was pounding, not so much from the climb, but from remembered apprehension, reliving that awful morning when she and her mama had come there together. It was the last time she had ever seen her mother.

The large stone building stood like a fortress, the chain-link fence surrounding it every bit as prison like and forbidding as she remembered. She had thought she could go in, make some inquiries, and see if she could gain any more information that might help her in her search. But the emotions that assailed her were too overwhelming. Laurel had turned around, practically run back down the hill and caught the next trolley that came along. The experience was too shattering to repeat, and she had never gone back.

Now Laurel suspected she had wasted valuable time that might have been better spent establishing herself as a student at the Music Conservatory. Her name had been placed on a long list of applicants, but her audition date was still weeks away. And she had learned that, in addition to giving a successful audition, one was required to supply three professional recommendations. Even with all that, there was no guarantee of acceptance.

Laurel's spirits were at a new low when she wrote to Mr. Fordyce, explaining her dilemma and asking him not to mention this latest delay to her parents. So far she received no reply.

But what could he do, after all? She had no other professional connections. Where had she sung except at church and school? And no one in the big city of Boston had ever heard of Meadowridge!

15

March blew into Boston like the proverbial lion, blustery days of cold rain which more often than not turned into sleet, coating streets and sidewalks with hazardous ice.

On one particular morning, the wind off the river was knife sharp as Laurel cut across the Common, her head bent, her umbrella slanted against the stinging rain. She had gone to the Conservatory to check the auditions list, in case her name had moved any further up. Of course, it had not. Neither had she heard from Mr. Fordyce yet. Perhaps she should see about getting a coach. That, of course, meant spending money. She had been holding onto her cash reserve, but now she wondered if she should not make that investment. Oh, there was so very much to think about, to decide.

Laurel had never dreamed living on her own in the city would be so expensive. The money Dr. Woodward gave her before she left Meadowridge seemed more than adequate, but everything cost so much more here than she had imagined. She knew she would have to find work soon or—or what? Laurel did not even want to contemplate what might happen when her money ran out.

The thought of returning to her small room at the boardinghouse on this dreary day was too depressing. There she would have nothing to think about but her troubles.

Besides, she was suddenly very hungry, so she headed for the small restaurant on the corner where she could get some lunch.

Pushing open the door of the restaurant, Laurel immediately felt its warmth enfold her. The delicious fragrance of freshly baked bread and the aroma of newly brewed coffee tickled her nostrils with their promise of satisfaction. A bowl of the thick vegetable soup made here daily and a slice of the crusty bread would revive her energy and her spirits.

She gave the pretty, dark-eyed waitress her order, then looked out the window. Laurel always chose a table by the wall near a window if it was available because she liked looking out on the busy street. It made her feel less lonely to watch other people, make up stories about them, where they were going, where they had been.

This was a game she had begun playing since she had moved here. After living in Meadowridge where she knew almost everyone and everyone knew her, it was a strange sensation to be alone in a city the size of Boston, where no one ever called you by name. Homesickness was a battle Laurel fought daily. Although she had only been here a few weeks, they had been the longest weeks of her life.

That's why she liked this cheerful little place with its friendly atmosphere. It was still early for the usual lunch crowd. Laurel enjoyed seeing the easy camaraderie between the staff and the customers, even though she was too shy to be a part of it.

As she sat there staring at passers-by, Laurel wondered what she could do to earn some money to stretch her small amount of cash beyond her rent and bare necessities. The first and most natural thought was to give piano lessons to children. But, in a city filled with aspiring musicians all in need of extra money to pay for their tuition and extra coaching, would there be an excess of them offering music lessons?

Refusing to be defeated before she even tried, Laurel decided she would place an ad in the newspaper. She would state her willingness to give lessons at pupils' own homes, both piano and voice.

All at once, the irony of her situation struck her. How similar to her mother's! Here in this same place, Boston, Lillian Vestal, too, had been forced to find work as a music teacher in order to support herself and her small child.

Laurel's memories of her mother were priceless, kept locked in her heart all these years like precious jewels. Now, she felt free to take them out, handling them delicately, examining, marveling and appreciating the magical childhood she had been given, even in the direst of circumstances.

She cherished the memory of being held in loving arms, of the pretty face above her framed in a cloud of dark hair, of the low, sweet voice singing her to sleep. At Greystone those memories had devastated her and yet, at the same time, sustained her. Then she had pretended their separation was only temporary, that soon they would be reunited. Even after she went on the "Orphan Train" to Meadowridge and was adopted by the Woodwards, her "real" mother had remained a phantom presence in Laurel's life.

Thinking about her, Laurel looked out the restaurant window into the rain-swept street, trying to bring that face into clear focus. But it was another one that superimposed itself on the vague image. It was Ava Woodward's face Laurel saw. Her face as she had last seen it—drawn, white, with alarming purple shadows ringing her eyes. The memory struck her conscience. She could hardly bear to think of Ava or of Dr. Lee. But if she had broken their hearts, her heart was breaking, too.

"Here we are, miss," announced the waitress in a cheerful tone.

Laurel turned away from the window as the steaming bowl of soup was set before her, and Ava's reproachful image disappeared.

Laurel ate, gradually feeling revived and more hopeful. Surely things must get better.

"Will there by anything else, miss?" the waitress asked. "For dessert today, we've got a lovely caramel custard and there's apple cobbler just out of the oven."

Laurel's mouth watered at the suggestion, but until she had a job she had to be careful, so she shook her head regretfully.

"No thanks, this will be plenty," she said, visions of Ella's delectable pies and cakes flashing tauntingly through her mind.

Just at that moment the door of the restaurant burst open and, with a gust of wind and rain, a young man dashed inside, closing his umbrella with a flourish as well as a great showering of water onto nearby patrons.

"Oh, sorry! I do beg your pardon!" he said in a deep, rich voice, bestowing an absolutely irresistible smile upon his victims.

His entrance in so small a place could not go unnoticed and Laurel, with the other customers, turned her head to look at the arrival. To her amazement, it was the same young man she had collided with on the steps of the Conservatory a few weeks before.

Mr. Pasquini, the restaurant owner, came hurrying forward, greeting him with the enthusiasm one reserved for a long-lost relative or visiting celebrity.

"Welcome, welcome! How went the tour?"

"*Bravissimo!*" replied the young man, divesting himself of his coat and hanging it on the wooden cloak-tree near the door. "It was better than we expected. Sold out crowds every night. But I missed your wonderful pasta...and no one can make bread like Maria!" He kissed the tips of his fingers in an extravagant gesture of praise.

"Well, come along, sit, sit! First some minestrone, yes? Then, some linguini, maybe?"

The young man rubbed his hands together in evident anticipation.

"Fine, fine!" Smiling, he looked around, and quite suddenly he met Laurel's gaze.

Aware that she had been staring, fascinated, she flushed and averted her eyes, looking down into her empty soup bowl. For some reason her heart was giving quick little leaps.

Her first impression of the young man was reaffirmed. He was extremely handsome. This time she noticed his teeth—very white against olive skin. Possibly he was of Italian descent, he seemed so at home here. There were quite a few Italian people living in the vicinity of her boardinghouse and the Music Conservatory.

Mr. Pasquini had mentioned a "tour." Did that mean the young man was a professional musician returning from a successful road tour? That day they had bumped into each other so unceremoniously on the steps of the Conservatory, Laurel had assumed he was a student. Although her curiosity about him was piqued, she had learned nothing more.

Having finished her lunch, she could not continue to occupy a table without ordering something more. Since it was near noon, the restaurant was beginning to fill up as all the "regulars" were arriving.

Reluctantly Laurel put on her coat and, taking her check, went up to the cash register to pay. There she noticed Mr. Pasquini hovering at the table of the young man, engaging him in lively conversation. Laurel got her change and with no further reason to linger, went out again into the stormy March day.

It seemed an odd sort of coincidence to see that young man again, Laurel thought, as she struggled to raise her umbrella. In this big city she rarely saw anyone twice. It was a city of strangers where she, too, was a stranger.

Her decision to advertise for piano pupils in the newspaper now settled, she knew she must get a newspaper to see how such ads were worded and how much it would cost. There was a newsstand on the corner about a block from where she lived. Braving the wind, she decided to walk to save carfare and by the time she reached the newsstand the hem of her coat and dress were quite soaked and she could feel the damp seeping in through her thin leather shoes.

Miserable and shivering, she hurried along the slick sidewalks, being splashed by the horses and carriages that went by the busy thoroughfare. For some reason she thought of her father who had been run over and killed on just such a stormy day in this very same city. Her father was still such a shadowy figure in her life. Laurel had no real memory of him, although she was two when he died. All she had was the picture in the locket.

When she had first come to Boston, Laurel had made the rounds of galleries and art dealers' shops, hoping that by chance, she might someday find one of her father's paintings.

But after she learned Mrs. Campbell's house had been razed by fire, she assumed they had probably all burned in the attic where they were stored.

Chilled to the bone, Laurel reached the boardinghouse and mounted the narrow stairway to her second-floor room. Longingly she thought of Ella's cozy kitchen where she had come in from school on many a rainy day to find hot chocolate or spicy tea waiting, and homemade cookies, still warm from the oven.

Quickly she got out of her wet things and curled up at the end of the bed, spreading the newspaper out in front of her. As she turned over the rain-dampened pages, going toward the classified section, something caught her eye, an item in the society news.

"Mrs. Bennett Maynard will be the hostess of a soiree next Tuesday evening to benefit the Symphony—"

The name seemed to leap at Laurel from the page. She noted the address—in the most exclusive residential section of the city. The brief article gave only the most discreet information: "Symphony supporters, only those holding season tickets, are invited to call between the hours of four and six. The Symphony's Music Director will speak on the selection of next year's program and possible guest artists to be featured in future performances."

Could *this* Mrs. Maynard be her grandmother?

Laurel determined that the next day she would take the trolley out to that part of town and look for the house matching the address given. Maybe, at last she would see the place that belonged to her mother's family, the house where Lillian Maynard had grown up and left to marry Paul Vestal.

Laurel was pretty well convinced now that her young parents had eloped. Why else the estrangement? A girl from Boston's Back Bay, with breeding and background, marry a penniless artist? Why, such an alliance would have been considered unthinkable in an earlier day. Yet the young couple was so madly in love, Laurel romanticized, that perhaps they knew there was no other way to be together. And in running away they had irrevocably broken all their ties. Yes, she would go and see. Maybe even tomorrow, Laurel decided.

But the next morning she awakened with a sore throat and fever and the next two weeks she was laid up with a heavy cold and laryngitis. When she finally made it shakily out of bed and went over to the Conservatory, she found to her despair that she had missed her scheduled audition date.

16

Laurel's disappointment over the missed audition was combined with unexpected relief. Maybe she really wasn't ready. It would be far worse to try and fail. After all, she could not be blamed for having a bad cold. But, if, unprepared and uncoached, she was rejected, that would be her fault.

What she had heard about the auditions was confusing. She did not know how the decision was made. Did the board base a student's acceptance on the difficulty of the piece or on the clarity of vocalization, on poise and stage presence or on one's presentation with integrity to the composer? Laurel had no idea.

Perhaps missing her audition was all for the best. Before the next auditions were scheduled, she would have time to find a coach to help her. But a coach cost money. That meant she must find a way to supplement her income.

Ever since her arrival in Boston, Laurel had received a small check from Dr. Woodward at the first of each month. Because of the circumstances under which she had left Meadowridge, however, she felt guilty using his money and so far she had resisted cashing any of the checks. But unless she found some way of earning some soon, she would be forced to do so.

To Laurel's delight the ad she had placed in the newspaper brought immediate response from many of Boston's socially active mothers. With their children industriously occupied at the piano at home, these ladies were free to be about their visiting or shopping or having tea with friends, a very convenient arrangement.

Laurel's first pleasure in receiving so many responses to her ad was soon diminished somewhat when she realized that teaching music in her pupils' homes meant hours of her time spent on trolleys, trams and on foot to reach the various addresses.

Neither had she imagined teaching to be so tedious. Listening over and over to clumsy little fingers stumbling over scales, or distorting such simple tunes as "Welcome, Sweet Springtime" sometimes made her feel like screaming. But her determination to be independent was more important than the boredom and weariness. It was a price she was more than willing to pay. Saving money for a coach meant practicing many small economies.

Her first resolution was that of eating only one full meal a day. It took some ingenuity for her to smuggle fruit and crackers, concealed in her music bag, past her eagle-eyed landlady, and make tea on a small spirit-burner bought in a second-hand store. For her one meal Laurel continued to frequent the restaurant on the corner, a few blocks from her rooming house.

After a short spring Laurel discovered Boston's summers were as extreme as its winters. Hot and humid days were followed by breathless nights when the air barely stirred the curtains of her bedroom windows. To make matters worse, several of her pupils canceled their lessons to vacation with their families at second homes on the coast of Maine or Cape Cod, where Boston's affluent spent their summers.

The unaccustomed heat and the prospect of the loss of extra income upon which she had come to rely were depressing, and Laurel struggled not to succumb to feelings of loneliness and self-doubt. She had to keep reminding herself of her main purpose in coming east.

With less traveling and teaching to take up her day, Laurel had more time to think about contacting Mrs. Bennett Maynard whom she had come to believe was her grandmother. She often took out that newspaper article and reread it. If this *really* was her Mama's mother, how did she go about approaching her? Since the woman must be advancing in years by now, it wouldn't do to show up on her doorstep, announcing herself. The encounter must be arranged with careful thought and tact.

One Saturday, Laurel decided to go out to the address given and see for herself what might have been her mother's childhood home. She took a trolley to the end of the line, then at the direction of the conductor, walked another few blocks. She strolled along quiet streets, lined with impressive homes set well back from the boulevard over which arched tall, shady elms.

Laurel walked slowly, looking for the house number in the clipping she held in her hand. Then, all at once she saw it! Displayed discreetly on a polished brass plaque set among climbing ivy in the post of a brick wall was the house number she was looking for.

Number 1573 was a stately pink brick of Federal architecture, its many windows covered with black louvered shutters. Curved double steps with ornamental black iron railings led up to a paneled front door flanked by tubs of espaliered trees.

There was no sign of life, not on the street itself, nor in the house. No movement at all behind those shuttered windows. Did Mama's family go to Maine or Martha's Vineyard, in the summer?

For a long time, Laurel stood looking at the house, then slowly turned and retraced her steps. She was hardly conscious when she left the luxurious serenity of that part of town inhabited by the city's wealthy and pretigious citizens and boarded the trolley to return to the workaday life of the rest of the population of Boston.

Laurel got off at her usual stop, still distracted by her pilgrimage, walked over two blocks to the little restaurant where she took her evening meal. Entering, she was glad to see her favorite small table in the corner vacant. Seating herself, she picked up the menu, looking at it without actually reading it.

Her thoughts were filled with the significance of her afternoon excursion. The grandeur of those mansions, guarded by ornamental iron fences or well-trimmed boxwood hedges, their manicured terraces and shuttered windows had cast a strange spell on Laurel. She tried to imagine the beautiful girl of her locket, with her laughing eyes and flowing dark hair, her dainty figure and exquisite clothes, who had lived in one of them and who had become her mother.

Now she began to see Mrs. Campbell's flat in all its shabbiness through the eyes of one once accustomed to luxury and comfort. She saw the shiny black of her mother's one coat with its worn fur collar and cuffs. The rare treats of cake or fruit to celebrate small occasions must have been eked out of a meager income. Yet Laurel had never heard her mother complain—not even when her living conditions brought about the illness that caused her death!

Laurel's thoughts were interrupted by a rich, male voice. "I recommend the lasagna tonight."

Laurel started and looked up at the waiter. She fumbled with the menu as she recognized him as no other than the young man with whom she had collided on one of her first times at the Conservatory. The very same one whom she had seen later right here in this restaurant.

Surprised speechless, Laurel simply stared at him. His smile widened and he said, "To answer your question. Yes, I am a student at the Conservatory, and I work here part-time to support myself *and* my voice coach!"

Laurel felt her face flame with embarrassment.

"Oh, well, I—" she stammered. "I'm sorry, I didn't—"

"Don't apologize, please! We all—at least most of us—have to work while we attend the Conservatory. It goes with the territory, as they say. Surely there is no such thing as an artist of any kind who doesn't have to struggle, is there? If so, I haven't heard of one, much less met one." His dark eyes sparkled with amusement. "Now, what about you? I mean, what would you like for dinner?"

Flustered, Laurel looked down at the menu, none of the selections making sense. It was usually her pocketbook that dictated her order anyway.

"May I make a suggestion?" he continued. "I've personally sampled the minestrone soup and found it to be, as usual, delicious. But then, perhaps, it's too warm an evening for soup. Maybe something lighter. The lasagna is delicious and, with a fresh green salad, perfect." He paused. "Even though we both know we have encountered each other before, may I introduce myself formally?" He gave a small bow. "I'm Gene Michela."

It would have seemed rude not to do the same. "I'm Laurel Vestal."

"Am I correct in assuming you are also a student at the Conservatory?"

"Well, not exactly. At least, not yet. That is, I haven't been accepted. I missed my audition and—I found out I should have a coach— So I've been teaching, giving piano lessons. I had ten pupils but now most of them are away for the summer and I—" Suddenly she halted, blushing. Why on earth was she talking so much, telling all this to a—a *waiter?*

But he was regarding her sympathetically, nodding with understanding.

"Oh, dear!" Laurel exclaimed. "I don't know what I'm saying, I mean, I don't know what I want to eat—" she broke off. Laurel closed the menu and handed it back to him.

"I'm sorry. I didn't mean to rush you. Would you like some time to decide? And while you're deciding may I bring you a glass of vino, perhaps?"

Laurel shook her head vigorously.

"No? Then a refreshing glass of lemonade instead?" His smile was disarming.

"Yes, that would be lovely," Laurel murmured, still blushing, wondering why she was making such a fool of herself.

She comforted herself with the thought that she did not have to come here again—that is, unless she wanted to eat! Actually there was no other eating establishment close by where she could get such delicious, inexpensive food. Oh, dear! Then why had she chattered on like that? Was it because she seldom had a chance to talk to adults, only the children she taught? She tried to avoid her garrulous and inquisitive landlady except when the rent money was due, and she had not really made any acquaintances among the other roomers who all seemed much older and not especially friendly. This Gene was very nice. Besides, he was a student at the Conservatory, which gave them something in common. No, it wasn't as if he were a total stranger.

By the time Gene was back, Laurel had managed to recover some of her composure.

"I've consulted with Mario, the chef—" He wisked a tall frosty glass off the tray and set it in front of her with a flourish— "and he has suggested the perfect selection for a summer evening—a combination plate of prosciutto, chilled asparagus, fresh tomatoes, cucumbers, cheese, bread. May I bring it out for you?"

Dazzled by all this attention, Laurel could only nod again, hoping that the price of a "chef's choice" would not make it necessary to eat crackers and oranges in her room for the rest of the week. She watched him as he waited on other diners. He handled each one with the same affability as he had with her.

The attractively presented plate proved tasty and delightful as well as filling. As Laurel was finishing, Gene appeared with a chilled dish of pistachio ice cream, garnished with a thin chocolate wafer.

"Compliments of the chef!" He set it down on a small round lace paper doily.

Laurel started to protest. But Gene, glancing over his shoulder, laid his forefinger against his mouth. Laurel followed the direction of his glance and saw Mr. Pasquini standing at the cash register, nodding and smiling at them.

There was nothing for Laurel to do but eat the ice cream with relish. However, it left her with a dilemma. Did she leave a tip? From their brief conversation Gene must know she was on as slim a budget as he. Would he be insulted if she tipped him, after all his tactful kindness in serving her? Or would he naturally expect one? And what amount? While she struggled with this, Gene reappeared with her check on a small tray, then stood behind her chair as she rose, thanked him, and moved over to the cash register.

He waited at a discreet distance while she paid, then escorted her to the restaurant door, which he opened for her with a little bow. "It was a pleasure serving you, Miss Vestal. I hope we meet again."

It was not until Laurel was back on the sidewalk and had counted her change, that she realized neither the lemonade nor the pistachio ice cream was included on her bill.

Laurel was halfway down the block when she heard her name called.

"Miss Vestal! Miss Vestal, wait, please!"

She turned to see Gene Michela sprinting after her. Had she forgotten something? she wondered, stopping and turning around.

He reached her, flushed and panting. "Miss Vestal, beg pardon, if this seems too personal but—but do you attend church?"

Startled, she nodded, then quickly amended. "Yes, I do, but I haven't since coming to Boston. I mean, I don't belong to one—"

Gene shook his head vigorously and held up a protesting hand.

"What I meant was—" and he held out a small card. "I'm singing at a wedding at this church next Saturday afternoon. It would be perfectly all right if you slipped in the side door and sat at the back." He smiled shyly. "I would like for you to be there…if you have no other plans."

Laurel looked down at the card he had handed her and read the scribbled name of the church, not knowing whether to laugh at this bizarre invitation. But Gene seemed so eager, so anxious, so appealing that her heart melted.

"Well, I'll try—" she began rather hesitantly.

"Oh, yes, *do* try." He smiled. "I'll sing as if you were there anyway!" Then with a wave of his hand, he backed away a few steps. "I've got to get back to the restaurant. I've diners waiting for dessert. Goodbye, Miss Vestal!" And he turned and ran back down the street.

What an astonishing young man, Laurel thought, amused. In spite of herself, in the days that followed, she found her thoughts turning more and more to Gene Michela. He certainly was impetuous and unconventional. Handsome, too, and terribly charming. Too good-looking, too assured, too charming?

Whatever conclusion she drew from this impulsive act, on the following Saturday, a little before three, Laurel found herself entering the side door of an imposing stone building.

The church, one of the oldest in Boston, was tall and stately, set back from the street, surrounded by an iron fence. It was completely different from the small, white frame Community church in Meadowridge, and yet there was something strangely familiar about it, Laurel thought as she opened the door at the side entrance and slipped inside.

The interior was dim and quiet, for it was a good forty-five minutes before the scheduled ceremony. Down the long aisle to the front of the church, about ten pews on either side were bowed with white satin ribbon, obviously reserved for the wedding guests.

Laurel felt a bit like an intruder, but finding a seat in the rear, shielded by one of the stone pillars, she sat down. She occupied herself by gazing around at the arched stained-glass windows. Sunlight slanted through, giving the colors only a pale radiance. Each window depicted a symbolic event in Jesus' ministry—the Feeding of the Multitude, the Healing of Jairus's Little Daughter, the Good Shepherd and—Laurel drew in her breath as her glance moved to the next window—Jesus with the Little Children.

From out of her past a pale memory struggled to break through. She had seen that window before. Could *this* be the same church she had attended with her mother?

Laurel felt excitement tremble through her.

Here in Boston everything seemed like a giant link connecting her to her past, to her childhood. Maybe everything was leading her back to her roots, to her family, to her identity.

The deep tones of the organ reverberated through the empty church and with a start, Laurel realized that the organist had arrived and was testing his chords for the wedding music.

It seemed strange to Laurel to be attending the wedding of strangers. Yet a few minutes before the bride entered, when Laurel heard Gene's rich tenor voice filling the whole building with its glorious sound, she knew it had been worth overcoming her timidity to come.

Listening to Gene sing, the beautiful words of "O Perfect Love," Laurel felt little prickles along her scalp and down her spine. Truly *his* was a God-given gift and she thrilled to its splendor. There was more to that young man than she had thought. Much more! One could not sing with such a voice and not be aware of its Creator.

Tears welled up in Laurel's eyes. Coming into this church, seeing the window, hearing Gene's voice had been an emotional experience. Before the wedding ceremony was over, Laurel rose and left quietly. She was too deeply moved to chance meeting anyone, especially Gene Michela.

In spite of herself, Gene was much in her thoughts over the next few days. But she carefully avoided Pasquini's Restaurant for a few days, not wanting to appear to be encouraging special attention from Mr. Pasquini's part-time waiter!

Still most of her thoughts that spring were centered on Mrs. Maynard. Week after week Laurel was drawn back to the street where the Maynard mansion stood. She would sit on one of the benches in the shady park across from it, staring at its impressive facade. If this *was* her mother's family home and Mrs. Bennett Maynard *was* her grandmother, would she not have wondered all these years what had happened to her own daughter? Surely, if Laurel presented herself, wouldn't she be happy to see her granddaughter at last? Or did she still harbor the old resentments? Had she cut off her emotions concerning the daughter as completely as she had cut off communication with her?

April passed into May, May into June, and each time Laurel took the long trolley ride, there was no sign of any activity around the house. Apparently the occupants were away.

During her "visits" Laurel pondered how she would go about contacting Mrs. Maynard upon her return to Boston in the fall. She had no desire to shock her. No, first she would send flowers and a note, saying she had reason to believe they were related and asking if she might call.

Of course, there was no way of knowing what Mrs. Maynard's response would be. What if, after the flowers and note, there was no answer? If not, Laurel decided, she would follow up with another note and, armed with a copy of her parents' marriage certificate, and her birth certificate would simply go to the house and ask to see Mrs. Maynard. Of course, it was very possible the woman would refuse to see her.

Then what would Laurel do? She could only guess that the old woman's curiosity would be aroused. Certainly Laurel's resemblance to her mother would not go unnoticed or overlooked. Then she would show her the pictures in the heart-shaped locket. After that, surely there could be no mistaking who she was.

Still, Laurel knew she should prepare herself not to get that far. Could she be satisfied that at least she *had* found her parents' graves, proof that they were married, that she was their daughter and their rightful heir?

The rest of the story, the lost fragments of her early life and background she had pieced together. Her parents—the wealthy debutante and the struggling artist—had fallen in love and risked everything to be together. How they had met was still a mystery. But Laurel knew that until her father's death, her mother had been happy with her choice. Why, after Paul Vestal's death, the young widow had never been reconciled with her family, Laurel did not know. Surely there had been no reason why their daughter had lived on the edge of poverty when the Maynards were perfectly capable of providing for her. The cold hard truth might be they had never forgiven Lillian for what she did.

As Laurel sat contemplating the austere, shuttered house across the street, she asked herself if it were possible, after all these years, for the needless bridge of bitterness to be crossed? And what did *she* herself actually want from all this? She searched her heart honestly. She wanted nothing. Nothing, more than the Maynards' acknowledgment that she existed.

With summer coming, Laurel had more immediate worries. Her pupils' long vacation would deplete her small savings and soon it would be time to register at the Conservatory to audition for acceptance as a student for the coming year. Even with all her scrimping, Laurel had not been able to return Dr. Woodward's checks.

Knowing that the new schedules for classes, auditions, and list of coaches would be posted before the opening of school, Laurel went to the Conservatory one sultry day in June.

In the Administration Office she spent a great deal of time filling out forms. She hesitated a long time over the question: "Who will be responsible for your tuition, to be paid before the start of each semester?" Laurel did not want to write in Dr. Woodward's name and yet, if she wrote her own, the next questions "What is your employer's name. The source of your income?" would have to be answered honestly.

Would she have to wait another six months before applying to become a student, when she was assured of having enough money to pay for it? And what about finding and paying a coach?

Laurel sighed and shoved all the papers into the portfolio in which she carried her music, and decided to think everything over before completing her application. Explaining briefly to the woman behind the reception desk that she would be back later, Laurel started out of the office. As she did so, she bumped into someone just entering. Her portfolio fell from her grasp onto the floor, sending her music sheets flying every which way. As she stooped to retrieve them, so did the newcomer and, in their combined attempt to gather up the papers, their two heads banged together.

For a moment Laurel was stunned. Dizzily she looked up and saw the other person holding his forehead, a pained expression on his face. As they stared at each other, his look of discomfort changed to one of amused recognition and with mock indignation he demanded, "Miss Vestal! Don't you ever look where you're going?"

"Oh, my goodness! Mr. Michela!" she exclaimed.

In her confusion Laurel bent down again in an attempt to pick up the scattered music and so did Gene. They bumped heads a second time. This time they both collapsed into fits of helpless laughter. As their laughter rose, surrounding them in a sensation of idiotic delight, their eyes met and a remarkable thing happened.

Why, it's like something straight out of a romantic novel, Laurel mused.

Of all the people in Boston, of all the possible students at the Music Conservatory, of all the days of all the weeks of the summer, why had her path crossed so often and so unexpectedly with that of this charming young man?

As this question flashed through Laurel's mind, all her girlish dreams of falling in love came into focus. She had imagined how it would be to meet the right person, had hoped that person was Dan, had mourned when it was over between them, had nurtured a secret hope that someday, in some strange new place, she would meet someone else. Now he was here. And it was not a dream!

17

It seemed natural for them to leave the administration office together, walk through the lobby and out the front door of the building into the blinding sunlight.

"It's really good to see you again, Miss Vestal," Gene said, "or should I say *bump* into you again?"

"I'm not always so clumsy, believe it or not!" Laurel laughed as she paused at the stone balustrade and set down her portfolio so she could tighten the ties. Without raising her eyes from the task, she said shyly, "I heard you sing."

"*Did* you?" Gene sounded pleased. "I so hoped you would."

"You *are* very good, you know." Laurel continued checking the ribbons of her portfolio to see if it was closed securely. "You really have to sing, don't you?"

"It's my life!" he replied.

"It shows," she said seriously, at last looking up at him.

Gene's dark eyes sparkled with enthusiasm as he suggested they sit down on the steps in the sunshine. Suddenly they seemed to have so much to say to each other, about music, about themselves. Gene told Laurel he had just returned from a month's tour with a choral group.

"It gave me a taste of what a concert singer's life would be like. On the road two weeks at a time, trying to sleep sitting up on a day coach, staying at run-down hotels, terrible food!" He laughed. "For an Italian boy the latter has to be the worst of all! Speaking of food, I'm hungry. How about you?"

It was past noon, and Laurel realized she had had nothing since breakfast.

"Come on." Gene stood up and held out his hand to her. "Let's go get a hot dog."

At the concession stand a ruddy-faced man in a limp chef's cap and apron, took their order. He forked sizzling weiners into long buns, then slathered them with mustard.

"My treat!" Gene held up his hand warningly when Laurel opened her purse. "Not that the menu is very elegant, but just wait until I have my debut at La Scala! Then we'll really celebrate!"

Buoyed by his playful optimism—that he would actually one day perform at the famous Italian opera house and she would be with him on that occasion—Laurel held their hot dogs while Gene bought two bottles of soda. Then they found a bench and sat down to eat.

As they continued to chat, Gene mentioned names of composers and famous singers as if they were close friends. Laurel found all this fascinating even though, by comparison, her own knowledge was very limited.

After they finished eating, they walked along the flower-bordered path down to the lake. Gene took off his jacket and spread it on the grass for Laurel to sit on. They went on talking as though they had known each other forever, yet in their conversation was the excitement of discovery.

The afternoon was slipping away when suddenly Gene scrambled to his feet.

"Laurel, I'm sorry, but I didn't realize it was getting so late. I can't take you home, or I won't make it to work on time!" he exclaimed. "It's not such a great job, but I need the money."

"Then maybe I'll see you later at the restaurant."

"Oh, this is a second job—just temporary. I'm, filling in for the regular who's sick." He seemed embarrassed. "I could make up something that would impress you, but the truth is I'm a night watchman at a warehouse."

"Oh, Gene, you don't have to try to impress *me!*"

"Of course you're right. My father always says all work is noble as long as it's honest."

"I believe that, too," she declared, although it was the first time she had thought much about the nobility of all work.

"But I did intend to take you home." Gene frowned. "I don't even know where you live. And I don't know how to get in touch with you—to see you again!"

"I can give you directions. You take the Number 10 trolley and—"

"Sorry, Laurel, but I don't have time to listen." Gene was already moving away, walking backwards as he spoke, "Could you meet me instead? Here? Tomorrow afternoon?"

"Yes!" she called. "Tomorrow afternoon! Right here." She nodded her head frantically as Gene, with a final wave of his hand, turned and made a run for it.

Laurel pressed both her hands to her mouth, giggling. How wild this was! And yet how happy she felt! She had not been this happy in weeks and weeks. She picked up her music portfolio and strolled in the other direction to the trolley stop.

She was still smiling to herself when she got off at her street and turned slowly toward the rooming house. Yes, this had been her happiest day since coming to Boston.

The next afternoon Gene was in the park waiting for her when Laurel arrived. Her heart gave a funny little flip-flop when she saw him pacing impatiently up and down. When he saw her coming, he broke into a big smile and rushed up to her, both hands extended.

"Laurel! I'm so glad to see you! I was afraid you might not come. To tell you the truth, I thought I'd dreamed the whole thing! The crazy way we kept bumping into each other— literally!" He threw back his head and laughed, a rich, full laugh. "And then last night, I kept kicking myself that I hadn't ditched the stupid job and seen you right to your doorstep. I thought maybe you'd think I was...I don't know...rude, irresponsible or something, and change your mind about meeting me."

Laurel shook her head. "Of course not! I told you I understood. Really!"

"Sure?"

"Positive." She laughed at his incredulity. "I wouldn't have come if I hadn't wanted to, if I thought you were...well, any of those things."

"Truthfully?"

"Yes, truthfully." She smiled. "Why don't you believe me?"

"I do." He squeezed her hands he was still holding. "Let's always promise to tell each other the truth, no matter what," he said earnestly.

Solemnly Laurel nodded, thinking how strange it was that it *didn't* seem strange at all for Gene to assume that there would be an "always" for them.

The rest of the afternoon flew by again. They never seemed to run out of things to talk about, to share and laugh about together. Gene had a wonderful sense of humor and was a raconteur. Everything that had ever happened to him seemed, in the telling, to be humorous, exciting, or an unexpected adventure. Laurel could not remember ever enjoying being with anyone so much.

By the end of the second day they had spent together, Laurel knew a great deal more about Gene. He had grown up in a small New England coastal town, part of a large, close Italian family with grandparents, many uncles and aunts and cousins. Although most of his relatives were fishermen, they were proud and supportive of Gene's pursuit of a singing career. Gene had won a scholarship to the Conservatory and had come to Boston right out of high school. But in spite of his paid tuition, he still had to work at odd jobs to support himself, pay for his coach, his rent. The Pasquinis, old family friends, were also kind, feeding him and giving him a job at the restaurant.

"Do you have a coach, Laurel?" he asked.

"No, not yet. I suppose I'll have to get one." She hesitated. "I—I really haven't done much about preparing for my audition either. Actually, hearing all you've done, all you've sacrificed to continue at the Conservatory makes me wonder about my own—well, my seriousness of purpose."

Gene looked puzzled. "I don't know if I understand what you mean—"

To her surprise, Laurel found herself confiding the roundabout way she had come to Boston. Her story just seemed to pour out, and before she knew it, she had told Gene the real reason for her move.

"I never really thought seriously about studying voice. But when my high school music teacher brought it up, it seemed like a good excuse to do what I'd been secretly planning all these years."

"And have you found out about your real family yet?" Gene asked.

Laurel told him what she knew.

"It's my grandmother, or the person I believe is probably my grandmother, that I still have yet to see." To be putting all this into words made Laurel realize she had never told anyone else in the world. And yet it seemed the most natural thing in the world for her to be telling Gene.

"I'm a little afraid, I think," she added.

"Would you like me to go with you when the time comes?"

Laurel felt the sweet surprise of his concern, the sincerity of his offer as if he were already a part of her life, and it touched her deeply.

As the days went by, they saw each other nearly every day, spending the afternoons together in the park. Within a short time Laurel realized being with Gene was the high point of her day—what she looked forward to each morning when she woke up, what she thought about the last thing before going to sleep at night. She was happier than she had ever been, happier than she had ever imagined possible.

Gene was everything Laurel wasn't—outgoing, optimistic, enthusiastic. His personality complemented hers in every way. Gene's drive and ambition, his willingness to work hard to achieve his goals influenced Laurel to make a decision. Feeling she should cut her old ties of dependency to the Woodwards, she determined to get a job that would give her a *regular* income, not accept any more of Dr. Lee's checks. Only when she could afford it herself would she find a voice coach and apply to the Conservatory. It was the only fair thing to do, the only right choice.

Often when they talked together, sharing their thoughts, the deep things of their hearts, Gene would say, "Everything happens for a purpose, Laurel, nothing by chance! Like our meeting the way we did. There's a reason for it all. God has a plan for each of our lives. Nothing is an accident, although it may seem like one. I've always believed that. He gave me my voice so that I could not only make my living, but so I could contribute something to other people's lives, too. I'm never happier than when I'm singing. That's how I know I'm fulfilling His purpose for me."

Although not completely convinced herself, something that happened shortly after she made her decision to look for a job made Laurel a believer. Taking what she thought was a shortcut back from the park to her rooming house one afternoon, she passed a Music Store with a sign in the window HELP WANTED, PIANIST.

On impulse, Laurel entered the store and found they needed someone to play the sheet music they sold to customers. When she sat down and sight read several pieces for the owner, Mr. Jacobsen, he hired her on the spot.

She could not wait to tell Gene the good news the next day. After congratulating her heartily, he told her he had some news of his own.

"Actually both good news and bad news."

"What do you mean?"

"Don't look so worried. The good news is I have a new job, a singing job! Just in the chorus, but at least I'll be singing. Gilbert and Sullivan. *The Pirates of Penzance.*"

"But that's wonderful, Gene!"

"Wait till you hear the rest." He held up his hand. "The bad news is that it's at a summer theater at the Cape."

"Cape Cod?"

"Yes, I'll be away for the rest of the summer—two weeks rehearsal, two weeks for the run of the show, maybe a chance to try out for the next one."

Laurel felt her heart sink.

"I hate the idea of being away from you," Gene said. "But, I can hardly turn down a chance like this."

"Of course, you can't," Laurel replied. "Anyway, it's only for a few weeks."

"That's right. The time will pass quickly."

"Yes, it will," Laurel agreed, not believing a word of it.

"I have to be there first thing Monday, so I'll leave Sunday on the morning train. But we've got today and Friday," Gene reminded her. "We'll go to the outdoor concert at Greenwood Gate Park on Saturday. We'll take a picnic supper and have a glorious last evening together. How does that sound?"

"Perfect." Laurel, already dreading the long separation, tried to sound happy.

Saturday afternoon Laurel dressed as carefully as if she were going to a ball. She chose one of the outfits Mrs. Danby had made for her the summer before and ironed it carefully. A short Spanish-style jacket of crisp, yellow cotton edged with trapunto embroidery, worn over a lawn blouse with delicate yellow featherstitching on the collar and cuffs, and a flared skirt belted with a wide green cumberbund. With it she would wear a basket-weave straw picture hat.

To avoid the probing curiosity of her landlady, Mrs. Sombey, Laurel tried to slip down the stairs to wait for Gene outside. There he might also escape running the gamut of the ill-concealed envy and criticism of the other roomers who gathered in the parlor whenever there was the slightest chance of anyone having a "gentleman caller."

She was unsuccessful. As if on cue, Mrs. Sombey appeared in the lower hall just as Laurel was coming down. Her ferretlike face creased in a saccharine smile as she remarked with exaggerated sweetness, "Oh, my, Miss Vestal, how nice you look. I expect you're going out again with your young man? I *do* like to see my young ladies enjoy themselves," she purred. "And what a lovely ensemble! It looks very—shall we say, 'tray sheek'? Cost a pretty penny, I'd imagine," she simpered. "Or did you make it yourself, you clever little thing?"

When Laurel had first taken a room at Mrs. Sombey's, she had managed to say as little as possible about herself except that she planned to attend the Conservatory. But every month when she went to pay her rent, she was subjected to what she came to think of as an "inquisition." She was sure Mrs. Sombey investigated her mail, certain that she examined the postmark and return address on every letter.

Laurel had thought of moving, but this place was clean, quiet and convenient to the Conservatory, and since Mrs. Sombey only rented to women, Laurel had felt comfortably secure staying there. Except for the annoyance of Mrs. Sombey's insatiable curiosity, Laurel had been reasonably content.

It was just since Gene had come into her life that the landlady's interest in her comings and goings had begun to irritate Laurel.

Still it was not in her to be rude, so trying not to be as abrupt as she felt inclined, Laurel murmured a thank-you and proceeded to the front door. Before she reached it, quick as a cat, Mrs. Sombey was there, parting the curtains on the glass partition and peeking out.

"Well, here comes your fellow now, Miss Vestal. And he's...yes, well, I do declare, he's carrying a hamper. Does that mean you're going on a picnic? Well, my, my, how very—"

Laurel gritted her teeth, and not waiting for more, slipped out and hurried down the steps to meet Gene just as he came up to the house.

As usual, Laurel caught her breath at her first sight of him—the dark, windblown hair, eyes dancing with anticipation, smile lighting up his whole face.

When he saw Laurel, he stopped and put one hand on his breast.

"What a vision you are!" He said dramatically. "I should have brought you flowers!"

"Flowers?"

"Yes, of course! Flowers are the accepted gifts of courtship, aren't they? Instead, I brought you food!" Gene held up the basket. "Thanks to Mrs. Pasquini, who packed us a lunch you won't believe. I kept telling her there would only be two of us, but Benigna, who is a realist as well as a romantic, assured me that music stimulates the appetite."

"Come on." Laurel slipped her hand through his arm. "Let's be on our way before Mrs. Sombey thinks of some excuse to come out here and interrogate you!"

At the park, they roamed over the acres of rolling hills dotted with lovely old trees above the semicircular amphitheater where the orchestra would assemble later for the program. After a few minor debates as to the ideal spot, they agreed upon one. Gene opened the large wicker basket, took out a small rug and spread it out on the grass, tossing two pillows upon it. Next came a blue checkered tablecloth, plates, napkins and silverware. Then Gene began setting out a platter of thinly sliced ham, squares of cheese, small containers of black olives, cherry tomatoes, pasta salad, sliced cucumbers.

Laurel's eyes widened.

"My goodness, you were right. That's quite a lot of food!" she exclaimed, thinking of the limited diet she had been living on for the past weeks.

Gene was busy slicing a twisted loaf of crusty bread on a small wooden cutting board. "Well, you don't have to eat if you're not hungry," he teased.

"Oh, I'll force myself!" Laurel retorted, dipping a tiny tomato into a fluted bowl of dilled mayonnaise and popping it daintily into her mouth. She was getting better at the kind of bantering repartee Gene delighted in.

There was a container of chilled lemonade and another of strong Italian coffee to have with an array of fresh fruit as well as lemon tarts.

They ate with relish, talking and laughing, completely relaxed and happy in each other's company. Laurel tried not to think that the next day Gene would be going away for weeks. Every time the thought threatened to spoil things, she determinedly pushed it to the back of her mind. There would be time enough to miss him when he was gone. Now, it was enough to enjoy him.

"What will you have for dessert, madam?" Gene held up a bunch of glistening purple grapes in one hand, a perfectly rounded blushed peach in the palm of his other.

"Oh, I don't know—I'm so full but—why don't we share a peach?"

"No sooner said than done," Gene said, deftly cutting it through, removing the stone, and handing half the fruit to Laurel.

"Oh, it's so juicy!" she said, as she bit into the luscious slice. The juice ran down her chin and she tried to capture it with her tongue.

Whipping out his immaculate white handkerchief, Gene leaned forward and gently wiped her mouth and chin. He was so close Laurel could see the spiky thick eyelashes shadowing his brown eyes.

Then Gene said huskily, "Oh, Laurel, I can't remember what my life was like before I met you. Now I can't imagine it without you!"

She caught her breath. "I know. I feel the same way," she whispered, knowing it was true.

Then his firm, cool mouth was upon hers in a tender, lingering kiss.

As the kiss ended, Gene murmured, "I hear bells ringing, music playing—"

"I do, too," sighed Laurel. "It must be some kind of spell."

"It's called being in love," Gene said softly and kissed her again. Then he chuckled. "Truthfully, I think it's the orchestra tuning up their instruments. The concert will begin as soon as it's dark. We'll want to go down closer," he told her, getting to his feet.

Gathering up the remnants of their picnic, they repacked the hamper, picked up their pillows and blanket, and moved down the hillside.

The sky had turned a hyacinth blue and a faint evening star had appeared by the time they were settled. Soon the snowy-haired conductor marched on stage to the podium, rapped his baton and the first haunting strains of Vivaldi's *Four Seasons* rose into the evening air.

Gene was humming the melody from the finale as he and Laurel walked through the park and toward the trolley stop at the close of the concert. It had been a glorious evening and now Laurel felt melancholy, knowing it was coming to an end, that tomorrow Gene would be gone.

They were quiet on the ride back to the rooming house, holding hands, gazing into each other's eyes with longing as the awareness of the parting deepened. When they got off, they walked the last block very slowly, until they could delay the inevitable no longer.

At the corner, Gene drew Laurel away from the circle of light shining from the lamppost into the shadows and took her into his arms. His cheek rested against hers, his lips moved along her temple, and she heard him murmur her name.

She closed her eyes and felt him kiss her eyelids, the top of her nose. Then he kissed her mouth and it was sweet and thrilling beyond anything she had ever imagined.

"Oh, Laurel, I love you so," Gene whispered, then sighed, "but I have nothing to offer you. I'm as poor as the proverbial church mouse. Even with my scholarship, and taking any odd job I can find, I barely make enough to pay board and room, to say nothing of my coach. It isn't fair when I have no idea how or when—"

Laurel placed her fingers on his lips, shutting off the flow of words. Then she put her arms around his neck, bringing his head down against her cheek, wanting to comfort and reassure him. Most of her life Laurel had been sheltered, cherished, protected. Now she was experiencing a new emotion—a desire to give. A strange new tenderness filled her heart so full she could hardly speak.

"It doesn't matter. I'm poor, too, Gene. But we'll both make it. We'll help each other. I feel it, I *know* it. It will take time, but we're young, and we have all the time in the world!"

18

The week after Gene left for Cape Cod seemed endless. On her half-day off, Laurel took the trolley out to the secluded neighborhood where the Maynards lived. To her surprise she saw a gardener clipping the thick boxwood hedge and a man on a ladder washing the outside of the downstairs windows. Preparations were obviously underway for the return of the owners.

The sight of all this activity both excited and unnerved Laurel. After a sleepless night, she decided it was now or never. If she was ever to find out if Mrs. Maynard was her grandmother, she should not delay any longer.

Laurel had learned from Ava, whose garden was her hobby and delight, about the legendary language of flowers. Together, they had enjoyed making up arrangements to convey secret messages as was the custom in old-fashioned times. So when Laurel went to the florist shop to order the flowers she wanted to send Mrs. Maynard along with her note, she recalled some of those meanings. Whether or not the lady would understand their significance did not matter. It gave Laurel a feeling of reaching out in a special way.

After much deliberation she chose a mixture of gladioli and white peonies, softened with maidenhair fern, symbolizing strength, sincerity and discretion. Laurel placed the note she had labored over composing to be delivered with the box of flowers.

> Dear Mrs. Maynard,
>
> I am writing because I have reason to believe we are related. I am the daughter of Lillian Maynard and Paul Vestal, born in this city September 1884. If you would be so gracious as to receive me, I would like very much to call upon you so that we may discuss this possibility further.
>
> Sincerely,
> Laurel Elaine Vestal

She used the double name on her birth certificate, which, she had been told, was given her in honor of her two grandmothers, though Laurel was not sure which of the two was Mrs. Maynard's name.

Underneath her signature, she had put the address of Mrs. Sombey's rooming house.

A week dragged by and every day Laurel hurried home from work hopefully. But no message came from Mrs. Maynard. She did, however, have one or two letters from Gene, all hastily written, telling of the thrills of rehearsals, the stimulation of being with other singers, and assuring her of his love. These she read over and over.

By the end of the week, Laurel resolved that she would not be put off nor would she wait any longer. There had been enough time for Mrs. Maynard to recover from any shock the note had given her and to consider the possibility that the writer *could* be her granddaughter. Now Laurel was determined to appear in person, and unless she was refused admission, she would confront her with the fact of her existence.

As she dressed for this momentous meeting, to bolster her courage, Laurel kept repeating to herself a Scripture verse she had memorized: "Ye shall know the truth, and the truth shall make you free."

It was as important for her as it was for Mrs. Maynard to at last confront the past, acknowledge it, face the truth then—Well, however Mrs. Maynard chose to react, she, *Laurel*, would be free, no longer haunted by the possibility that her mother had never told her parents of her baby's birth. Maybe the estrangement had been too bitter, the parting too harsh, the pain too deep. Laurel remembered asking her mother once about the grandmothers for whom she was named and if she would ever meet them. Now she recalled the reply. "Someday...when all is forgiven."

Forgiven? Did Mama mean that she must forgive her parents, or that she needed *their* forgiveness?

At last, dressed in a dove-gray linen suit, a dainty white blouse, and wearing a polished straw hat ringed with white daisies, Laurel was ready. For a minute she stood thoughtfully, fingering the chain of her gold locket. Then she carefully pulled on white cotton gloves, picked up her handbag containing the copies of her parents' marriage certificate and her birth certificate, and went downstairs and out of the house. She walked resolutely to the corner of the street where she took the trolley out to the quiet neighborhood, to one household whose serenity she was about to shatter.

The butler answering the door was tall, his demeanor haughty. He held out a small silver tray for a calling card which Laurel could not supply.

"I have no card," she replied with what she hoped was suitable poise. Inwardly she was trembling. "But I think Mrs. Maynard will see me."

The man looked coldly suspicious. "Then whom shall I say is calling?"

"Miss Laurel Vestal."

"One moment, miss." He started to close the door, but Laurel slipped inside before he could leave her standing on the porch.

He gave her a withering look, turned sharply on his heel, and disappeared down the hall. Laurel clenched her hands together nervously. She strained her ears and thought she heard the murmur of voices coming from beyond the closed door at the end of the hallway.

Left alone, she looked around her. The foyer was oval in shape with recessed alcoves in which were placed marble busts. The parquet floor was partially covered by a runner of dark red carpeting extending from the doorway and up a broad staircase with wide polished banisters, leading to the second floor. At the curve of the balcony was a tall window with stained-glass panels through which a milky sun shed pale light into the otherwise shadowy interior.

It seemed an age since she had been left there, stiffly waiting, until the door at the end of the hall clicked, and she saw the figure of the butler returning. His expression had settled into what seemed to be permanent disdain.

"Although this is *not* Mrs. Maynard's regular 'At Home' day, she *will* see you," he addressed her in an icy tone. "Come this way, please."

Laurel followed, though the impulse to flee was strong. She fortified herself by remembering why she had come and why it was necessary to see it through.

At the end of the hall, the butler opened a door and announced, "Miss Vestal, madam," then stepped back for Laurel to pass into the room.

Her first impression was of overpowering ostentation—thick Oriental carpets, heavy carved furniture, gold-framed portraits on paneled walls. Then she saw that there were three people instead of the one she expected.

As she advanced a few steps, a man got to his feet and moved slowly behind the chair of one of the women. All of them were regarding her with curiosity and something else. Obviously she was an unwelcome intrusion, her ill-timed appearance interrupting a pleasant summer afternoon.

But at least *one* of them *should* have been warned of her coming. Laurel looked from one lady to the other. Which one was Mrs. Maynard? Which one was, possibly, her grandmother?

Her hands tightened on the tortoise-shell rim of her handbag. It somehow gave her strength, knowing that inside was the proof that she belonged here as much as any of them—or at least, that she had the right to come. "Ye shall know the truth and the truth shall make you free" flashed through her mind again, giving her added courage.

"Mrs. Maynard?" She spoke in a low, steady voice.

There was silence. The man made a slight impatient movement, as if shifting from one foot to the other. There was a moment's hesitation before one of the women spoke, "*I* am Mrs. Maynard."

Immediately Laurel focused her attention on the speaker.

Mrs. Maynard was thin, everything about her finely honed—the aristocratic nose, the unrelenting line of her mouth, the erect posture, the proud way she held her head, all bespeaking self-discipline and a certain inflexibility. She was a splendid-looking woman, who might have once been beautiful, Laurel thought, with her features, her beautifully coiffed iron-gray hair.

But as they regarded her, Laurel wondered what secrets were hidden behind those pale-blue eyes.

Then Mrs. Maynard spoke again. "This is my cousin, Mrs. Farraday, and her son, Ormand."

Only the man acknowledged the introduction with a nod. Mrs. Farraday merely stared at Laurel with wide-eyed annoyance.

"You wished to see me?" Mrs. Maynard's voice was cool with a distinct Boston accent.

"I am Laurel Vestal, Mrs. Maynard. You may recall I wrote to you a few weeks ago, asking if I might call?"

It was an effort for Laurel to keep her voice from shaking. She sensed she was on dangerous ground and that Mrs. Maynard was not going to make it easy for her. Nor did Laurel want to embarass her in front of the two who were eyeing her visitor with undisguised suspicion.

When Mrs. Maynard did not reply, Laurel had to push further. "You *did* receive my note, did you not?"

Mrs. Maynard inclined her head slightly, but did not speak.

Laurel could sense the hostility mounting in the room and she rushed on hurriedly, before her courage failed altogether. "I have been waiting for an answer. When I did not hear from you, I decided to come in person."

There was a sharp intake of breath from the other woman, who straightened up in the tapestried armchair in which she was sitting. "The very idea!"

Laurel froze momentarily. No doubt she had committed some terrible social blunder. In this echelon of society, if someone did not reply to one's request to call perhaps it meant they did not wish to receive that person. But it was too late to worry about that now. She had come for some kind of answer, and she would stay until she got it. Unconsciously Laurel squared her slender shoulders.

Mrs. Maynard laid a restraining hand on her cousin's arm. "Gertrude, please, I'll handle this." Then waving one ringed hand toward a straight chair near the door, she asked, "Would you care to sit down, Miss Vestal?"

Still standing, Laurel suggested, "Perhaps I could come back at a more convenient time?"

At this suggestion, Laurel thought she saw a flicker of relief in the otherwise rigidly composed expression. Mrs. Maynard rose from her chair. "Yes, perhaps that would be best. We are due at a meeting of the Symphony Society very shortly and as Chairwoman I cannot be late."

"Would you care to give me another day and time?" Laurel persisted, unwilling to let this opportunity pass without some definite commitment.

Mrs. Farraday made a clucking sound to indicate her irritation.

Ignoring her, Mrs. Maynard moved toward the door, extending one arm toward Laurel as though ushering her out. "I will send word when that can be arranged."

Having come this far, Laurel was not to be put off. As the older woman's hand rested on the doorknob, Laurel drew out the envelope containing the extra copies of her parents' marriage certificate and her birth certificate and handed it to her. "In the meantime, Mrs. Maynard, perhaps you would find these interesting."

The thin, controlled mouth seemed to quiver slightly, and there was a second's pause before she held out her hand to take the envelope.

When the drawing room closed behind her, Laurel heard Mrs. Farraday declare, "The nerve of the girl!"

And in an entirely different context, Laurel agreed. It had taken nerve—all the nerve she could muster.

Outside again and in the warm summer afternoon, Laurel realized she had been holding her breath. She let out a long sigh. After the dimness of the shuttered interior of the Maynards' house, the bright sunshine was dizzying. She leaned against the brick wall for a moment to gain her equilibrium.

Well, it was done! She had carried out her part. The rest was up to Mrs. Maynard.

19

Laurel was thrilled to see a letter from Gene waiting for her on the hall table of the rooming house when she returned. She had never needed something to lift her spirits more. Gene's letters always did that. He wrote easily almost as if he were talking to her. From his descriptions of some of the people in the operetta cast, funny incidents that happened in rehearsals or even during the performances, Laurel could get a picture of backstage life.

She ran upstairs to her room, tore open the envelope, and devoured every word. But this letter was different from most of the others she had received from him. It was short and contained an unexpected message.

"I am making a quick trip to Boston. Since the theater is 'dark' Sunday and Monday, I'll leave right after the performance on Saturday night and be there some time Sunday. I have a surprise for you. I can't wait to show you."

Anticipating Gene's coming brightened what proved to be a depressing week for Laurel. Mrs. Maynard's promise to get in touch with her and arrange another meeting had not been kept. As each day passed without word, Laurel's disappointment turned into a kind of indifferent resentment. Their brief encounter had not endeared Mrs. Maynard to Laurel.

Maybe it was her own fault. Her expectations had been high. Laurel had imagined that once her grandmother saw her, recognized the unmistakable resemblance to her own daughter, there would be a joyous reunion. But it had been anything but joyous.

In spite of her initial cool reception by Mrs. Maynard, however, Laurel persisted in her desire to be acknowledged for who she was. Now it was much more than a validation of her identity; it had become a vindication of her parents' cause. Mrs. Maynard should take the responsibility for the unhappiness she had caused her daughter, for the way that courageous young woman had been forced to live—and die. She should face up to the fact that, because of her own arrogance and unforgiveness, her granddaughter had been placed in an orphanage to be reared by strangers.

Though in her heart Laurel knew these were less than ideal motives, she held to them stubbornly.

The night before Gene's arrival, Laurel was restless. He had been away for so long—nearly three weeks now. What if he had found someone else among the pretty actresses and singers in the cast? If not, there were always the summer people, many of whom entertained at lavish parties in their homes during the run of the play. Gene was so attractive, so talented. He was sure to be showered with flattering attention. The more she thought of it and of the mysterious note announcing his visit, the more Laurel imagined the worst. This, combined with the depressing circumstances of her heritage, sent her into an unaccustomed decline and she paced the floor, sleepless.

Toward morning, her gaze fell on the little slip of paper on which she had copied the Scripture verse she had memorized before her encounter with Mrs. Maynard: "Ye shall know the truth and the truth shall set you free." Well, she would soon know the truth about Gene, too, and about the love he had declared in his letters. Breathing a hopeful prayer, she fell into a deep sleep and awakened refreshed.

Rising hurriedly, she put on a pink linen that was one of Gene's favorites, then posted herself at her bedroom window to watch for him. While she waited she patted her hair distractedly, gave the bow on her sash an extra fluff, and fiddled with the frilled ruffle outlining her bodice.

He had mentioned a "surprise" in his letter. Just what kind of surprise? But she shook off the persistent dark thoughts. If she truly loved Gene, she would just have to trust him until he had a chance to speak for himself.

Spotting him coming down the street, Laurel flew down the stairs, slid the lock noiselessly back, and slipped out the front door. She was waiting for him at the top of the porch steps when he came through the gate, a square, brown paper-wrapped parcel under his arm.

One foot on the first step, he looked up at her, and her heart melted. He was regarding her with eyes filled with love, as if she were the only woman in the world. His mouth, parted in a smile, was as sensitive and sweet as she remembered.

"Hello, Laurel," he greeted her softly as she came down the steps toward him. "I've missed you, more than I can tell you, more than I thought possible."

Such a wave of relief swept over her that she was giddy.

"I've missed you, too, Gene," she confessed breathlessly.

"Then no one stole you away from me while I was away?"

The question was posed with such guilelessness that Laurel had to look deep into his eyes to be sure she had not asked it herself! Overcome by the irony of his question, Laurel began to laugh and soon Gene was joining her in a hearty duet, laughing uproariously.

"I see someone peeking through the curtains of an upstairs window," he said at last, when the last ripple of merriment had subsided. "Come on! Or I'll give Mrs. Sombey the first shock of the day by kissing you right here in broad daylight!" He grabbed her hand.

"Better not!" Laurel protested in mock alarm. "Or I'll be thrown out bag and baggage!" Then, in her best imitation of her landlady's voice, she said, "I run a respectable establishment, I'll have you know!"

And suddenly Laurel thought of Toddy. How like something her old friend would have said! Yet the laughter and the jesting had come spontaneously, bursting into bloom in the fertile soil of Gene's love, his approval. She felt so free!

"Let's walk over to the park where we can find some privacy and you can welcome me back properly," he suggested with a mischievous gleam in his eye.

After Gene's first suggestion had been carried out as promptly and satisfactorily as both had hoped, Gene put the package in Laurel's lap.

"Go ahead, open it," he directed, watching her eagerly.

"What is it, Gene? You shouldn't really be spending your money on presents for me." Laurel's fingers tugged at the knotted string.

"Stop fussing," he ordered "Open it!"

She laughed and pulled at a knot. Impatient, Gene whipped out his pocket knife and cut the string. "There!" he said and Laurel tore away the paper.

For a minute she simply stared. Then she turned to Gene. She opened her mouth as if to say something, but no words came. Looking down at the contents of the package, she slowly put both hands on either side of the narrow wood frame and lifted the little painting from the box.

The canvas was small, perhaps twelve by fourteen inches, the style Impressionistic. It might have even been a preliminary study for a larger, more detailed painting to be done later. This was done on the spot in daylight, without special attention to props or artificial lighting.

The subject was two figures—a woman and a sunbonneted child on the beach. The woman's face was shadowed by a wide-brimmed straw hat and the parasol she was holding; one graceful arm was extended to help the little girl make a mound in the sand. It was simple and heartfelt and absolutely delightful.

As Laurel gazed at it, a dozen emotions assailed her, prompted by the vaguest memories. In the lower right-hand corner were the tiny initials PV/86.

"Turn it over, Laurel," Gene said softly.

On the back, written with casual brush strokes, were the words—"August 1886, Lil and Baby L. at C.C."

Eyes brimming with tears, Laurel looked at Gene. "Where did you find this?" she asked in a barely audible voice.

Gene's face was animated as he replied, "In a little art gallery at Martha's Vineyard. I was just wandering around one afternoon when we didn't have a rehearsal. Actually, I was looking for some kind of little gift to bring you when I spotted this in the window."

"Oh, Gene, I'm sure this is one of my father's paintings!" Laurel exclaimed. "Do you suppose there are more?"

"I intend to go back and take a good look," Gene said seriously. "The new owner has stacks of unframed canvases in the storage shed behind the shop that he hasn't had time to sort through. He says this is one of the finest examples of Impressionist paintings he's seen."

"The style is very like the painting that hung over our piano when I was a little girl. The same sky and sand and feeling of lightness and a certain...serenity, I guess you'd call it." Laurel sighed, returning the painting to the box. "When I asked Mama why Papa painted so many seascapes, she told me that every summer a group of their artist friends would rent a house at the beach and take turns living there. It was something they looked forward to all year—a break from the humdrum routine of the rest of the year."

"Then we may be on to something. When I told this fellow, Ed Williams, that I knew the daughter of the artist, he told me he would get in touch with you when he had had a chance to evaluate all the paintings. He seemed to think your father's work may be quite valuable."

"Gene, how can I ever thank you?" Laurel asked as she began rewrapping the canvas.

"Seeing you so happy is all the thanks I need." Gene took the package from her and retied the strings tightly. "In fact," he said, giving her a long look, "I want to spend the rest of my life making you happy."

Laurel held her breath, not daring to speak. It was a moment of knowing for them, a moment of decision, of choice and commitment.

"I love you, Laurel. I think I knew it from the first day. Do you...would you...can we be—" he faltered.

"Yes, yes, yes!" Laurel answered every question in a breathless rush. "I want that too. But how—"

"We'll work it out, my darling—" Gene drew Laurel close, kissing her with a new tenderness. When it ended, they searched each other's eyes as if in confirmation of the sweet promises they had just made.

Gene jumped to his feet, tossed his hat up in the air and caught it by its brim as it came sailing down again. "I'm the happiest guy in Boston!" He grinned.

"Oh, Gene!" Laurel sighed happily.

"I'm also the hungriest! Come on, let's go get some breakfast!" He took her by the hand, tucking the wrapped picture under his arm and together they left the park.

Late that afternoon Laurel went to the train station to see him off again.

"No more of these partings," Gene told her. "I have enough money now to last me through the next semester at the Conservatory. I'm not going to take any more jobs that mean going out of town or on tour. That is unless—"

He halted, took both her hands and held them tightly.

"I want us to be married, Laurel, as soon as possible. I don't know how we'd manage or how—"

Caught up in his declaration, Laurel ventured, "I have my job and Mr. Jacobsen talked about giving me a raise."

Gene frowned. "But your own plans to start in at the Conservatory—"

She took a deep breath, casting about for words to express what was only now becoming clear to her. "Gene, I realize that I don't have the same urgent desire as you to pursue a career in music. That drive, that belief that my voice is my priority is just...missing. I love music, I enjoy playing and singing, but I don't think it could be the focus of my whole life. Not the way it must be to succeed. I just don't think I want it that much—" She paused, hoping he would understand. "Or maybe it's just that I've found I want something else more."

Just then the train whistle blew and the conductor was announcing, "All aboard!"

Pulling Laurel to him for a final kiss, Gene shouted above the noise of hissing steam and grind of gears. "I must go darling! See you in two weeks!" And he was gone, swinging up the steps and disappearing through the door of the car.

20

Two days later, Laurel propped the painting against the mirror of the bureau, then stood back to study it. She felt a deep thrill and pride knowing that Paul Vestal, the father she could not remember, was the artist.

She had recognized it as his right away. But she had not been prepared for her emotional response. Laurel ran her fingers lightly over the canvas, feeling the rough brush strokes. Looking at it, she could almost recall the warmth of the sand under the small bare feet of the chubby baby her father had captured in the painting. Strangely, she seemed to be experiencing again what could only be the vaguest kind of memory imprinted somewhere in the innermost part of her brain—the salty scent of the sea breeze bending the tall dune grass behind the figure of her mother, the clarity of the light, the cloudless blue of the windswept sky, the sun-washed roof of the weathered shingled cottage in the distance.

The fact that this painting now belonged to her, and that there might be more to come, sent a thrill shivering through Laurel.

The amazing coincidence of how Gene had found it made Laurel's head spin. She ticked off all the unrelated events that had brought this painting into her possession—What if she had not bumped into Gene on the steps of the Conservatory? What if she had never gone to Pasquini's to eat? What if they had not again collided in the administration office that day? What if? It could go on and on. Gene had not come into her life by chance, Laurel was sure of that now.

She thought of him now—back on the Cape—and the power of their love cast out all fear. He would be appearing in the next presentation of the summer light-opera series, with time to check again with the gallery owner to see if there were any more of Paul Vestal's paintings available. After the run of the second operetta, Gene planned to go to New Bedford for a short visit with his parents before returning to Boston. He was earning good money, and Laurel was proud he had been selected from the chorus of *The Pirates of Penzance* for the other show. She missed him, of course, but their time would come. Meanwhile, she was content to wait for him.

All this came back to Laurel as she stood looking at the painting. It all flowed together somehow—her coming to Boston to trace her heritage, her early plans for the Conservatory. Then she had met Gene and everything had changed. Her world circled around Gene now, everything else seemed less important. Finding a way to be together was all that mattered.

The next day when Laurel came in from work, Mrs. Sombey, twittering with excitement, was waiting for her in the downstairs hall.

"This came for you today, Miss Vestal," she said, her curiously light eyes protruding with greedy interest. "A handsome carriage drove up and stopped right out front and a driver in a fine, dark blue coat come right up to the door and asked if this was where Miss Laurel Vestal lived! When I said it was, he handed me this." Mrs. Sombey's hand was quivering as she handed Laurel a creamy vellum envelope with a red wax seal.

The handwriting on the envelope was in a fine Spencerian script, and Laurel knew instinctively it was from Mrs.

Maynard. Not about to open it in front of Mrs. Sombey, Laurel simply thanked her and started up the steps.

Mrs. Sombey's face crumpled with disappointment. Abandoning her usual put-on airs of prissy refinement, she blurted out, "Ain't you going to see who it's from?"

"Of course," Laurel replied over her shoulder, continuing to mount the stairway. She felt no obligation to satisfy her landlady's curiosity.

Ripping open the envelope, she noted the formal salutation:

> My dear Miss Vestal,
>   I have cleared my social calendar and will be at home Monday next from 3 to 5 in the afternoon if you would care to call. I shall send my carriage and driver if your reply is affirmative.
>
> Cordially,
Elaine Maynard

Elaine! So *she* was the Elaine Laurel had been named for! She folded the note and replaced it in the envelope. Now that the long-awaited invitation had come, strangely enough it did not give her the satisfaction she had expected.

That evening she penned a reply as brief and impersonal as Mrs. Maynard's had been. She agreed to the meeting, but declined the offer of the carriage, stating simply that she would arrive on her own between three and four.

Coincidentally, the next day's mail brought a letter from Ava, the first Laurel had received from her since leaving Meadowridge.

> My darling girl,
>   This letter should have been written months ago, but I was too preoccupied with my own sorrow. My main and inexcusably late reason for writing now is to assure you of my love and to ask your forgiveness if my actions caused you any needless guilt.

It has taken me a long time to face myself and to come to terms with the unhappiness I have caused those I hold most dear in the world.

For ten years you have given me enormous joy and never a moment's distress. You filled our home and my heart with more happiness than I ever thought I would know again. For this I am truly grateful.

Lee brought you home from the Orphan Train that day with the hope that you might take the place of our little daughter who died. Let me say you did not do that. Instead, you created your own special place and we could not love you more if you had been born to us.

Lee showed me the check you returned with your sweet note, saying you had been dependent on us long enough, and since you had left home without our approval, you did not feel it was right to continue accepting support.

How can I put this so you will understand? I was wrong not to let you go with a glad heart, allow you your freedom and your chance to be independent. It is your Papa Lee's and my pleasure to help you financially or any other way we can while you pursue your voice studies. We *are* your family and we want to support you wherever you are, whatever you choose to do.

I regret that my own sorrow at parting with you kept me from giving you my full blessing. I was like the Chinese princess in one of your favorite stories that I used to read to you, do you remember? She clipped the wings of her beloved songbird so he could not fly away and leave her. What happened, I'm sure you remember. The bird stopped singing! It is *I* who forgot!

So, now as you read this, I hope you realize that I, who love you so dearly, release you from the bonds I tied around you. Love should make us strong, capable and free to do whatever God's gifts enable us to do.

Be free, my darling, to be whatever you can be, desire to be, want to be. I believe, whatever makes you happy will bring happiness to others. I pray God's special blessing on you now and always.

Your loving mother,
Ava Woodward

Laurel read the letter over two or three times, savoring each sentence, almost memorizing each word. Her heart swelled with love and tenderness for the one who had written it. For this to have arrived the day before she was to meet with Elaine Maynard seemed remarkable. It gave Laurel the inner confidence she needed to face whatever the next day held for her. Regardless of her grandmother's attitude, whether she accepted Laurel or denied her did not seem quite as important, quite as necessary to her now.

Again Laurel dressed with exquisite care for her interview with Elaine Maynard. A navy blue silk with embroidered collars and cuffs, a matching straw sailor hat with crisp grosgrain ribbons, white gloves and dark blue handbag.

Her appearance and departure in the early afternoon caused more inquisitive glances and raised eyebrows on the part of Mrs. Sombey, who did everything but ask Laurel why she had not left for work that morning and where she was going now and if she could afford to lose a day's pay.

"When you wasn't down at the usual time, I almost come up to see if you was sick, Miss Vestal," the landlady said, her eyes traveling impertinently up and down Laurel, taking in every detail of her costume. "I know you always leave promptly at eight to catch the eight-fifteen trolley so you won't be late for work, so I couldn't help wonderin'—" Her voice trailed off, begging an answer.

Laurel smiled complacently and shook her head. "No, I'm quite well, thank you, Mrs. Sombey," she replied calmly and went out the door.

Her landlady would have been even more curious if she had seen that just around the corner, Laurel hailed a hackney cab and rode out to the Maynard residence in extravagant style.

It was precisely two minutes before three when Laurel mounted the steps and lifted the polished knocker of the front door. She turned and looked down the street at all the other fine houses lining this sedate enclave of the wealthy. There was a subdued splendor in the atmosphere, an understated but clearly defined exclusivity about the Square, setting it apart from the workaday world Laurel knew.

Standing there, waiting for the door to be opened, Laurel could not help wondering how different her own life would have been if Lillian Maynard had not been banished by falling in love with—"the wrong man."

"Good afternoon, miss," came a quiet voice from behind her, and Laurel recognized the same aloof butler of her last visit. This time he did not regard her coolly or skeptically, but stepped back immediately and opened the door wider.

At least she was expected, she thought, stepping inside.

"Mrs. Maynard will receive you in the parlor, if you will come this way."

The butler's manner was pointedly different, she observed, not condescending, but deferential. He opened the double door leading into a smaller room than the one into which she had been shown the last time. It was beautifully if less formally furnished, with a more intimate atmosphere, enhanced by the afternoon sunlight shining in. There was a piano in one corner, graceful chairs covered in needlepoint, bookcases flanking the fireplace, a hearth now hidden by a Japanese fan-screen.

"Good afternoon, Miss Vestal." Mrs. Maynard's thin, high voice greeted Laurel from where she sat in one of the high-backed chairs. She did not rise to offer her hand or in any way to make a gesture of welcome. She merely waved toward the oppposite chair. "Do be seated."

Laurel tensed. All the confidence she had built up began to evaporate under Elaine Maynard's ice-blue gaze.

Mrs. Maynard seemed to be waiting for Laurel to speak first. Laurel, acting on some inner reserve, waited for Mrs. Maynard to open the meeting she had called.

Silence stretched between them. Mrs. Maynard's eyebrows lifted slightly. Then she spoke. "Well, Miss Vestal, I understand from your note you have some reason to believe we are related."

"Yes, Mrs. Maynard. I assume you have had time to look at the papers I left with you. They are copies of a marriage certificate and birth certificate — proof that my mother was Lillian Maynard and that *I* am your granddaughter." Laurel's voice was surprisingly steady.

Mrs. Maynard waved a dismissive hand. "My dear young lady, certainly you must know papers can be forged! That is not proof of anything! What do you hope to gain by such a claim?"

Laurel was shocked. She thought she had prepared herself for any of several possible reactions from Mrs. Maynard, but not this cynical sarcasm.

"I have the originals —" she protested. She started to open her handbag, then remembered she had left them locked in her bureau drawer. She stared at Mrs. Maynard incredulously.

"Did you really think I would accept this? Someone walking in here off the street making all sorts of assertions? Do you take me for some kind of gullible, sentimental fool? Naturally, I would seek legal advice. I have my lawyer checking your shoddy copies. He was very skeptical of the whole matter, but promised to pursue it. But I *am* curious — what *did* you hope to gain by coming here and making this — this announcement?"

Laurel's slowly rising indignation at these insinuating accusations was suddenly overcome by a curious calm. She stood up.

"I did not come here for any reason other than to satisfy my own conviction that you are my grandmother, my mother, Lillian Maynard's mother. I thought you would be glad, yes, *happy* to meet me! Perhaps, you never knew you even had a grandchild. Did you not ever wonder? Did you not care what had happened to your daughter after she left this house? After you drove her out?" Laurel's voice rose in spite of her effort to maintain her composure. "I look around me at this place, with all its luxury, all its obvious wealth—and I think of the shabby little flat where my darling mama and I lived, where she struggled to support us both by giving music lessons! And I wonder if you ever gave us a thought all those years! Did you know she died in the charity ward of a State Tuberculosis hospital? That I was put in an orphanage? And later on, an Orphan Train, to be adopted by strangers?"

At Laurel's words Mrs. Maynard visibly paled. Her mouth twitched and her bony hands gripped the chair arms until the knuckles were white and the huge sapphire ring flashed fiery lights.

"Orphanage?" she repeated.

"For two years I lived at Greystone Orphanage."

"Greystone?" The woman's jaw dropped slightly.

"Yes, Greystone…only a few miles from here, Mrs. Maynard." Laurel drew herself up, breathing hard, thinking of the cold stone buildings, the yards of bare floored corridors, the high curtainless windows.

"Mama never said a word against you or my grandfather, never explained why you had become estranged from her. I suppose she thought I was too young. Perhaps if she had lived, she might have told me the truth—that you could not find it in your cold hearts to accept the young man she loved. Could not accept the fact that their love was so strong she had to choose between him and her parents." Laurel's voice trembled and she shook her head. "I'm sorry for you, no, I *pity* you! You missed so much. You missed knowing a beautiful young man, a talented artist, who may still become famous! Worse still, you lost your only daughter—"

"Enough!" Mrs. Maynard put one shaky, blue-veined hand up, shielding her face. Her voice, sharp and keen as a knife, cut through the breathless words.

Laurel's whole body quivered with the strong emotions coursing through her. "Don't worry. I'm going now, Mrs. Maynard. If I upset you, I apologize, but I'm not sorry I came or that I told you the truth. Because it *is* the truth—all of it. You asked me what I hoped to gain by coming. Actually nothing. I don't need anything you have, Mrs. Maynard. I have the tenderest memories of my real parents who loved each other and me dearly. I have loving adoptive parents, and I'm engaged to marry a wonderful young man. I don't need you. I don't want anything from you. Good day, Mrs. Maynard."

Still trembling, Laurel cast a pitying look at the old woman who was leaning to one side of the massive chair, her face covered with both ringed hands. Laurel moved toward the door. Her hand was on the knob when the imperious voice rang out once more.

"Wait! Stop!" A pause, then, "Please, Miss Vestal—Laurel, come back."

Struck by the change in the tone, the hint of a plea in the request, Laurel dropped her hand and, turning slowly around, faced Mrs. Maynard. The older woman's face looked deathly pale, almost gray, the eyes haunted.

"You are right. Lillian *was* my daughter. All these years I've tried to forget that—forget her, but—the minute you walked in that day, I knew it was impossible. You look so much like her—But it was a great shock. A terrible shock." Her hand shook as she put it up to her forehead where a vein in her temple pulsed. "I must admit my cousins, who were visiting that day, as you may recall, tried to convince me you were some sort of an impostor, a fortune hunter, urged me to have my lawyer check you out." She paused and toyed with the double strand of amethysts and pearls about her neck. "Of course, I followed their suggestion because...well because I hoped it was not true." She closed her eyes wearily. "You see, you must understand—it's been so long ago—"

Laurel did not reply, but listened.

"Lillian was our only child, born late in our marriage. My husband—my late husband Bennett—adored her. She was literally the 'apple of his eye.' A beautiful, happy child, a great joy to us—She was so gifted, so bright—Bennett took her everywhere with him....We dressed her like a doll in French-made clothes...she was...exquisite—" Mrs. Maynard's voice broke.

After a moment she began to speak again.

"That's why it was so hard to accept...what happened. She was only eighteen...her whole life ahead of her—We were planning her debut, a magnificent ball, to introduce her to Boston society. It was all arranged when she told us she was in love—" Mrs. Maynard's voice grew strained, husky. "Bennett flew into a rage, demanded to know how she had met this fellow. We had given her every advantage—piano lessons, voice and art lessons...it was there she met...Paul Vestal." The name was uttered with contempt. "When Bennett discovered he was her art teacher, penniless, with no background, no prospects, he decided he could not let her throw her life away. He forbade Lillian to see him—immediately made plans to take her away to Europe, hoping the distance between them would make her forget him, cool the romance. Of course, in retrospect, it was the worst thing he could have done. Lillian was sweet-natured but also strong-willed. And the result was on the eve of our sailing date, she ran away—eloped."

The room was still, absolutely quiet. Laurel waited for Mrs. Maynard to continue.

"Bennett never got over it. It broke his heart, hastened his death, of that I'm positive. And he never forgave her. He died only a year and a half later. He had forbidden me to answer the letter she wrote us after she was married, forbade me to contact her in any way." Mrs. Maynard sighed heavily. "I obeyed. What else could I do? I had always obeyed him. We had been married nearly thirty years, and that is how I was brought up to believe, that a wife obeys her husband."

Laurel said nothing and eventually Mrs. Maynard went on.

"Bennett suffered through a long agonizing illness. He lingered for months and I was with him almost every minute. When the doctors told me the end was near, I thought about Lillian, wanted to get in touch with her, bring her home to say goodbye to her father. But Bennett was adamant. When I suggested trying to find her, he got very upset, said we had no daughter. And he made me promise I would not ever attempt to contact her—even after his death."

Hearing this sequence of events, all the missing pieces she had wondered about for so long, Laurel was overcome. As she saw tears fill Mrs. Maynard's eyes and roll down the wrinkled cheeks, her heart wrenched. All this unnecessary suffering and sorrow. What a terrible, twisted thing so-called love could become.

"When last week my lawyer came to me, authenticating all the same things you said…that my daughter had died in a tuberculosis sanatorium, that there was a child—" Mrs. Maynard bit her trembling lip, dabbed her eyes with a dainty, lace-trimmed handkerchief. "But it was just now when you—you mentioned Greystone Orphanage that something inside me—to think I've been on the Fund-raising Board of Greystone Orphanage for years—and not to know my own grandchild was there, only a few miles away all the time—"

At this, Mrs. Maynard bowed her head and put both hands up to her face. Under the lacy shawl the old woman's shoulders shook convulsively.

All at once, Laurel was moved by compassion and in another minute she was on her knees on the floor in front of Elaine Maynard, her arms around her.

21

It was still light when early that evening, to Mrs. Sombey's complete astonishment, an elegant landau, glistening black with red-rimmed wheels drawn by a handsome dapple gray horse halted in front of her rooming house. The rig was driven by a haughty-nosed driver in gray broadcloth coat, black high hat, gloves and high shiny black boots. From her post behind her stiff, lace curtains she watched in open-mouthed amazement as he climbed nimbly down, opened the carriage door, and assisted one of her boarders out. When she saw it was Laurel to whom he bowed slightly and tipped his hat, she could hardly contain herself. So mesmerized was she by this unusual occurrence that Laurel was up the porch steps and coming in the front door before Mrs. Sombey had a chance to do more than back up a few steps to save herself a bump on the nose as Laurel opened it.

"Oh, Mrs. Sombey, I'm glad you're here," Laurel exclaimed.

Something was up, that was for sure, the landlady told herself, seeing the girl's flushed cheeks. Hastily she assumed nonchalance, flopping her feather duster, pretending she had been dusting the hall table all along. But Mrs. Sombey would never have guessed the explanation Laurel was about to give her.

"I'm moving out. I have just come to get my things."

"Moving out?" Mrs. Sombey repeated, nonplussed. "Just like that? Without giving any notice?" She drew herself up huffily. "I'm sure I had no idea you wasn't satisfied with your lodgings, miss. You certainly never gave the slightest indication—"

"Oh, it's not that, Mrs. Sombey. My room has been...well, fine...that is, until now. You see I'm going to stay with my grandmother on Wembley Square."

Laurel had no way of knowing what the name of that prestigious residential section meant to someone like Mrs. Sombey.

"Wembley Square?" she repeated through stiff lips. "Your *grandmother!* Well, indeed, Miss Vestal, you never said nothing about having relatives in Boston before. I thought you was— I mean, you being from the Midwest and all, I naturally assumed—" the landlady was, for perhaps the first time in her adult life, at a loss for words.

"I know. But it's really too complicated to explain, Mrs. Sombey." Laurel smiled apologetically and then breezed by her and ran up the steps. "I'll just pack up my things now. My grandmother's driver is waiting for me," she called back over her shoulder.

Indignant at being taken so off guard by all these unexpected events, Muriel Sombey vented her furious frustation by hurrying to the foot of the stairway and, losing her pseudogentility, shrilled up after Laurel's departing figure. "There'll be no refund for the rest of the month, Miss Vestal, you understand? If I'da known you was leaving, I could have rented that room twice over for what you've been payin.'"

At the landing Laurel stopped and leaned over the banister, saying sweetly, "Of course, Mrs. Sombey. I understand. I did not expect any refund."

Laurel was not sure what awakened her—muted sounds from somewhere deep in the house, the snip-snap of a gardener's clippers in the garden just below the bedroom window. Or maybe it was the quietness itself, accustomed as she was to waking to the sound of delivery-cart wheels on the cobblestone street outside Mrs. Sombey's boardinghouse, the shouts of the drivers on the delivery wagons, the voices of the other roomers standing in line outside the hall bathroom, the repeated slam of the front door as they left the house on the way to work.

Laurel had noticed many times before the sedate pace of life on Wembley Square. Even the horseless carriages seemed to run noiselessly, while pedestrians moved with a purposeful dignity. The whole neighborhood exuded an aura of quiet charm and permanence.

In contrast, Laurel lay in bed in a kind of daze, thinking how quickly everything had changed since the previous afternoon. Three hours after her arrival at the Maynard residence, she had been on her way to her rooming house to pack up all her belongings and move in here with her grandmother!

"Grandmother," Laurel whispered the word, feeling its taste on her lips as she said it. Mama's mother.

Her eyes roamed the room, sweeping up through the lacy crocheted canopy of the dark mahogany four-poster to the little desk between the two windows, the small white marble fireplace. Mama's girlhood room, where *she* had slept— in this very bed—played with her dolls, studied her lessons, dreamed her romantic dreams! Here, in this spot!

After all the years of imagining, the reality was almost overwhelming. Laurel sighed and stretched, then snuggled once more into the lavender-fragrant sheets, the satin-covered feather quilt.

When she had returned with her belongings last evening, Laurel had found Mrs. Maynard looked very tired. They had a quiet supper together before the fire in the small parlor— delicious, delicate food, well-prepared and tastefully served. But neither of them had eaten very much. At length

171

Mrs. Maynard had regretfully admitted, "If you will excuse me, my dear, I really think I must retire. This has been quite an emotionally exhausting day for me. I'm no longer young nor very resilient, I suppose."

"Of course, Grandmother, I understand."

Mrs. Maynard rose and passed by the place where Laurel was sitting. Laying her hand, as light and dry as a winter leaf, against Laurel's cheek she said, "At least I can look forward to many such evenings with you in days ahead, and tonight sleep peacefully, knowing my grandchild is under the same roof." She sighed and seemed about to say something else, but did not. Then she drew from her pocket an envelope, yellowed with age, worn around the edges.

"I think you should read this, Laurel," she said. "I've kept it all these years, wept over it, if the truth be known, and wished with all my heart that I had acted upon my real feelings at the time. Maybe reading it will help you understand—Well, I'll leave that to you, my dear."

Her grandmother left the room in a lingering scent of violets. Laurel held the envelope, looking at the familiar handwriting. Even before she opened it, she knew who had written it. Carefully she took it out and, by the light from the fireplace, read the letter.

She had taken it upstairs to the bedroom and read it again before going to sleep. It was lying on the table beside the bed where she had put it, and now Laurel reached for it again.

With the early autumn sunlight streaming through the windows, Laurel read the words her mother had penned so many years ago, feeling her own young, in-love heart respond with special understanding.

Dearest Mother and Father,

By the time you read this, Paul and I will be a long way from Boston. We were married by a justice of the peace at the Court House a few days ago. It was not the church wedding I'd always dreamed of having, with my beloved and loving parents in attendance. But since you have made it clear that you would never accept Paul as the man I love and have chosen to be my husband, we felt we had no other alternative.

As you must know, I would rather have had your approval and blessing, but since you withheld it and declared it would never be forthcoming, I had to make the hardest decision of my life. It breaks my heart to have to choose between my parents and Paul, and I still feel it did *not* have to be thus.

I thank you from the bottom of my heart for my happy childhood and home and all the loving care, the many advantages and privileges you showered upon me. Whatever you may think now, I am not ungrateful.

I love you both dearly and never wanted to hurt you in any way. I hope there will come a time when you will forgive me and know that you have not really lost a daughter but now also have a wonderful, gentle, kind, talented young man, willing and anxious to be a son to you both. Always,

Your loving Lillian

Laurel was still holding the fragile, thin sheets of paper when a soft tap came on the bedroom door, and a maid in a ruffled cap and apron peered in.

"Morning, miss. Just came in to light the fire and warm up the room before you got up, then to tell you your grandmother would like you to join her for breakfast."

Laurel sat up smiling and motioned the young woman regarding her so curiously to come in. She guessed the household staff was all agog over the news of the sudden, unexpected appearance of a Maynard granddaughter.

One of the first notes Laurel wrote, seated at her Mama's little desk in her former bedroom, was to Gene.

"You are simply not going to believe all that has happened to me since you left," she wrote. "You will first wonder at my change of address, I know, so I must tell you the wonderful thing that has happened."

Laurel's pen skimmed over the stationery as she told Gene all that had taken place since they parted. "I can't wait until you meet her! She's very grand, so be prepared! Most of all, I want *her* to meet *you*."

If Laurel's letters about her new life with Mrs. Maynard were exuberantly enthusiastic, they only reflected her own euphoria. One day followed the other in a kind of sunlit splendor. Mrs. Maynard had so much to show Laurel—keepsakes, photos, the portrait that had been painted of Lillian as a child and had once hung over the fireplace in Mr. Maynard's study, even her baby clothes that had been kept in a locked trunk. They spent many happy hours together, poring over these and albums and scrapbooks of Lillian's school days.

"You can see why it was such a blow to us, can't you, my dear?" Mrs. Maynard would ask Laurel over and over. "To lose her was like losing a part of ourselves."

Laurel longed to ask why it was necessary, why they had never given her father a chance, never even met him. But the harmony existing between her grandmother and herself was so comforting, so sweet, Laurel was loath to break it. There would be time for some of those hard questions later, after they were better acquainted. Just now they were moving slowly, cautiously into this new relationship.

Afternoons were spent in any number of pleasant ways— a carriage drive in the afternoon, or shopping in some of the lovely, exclusive stores where Mrs. Maynard was immediately recognized or stopping for tea at one of the luxurious hotels where they were always greeted by the maitre d' and ushered to Mrs. Maynard's special table overlooking the park, now brilliant with autumn colors. Here they were served by solemn, uniformed waiters an elaborate medley of dainty sandwiches, hothouse strawberries dipped in chocolate, truffles or glazed fruit flan or iced petit fours, with fragrant oolong tea.

Sometimes in the evenings, at Mrs. Maynard's request, Laurel would play the piano for her.

"You have Lillian's musical talent, that's evident," Mrs. Maynard sighed. "You must go ahead with your plans to attend the Conservatory. Of course, I will take care of all your fees, arrange for a coach—"

Laurel began to feel like Cinderella. What would Gene think of all these offers? Would her grandmother's generosity extend to him? He was actually the one with the *real* talent. She had mentioned him often, but her grandmother had not seemed interested in pursuing the discussion. In fact, she seemed to have forgotten all about Laurel's engagement. There was so much else to talk about and enjoy together. Her grandmother liked to play chess and taught Laurel the intricacies of the game. With their time so pleasantly occupied Laurel did not notice how quickly it was passing until one day she received a short note from Gene, saying he would be back at the end of the week.

"And where did you meet this young man?" Mrs. Maynard asked, a slight frown puckering her thin, high-arched brows.

"At the Conservatory, Grandmother," Laurel replied, deliberately omitting an account of the unorthodox manner in which she and Gene had really met. Somehow Laurel did not think Elaine Maynard would approve of so casual an introduction. Neither did she tell about their further meeting at Pasquini's Restaurant where Gene waited on tables.

On this afternoon when Gene was expected, Laurel and her grandmother were in the small parlor, awaiting his imminent arrival. Mrs. Maynard was seated in her favorite wing-back chair, her hands busy with needlepoint while her eyes keenly observed her granddaughter. Laurel was too excited to sit down. Everyting about her fluttered—the ruffles on her skirt, the tendrils of waves escaping from her coiled hair, the handkerchief she carried as she moved back and forth from door to window.

"Do light somewhere, child. You are as nervous as a butterfly," complained Mrs. Maynard.

"I'm sorry, Grandmother. It's just that I'm so anxious for Gene to come, for the two of you to meet." Laurel turned a radiant face on her. "Oh, I know you'll be impressed. He's so handsome, so charming, has such a wonderful personality. And, oh, Grandmother, you should hear him sing!" Laurel sighed rhapsodically.

"Is he planning a professional career?" was Elaine's next question.

"Oh, that's inevitable! He has a glorious tenor voice. He's already been on tour twice—only in the chorus, up till now. But a career has to be built slowly. This summer at the Cape theater he was in *The Pirates of Penzance*."

Mrs. Maynard pursed her lips "Very few ever actually make it, you realize, don't you, Laurel? Only the very best, and that after years of training and study, and certainly a year or two in Europe—"

"Oh, I have no doubt Gene will make it. He is determined and certainly has the talent."

"But does he have the means to finance such a long period of training, a family willing to support him until he is at a point where he can demand...shall we say...a living from his voice?"

Laurel hesitated. Should she tell Mrs. Maynard that she knew very little about Gene's family, only that they were hard-working Italian fishermen, that Gene had to work at menial jobs to support himself, that they had already discussed the future of his career and her part in helping him attain his goals?

Even as she considered how much to confide of their plans, the sound of the knocker echoed through the downstairs. A bold, confident knock. Laurel smiled, thinking that neither fancy facades, shiny brass knockers, nor formidable butlers would ever intimidate Gene. She started over to the parlor door, ready to rush into the hall.

"Thomas will show your guest in, Laurel," her grandmother said sharply.

Laurel halted, surprised by the reprimand in Mrs. Maynard's voice.

A minute later there he was, right behind the solemn Thomas. Laurel's heart spun at the sight of him. He looked marvelous, his skin still attractively bronzed from days on the beach. Nor could her grandmother fault his attire. He was dressed for the occasion in a light beige twill suit, crisp striped shirt with snowy stiff collar, a waffle-straw hat tucked under one arm.

Laurel swelled with pride as she reached for his hand and drew him into the parlor. Then, turning to Mrs. Maynard she introduced him.

"Grandmother, I'd like you to meet Gene Michela. Gene, my grandmother, Mrs. Maynard."

Elaine held out her hand and Gene walked over and bowed over it as he spoke in his clear, rich voice. "A pleasure, Mrs. Maynard."

"Mr. Michela." Elaine was politely formal. "Please be seated. Laurel tells me you have spent the last several weeks at the Cape."

It was only then that Laurel was conscious of the chill in the room. It was as if someone had opened a door and a winter wind had swept through. Somehow Mrs. Maynard had deftly taken control of the conversation and begun to conduct what amounted to an interrogation. The situation took Laurel unawares at first, but once she had grasped what was happening, she grew tense with anxiety.

Thomas brought the tea service in on a round silver tray and set it down on a low table in front of Mrs. Maynard. Alerted that Gene was under some kind of scrutiny, Laurel watched with mounting apprehension as he took one of the dainty napkins, flicked it open, placed it on his knee, asked for lemon instead of cream, accepted one of the tiny triangles of watercress sandwiches, answered all Mrs. Maynared's probing questions with ease and never with his mouth full. Laurel was ashamed of herself for fretting. Under any other circumstances, it would never have occurred to Laurel to worry about the kind of impression Gene was making. He was always the perfect gentleman, had impeccable manners. Still, it was her grandmother's unrelenting observation that made Laurel uneasy, and she couldn't help the image that came to mind—that of the spider spinning her fatal web.

Then quite unexpectedly Laurel heard her grandmother say as though puzzled.

"Michela? Is that an Italian name or perhaps Portuguese? I understand there is quite a large Portuguese population in the coastal communities. Where did you say you were from originally? New Bedford?"

Laurel snapped to attention. She felt a strange sense of déjù vu. Of time turning backward. Weren't those the same words her grandmother had quoted Bennett Maynard as having said in the confrontation with her mother so long ago? A confrontation that had probably taken place in this very room!

"Paul *Vestal*? What kind of name is *Vestal*? Polish? Hungarian? Is he from one of those Balkan countries always in revolution? How long has he been in this country? A year or two? You mean he's an *immigrant*? Lillian, your ancestors came here on the Mayflower! Men of quality, old families, men of the cloth, lawyers, teachers—you have a long and illustrious lineage. And you want to marry this man with no background, some *foreigner?*"

She imagined the same icy tone she was hearing now in Mrs. Maynard's voice, and felt a blaze of anger ignite within her. How insulting Mrs. Maynard was being in her cool, civi-

QUEST FOR LASTING LOVE

lized "drawing room" manner! Laurel glanced over at Gene to see if he was feeling it, reacting to it. But he looked perfectly relaxed, listening to Mrs. Maynard with polite attentiveness. Of course, he was too sensitive not to feel the sting, but too gracious to show any emotion. He was behaving as a perfect guest. It was her grandmother who was taking advantage of her position as hostess. Hostess? The Grand Inquisitor, rather! Gene was not on trial here, Laurel thought indignantly.

Or was he? Quickly Laurel remembered an enigmatic conversation she and her grandmother had had over tea one afternoon. Mrs. Maynard had remarked casually that soon she wanted to introduce Laurel to some young people of her acquaintance, daughters and sons of some friends in "our set."

So that was the game? She was trying to prove Gene unsuitable. No wonder she had ignored Laurel's mention of her engagement.

Laurel felt a chilling reality, as if a smothering cloak, were dropping over her head, almost heard the clang of a trap bolting, locking her in, shutting Gene out. It was history repeating itself. Lillian and the unsuitable "foreigner" Paul Vestal all over again. But this time it was Laurel and Gene Mrs. Maynard was trying to break up.

Laurel felt her smile freeze on her lips as she sat there holding the delicate handle of her teacup balanced on her lap. Her eyes moved from Gene to her grandmother, back and forth, like watching a tennis volley. She was pleased to see that Gene was holding his own, replying to all Mrs. Maynard's outrageous questions with complete poise.

Her heart warmed and melted. What a true gentleman he was! Never mind he was probably not measuring up to all her grandmother's invisible criteria, possibly missing the mark of her prerequisite targets for approval and acceptance. What did that matter? Her mother had been brave enough to withstand such pressure, to follow her own heart, to find happiness with the good man she had loved and married. Laurel remembered Mama saying once that to have known even a short time of perfect happiness was worth the sorrow she had known afterwards.

Apparently her grandmother was only looking for shallow externals. In Gene, Laurel had found more than a pedigree or even a handsome face and courtly manners. In him, she had found inner goodness, gallantry, lasting values.

Then Gene was on his feet. "I must be on my way now, Mrs. Maynard. Thank you for allowing me to visit Laurel here, and for the honor of meeting her grandmother."

Laurel rose with him. Setting down her cup, she said, "I'll walk you to the door. Excuse us, Grandmother." She slipped her hand through Gene's arm and together they went out of the parlor and into the hall.

"Gene," she whispered, "I want you to meet me tomorrow at our old place in the park. We must talk, make plans. It is impossible here."

He squeezed her hand, his eyes darkening with understanding. "Yes, of course. I'm working tonight at the restaurant and a private party tomorrow night, but shall we say two tomorrow afternoon?"

"I'll be there."

Laurel did not return to the parlor but went upstairs to her bedroom. She closed the door, went over to the window, and watched Gene's departing figure on his way to catch the trolley.

"I love you!" She blew a kiss, then turned and resolutely got out her suitcase and began packing.

22

Gene was waiting for Laurel when she arrived in the park, flushed and breathless from hurrying. He caught both her hands and raised them to his lips. Then, putting his arm around her waist he led her over to a bench where they sat down.

"What is it, darling? What's troubling you?" he asked, all tender concern.

In as few words as possible, Laurel explained her feelings. "It's almost eerie, Gene. It's starting all over again, just like it was with Mama—at least, the way I imagine it was with Mama. My grandmother doesn't even realize what she's doing." She paused, looking worried. "I don't want to hurt her, but of course I can't stay." She hesitated, not wanting to tell Gene it was specifically Mrs. Maynard's attitude toward him that had brought about her decision. "I don't want to go back to Mrs. Sombey's, so I must find another place to live."

Gene was silent for a minute, his brows furrowed as if in deep thought. Then he said slowly, "This is too important a decision to make impulsively, Laurel. You've waited too long to find your mother's family to walk out."

"But—"

"Wait, let me finish." Gene held up his hand to stem her protest. "Granted, your grandmother is old and set in her ways. She's used to managing things, servants, other people's lives. Your leaving won't change her, Laurel, except in ways you don't want to be responsible for. I could see you mean a great deal to her. After so many years of denial, having you, her own granddaughter in her home...can't you see? It's given her a new lease on life. Of course, she's full of plans for you. Just think what her life must have been like all these years before you came. Think—" he lifted her chin with his thumb and forefinger and searched her face— "Think what they will be like if you leave her now."

"But, Gene, she wants me to become something I'm not! At least Mama was raised to be a socialite. I wasn't." She smiled ruefully. "And I used to think Mother—my *adoptive* mother—was possessive!"

Gene laughed. "See?"

"But what shall I do?"

"I think you should be patient with her—gentle and understanding the way you always are. Give your grandmother time to get to know you. Gradually she will loosen the tight grip she has on this newfound happiness. Right now, she's afraid it will slip out of her hands, and that would be like losing her daughter all over again." When Laurel began to weep quietly, he held her close. "Don't worry, I'll help you darling. Together we can win your grandmother over. I'm sure she doesn't want to make the same terrible mistake *twice*."

"Yes, I suppose you're right, Gene—in fact, I *know*, you are." She sniffled and he whipped out a huge white handkerchief to mop her tears.

He took Laurel's hand, smoothing out the fingers, one by one.

"It may be a few weeks before everything can be worked out...and I didn't want to say anything about it until I was sure. But there's a very good chance that I'm going to be hired by the Conservatory as one of their coaches on a good salary plus, of course, coaching fees. If that happens, we could get married right away." He looked at her hopefully. "Unless you've changed your mind?"

"Of course I haven't changed my mind. But can we really afford it? To get married, I mean? We discussed it before and never thought we could. This wouldn't mean your giving up your singing career, would it? I wouldn't want to do anything to delay your dreams coming true."

"Laurel, don't you know by now? You *are* my dream come true! You *inspire* me, make me want even more to succeed, in my career. Actually, this would provide me with more time on my own to practice, study languages, like German and French for example, in which so many operas are written. But the main thing is, we would be together." He raised her hand and kissed it. "Besides that, I have some very good news for you from Ed Williams, the owner of the art gallery at the Cape."

Laurel was all eager attention.

"I didn't know this before, but he has a gallery here in Boston. He has a partner who is actually an expert, a real art expert and critic. It seems his partner came up to look over this cache of paintings I told you about, your father's among them." Gene paused significantly. "Well, this other gentleman, Karl Sandour is his name, became very excited when he saw Paul Vestal's paintings. There are quite a few—most of them beach scenes—very light, vivid colors, local scenes, families and children, all in very natural, appealing settings. Williams's partner, this Mr. Sandour, wants to have what they call a retrospective of American Impressionists and particularly of your father's Cape Cod pictures."

"Oh, how wonderful, Gene! But—" her sunny smile faded—"I wish it could have happened while he was living."

"Yes, well I'm sure he would be happy to know the daughter he painted so often will be receiving the benefits."

"What do you mean?"

"Williams and Sandour want you to see all the paintings, decide which ones you want for yourself, then give them permission to put the others on exhibition and for sale. They will take care of all the expense of cleaning the canvases, framing them, the cost of brochures, advertising, everything, and of course they will take a percentage of all sales." Gene paused again and said quite carefully. "But from what they tell me, Laurel, even with that, you should be a very wealthy young lady."

Laurel stared back at Gene. It was taking a long time for all he had said to sink in. For so long she had hoped to trace her parents, find her identity, claim her true heritage. But she had never expected anything like this. Emotion swept over her, she felt her eyes fill with tears, her mouth tremble as she tried to speak. With a look of complete understanding, Gene took her in his arms and held her, while she put her head on his shoulders and wept.

"But I don't understand, Laurel. Why must you go?" Elaine Maynard's expression was a mixture of bewilderment and distress. "I've tried to make you comfortable here, assured you of my intention to support you at the Conservatory, provide you with anything you need—"

"I know, Grandmother, and I appreciate all you've done, all you want to do for me. But I have other plans now. Gene Michela and I are going to be married. He has been offered a position now at the Conservatory and will be well able to support me. I want to share this with my adoptive parents, have Gene meet them. We'll be married there in Meadowridge in November and then come back to live in Boston."

Mrs. Maynard shook her head as if not comprehending. "But, Laurel, I had it all planned, I intended—*wanted* you to make your home here with me until such time as you met some suitable young man. I planned to give you a reception to introduce you to people of our class, our kind—" Her words faded away as if she realized she was saying all the wrong things.

"Grandmother, it's not that I'm ungrateful. I know you have the best intentions in the world, but your plans are not my plans. We don't see alike, don't value the same things." Laurel spoke with quiet dignity. "I have found the person I love, the one with whom I want to spend the rest of my life. Gene Michela is everything I want, everything I've always hoped for, or need. When you get to know him better, you'll see I'm right. In fact—" Laurel leaned forward, looking intently into her grandmother's eyes. "I wanted to find my roots to satisfy my own longing to belong. Gene taught me to look for ways to give back what I already *have*. Both of us want you to be part of our life."

That sincere request seemed to touch a chord in a heart that had protected itself for years from feeling pain, regret, love. The long-suppressed vulnerability gave way. Speechless, Elaine Maynard held up her arms to her granddaughter. A minute later the fragile old woman was held in the young one's strong arms. Tears of forgiveness and reconciliation mingled on cheeks pressed close. Love withheld, love given, love renewed encompassed in a healing embrace.

Though outwardly reconciled to the inevitability of Laurel's leaving, as the time grew near for Laurel's departure for Meadowridge to prepare for her November wedding, Elaine Maynard's resistance to the idea stiffened. Laurel knew she had to somehow break through the wall her grandmother was building to shut out acceptance of Gene.

One Saturday evening in early October, she approached her. "Would you like to attend church with me tomorrow, Grandmother? Gene has been hired as soloist, and you've never heard him sing. I wish you'd come with me."

A shadow seemed to cross Mrs. Maynard's face and she turned away, visibly distressed.

"Is something wrong, Grandmother?" Laurel asked anxiously.

"It's just that—well, I haven't been...for a long time." She sighed. "Your grandfather was so bitter after...Lillian...we stopped going. Then when he was so ill and died, I felt God had—" her voice broke. Then, straightening her thin, elegant shoulders, she lifted her chin. "Yes, Laurel, perhaps that's what I *should* do, go back to church."

Sunday morning, looking regal in a gray, fur-trimmed coat and a feathered toque, accompanied by her granddaughter, Elaine Maynard took her place in the pew identified by a small brass plaque engraved with the MAYNARD family name.

It was a magnificent church, she thought, contemplating the stained-glass windows and, at the opening chords of the magnificent organ, she reminded herself that she and Bennett had contributed generously to its purchase. But when she heard the rich fullness of the tenor voice raised in worshipful praise, she knew *that* was the true contribution, the real gift.

She felt tremors coursing through her as the words of the first hymn resounded into the rafters: "All creatures of our God and King, lift up your voice and with us sing, Alleluia! Alleluia!" But it was when Gene sang the stirring lyrics of "It Is Well with My Soul" that Elaine was most deeply touched. Unexpectedly, the woman who had always prided herself on never publicly displaying emotion was moved to tears as the words reached the innermost places of her heart.

Believing no one was aware, she was surprised and comforted as Laurel's hand pressed hers. Looking at her granddaughter, she smiled. *How blessed I am,* Elaine thought. *Thank You, Lord, for bringing her into my life—and the young man she loves. Forgive an old woman her past sins.* With a sigh of thankfulness, Elaine briefly closed her eyes, listening to the words of the hymn repeating them in her own heart: *Yes, it is well with my soul—*

23

Meadowridge was riotous with changing color—gold and russet and bronze—when Laurel returned just before Thanksgiving to await her wedding day.

Ava had insisted on commissioning Mrs. Danby to make the wedding gown and it hung now, a splendor of ivory lace and taffeta, in the closet of Laurel's old room. In fact, every moment since her homecoming had been filled brimful with preparations for the ceremony that would take place in the Community Church the week after Thanksgiving, not to mention plans for that most New England of all holidays. Ella had been cooking for days, eager to make a good impression on "Mr. Gene," and Jenny had come back to lend a hand with fall cleaning and polishing until the house fairly sparkled.

On Thanksgiving morning, when Gene was scheduled to arrive, Laurel insisted on going to the station by herself to meet him. A glance from Dr. Woodward stilled Ava's suggestion that they all go down in their newly acquired motor car to welcome Gene to Meadowridge, and Laurel set out on foot alone.

The yellow frame Meadowbridge train station was a nostalgic symbol to Laurel. Imprinted on her memory forever was the day she and the other orphans, shepherded by Mrs. Scott, were paraded out on the platform. Laurel remembered that shivery sensation inside, in spite of the fact that she was holding Toddy's hand on one side, Kit's on the other. Seeing it now, ten years later, brought all those feelings rushing back. Still, she knew she had been one of the lucky ones.

She thought also of the morning she had left Meadowridge to go to Boston, not sure she would ever come back. The empty heartsickness she had felt that misty morning gripped her as the slant-roofed station building came in sight.

But today there was not the slightest tinge of sadness in Laurel. Her step was as light as her heart, her pulses racing with excitement. Her anticipation mounted as she heard the train whistle in the distance. Clasping her hands tightly together, she moved to the edge of the platform peering down the tracks for the first sign of the engine rounding the bend. In her head she could hear the conductor's voice. "Meadowridge! Next stop, Meadowridge!"

And then she saw him, swinging down from the train's high step minutes after it had screeched to a stop, steam hissing, the grinding noise of steel against steel.

"Gene! Gene!" she called, waving her hand. She caught her breath as he came toward her, seeing his dark eyes sparkling and the smile that always made her heart turn over. Then she was swung up in his arms and she heard him whisper her name. Foolish tears gathered in her eyes as he set her back down on her feet.

"Let me look at you! These have been the longest weeks of my life!"

They said all the little, inconsequential things lovers say to each other, then Laurel gathered her wits about her enough to give directions to the baggage clerk to have Gene's luggage sent up to Meadowridge Inn where Dr. Woodward had made reservations for him.

"The house isn't far, so I thought we'd walk. I want to show you everything," she said almost shyly, hardly able to believe that he was really here with her in Meadowridge.

"It looks like I thought it would, only more so—" Gene remarked on the way. "Like everyone's dream 'hometown.'"

"Well, yes, maybe it does!"

As they strolled, hand in hand, Laurel realized she was seeing things with the long familiarity of childhood and Gene with fresh eyes. He marveled at the size of the elms, the willows on the sloping banks of the river when they crossed the arched stone bridge leading up to Main Street. The sun was out strongly now brightening the paint on all the houses along the way. Shining through the fretwork of gabled dormers, it cast lacy shadows on the clapboard. Autumn had been mild here, and most of the gardens still boasted flowers. Heavy-headed dahlias in various shades of orange, purple, yellow and white nodded in the brisk breeze.

Then finally they turned onto a winding lane with tall, arching trees and Laurel pointed to a white frame house with dark green shutters at the end.

"There it is." She smiled up at him. "Come on."

As they approached Gene saw a bunch of colorful Indian corn tied with wide yellow satin ribbon hanging on the front door that a minute later was flung open by a slender, dark-haired woman. Behind her stood a handsome, gray-haired man.

Laurel and Gene came up the porch steps together.

"Gene! How wonderful to meet you at last!" Ava said warmly and Dr. Woodward shook Gene's hand, saying, "Welcome...son."

Laurel felt tears again and her throat felt thick with emotion as she looked at these two she loved so dearly, then at the man she had chosen. A gladness surged up in her and a heartfelt prayer.

"Thank You, God, for all my blessings." The words of her favorite Psalm rushed into her mind, its beautiful words echoing in the fullness of her happiness: "Trust in the Lord, wait on him and he will bring it to pass. Trust him and he will give thee the secret desires of thy heart."

Dinner was served promptly at four. Jenny had come to help and could not seem to stop smiling as she served them. Every time she happened to catch Laurel's eye, which was often, she gave her a solemn wink.

Everything was perfect, Laurel thought, glancing to see if Gene appreciated Ava's artistry in arranging the table with its centerpiece of fruit and flowers—purple asters, marigolds combined with golden pears, and flame Tokay grapes. Her best Devonshire lace and linen cloth and napkins had been brought out, polished silver and glistening crystal, the good china that as a child Laurel had always admired—its design of the East Indian symbol of the Tree of Life in burnt orange and blue.

The food was a triumph of Ava and Ella's combined efforts. Ella herself brought in the turkey—golden brown, smelling deliciously, surrounded by tiny crabapples and parsley—then set it before Dr. Woodward with an air of deserved pride. This was followed by bowls mounded with snowy-white, light-as-air mashed potatoes, squash and creamed peas and pearl onions. Gravy boats were passed as well as numerous cut-glass containers of condiments—watermelon, pickles, peach chutney, quince jelly, and of course cranberry-orange relish. Two carafes of sweet apple cider were set at each end of the table to be poured into delicate, thin-stemmed goblets.

"Let us give thanks," Dr. Woodward said, bowing his head, holding out his hands to Laurel on his left and Gene on his right as was their custom. Ava completed the circle.

"Most gracious Father," he began. "We are more aware than ever of Your unmerited favor, the many blessings You have lavishly given us. We thank You especially for our daughter, Laurel, and for the fine young man who will be her husband and our son. We thank You for the blessings of health, food and shelter, love of family and friends, and unwarranted bounty. We ask to be led by You in all things and be worthy to be called Your children. We ask this in the precious name of Your Son, Jesus Christ. Amen."

In a blur of happiness Laurel ate, not being entirely aware of what she tasted, filled as she was with a warmth and contentment that seemed to take up all the space within her, leaving very little for food. She looked at each of the people at the table, smilingly, silently loving them with a complete acceptance and gratitude.

Ava suggested they wait until later to have a choice of pie—pumpkin, apple or pecan—since everyone claimed they could not eat another bite just then. So taking their coffee the four of them went into the parlor.

It was getting dark outside with the quick falling darkness of an early winter day. The curtains were drawn, lamps lighted, and Dr. Woodward put a match to the fire that had been laid earlier. The kindling caught immediately with little snapping sounds, sending up spurts of bright flame. Soon a nicely burning fire glowed brightly in the hearth, reflecting on the brass fender and andirons in the shadowy room.

"Why don't you play for us, dear?" Ava suggested and Laurel took her place at the piano.

For a few minutes her fingers roamed the keyboard as if trying to find exactly the right melody for this special time. As she began to play a piece she knew was one of Dr. Woodward's favorites, her eyes circled the familiar room—the firelight burnishing the frames of the paintings, the polished furniture, the prisms of the candlesticks on the mantlepiece. Memories came flooding back—the first time she had seen this room, had discovered the piano, lifted its lid and let her fingers grope for the keys to play the simple little tune her mama had taught her years and years ago, guiding her tiny hands.

She played on, moving from one song to the other, an almost forgotten medley of music that the Woodwards most enjoyed. As her fingers moved across the keys, her mind wandered back and forth, in and out, everything coming together, past and present. All the varied experiences of her life, all the things that had happened began to take shape, form, fit into a whole.

As she played on, unconsciously a thrilling rightness of this moment she was sharing with the three people she loved most in the world swept over Laurel. All at once Laurel knew the joy of homecoming.

She had been on a lifelong journey to find her "real family," her "real home," and now she realized with a heart filled with understanding that her Heavenly Father had done "abundantly above all that we ask." He had given her more than one family and one home.

Sitting at the piano, in the comforting warmth of this familiar room, with the family He had provided for her, Laurel realized at last that she was no longer an orphan, but a lost child who had finally come home.

DREAMS OF A LONGING HEART

JANE PEART

Fleming H. Revell
A Division of Baker Book House Co
Grand Rapids, Michigan 49516

Scripture quotations in this volume are from the King James Version of the Bible.

ISBN 0-8007-5373-9

Copyright © 1990 by Jane Peart
Published by Fleming H. Revell
a division of Baker Book House Company
P.O. Box 6287, Grand Rapids, MI 49516-6287

ISBN: 0-8007-5373-9

Printed in the United States of America

DREAMS
OF A LONGING HEART

1

Boston
Greystone Orphanage

Kit felt her toes push painfully against the end of her too-small boots. Stopping for a minute, she lifted one foot at a time and wiggled them. Grateful for the halt, her little brother leaned his small body heavily against her. The steep hill had been quite a climb for his short, five-year-old legs. Even Kit, at nearly eight, was feeling the strain and was only too happy to let Jamie rest while she herself caught her breath.

Several strides ahead of them, her father carried their baby sister, Gwynny, her round little face bobbing over his shoulder at each step.

At the top of the hill he turned around and called back to them, "Get a move on, you two. Don't be laggin' behind like that. We're almost there."

Something cold and hard lodged in Kit's chest. She was the only one of three children who knew what *there* was. Her father had explained it to her the night before.

Telling her to sit down on the other side of the kitchen table, he had leaned across it, his big workman's hands clasped tightly in front of him, and keeping his usually loud voice low, he had told her.

"'Tis the only thing there is to do, Kit. There's no work here for me. I've got to go over to Brockton and see if I can get on at the shoe factory. And there's no one to look after you kids. They'll keep you there 'til I find a job and a place to live, then I'll come and get you."

"Why can't we come with you, Da?" Kit wanted to know.

Sean Ternan took out his red handkerchief and wiped his nose, then his eyes before answering. "There's no way I can do that, girlie. I don't even know for certain if there *is* work—" his mouth twisted as he added bitterly— "or maybe there'll be signs over there as well as here that they're not hiring *us*."

Kit knew what he meant. She had seen the postings that read: NO IRISH NEED APPLY on some of the businesses and construction sites around the city. Her father had been a journeyman bricklayer by trade in Ireland. Mam had told Kit that when he'd first come to this country as a young fellow, he'd walked with a swagger, sure of himself, sure he could make a good living, and like so many of his countrymen, sure he'd find the proverbial pot of gold at the end of the American rainbow.

But it had all turned out so much differently. Her father was forced at length to go to work in one of the mills at low pay, long hours, subject to frequent layoffs. "Last hired, first fired" was the rule of thumb and most often it was the immigrant Irishmen who went when production fell off.

Things had gone from bad to worse the last two years. After Gwynny's birth Kit's mother, Eileen, had sickened and three months ago she had died. Soon after this, Sean Ternan had lost his job.

Her father's voice echoed in the empty street, jarring her back to the dark, chilly morning, the frightening present.

"Kit, come along, girl. We've not got all day!"

She tugged at her brother's hand. "Come on, Jamie, it's not far now," she encouraged.

"I'm tired, Kit. Hungry, too."

"Like as not, they'll give us something to eat when we get there," Kit assured him. Her own stomach felt hollow. She hadn't been able to eat much of the oatmeal she had fixed for them all before they left the flat earlier. There was a heavy lump in her throat that would not go away, over which she could not swallow more than a spoonful of oatmeal.

Jamie dragged on her as they trudged along, trying to catch up with their tall father.

"I'm cold," he whimpered.

Kit pressed her lips together. She wanted to scold him. *Shut up! I'm cold and tired, too. But there's worse waiting for us where we're going!* But she couldn't. Her heart was too sore, aching with the knowledge that was *her* burden, not her little brother's.

Then suddenly she saw the black iron arch over the gate. Even though Kit had to leave school to take care of the younger children when her mother died, she had kept up with her reading and now she could make out the words on the sign:

GREYSTONE COUNTY ORPHANAGE

For the first time something inside Kit rebelled. "But *we're* not orphans!" Suddenly she ran forward, the reluctant Jamie stumbling after her. When she reached her father, she looked up at him, tried to slip her cold, ungloved hand into his.

But he was staring straight ahead, his face like granite. Kit followed the direction of his glance and saw his lips moving silently. Sean Ternan was also reading the sign.

A minute later they were standing on the stone steps in front of a massive door and he was ringing the bell. It was answered by a harried-looking girl in a mobcap and blue-checkered apron, and they stepped inside the front door. The next thing Kit knew they were ushered through a door marked HEAD MATRON, MISS AGATHA CLINOCK. There a severe-looking, gray-haired woman behind the desk was regarding them all over glasses that pinched her rather large nose.

Kit heard Father say, "'Tis only temporary, you see, ma'am. As soon as I've found work, I intend to come back for my family. I promised my wife, God rest her soul, that I'd do my best to keep us all together."

Miss Clinock inclined her head slightly, fingering the black cord that hung from her glasses to a pin on the starched front of a high-necked gray blouse.

"Of course, Mr. Ternan. You understand, we are obliged to give *temporary* shelter to children of indigent families, but we make very clear it is for six months *only*. If they are not reunited with their parents by then, we are forced to seek suitable adoptive homes for them. This institution is almost at its capacity now. You were fortunate, indeed, that we are able to provide for *three* children at this time."

Kit's father nodded, his hands twisting nervously. Gwynny was sucking her thumb, Jamie fidgeting. Kit felt stiff, as if she had turned to wood. She could not take her eyes off her father. He looked at her once and his eyes were shiny. Then he turned his head and would not look her way again.

Another woman in a black dress and gray apron opened the office door, summoned as if by magic, and Miss Clinock spoke to her.

"These are the Ternan children, Miss Massey. The little girl goes to Nursery, the boy to Primary and—" She scrutinized Kit. "How old are you, child?" she asked.

"Seven," Kit murmured shyly.

"Speak up, child, don't mumble," Miss Clinock corrected.

"She's near eight. Smart as a whip." Kit's father said, his voice sounding almost too loud and hearty.

"All right then, take her to Third," Miss Clinock directed.

Her father lifted Gwynny out of his lap, set her on her feet, gently shoving her toward Miss Massey who stood waiting at the open office door. When Gwynny did not budge, he spoke to Kit.

"Take her hand, Kit. She'll go with you."

Kit heard a roaring in her ears, not realizing it was her own heart pounding frantically.

"It will be all right, mind you." Her father's voice sounded as if it came from a long distance. "Jamie, lad, do as you're told. Now, Kit, go along."

Kit felt strong fingers clamp on her thin shoulder, turning her around to face the door. Gwynny's soft little hand curled into her palm. Kit took one or two hesitant steps, then looked back at her father. She halted, desperately hoping that somehow this was all a mistake, that he would gather them all up and out they'd go, away from this strange, grim place.

But Sean Ternan was sitting like a stone in the chair opposite Miss Clinock's desk, looking down at his hands. He neither moved nor spoke.

"Goodbye, Da!" Kit called over her shoulder, her voice cracking a little.

They were out in the hall now, and Miss Massey closed the office door firmly. Then, placing a clammy hand on Kit's neck, she urged her forward.

"Go along, child," she ordered and Kit looked down a long corridor of gray walls to which there seemed to be no end.

2

Meadowridge

Cora Hansen came out of church into the bright April sunshine and, calling her three younger boys from their play under the budding maple trees in the churchyard, went straight over to their wagon where the two horses were hitched to the fence. She helped the boys into the back, then she climbed up into the wooden seat in front. Shivering, she pulled her shawl around her thin rounded shoulders. Seems like she was always cold, even on a warm day like this.

She'd left her husband talking to some of the other farmers outside the church. Not that Jess was one to socialize much. Just getting him in town to church on Sundays was about all Cora could manage. But since the individual farms around Meadowridge were all pretty isolated from one another and the men busy from sunup until the last chore was done at sunset, Sunday after service was about the only time they had to congregate, discuss the weather, crops and livestock.

Usually Cora took advantage of this to pass the time of day with some of the other wives. It was her only chance to visit because Jess didn't like her going off to the quilting bees or the get-togethers for canning or jelly-making like some of the others did.

"Too much gossipin' and gabbin' and meddlin' in other folks' business," he would say. "You got enough to keep you busy at home with the young'uns and your own chores."

Whether that was true or not of those gatherings, what Jess thought became law in the Hansen household, and Cora had always gone along with whatever Jess thought.

But this Sunday she had not stopped to speak to the few women she knew because she had some thinking to do, and she needed to be by herself to sort out her thoughts.

Most of the time during the sermon, Cora's mind was on the Sunday meal she would have to get on the table the minute they got home from church. But this time there wasn't Reverend Brewster's familiar drone to lull her into a half-attentive state. Instead, an earnest young man from the Rescuers and Providers Society riveted them all with dramatic stories of city children lost and abandoned, without homes or families. He had ended with a plea that Cora simply could not put out of her mind. Especially since responding to it seemed a way of solving her own problem.

At thirty-five, Cora looked a good dozen years older. Her straight hair, the color of a field mouse, was pulled straight back into a knot. Her skin was parched-looking, etched with sun-squint wrinkles around her lackluster eyes. She was worn-out, overworked, had an acid tongue and an attitude to match.

She had married Jess, a widower twelve years older than she, when she was fifteen. That was twenty years ago. Now there were five children, all boys.

Cora rarely thought about her life in any conscious way. She had come out West as a nine-year-old child with her father, two brothers, and their stepmother. Lured by the promise of gold in the hills around Meadowridge, her pa had prospected for a few years with no luck. He had then turned to homesteading and a safer life, if no easier. It had also proved no more profitable.

As a child Cora grew up working alongside her brothers—hoeing, sowing, weeding. It had been a joyless, dirt-poor, bone-tiring childhood, but it was all she knew. When her father died her stepmother had sold the land to Jess Hansen, whose property adjoined theirs. Jess had already built a house and barn and wanted the additional acreage to provide extra grazing pasture.

Cora's stepmother, who was glad to pack up and leave the sod house, give up the endless struggle, the cold winters, to go back to her kin in Tennessee, had told Cora, "You kin come with me, or stay."

Since Cora had never gotten along with her stepmother, it did not take her long to decide to accept Jess's laconic offer of marriage. She had moved from her father's home into her husband's without much change from the relentless drudgery and monotony of life she had always known.

Until now, she had never expected anything to be different. Until today, when she heard that man from the Providers and Rescuers Society talk about taking an orphan into your home. She could sure use some help. Cora straightened her hunched shoulders, unconsciously easing the almost constant ache in her back. It bothered her just as much sitting as standing, whether she was lugging in buckets of water from the well or full milk pails from the barn. Years of backbreaking work had begun to take their toll.

Even the two big boys were not much help with her chores. Jess had them working alongside him in the fields now. And the three little ones couldn't do a whole lot except feed the chickens, gather eggs, and do some occasional weeding.

What she needed was a good, strong girl to take some of the load—somebody to churn, help with the canning, haul out the heavy baskets of laundry on washday.

But what would Jess say to them taking in one of them orphans? From what the speaker said, the Society would provide enough clothing for them for a year until the family who took them decided whether or not to adopt them. All the family had to do was feed them, bed them, see that they got their schooling and attended Sunday service.

They certainly had enough room, Cora knew. The attic had plenty of space to put a cot up there, and another mouth to feed on a farm was no problem. In fact, with some help, Cora figured she could put in a bigger vegetable garden.

Just then Cora saw Jess heading for the wagon. He had rounded up the two older boys who had been playing with some of their friends from Sunday school. Cora decided to wait until after they had eaten their big Sunday midday meal before broaching the subject of taking in one of the orphans when the train came through Meadowridge. He'd be in a better mood then, more likely to see things her way.

3

Orphan Train
En Route to the Midwest

"No one will ever adopt me," Kit said to herself, staring out the window as the train roared through the flat Kansas prairie. No matter what Mrs. Scott said, Kit was sure of it. She was too tall, too skinny, too shy. Hadn't they made three stops already, all the children lined up on the station platform, while groups of people in each of the towns walked around, looking at them, making comments to each other—sometimes behind hands held over their mouths, other times right out loud?

Kit had tried to smile, although she was careful not to show her teeth, because she had a space between her two front ones. Some of the boys teased her, calling her "snaggletooth." And she had made her eyes wide to look alert and intelligent.

Still, so far, she was among the ones marched back on the train to settle in for another long ride until the next town. Each time, the certainty that no one would ever want her lodged more stubbornly in her heart.

Kit looked over to where Toddy was organizing some of the children for a game. Maybe if she were lively and clever like Toddy, or pretty like Laurel—Kit sighed. She remembered that day at Greystone, the first time she realized what "adoption" meant.

It was during recess and they were all out in the fenced-in side playground. Kit was taking turns skipping rope when someone had yelled, "Come look!" They had all rushed over to the fence in time to see a carriage pull up in front of the main entrance and watched as a well-dressed couple got out and climbed the steps into the building.

"Who do you think they are?" Toddy had wondered aloud.

"Somebody's parents coming to get them?" suggested Laurel, an edge of longing in her voice.

"No, stupid!" Molly B. retorted disdainfully, her freckled face pressed like the others against the wire fence, gawking at the strangers. "They're folks come to visit the Nursery and pick out a baby."

"What do you mean?" Kit asked through stiff lips.

"Just what I said, ninny." Molly B. turned to Kit, squinting her eyes and making a face. "They're gonna take one home with them, what did ya think I meant? They always pick the little ones, ya know. The cutest ones."

Kit felt her stomach lurch sickly. Immediately, she thought of Gwynny, with her rosy cheeks and dimpled smile and tumbled curls. Surely they wouldn't let Gwynny be adopted! Not when their Da was coming back for them all soon!

Her terror must have shown on her face because Molly B., smelling the scent of fear, lunged for an attack.

"Bet your little sister'll be 'dopted," she smirked.

Kit left the fence. She heard Toddy defy Molly B. "What do *you* know?" And the next thing Kit felt was Toddy and Laurel on either side of her, walking her away from the sound of Molly B.'s taunting voice.

"I been here longer than any of you, and I do so know! The Nursery babies *always* get 'dopted!"

That was on a Thursday. On Sundays at Greystone, children with brothers or sisters in the other sections were allowed a "family visit." As long as she had been at Greystone, Kit had looked forward to Sundays when she could see Jamie and little Gwynny.

It had surprised her to see how quickly Jamie had settled in at Greystone and that he actually seemed happy. But, of course, he was with other boys for the first time in his life. When their mother was ill and after she died, Jamie had been confined to their small tenement flat with only his baby sister and Kit. Kit, placed in charge of the two younger ones while their father was at work, burdened as she was with grown-up responsibility, tended to be "bossy," Jamie complained. He had chafed under her care. Now he was experiencing a kind of freedom, a well-ordered life, three meals a day, boisterous play with companions his own age and sex.

Jamie became restless and bored during their family visits. Even Gwynny squirmed down from Kit's lap after a few minutes and seemed just as willing to go back to the Nursery when the hour was up. This hurt Kit's feelings more than she cared to admit. She prayed their Da would come soon so that they could be a family again. But with each passing week that hope grew dimmer, and Kit felt a strange uneasiness.

The Sunday following the day she had seen that couple arrive, Kit went as usual to meet her brother and sister. Only Jamie was waiting for her.

"Where's Gwynny?" she asked, the words almost choking her.

Jamie shrugged and said, "Dunno. When I stopped at the Nursery to bring her over, Miss Driscoll told me she was on a 'probation visit.'"

"A probation visit? What's that?" Kit gasped.

Jamie shrugged again. "Dunno. That's all she told me."

Kit grabbed him by the shoulders and shook him. "What's the matter with you, Jamie? Why didn't you ask? Find out?

That's our Gwynny they're talking about! Where's she visiting?"

"Leggo of me, Kit! You're hurting me!" Jamie shouted, wriggling out of her grip.

Kit dropped her hands, clenching them into fists. "I'm sorry, Jamie. I didn't mean to hurt you. But listen to me!" Hot tears were stinging her eyes now. "We got to find out about Gwynny, don't you see that? What if Da comes and finds her gone?"

Jamie rubbed his shoulder and glared at her. "Da's not coming back," he mumbled.

"That's a wicked thing to say, Jamie."

"It's true," Jamie protested. "We're all goin' to get 'dopted."

"It's *not* true and Da *is* goin' to come back. He promised!" Kit said more to herself than to her brother. "Who told you such a thing?"

"My friend Tom. He heard 'em talkin', them people that come to look at the babies the other day. He's been here since he was two and he told me that we're way past 'temporary' now. That means you either stay here or else you get 'dopted. Boys are more likely to get 'dopted than girls."

Kit swallowed. Her mouth felt dry with fear. Somehow what Jamie was saying rang true. She'd heard much the same kind of talk among the girls in her section. It had been months since their father had brought them here. She had tried to keep track of the time, but somehow she had gotten mixed up. That cold, sick churning began in her stomach again.

"Can I go now?" Jamie asked. "We wuz goin' to play ball 'fore I had to come over here—" He slid off the bench and hopped from one foot to the other.

Kit nodded. There was no reason for him to stay any longer. Sadly she watched him push through the gate and start running. Suddenly Kit was clutched with an awful fear that she might never see him again, and she jumped up. Flinging herself against the fence, she called his name. But Jamie kept on running and didn't look back.

"He must not have heard me," Kit said to herself.

Remembering that scene, Kit felt her throat constrict. Two weeks later Jamie, too, was adopted. When she was told, Kit burst into tears.

"What will my Da say when he comes and they're not here?" she had asked, almost hysterical.

Finally Miss Clinock told her as gently as possible that her father had been notified of both Gwynny's and Jamie's adoption requests and had signed their releases.

"Then, is he comin' for *me*?" was her next question.

"I'm sorry, Kit, but I'm afraid not," the matron said quietly.

And now Kit had a chance to be adopted, too. Mrs. Scott had assured her they had only chosen the most suitable children to take on the Orphan Train, ones that would fit in nicely with the families that had agreed to adopt. But Kit's uncertainty lingered. If her own Da had not wanted her, who would?

4

Meadowridge

Cora Hansen lifted the heavy blue enameled coffeepot from the stove, brought it to the table, and refilled her husband's cup. Jess was scraping the last of the sausage and eggs onto his fork, helping it along with the remainder of a biscuit held in his other hand.

Setting it back down on the stove, Cora took a seat across from him. Crossing her arms on top of the table, she leaned forward.

"You'll be sure to quit afore noon so's we can eat and get into town in time, won't you?" she asked anxiously. She was worried, had been all along, that Jess might change his mind about them taking in a girl from the Orphan Train.

He didn't answer, just continued to chew, not looking up from his plate.

"Jess? You didn't forget, did you? Today's the day that Orphan Train gets here. We need to get into town early so's we can look 'em all over good."

Jess wiped his mouth with the back of his hand, then pushed his chair away from the table. He looked at his wife with narrowed eyes.

"You shure you want to go through with this? Don't seem like we need no other child 'round here."

"I told you, Jess. It'll be like havin' another pair of hands. There's enough work for two women here now with five young'uns, the garden, and all. And especially come harvest time, when we have the hired workers to feed. I mean to pick out a half-growed girl, strong, sturdy. She'll be a big help. You'll see."

In spite of everything, her anxiety that after all the talking she'd done to persuade him might not be enough, trembled in her voice.

"I'll lose pretty near a day's work goin' into town in the middle of the week like this," he grumbled.

"It'll be just this once, Jess."

"We gotta sign some papers, don't we? Put money out?"

"No, Jess, I explained it to you. We've jest got to agree that she gets her schoolin', gets fed and dressed proper. And we make two reports a year to the Society that she's bein' taken care of—until she's eighteen. That's all there is to it."

Jess stood up and walked toward the back door. With his hand on the knob, he turned and fixed a level gaze on his wife for a long minute.

"Well, if you're sure we ain't takin' on mor'n we can handle—It's up to you. I got my hands full with the farm and the livestock. The boys ain't that much good in the fields yet—"

"Oh, she'll pull her weight. I'll see to that," Cora assured him as she followed him out onto the back porch, wiping her hands on her blue checkered apron. "She'll do her share of the chores. You don't have to fret none about that."

Jess grunted again, clomped down the steps and started toward the barn.

Cora sighed with relief. Satisfied that there'd be no last-minute hitch, she went back inside. She hurried over to clear the table of her husband's plate and cup. Then she set out bowls and went over to the stove to stir the pot of oatmeal.

As she stirred Cora stared out the kitchen window. It was getting light now. The children would be waking up soon,

24

coming down to eat. One thing that girl could do when she came was cook the kids' breakfast.

Cora sighed again. She couldn't imagine what it would be like to have some of the burden lifted from her—the constant round of chores, going from one thing to the other with never a breathing space between.

Of course, come fall, the girl would have to go into school every day with Lonny and Caspar and little Seth. They'd had to agree to that in order to get one of the orphans. But it was in summer that farm work was heaviest anyway, and then Cora's chores would be lightened considerably with someone young and strong to help.

Cora wondered what it would be like to have another female around. She was used to a houseful of boys and no other woman for miles around to talk to. Not that she meant to make a fuss over the girl. That wouldn't do. They were giving a homeless girl a permanent roof over her head, and that was more than she had now.

Cora had always felt herself an "outsider" among the Meadowridge folks somehow. As if she weren't as good as some of the women who lived in town. It gave her a smug feeling that the Hansens were among the families willing to offer to shelter "these poor abandoned waifs" Mr. Scott had talked about.

Not that she had gone to a lot of trouble getting ready for the orphan. But she *had* fixed up a place for the girl. Cleared out the clutter from a corner of the attic to make a sleeping room. She'd been careful not to ask Jess for anything extra. Just got out the old iron bedstead that had been stored there since goodness knows when, cleaned it, and made it up with muslin sheets and some of her older quilts. It wasn't much, but probably better than the girl was used to in whatever orphanage she come from. Surely she wouldn't expect too much.

Besides, she'd learn soon enough that the Hansens were plain folks, living a simple farm family's life. They were offering the girl a sight better than her own childhood had been, Cora thought, remembering the sod house she'd lived in with her family before she'd married Jess and moved into the frame house.

They'd added on rooms as the children had come along, and it was as nice as most of the other farmhouses around. Well, maybe not so fancy as some who had put in parlors and front porches. Of course, no use for them to have either one. Jess didn't hold with having company, so buying that mail-order parlor furniture would have been a waste of money. He put most of what they earned from their crops right back into buying good livestock and better farm implements. And he wanted to build a new barn—

Cora's thoughts were interrupted by the sound of bare feet running down wooden steps as the two older boys came tumbling into the kitchen, tussling with each other as they usually did.

"Now, you boys, stop that carryin' on and set down and eat," she ordered.

The two rumpled-haired boys, ages nine and ten, stopped jostling each other, pulled up their overall straps and slid into their seats, thumping their elbows onto the table.

"Where are the others?" Cora demanded as she spooned cereal into their bowls.

"Seth's comin'. Chet and Tom's still sleepin'.'" Caspar replied, grabbing a spoon.

"Well, they'll have to git up. We all got to go into town today and fetch that girl who's comin' to live here."

Both boys looked up in surprise. "You mean that girl from the *Orphan Train* you been talkin' about gettin'?" Lonny stopped eating long enough to ask.

"The very one," Cora answered briskly. "Now eat up. You got to feed the chickens and collect the eggs afore we go."

"How long is she goin' to stay, Ma?"

"She's goin' to *live* here, for pity's sake."

"Forever?" Caspar persisted.

"Well, I should think so. At least 'til she's full-growed. I'm sure she won't want to go back to that orphan asylum. I expect she'd have to be pretty miserable to want to do *that!*" Cora said sarcastically, adding, "I should think she'll like livin' on a farm after where she's been."

Turning back to the stove, Cora missed the sly look the boys exchanged. A look of silent consent, mischievous intent, a look of mixed anticipation and malice, a look that implied trouble for their unsuspecting victim—the girl from the Orphan Train.

5

Summer, 1890

"Come along, Kit, you've been adopted!"

Kit turned around and looked up at Mrs. Scott; her heart gave an excited little jump.

"I have?" she exclaimed, slipping down from the chair she'd been sitting on so long, tense with anxiety as one after the other of her fellow orphans had been selected and taken out of the Social Hall to their new homes. Her secret fear that she was too plain, too tall, too skinny for anyone to want was laid to rest. She had seen Toddy happily skip away with the elegantly dressed woman and the pretty, dark-eyed older girl. Then Laurel had left, hand in hand, with the doctor who had examined them all. Kit had been the only one of the trio remaining.

"Yes, you are going with the Hansen family. They live on a farm just outside Meadowridge. But you'll be coming into town to go to school, so you'll be seeing Toddy and Laurel again soon." Mrs. Scott seemed a little nervous as she helped Kit gather up her things.

Kit had read stories about farms. They had always sounded so nice. Now she was going to live on one!

Mrs. Scott took Kit's hand and led her over to where a tall man stood with Reverend Brewster and Mr. Scott on the other side of the room. As they approached, the man turned and stared at Kit. Kit's fingers gripped Mrs. Scott's hand tightly as she met the man's narrowed gaze.

But Jess Hansen didn't look like any of the farmers Kit had read about. Those storybook characters had been jolly and kind, working hard, but coming in at noon and night to eat hearty meals with the family. This Mr. Hansen looked as if he had eaten a sour pickle! He had a sallow face and thin lips that curled when he spoke. Lank, wheat-colored hair fell in a shock over his forehead, and he brushed it back impatiently from his dull, deep-set eyes.

"This is Kathleen Ternan, Mr. Hansen," Mrs. Scott introduced Kit, loosening Kit's clinging grasp and pushing her gently toward him.

Jess gave a brief nod, then stuffing the papers he had just signed into his coat pocket, he jerked his head toward the door and said gruffly, "Well, then, let's git goin'."

"She's called Kit, Mr. Hansen. I'm sure you'll find her sweet-natured, obedient and willing," Mrs. Scott began, but Jess was already moving toward the door.

Mrs. Scott bent down and took Kit's face in both hands and kissed her cheek. "You'll be fine, Kit, don't worry. Any family would be lucky to get you. I'm sure Mrs. Hansen will love having a little girl since she has five boys. So you'll be a welcome addition."

Kit's heart was hammering now. She wasn't at all sure she wanted to go with this unpleasant man, even if he *did* live on a farm.

"Come on," Jess called from the doorway.

Mrs. Scott gave her a final hug. "Go ahead, Kit, and God bless you!"

Kit hurried toward the tall man waiting for her. At the door she turned for one last look at Mrs. Scott and tried to smile. Mrs. Scott waved encouragingly and Kit waved back, then followed Jess outside.

It was hard for Kit, lugging her suitcase, to keep up with his long strides as Jess headed for a buckboard hitched to the rail fence. He untied his horse and climbed up into the wagon seat.

"Well, come on, girl, git in!" he called to Kit, standing a few feet away. *Cora's going to be mad as a wet hen when she sees the size of her,* Jess thought grumpily.

Things hadn't gone right all day. It was bad enough that he'd got a late start coming into town. Not that it was his fault. One of the boys had left the pasture gate open and three of the cows had got out. It had taken him the good part of an hour to round them up again. Jess felt the anger rise in him again. Neither one had owned up to doing it, so he'd had to lick both of them.

All that had taken so much time, he'd sat down late to the midday dinner. And had no peace then with Cora, persimmon-lipped, banging pots and pans around to show she was upset with the delay. It was a miserable meal and he'd had indigestion 'fore he finished.

Cora was so distracted with her fuming that she hadn't been paying attention to what she was doing, and the smallest young'un got too near the stove and pulled a pot of soaking beans over on himself.

At that point Cora had told Jess to go on without her. She had to see to the mess on the floor, and the child had to be tended to. So Cora, busy with scolding the boy and cleaning everything up, couldn't go along with him.

The last thing Jess had heard as he pulled out in the wagon had been Cora's strident voice yelling from the kitchen window, "Now you can see why I need help, can't you?"

Well, Cora was going to be none too happy with the girl he was bringing home, Jess thought morosely. She wanted a strong, strapping girl and this one—Jess shook his head— why she looked like a strong wind might blow her down.

But when he'd finally got to where they had all them orphans, there were just a few of them left. No boys at all. Jess would have preferred a boy himself, one twelve, fourteen, big enough to really give him a hand with the farm chores. But Cora had been pickin' and naggin' and complainin' so that he'd been wore out with hearin' it and there weren't nuthin' to do but give in.

"You deaf, girl?" he frowned down at Kit. "I said, git in." His tone was irritable.

Struggling with her cardboard suitcase, the coat she hadn't had a chance to put on slung over her arm, Kit grabbed the handle on the side of the wagon with her free hand and hoisted herself up beside Jess. Her bonnet had slid off and was dangling by its ribbons around her neck. But before she could secure it or was hardly settled on the narrow plank seat, Jess flicked the reins and the wagon jerked forward. Kit had to grip tight to the rough sides to keep her balance as they rumbled through the streets of Meadowridge and headed out of town.

She hadn't even been able to say a proper goodbye to either Toddy or Laurel, Kit thought sadly. But Mrs. Scott had assured her that they would see each other often, that they would be going to the same school and church.

"We will keep track of all of you to see how you're doing, you know!" she had told Kit comfortingly.

As they left the town behind, Kit became aware of her surroundings. The road had narrowed and everywhere she looked were fields and meadows and orchards, stretching as far as she could see on either side.

Kit had grown up in a grimy, industrial city, its air thick with acrid odors spewed out in yellow-gray clouds from factory smokestacks, darkening the atmosphere, obscuring the sunshine. Before Greystone, all she had known was the small, crowded tenement flat, its labyrinthine halls and dark stairways heavy with the greasy smells of cooking cabbage, the musty smell of rotting wood, airless passages.

What she was seeing was all new to her and she breathed deeply of the pure, clean country air, scented delicately with the blossoming apple trees in the orchards beside the road.

It was all so beautiful! Kit felt delight swell inside her, a pleasure she had never experienced before spread all through her body. She could not resist smiling, enjoying each new thing she noticed, the grazing cows who looked up as the wagon rolled by, a hillside of fluffy sheep with a few lambs trotting alongside the big ones, a pasture where several horses ran tossing their manes.

Kit started to point and exclaim at everything she saw, then glanced over at the silent man beside her. He was staring straight ahead, his face like one of those wooden Indians Kit had once seen in front of a store. So Kit swallowed her excitement and they rode on with never a word spoken the whole way.

Cora had been to the kitchen window at least a dozen times. Shielding her eyes from the afternoon sun with her hand, she searched down the lane to the road for some sign of the returning wagon. Where in the world was Jess?

Gradually Cora's uneasiness turned to anger. If he had got into town too late and missed being in time to get one of them orphan girls—her thought drifted away unfinished as just then she saw, rounding the turn of the road in the distance, the familiar wagon rolling into sight.

She watched as it rattled up toward the house and strained to get a good look at the figure sitting beside Jess on the open wagon seat. As it came closer Cora's hands balled into fists. Standing on the edge of the porch, she stiffened as Jess reined the horse to a stop. Without looking at his wife, he got down and came around the other side of the wagon. There he stood, hands hanging at his side, while a little girl climbed gingerly down.

My land! Cora bit her lip. Disappointment and frustration battled with rising fury. What was Jess thinking of? Bringing home a wisp of a girl like that? Why, she didn't look hardly stronger than Seth. Not fit to do a day's worth of chores, if Cora was any judge.

She threw Jess a withering look as the two of them approached the porch. At the bottom of the steps they both halted.

"This here's Kit," mumbled Jess, jerking his thumb at the child.

Cora heard the rush of the boys running out from the house behind her to stand staring curiously at their father and the little girl.

Cora wrestled helplessly for words. She wanted to dress down her husband proper for his lack of good sense. She might as well have no one as this slip of a thing. It would be just another mouth to feed, a child to cope with! He must have been plumb out of his mind to take this one.

While she struggled Cora wondered if they could return her, or had the Orphan Train already left, after depositing its passengers?

"Is that her?" Caspar demanded in a loud voice.

"Is that our orphan?" asked Lonny.

Cora felt the younger boys clinging to her apron. The stunned silence lengthened agonizingly.

Then for the first time Cora let herself look directly at the girl. She was startled to see wide, clear eyes—the color of a mourning dove's wing—regarding her. Then the child smiled a spontaneous, radiant smile that transformed her small, plain face. Momentarily unsettled by its warmth, Cora spoke brusquely.

"Well, you might as well come in. Supper's near ready."

She'd deal with Jess later, she decided. See what could be done about this terrible mistake.

"I'll show you where to put your things," she said, bustling into the house. Still lugging her belongings, Kit followed more slowly. Motioning Kit by the line of gawking boys, Cora led the way up the stairway to the second floor. There she stopped and, opening a wooden door, stepped aside and indicated a narrower flight of steps to the attic.

"Up there's your place," she told Kit. "When you've washed up, you can come down and eat."

Breathless by now from the climb, Kit went the rest of the way up alone. When she reached the top, she dropped her suitcase, flexed her cramped fingers, and looked around.

Under the slanted ceiling was a small, black iron bed with a white coverlet and a striped blanket folded at the end. There was a pine chest with a tiny mirror above it. On top was a plain white pottery washbowl and pitcher, and a dish with a cake of yellow soap. On the wall hung a wooden rack with a washcloth and two towels. A small bench was placed under the window, set into the eaves.

Kit walked over to the window and, unlatching it, pushed it open. Leaning her elbows on the sill, she looked out.

She had never seen anything like it! The sun was just touching the treetops around the farmhouse with a golden haze, and beyond it squares of farmland, all different shades of green, spread out before her like a patchwork quilt. The air, sweet and dewy fresh, rose into her nostrils, and Kit inhaled it as though it were some kind of rare exotic perfume.

A new emotion suffused Kit's very being. If it was not quite happiness, erasing all the old sadnesses, the constant aching wonder about Jamie and Gwynny, it did fill Kit with a nameless joy. It was a sense of discovery, of finding something she had not even known existed.

Taking another long breath, Kit turned from the window and glanced around with satisfaction. She had never before had a room to herself, a room all her own! Kit sighed with contentment. Oh, how lucky she was to be "placed out" here!

6

Kit shook out a clean sheet from the pile in the basket and, stretching up her arms, pinned it awkwardly to the line.

All morning she had helped Cora with the washing. They had begun right after breakfast. First, carrying bucket after bucket of water from the well into the house and pouring it into big pots to heat on the stove. Then Cora had posted her at the kitchen stove to watch until the water began to boil. When that happened, she was to lift it carefully and take it out to the side of the house, where Cora was bent over a huge, copper tub set on a wooden sawhorse, scrubbing vigorously on a metal washboard. It was hot, heavy work on this warm summer day.

When each load was done, it was piled into a big oak-chip basket and Kit was told to hang the wet laundry on the hemp rope, strung in lines from the corner of the house to posts near the fence. Kit liked being outside in the sunshine better than inside. Out here, the fresh breeze brought the sweet smells of wildflowers and turned earth from the fields beyond.

As she worked Kit thought about her life with the Hansens.

Jess had hardly said a word to her since she had arrived, barely acknowledged her presence. Even at mealtimes when she sat down after placing the serving bowls on the table, he never so much as glanced her way.

Mealtimes were silent affairs. That seemed strange to Kit and not at all the way she had thought it would be in a family. Her own family had been different. Even though they had been poor and the meals never as abundant as here at the Hansens, there had been lots of talk. Before her Mam had taken sick, she and Da carried on long conversations. Kit didn't remember what they had been about, but she remembered laughter and a warmth that was lacking here.

There never seemed to be any laughter at the Hansens. Unless you'd call laughter the boisterous jeering of Caspar and Lonny when they'd played some kind of trick on her.

Tricks and teasing were a way of life here at the Hansens, Kit was beginning to accept. Those two were always doing something to make things difficult for her—whether it was slyly kicking over the basket of beans she'd been sent to pick out in the vegetable garden, or sneaking up to her room and putting a frog inside her shoe so that she'd let out a shriek when she slipped her foot into it first thing in the morning. Worse still, was the time they had put a dead mouse in her pitcher and it had plunked into her washbowl when she poured in the water.

She never knew when the next attack was coming. Even though she was growing more wary, she hadn't always been able to second-guess the devilment the two boys between them could devise.

But she never tattled on them. Kit had learned at Greystone never to "snitch" on anyone. But instead of discouraging the boys, that only seemed to egg them on to worse mischief. Where no punishment was inflicted, the persecution continued.

Why didn't they like her? Kit wondered, sighing as she dragged another heavy damp sheet out of the big wicker basket and struggled to hang it straight. She had made some headway with the *little* boys, even Seth, the middle one, who wanted to tag along with his big brothers, only they wouldn't let him. But the rest of the Hansens, including Cora, seemed cold and distant.

It certainly wasn't how Mrs. Scott had said "placing out" would be like. With the familiar twinge in her heart, Kit thought about Jamie and Gwynny. She wondered where they were and how they were getting along in their new homes. She missed them awfully. She hoped they were loved and well cared for. She knew Jamie would love being on a farm like this with all the animals—the baby chicks and the ducklings down at the pond, the new calves. If she knew where he was, she could write and tell him about them. None of the Hansens seemed to think any of this was special at all.

Kit felt dreadfully lonely sometimes, with no one to talk to. She particularly missed her Greystone friends, Laurel and Toddy. She saw them once a week at Sunday school when she went into town to church with the Hansens. But they did not have much time then to be together to talk.

Kit sighed. She could tell that Toddy and Laurel were happy in *their* new homes. Laurel wore such pretty dresses, and Toddy was always talking about the big house on the hill where she lived now as Helene Hale's "little sister."

Kit thought back to the day of the Fourth of July. She had been surprised to learn that the Hansens were going into the town park for the annual picnic. There was a flurry of extra baking that morning. Pies and a cake were set out to cool and a ham brought out of the cellar. Cora was up at dawn getting things ready, packing the big wicker hamper with their food. While Cora stewed, Jess grumbled more than usual, and Lonny and Caspar ran in and out of the house to the wagon that had been hitched up early and brought around to the back.

The three smaller boys were underfoot in the kitchen, getting in the way, impatiently asking, "When are we goin' to go?" until their mother snapped, "When *I'm* good and ready! Quit that whinin' and go git in the wagon, or you won't go at all!"

Kit stood quietly, awaiting directions, as Cora's eyes swung around the kitchen, checking to see if anything could possibly have been forgotten. Kit had learned not to ask too many questions. Her new mother did not like to be anticipated nor did she like suggestions.

Finally she said, "Well, I 'spose that's it. Iffen we forgot sumpin', it'll have to be forgot."

With this, she picked up her sunbonnet and tied it firmly under her chin, took down her shawl from its peg on the door, then motioned Kit to take the other handle of the hamper. Together, they carried it out to the wagon.

All the way into town Kit looked forward to seeing Toddy and Laurel, who told her they would both be there. Caspar and Lonny had whispered behind their hands, giggling mischievously, and Kit felt sure they were plotting something. But the day itself had been fun. Especially when she had had dessert with the Woodwards at their picnic spot. Laurel's new "mother" was so pretty, with a sweet face and kind eyes. But when she had come over to ask Cora if Kit could go with them to watch the fireworks from the Hales' veranda, Cora had said no. She had been very abrupt, as if she didn't like Mrs. Woodward at all. It had been a real disappointment to Kit to have to leave with the Hansens. But Mrs. Woodward had leaned down and kissed her and whispered, "There'll be another time, Kit, I promise." So maybe there would be. Anyway, she could hope.

At last the overflowing laundry basket was empty, and Kit picked it up and started back to the house. She had just reached the porch steps when she heard a peal of hooting laughter. Whirling around, she saw the clothesline had been untied and all the clean sheets she had just finished hanging up were dragging on the dusty ground. At the same time she saw two overalled figures running down toward the barn.

Hot, helpless rage shot through Kit. She ran after the fast-disappearing boys, shouting furiously. "Just you wait!" But they were already far beyond her reach. Breathing hard, she stopped on the path, angry tears crowding into her eyes.

What could she do? Didn't they realize their own mother had spent hours doing the work they had ruined in less than a minute? Shoulders sagging, Kit turned slowly around just as Cora came out onto the porch. Seeing the drooping clothesline, the sheets in the dust, her face reddened angrily.

"Land sakes, girl, can't you even hang up clothes proper?" she demanded. "Didn't they teach you nuthin' in that orphanage?"

7

Cora wiped the beads of perspiration from her forehead with the back of one arm while she stirred the bubbling contents of the kettle—blackberries. These berries were the last of the season. The smaller boys had brought her in two full buckets of them yesterday. You couldn't let things like that go to waste. 'Specially when it was free. Blackberry jam would come in handy on buckwheat cakes, biscuits, and such come wintertime.

In this first week of September, the days were cooler, but even so the heat was getting to her. Maybe she should have had Kit do the stirring for a while instead of sending her out to weed and pick the last of the summer squash.

She turned and looked out the kitchen window and saw Kit bending over the vegetable garden, her skirt puffed out behind her like small sails in the brisk wind. Must be a sight cooler out there than in here, Cora sighed.

Cora turned back to the stove, lifted a spoonful of the dark purple liquid, examined it, then let it drip back into the pot. Still not thick enough. As she went on stirring, Cora's eyes wandered back out to Kit. She was a good girl. Minded. Didn't sass. Did her chores and whatever else Cora told her without a fuss.

She hadn't even been sullen about missing that Fourth of July thing. Cora felt real bad about that now. She could have let her go with her friends.

"If the doctor's wife just hadn't got my dander up like she did, I might have let her go," Cora argued with herself. But then maybe she'd done right by the girl after all. Going up to that big hilltop house of the Hales' might have given her ideas. They and the Woodwards—although Doc Woodward was as nice and plain-talking as could be—lived in a different world from the Hansens. And there was no use trying to mix the two.

It was sure different having a girl around. Restful. Boys were always making some kind of racket. Pushing, shoving, wrassling each other. Like to drive a person crazy with the noise sometimes.

When just the two of them were working together in the kitchen, Kit was just as quiet as could be. But she was right there when you needed her. Didn't have to be told twice. Caught on real quick to how Cora liked things done, she did.

She certainly wasn't what Cora had expected when she'd talked Jess into taking one of them Orphan Train kids. There was something unusual about Kit. Cora shook her head wondering how long Kit had been in that orphanage? And before that? *Someone* must have taught her some of the nice little ways she had. Things like fixin' up her room like she did.

Kit didn't talk much. Not about her life before the Orphan Train anyhow. And Cora didn't ask. Except that one time when she saw the picture Kit had thumbtacked over her bed. It was a picture of an angel hovering over a little boy and girl as they crossed a bridge.

Cora had gone to the attic to put away some heavy winter clothes and wool blankets in the cedar box up there. When she saw the picture, she had asked Kit about it.

"Where did you get that?"

"It was a prize at Sunday school," Kit answered shyly.

Imagine that! The girl had won a prize! And not a word to anyone about it. If one of their boys had won something, *anything*, particularly in *Sunday school,* they'd never have heard the last of it.

"Teacher give it to you?" Cora asked.

"No ma'am, I picked it out. There were three to choose from."

"You liked that one best, huh?"

"Well—" Kit seemed to hesitate, then said slowly, "It reminded me of my little brother and sister."

Unexpectedly Cora's throat tightened. She'd turned away and gone back downstairs fast. The attic had been warm on that early summer day, but not *that* hot. Not hot enough to make Cora feel suddenly suffocated, so's she couldn't get her breath.

She had walked out on the porch and stood there for a long time. Thinking. Thinking about Kit and way back to her own childhood. She stood there for another few minutes. Then she had gone into hers and Jess's bedroom downstairs, lifted the lid of the old trunk set at the foot of the bed. She knelt down, reached into it and brought out the afghan she had crocheted. It had colorful zigzag stripes. The pattern was called "Joseph's Coat." Cora had seen one like it at a County Fair and copied it. It had taken her all one winter, collecting the right colors of yarn, working on it catch-as-catch-can between her chores. But when it was finished, she had put it away and never used it. She didn't know why. It's just that Jess preferred the quilts piled on top of the bed, and Cora had never had any woman friend to come admire it. Oh, for land's sakes, she didn't really know *why* she had not put it out for a bedspread herself!

Cora looked at it for another minute or two, then before she could change her mind, she had marched back up to the attic and handed the afghan to Kit. "Here, you might like this to put over your bed."

Kit's eyes had lighted up like twin stars.

"Oh, thank you! Thank you! It's beautiful!" she had said, running her hand over it, laying her cheek against its softness.

Recalling the incident as she stirred, Cora said out loud to herself, "Never saw a youngster so grateful for the least little thing."

Cora glanced out the window again. Kit, with a full basket of vegetables beside her, was now picking some wildflowers growing along the fence.

That evening when Kit set the table for supper, she arranged the flowers she'd picked—daisies, purple wild asters and Queen Anne's lace—in a wide-necked green bottle and placed it in the center of the table. She had found the old glass bottle half-buried in the sand near the barn and, liking the iridescent glow of it, she had washed and polished it to use as a vase.

Cora noticed, but busy pouring the jam into her jars, didn't say anything. It was nearly time to start supper. It wasn't until the boys were rounded up, Jess seated, and she and Kit began to serve that the ruckus started.

Jess had rattled off his usual mumbled blessing before meals, and the words were hardly out of his mouth before he growled, "Who put them weeds in here?"

Cora, turning around from the stove, saw Kit's face go scarlet. Caspar and Lonny clapped their hands over their mouths, pointing at Kit.

"Weeds! Lookit the weeds!" hollered Lonny.

"Betcha she thinks they're *beautiful*, jest like she does the cows!" hooted Caspar.

Cora felt a rush of rage course through her at her own children. She saw the flowers for the first time and something quickened inside her at the delicacy of their shapes, the blend of colors, the way the light struck the mottled green of the bottle.

Then it struck her forcefully that she would never have noticed if it hadn't been for Kit.

Frying pan in hand, Cora silenced the boys with a threatening look they both recognized and feared. "I think they look right pretty," she said sharply. "And you boys just keep your opinion to yourself."

After supper, as she and Kit were clearing away the dishes, Cora said to her, "School will be starting soon. I've got a piece of flowered calico put back that would make up for a dress for you. Think I've got a pattern we can cut down that'll do too."

Kit murmured, "Thank you."

Nothing else was said. Nothing else needed to be said.

Cora was bewildered by her own feelings. In spite of herself, she was drawn to the girl in a way she could not understand.

Something in Cora had been frozen through the years. Now vague longings she had never expressed began to emerge. Like the hard earth in spring after a cold winter, she began to thaw.

8

Miss Millicent Cady looked over her classroom full of students in Meadowridge Grammar School. The windows were open to a gentle May breeze. Outside, beyond the schoolyard fence, she could see the faint pink of budding apple trees in the nearby orchard. The young teacher straightened her shoulders, resisting the urge to yawn. *Spring fever!* she chided herself sternly.

The children were finding it hard to concentrate, too. Every few minutes one little head or the other would glance up from the workbooks, and gaze yearningly outside.

Milly suppressed a smile. Maybe she should ring the dismissal bell early, let them go out and enjoy the beautiful afternoon. What harm would it do if she deviated from the curriculum for one day?

The County Superintendent of Schools had already made his annual visit and declared her students' progress well within the county average. Indeed, he had commended her, saying it was somewhat above average in some cases. He had complimented her on her students' grasp of the subjects on which he had quizzed them and their remarkable performance during the Spelling Bee.

It had been a good year, all told, Milly had to admit. Maybe the best of her six years of teaching in Meadowridge. Last year she had felt restless, had wondered if it might not be a good idea to make a change, apply to another district for a new position. She realized teachers got stale. She was still under thirty, and not married. Perhaps it was time for her to move on while she was young enough to seek new horizons.

But she had stayed on and now she was glad she had. If she had not, she would not have experienced the restored enthusiasm for teaching, the unexpected joy in her profession, brought about by the entrance into her classroom of three interesting new pupils.

Milly's eyes rested on Laurel, Toddy and Kit—the Orphan Train trio—as she called them privately.

She recalled her own reservations when she had first heard they were coming. Milly had heard stories of the dire conditions from which some of the orphans came and had been apprehensive of their influence on the rest of the children.

After all, who knew what their background might be? What bad habits they had picked up. What ingrained attitudes might they bring with them? How would they fit in with the Meadowridge children? But none of her anxious premonitions were confirmed. Instead, the three little girls had proved themselves valuable additions to the class.

In spite of priding herself on never having any favorites among her students, no "teacher's pet," Kit Ternan was an exception. Milly saw in her a creative imagination, a fluidity in expressing herself in her compositions that was truly outstanding.

The fact that she had been "placed out" with the Hansen family gave Milly some concern. She had had Caspar and Lonny in her classes and denser, less teachable children would be rare to find. They seemed to have no intellectual stimulation at home and found their studies tedious and dull. The papers she returned to them were always full of red-penciled corrections, though she always suggested they "try harder next time."

Yet, Kit was special and Milly encouraged her writing. When she saw how Kit loved to read, she loaned her books from the school library as well as from her own personal collection.

If only Kit did not get bogged down by the chores Milly knew she was responsible for on the farm, did not get discouraged by the lack of intellectual stimulation in her environment. So far, neither of the Hansens had ever shown much interest in their own boys' education. Only once had Jess Hansen shown up, offering to "whup 'em good" when she had sent a note home with Lonny, complaining about his arithmetic sums.

Milly determined she herself would see that Kit's avid thirst for knowledge was nourished. The girl was too intelligent, and a mind was a terrible thing to waste!

Just then, Kit looked up and smiled at her, and Milly sensed that sweetness that always seemed to emanate from her, and smiled back.

How pretty Miss Cady is, thought Kit. *I want to be just like her when I grow up. I guess I'll be a teacher, too. When you're a teacher, you can read as many books as you want. You can live in a nice little cottage and have just flowers in your garden. You can wear frilly blouses, a fresh one every day, and combs in your hair and flowered hats on Sunday.*

Unconsciously Kit sighed. She had only been in Miss Cady's little house twice, and it was so different from the Hansens' farmhouse that she would like to have stayed forever. Miss Cady had offered to lend her some books and, even though Kit knew she would miss a ride home on the Wilsons' wagon and have to walk instead and probably be scolded for being late, it had been worth it. Miss Cady had let her pick out whichever two books she wanted. Kit had knelt for a long time in front of the bookcase in Miss Cady's parlor trying to make up her mind.

Afterwards they had had tea, real tea in pink china cups, sitting in front of a dear little polished stove. There was a plate of lemon circles stuck with cloves, and delicious wedges of thin cinnamon toast, all served on a small round table covered with a crisp linen cloth with a border of cross-stitch roses.

Kit's chest had seemed to swell with happiness so that it was almost hard to swallow. Everything about that afternoon stayed in her mind, like a picture she could take out and look at and enjoy all over again, times when she was lonely or life out at the Hansens was particularly dismal.

Kit bent her head over her workbook, her fingers tightening on her pencil. Maybe it wasn't right to wish such things, but, oh, how she wished she'd been "placed out" with Miss Cady. That was Kit's idea of pure heaven.

She bit her lip. Some days were really hard. School was a welcome relief from the joyless routine on the farm. Kit got up before dawn to do her chores before it was time to walk down to the gate to get a ride into town with the Wilsons. Mr. Wilson went every day to do his milk deliveries and he would let his children and the Hansens off at the schoolyard.

Kit hated that ride. Of course, Lonny and Caspar either ran ahead or lagged behind her, making teasing jibes all the way. Then when they got on the back of the milk wagon, the Wilson girls, Susan and Ruby, were so mean. They had made it plain right from the start that they had no intention of making friends with her. The very first day of school they had drawn their pinafores away from Kit when she sat down beside them, put their noses in the air and sniffed, saying spitefully, "Orphan Trash."

At least when she arrived at school, she had Laurel and Toddy, Kit thought gratefully.

Suddenly the school bell clanged and Kit and everyone jumped, looking up in surprise to see Miss Cady standing by the classroom door, a smile on her pretty face.

"Early dismissal today, boys and girls," she announced.

All the children scrambled to their feet, pencils dropped, workbooks slammed shut. The room emptied as if by magic as everyone went running out. Only Kit remained. She came up to Milly's desk.

"Miss Cady, I wanted to ask you about the composition tablets," she began shyly. "I noticed most of them have a few pages left in them even though we've done our last essay for the year."

"Yes, what about them, Kit?" Milly asked.

"I wondered if I could go through them, tear out the blanks and have them?"

"I don't see why not. I was going to discard them anyway."

"Oh, thank you, Miss Cady. May I do it after school?"

"Certainly. But, I'm curious. Why do you want them?"

Kit lowered her eyes and color crept up into her cheeks. "I want to use them to write to my little brother and sister."

"Oh? I didn't realize you had a brother and sister, Kit. How old are they and where do they live?"

Kit shook her head. "I don't know. I mean, I know how old they are or how old they *must* be now. But I don't know where they are." She hesitated, then said slowly, "You see, they were adopted, and it's a secret where they're placed. But someday, when I'm a grown-up, I'm going to try to find them. And in the meantime, I write them letters telling them about things, where I am, what I'm doing. I know how much Jamie, my brother, would love the farm. So I tell him things about the animals and all. And Gwynny, I'm afraid she will forget me, she was so little. So I write about things she wouldn't know about unless I told her. About our Da and our mother who Gwynny wouldn't remember at all—" Kit paused, her cheeks flushed, embarrassed that she had said so much. "That's what I write. That's why I want the paper."

Milly turned away, busying herself by erasing the blackboard. Her eyes stung. She felt like going to the teachers' supply cabinet and taking out a ream of fresh paper and giving it to Kit. But she knew that would further embarrass the child. So she went to the discard bin and took out an armful of used copybooks.

"If you'll wait a minute, Kit, I'll help you tear out the pages" was all she could trust herself to say.

Later, up in her room under the eaves, Kit read over some of the "letters" she had written over the past few months.

Dear Jamie and Gwynny,

First, I'll tell you where I went after I left Greystone. They put us on a train going West and it was very interesting and exciting as I've already written.

When we got to Meadowridge, I was placed out with a family who have a farm about three miles from town.

There is a barn and a big house. My room is on the top floor with a window where I can look cut and see the whole farm—the fields, the orchards, the river, the pasture.

There are lots of different kinds of animals on the farm. In the pasture there are cows with lovely, soft velvety-brown eyes. There are a couple of workhorses Mr. Hansen uses to pull his plow and two more for the wagon when he goes into town. There are lots of chickens, and a cross old rooster who squawks and chases me every time I go out to feed them. But there are sweet, fluffy little baby chicks that Gwynny would love to pet.

Kit tried to describe all the good things about the farm she could think of, but there were things she didn't tell, things that made her sad even to think about. Like how the cows mourned when their calves were taken away to market.

The first time she had heard the pitiful sound of loud mooing, she had rushed in to tell Cora that something must be dreadfully wrong with them. They must be sick or in pain. Cora matter-of-factly explained that they missed their calves.

"You mean like a mother would miss her baby?" asked Kit with tear-filled eyes.

Cora had given her a strange look, then nodded, her lips pressed together tightly.

Kit had crawled up in her bed, crying, too, as the mournful sound continued all the next day. She wondered if their Da ever missed *them* like that. But of course she didn't write that in her letters, either.

Sometimes what Kit wrote was more for herself than for her brother and sister. Some of her heart's deepest longings, her mind's most puzzling thoughts. After all, she wasn't at all sure Jamie and Gwynny would ever get to read the letters anyway.

The Hansen family has five boys. The two oldest, Caspar and Lonny, are terrible teases. I didn't think they liked me at all at first, but now I think it's just that they're boys and have to prove something. Still, I hope you'll never be that way, Jamie. The three younger ones are Seth, Chet, and Tom, who are turning out to be my friends.

When they had the measles and had to stay in bed with the curtains pulled, so the room would be dark and not damage their eyes, I read to them. Listening to the stories kept them quiet. I pretended I was reading to you and Gwynny. Anyhow, after they got well, they still wanted me to read to them. Mrs. Hansen says she hasn't time to do it.

But sometimes she'll have me sit in the kitchen while she's making bread and read out loud to all of them. She says it keeps them out of mischief and from underfoot. But I think she likes the stories, too.

I wonder a lot about you two. Where did you go? Who adopted you? Are you happy? I daydream that one day we will find each other again, maybe not until we're all grown up.

I hope you haven't forgotten me.

Your loving sister,
Kit

Kit settled herself comfortably by the window, smoothing out the first copybook from the pile of used ones Miss Cady had given her, and began a new letter:

Dear Jamie and Gwynny,

School is nearly out for the year. Next week we have report cards and Promotion. I got promoted to the Fifth Grade. I will have the same teacher, Miss Cady, the one I told you about because she teaches both Fourth and Fifth. She is so nice. I think I will be a teacher when I grow up, or maybe a writer—

9

The Class of 1900

Kit Ternan, at nearly nineteen, was a willowy brunette. Her hair, the color of polished maple, was swept back from her face, emphasizing her wide, gray eyes and lovely brow.

Her arms full of books, she came out of the main door of Meadowridge High School. Seeing groups of students who, lured by the warmth of the early June day, were sitting all over the steps, she paused at the top for a minute, wondering how to pick her way down through them.

Hearing the thunk of a tennis ball, she turned to look over at the school's tennis court where two couples were playing mixed doubles. She recognized her friends, Toddy and Laurel, at once. It was easy to guess who their partners were—Chris Blanchard and Dan Brooks.

Toddy sprinted toward the net, with the lightness of a butterfly, her blonde hair swinging like a silken bell from its bow glinted with golden lights in the sunshine. Laurel, slender in her fashionable white tennis blouse and skirt, moved with graceful ease.

Kit moved to the other side of the porch for a better view and stood watching them. Laurel was poised with her racket at the base line, Toddy shifting her position in anticipation of Chris's serve. Dan's lean body, crouched at the ready, twirled his racket waiting tensely for the play. A fast volley followed until Chris slammed a wicked backhand into the net, then raised both his hands and let out a frustrated howl. The others laughed and game was called. Still laughing the foursome walked toward the edge of the court.

Kit shifted her load of books, then threaded her way down the steps, stopping here and there to exchange a greeting as she did. As she went by the tennis court, Toddy saw her and waved.

"Wait, Kit!"

Leaving the others refreshing themselves at the water fountain, Toddy ran up to the wire-mesh door of the court, opened it, and came out.

"Can you?" Toddy asked. "Stay over with me after the Awards Banquet?"

Kit hesitated. "I haven't asked Cora yet. I will when I go out to the farm this weekend."

"She'll have to say yes. After all, it's part of Graduation Week," Toddy reminded her.

"I know, but we bake on Saturdays and she—"

"You can't miss the Awards Banquet, Kit!" Toddy protested. "Surely—"

"Oh, I won't miss it. It's just that staying over in town Friday night would put me late getting out to the farm Saturday morning and—"

"But it will be late when it's over and Laurel wants us all to come over to the Woodwards' house afterwards for our own party. You *must* stay over, Kit," Toddy insisted. "Do you want me to have Mrs. Hale write her a note, inviting you?"

Kit shook her head. "Cora hates getting notes. I'll ask her and explain. I think she'll understand—"

Toddy looked at her friend, for once her pert face serious. "You're over eighteen now, Kit. You know you don't have any further obligation to the Hansens. They haven't taken any responsibility for *you* since then, have they?" she demanded. "I mean, you *have* been living with Miss Cady this year."

Kit nodded, "I know. It's just that…well, Cora has so much to do, Toddy. You can't imagine what goes on every day at the farm. With those five big boys there's so much cooking, baking and—"

"But you aren't their hired girl, Kit. If it hadn't been for Miss Cady, they might not have even let you finish high school!" Toddy sounded indignant.

"I think Cora would have, she wanted to, it was Jess—he just didn't, *doesn't* understand, that's all."

"Well, anyway, they haven't lifted a finger to help you finish your senior year and they're not doing anything to help you earn the money you'll need for college." Toddy paused and put on a severe expression. "They certainly aren't paying you for all the weekends you go out there and work, now are they?"

Kit shook her head. What Toddy was saying *was* true, but she felt disloyal admitting it. After all, the Hansens *had* given her a home all these years, fed, clothed her. So, instead of telling Toddy she was right, Kit changed the subject.

"Speaking of getting paid, I'd better run or I'll be late for work at the library and Miss Smedley will give me one of her famous lectures on a 'prompt and willing employee.'" Kit groaned.

"Looks like you're taking books back, not checking them out. I guess you've got the perfect after-school job for *you*."

"I know—'bookworm,' that's me." Kit smiled, not annoyed by her friend's teasing.

"I should probably be at the library studying instead of playing tennis!" Toddy made a dismal face. "Two more final exams to get through."

Kit nodded sympathetically.

"Oh, *you* should worry, Kit. You'll pass with honors in everything. I'm the one who has to worry, especially about History. All those dates!" Toddy rolled her eyes.

Kit smiled. "Soon it will all be over and we'll be graduating."

"The Class of 1900! Just think!" Toddy grinned.

"I really have to go now, Toddy. I'll let you know about Friday," Kit promised as she set off down the shady street toward the town library.

On her way, Kit thought about what she and Toddy had discussed. Especially about Millicent Cady, who, ever since Kit was in her grammar school class, had taken such a special interest in her. Not only had she been Kit's ideal, she had been her mentor, guide and friend. It was Miss Cady who kept encouraging Kit to set goals, make plans, who fueled Kit's fire for learning.

"You've got a fine mind, Kit. It's God's gift to you, so you must develop it and then you can share it with others," Miss Cady constantly told her. She urged Kit to apply for a scholarship to Merrivale Teachers College.

At first, that had sounded like an impossible dream. But, spurred on by Miss Cady's belief in her ability, Kit had pushed herself and worked hard so that her high-school marks were consistently excellent. This winter Miss Cady had helped her fill out the scholarship application. All that was needed now were her final exam grades. If she qualified, she would then go for a personal interview with the Dean of the Teacher's College. After that, she would just have to wait to see if she were accepted.

This had been the best of all her years in Meadowridge. But, if Miss Cady had not offered her a home, Kit might have had to quit school entirely.

Jess didn't set much store by "book larnin'," as he called it. Lonny and Caspar dropped out at Sixth Grade and now worked full time on the farm. Living there, Kit found it harder and harder to find time to study, do the required papers. The workload of chores—washing, cleaning, cooking, baking, sewing, mending—became heavier as the boys got older, bigger, hungrier and outgrew their clothes more rapidly.

Although Kit felt sorry for Cora, she knew if she stayed, she would be trapped. An existence that ignored the life of the intellect and spirit would be an imprisoning life for someone of Kit's sensitivity. She was indebted to Miss Cady, and each time she went back to the farm to help out, she realized more and more just how *much* she owed her.

Kit reached the old brick, ivy-covered library building, hurried up the steps, and went through the etched glass and wooden doors.

Once inside, Kit felt "at home." There was something familiar and comforting about the smell of paste, paper, old and new books, and the furniture wax that kept the golden oak tables and chairs gleaming. That was Amelia Smedley's doing. She felt she owned the public library after all the years she had worked here as head librarian. She took as much pride in its appearance as if it were her own home.

Ever since she had discovered it years before, the library was one of Kit's favorite places. She could still remember her sense of awe and wonder at first seeing shelf after shelf of books, learning they all could be taken out and read!

She still loved coming here, felt lucky to work here, even though Miss Smedley was considered a veritable "dragon" by most people.

As Kit slid her armload of books into the RETURN slot, Miss Smedley looked up from a pile of books she was cataloguing. Surveying Kit sternly over her pinch-nose glasses, she glanced at the wall clock. "You're late."

Kit's eyes followed the glance, saw the minute hand jerk a little past four. Only three minutes late!

"Sorry, Miss Smedley."

Miss Smedley pointed with her stamper. "Get to work then."

Suppressing a smile, Kit went straight over to the book cart loaded with books to be shelved.

Kit looked out from the stacks where she was shelving books when the door opened and Dan Brooks walked into the library. Her hands started to shake so that she almost dropped the books she was holding. Her face flamed and her heart thundered.

That always happened when she saw Dan unexpectedly—coming toward her down a school corridor, or out on the school grounds, or walking along the sidewalk on the opposite side of the street in town, it didn't matter.

She was ashamed of the quick dart of envy she felt for Laurel, because she loved her friend dearly. But Laurel didn't even seem to notice Dan's worshipful attitude toward her. For some reason Laurel always seemed to have an air of detachment about her. It was almost as if she were a bird of passage, only temporarily among them.

It wasn't that Kit wished she could replace Laurel in Dan's affection exactly. It was just that her romance-starved heart secretly yearned for someone to gaze at her with such unconditional adoration. If it couldn't be Dan, then maybe someone just like him.

10

The day of the Senior Picnic, Kit, dressed in a crisp pink-checked gingham dress and swinging a wide-brimmed straw hat by its strings, walked from Miss Cady's cottage over to the high school feeling happier and more carefree than she could ever remember.

The blue sky, washed clear of clouds by a light rain that had fallen during the night, promised a perfect day ahead for the class outing. Even if it had been cloudy, nothing could have spoiled this day for Kit. Since yesterday, all of her dreams seemed possible.

Yesterday had been the last regular day of school in the last week before Graduation. Exams were over and, with most classes suspended, all the Seniors had to do was practice the processional and rehearse the songs they were to sing at the program.

The Seniors had filed into the auditorium for morning assembly with more than the usual amount of chatter. An undercurrent of excitement buzzed among them.

Mr. Henson, the principal, standing at the lectern on the stage, had to rap more times than usual for things to quiet down enough so he could be heard.

"Students, your attention, please. Before I dismiss the rest of you except for the Seniors, who have to rehearse for Graduation, I want to make the announcement I'm sure you have all been waiting to hear—the names of the Seniors who will represent the Class of 1900 as Salutatorian and Valedictorian."

A murmur of anticipation rippled through the room.

"Actually there was very little difference in the grade point averages of the two top students. The Salutatorian, as you know, makes the welcoming speech. The Valedictorian will give the speech summing up the feelings, thoughts, future goals of our departing Senior Class."

Mr. Henson cleared his throat, adjusted his spectacles and, referring to the paper he held, said, "This year's Salutatorian of Meadowridge High's graduating class, we are proud to name—Daniel Brooks."

Kit's hands became clammy as the announcement hit her like a blow, knocking the breath out of her. Only the evening before, Miss Cady had confided excitedly that when she had gone into the high-school office on some pretext, she had seen some of the Senior grades.

"Yours were very high, Kit! You have a very good chance of being named Salutatorian even though a girl has never spoken at Graduation before."

Just that morning before Kit left for school, Miss Cady had hugged her impulsively. "I just know you'll be named Salutatorian, Kit. And now there'll be no question of your getting a scholarship to Merrivale," she assured her.

Kit fought back tears, battled her disappointment while all around her their classmates began applauding as Dan stumbled to his feet, looking both bewildered and pleased.

Kit started clapping, too. Of course, it would be Dan, she told herself. Dan was outstanding, intelligent, a brilliant student. He deserved it. It had been foolish to hope. Kit clapped harder so that her palms stung.

Mr. Henson let the clapping go on for nearly a full minute before holding up his hand for silence.

"And now, for a precedent-setting announcement, which seems particularly fitting for the first class graduating in the beginning of a new century. After tabulating the grades repeatedly to be sure there was no possible mistake, we have come to the conclusion that this year's Valedictorian will for the first time be a young woman—Miss Kathleen Ternan."

Kit had sat there, completely motionless, her hands pressed against her mouth, while pandemonium broke all about her. She heard a roaring in her ears as her heart thundered, beating in her chest as if it might explode.

It couldn't be happening! Had she really heard it right? Had Mr. Henson announced her name?

"Kit! Kit!" Someone was tugging her arm. "Mr. Henson wants you to come up on the stage."

It was Toddy and, on the other side, Laurel was hugging her. The sound of applause rose in crescendo as Kit somehow managed to get to the end of the row and make her way up the steps of the stage. As she reached its center, Mr. Henson was holding out his hand to shake hers, and Dan, standing alongside the principal, was grinning and clapping like the rest.

Kit turned toward the assembly and, through happy tears, she saw that all the student body had risen in a standing ovation.

Yes, yesterday had probably been the happiest day of her life. If only Da could have known and Jamie and Gwynny could have seen their big sister receive such an honor! Of course, Toddy and Laurel had been thrilled, treated her to a soda at Shay's Ice Cream Parlor after school to celebrate. But it would have been nice to have *real* family there.

In sight of the schoolyard now, Kit was hailed by some of the other Seniors arriving for their class picnic. Kit was admired and well-liked by her classmates, and several of the Senior boys would have been eager to claim her as a girl friend. However, Kit never had any time for anything but school and her work at the library. Her weekends were spent out at the Hansens' farm, helping Cora.

Some of the more enterprising fellows who ordinarily did not care much for extra reading frequented the library, hoping Kit would be checking out books that evening.

Although Kit did not have Laurel's "candy-box" prettiness nor Toddy's gamine appeal, she was attractive. Today the sun gave her rich brown hair a golden sheen, and her clear skin had a becoming apricot glow. But her eyes were her best feature—large, beautiful, a silvery gray set in thick, dark lashes.

Today, Kit was so filled with joy that she radiated happiness and her fellow classmates felt drawn to her in a new and special way. Everyone wanted to sit with her as they climbed into the wagons filled with hay to ride out to River Park, sit beside her on the rustic benches at the tables in the park where a lavish picnic was set out.

But it was with Toddy and Laurel that Kit always felt most at ease. Wherever those two were, Chris Blanchard and Dan Brooks could usually be found. After lunch the five friends left the picnic area to climb up the hill leading to the bluff overlooking the river.

"Written your speech yet, Kit?" Dan asked in mock seriousness.

"Of course! A hundred times, haven't you?" she laughed in return.

"I'm so proud of you two!" declared Toddy. "Imagine being friends with two celebrities!"

"Are you going to be a suffragette, Kit?" asked Chris. "Votes for women and all that sort of thing?"

"She'll probably end up being the first woman President of the United States," Toddy told him as they reached the top.

Kit stretched flat on her back, tilted the broad-brimmed straw hat over her face. Her hands at her sides stroked the grass on which she lay. She breathed deeply, as if she could take everything—the sun, the scents, the cloudless sky—into her very being, wanting to hold onto it forever.

The thought drifted through her mind to try, because instinctively she knew it was the kind of day to be looked back upon and remembered at some distant time.

Kit heard the voices, muted laughter coming up from the river where Chris and Toddy were skipping rocks across its sun-sparkled surface. She heard Laurel softly humming some melody. She wondered if any of them were as aware as she of the swift passage of time. This week they would graduate from high school and then everything would change. She wanted to cry out to them, but what would she have said? They would have thought her ridiculous if she had stood up and shouted, "Behold! This, too, shall pass."

Kit smiled to herself. Yes, they would have thought her mad. But her own awareness gripped her in an urgent need to savor this day.

"Penny for your thoughts, Kit!" Dan interrupted her reverie.

Would Dan understand if she shared them with him? Maybe. But not being sure, she raised herself on her elbows, pushed back the brim of her hat, smiled over at both him and Laurel, and quoted softly from one of the poems in the book of collected verse of Elizabeth Barrett Browning Miss Cady had given her.

> The little cares that fretted me.
> I lost them yesterday
> Among the fields above the sea,
> Among the winds at play,
> Among the lowing of the herds,

> The rustling of the trees,
> Among the singing of the birds,
> The humming of the bees,
> The foolish fears of what may happen.
> I cast them all away.
> Among the clover-scented grass,
> Among the new-mown hay:
> Among the husking of the corn,
> Where drowsy poppies nod,
> Where ill thoughts die and good are born—
> Out in the fields with God!

"That's beautiful, Kit." Toddy's voice was enthusiastic as she and Chris reappeared. "Will you write that down for me, please? Mr. Allen asked me to find something appropiate to recite at the Baccalaureate Breakfast, and that would be perfect."

"Sure," agreed Kit.

Just then they heard the shrill sound of a whistle, the teachers' signal to come to the main picnic area for the ride back to town. Reluctantly, they began to straggle back down the hillside.

Kit was the last to leave. She stopped, and looked back. The sun's rays were beginning to touch the hills, sending long, purple shadows across the waving meadow grass. She had the feeling of saying goodbye to something precious. To what? Youth? Freedom? Or only a perfect day?

She had to smile at her own dramatizing. Surely there would be other days when the five of them would come back to this hill during the coming summer. But she knew it would never be quite the same as this one idyllic day. For some reason Kit shivered and hurried after the others.

11

Hairbrush in hand, Kit studied her reflection in the mirror and frowned. Her arms were weary from practicing doing up her hair as she wanted to wear it for Graduation. It was much too thick and heavy to pouf up in front, combing it over the wire "rats" some girls used to achieve the popular pompadour style. So she had brushed it to a satiny sheen, braided it, and turned it under at the nape of her neck, securing it with tortoise shell hairpins.

This style was not in fashion, she knew, but it was all she could manage and looked well enough, she decided. Even if her hairdo did not satisfy her, Kit felt pleased and happy with her graduation outfit. The white tucked blouse was simple but dainty, and the white skirt fit her slim figure perfectly.

Miss Cady had suggested that she buy a good quality material for a skirt, then make two blouses. That way she had had two outfits to wear to the events. Miss Cady had given her the lace for the blouse—*real* lace! Miss Cady said a lady *never* wore *machine-made* lace. Of course Kit would not have known that unless Miss Cady had gently told her. The lace simply *made* her blouse.

Yes, Miss Cady was right as she was about all the fine points of being a lady. "Understatement" was so much more in good taste than the flamboyant patterns and fabric the clerk at Donninger's Dry Goods had tried to sell her.

"Half the girls in the graduating class will go for that sort of thing," Miss Cady told Kit. "But you will stand out in your elegant simplicity. People will see *you*, not what you're wearing. They'll remember your words, not your dress. And, after all, that's the important thing. You will be the first female Valedictorian Meadowridge High has ever had! Just think, Kit!"

Miss Cady had gone to her weekly Wednesday Night Prayer Meeting, and Kit was alone. She was giving her blouse and skirt a final careful pressing in the kitchen when the front doorbell rang. She set the iron on its heel, then slipped her blouse off the ironing board, hung it on a hanger, hooked it over the doorknob, then ran to answer the door. Maybe Miss Cady had forgotten her key.

To her surprise, it was Cora.

"I almost left, thought nobody was home," Cora said. "I wuz just goin' to leave this, but now I see you're here, I'll jest bring it on in myself and see you open it." She bent down and picked up a large cardboard box she had propped beside the front door and, as Kit held the door open wider, Cora squeezed in carrying it.

"There now!" Cora let out her breath as she put the box down. "Where's your bedroom, Kit?"

Kit realized Cora had never been to Miss Cady's cottage before. Still astonished by this unexpected visit, she led the way down the short hall to her room.

"This doesn't mean you're not coming tomorrow, does it?" Kit asked, turning to Cora with a worried frown.

"Oh, no, we're comin' all right. But I jest come in myself to bring you this." Cora laid the box on Kit's bed. Then she stood back, hands on her hips, and pointed to the box. "Well, go ahead. Don't you want to see what's inside?" Her thin lips twitched a little.

Still puzzled, Kit undid the string tied around the box and lifted off the lid. Then she pushed aside the tissue paper on top. A wave of dismay washed over her when she saw the contents.

"Oh, Cora, you shouldn't have!"

"Well, aren't you goin' to take it out, try it on?" prodded Cora, hardly able to contain her own excitement.

Kit reached in and slowly unfolded the most impossible dress she could have imagined. At the same time, she knew Cora thought it the most beautiful.

"I thought you should have a store-bought dress for once, Kit. So I ordered it out of that mail-order catalog from Chicago. They have the latest fashions, you know," Cora said, reaching out to touch the gleaming sateen surface of the tiered skirt trimmed with row after row of *machine-made* lace.

Unable to speak, Kit held the dress up to herself, turning away so Cora could not see her face betray her true feelings about this disaster of a dress.

The leg-of-mutton sleeves were ribboned to the elbow, the cuffs banded with the same lace as the skirt and bodice. For a minute Kit closed her eyes and prayed desperately for the right words to say.

Cora, her head to one side, was surveying the dress from behind.

"You'll have to slip it on with the shoes you'll be wearin' so's we can see if the length is right. We still have time to take up the hem if needs be."

Speechless, Kit got out of her cotton skirt and shirtwaist, and stood in her camisole and petticoat while Cora, humming under her breath, dropped the dress over Kit's head and proceeded to do up the buttons in the back.

"Well now, I think it's goin' to fit just fine," Cora said with satisfaction.

Kit, who had hoped against hope that it would be too big or too tight, suppressed a groan of despair. She dreaded looking in the mirror. She could only imagine how wrong in every way this awful dress was.

"There now, Kit, what do you think?" asked Cora.

It was the ultimate test. It took Kit only a second to conquer her own self-will, the length of a whispered prayer. Then she turned around and gave Cora a hug. "Oh, Cora, thank you! It was such a thoughtful thing for you to do. I just can't tell you how much I appreciate your doing it." All the words were true but every one cost Kit dearly.

"Well, no need to make such a fuss." Cora pulled away self-consciously. "I just didn't want you up on that platform lookin' dowdy beside the doctor's girl and that sassy little baggage from the Hale's." She took a step back and surveyed Kit again. "If I do say so myself, not another girl graduatin' will hold a candle to you in *that*." She pursed her lips, which was Cora's way of showing she was pleased. "Well, I best be goin' if I'm to get home afore dark. I was waitin' and waitin' for this to come. Don't know how many trips I made to the Post Office to see if it had got here yet," she exclaimed with a shake of her head. "T'would've been a real pity if you hadn't had it to wear fer your Graduation."

Oh, if only it *hadn't* come, thought Kit miserably.

She walked to the door with Cora, stood there and watched Cora climb into the wagon and drive off. Then she shut the door and leaned against it, her head pressed on the wood, wanting to bang it in frustration.

Of all the years, of all the times she might have been thrilled that Cora thought enough of her to spend the money to order her a dress, *why now?* When it didn't matter, or rather, when it mattered *so much.*

Kit walked slowly back into the bedroom and stared at her reflection in the mirror. The material felt sleazy against her skin, the cheap lace scratched her chin and wrists. Her face crumpled. She *hated* this dress! She looked—like an over dressed, over frilled—floozy! Kit slid to her knees, buried her face in her hands as bitter tears forced themselves up through her throat and broke out in hoarse sobs.

The occasion when she had planned to look her very best, when she would be standing in front of all Meadowridge to give the Valedictory speech she had worked so long and hard over, was ruined for her.

Finally she wiped her tears. Sighing heavily, she got to her feet, stumbling a little over the ruffled hem. As she did, her eyes caught sight of the white blouse with its dainty *real* lace on its hanger on the doorknob, and a new wave of despair swept over her. Kit thought of the hours she had spent sewing it, laboring over its tiny tucks and delicate stitches. All wasted time now.

There was no way out. She would *have* to wear the dress Cora had chosen for her. Kit could imagine how she must have sat at the kitchen table in the light of the oil lamp, poring over the pages of the huge mail-order catalog. How she must have got Lonny or Caspar, no, probably Seth, to print out the order for her, address, and mail it. And that would have taken some humbling for Cora to do, Kit knew. When Kit had been at the Hansens' less than a year, she had discovered Cora's shameful secret, the one she kept well-hidden. Cora could not read or write.

She understood what a gift of love this was from Cora, even if it was tinged with self-pride and the oft-revealed resentment she had toward the other Orphan Train adoptive homes. It was a gift Kit must receive with gracious gratitude, no matter what.

As Kit started to unbutton the dress, she heard the front door open and Miss Cady's light step coming down the hall.

"Kit, are you still up? Did you realize you left the lamp lighted in the kitchen and the ironing board up?" Miss Cady stopped at her half-open bedroom door.

"What on earth are you doing in that dreadful dress?" she asked with undisguised horror.

Kit lifted her chin, straightened her shoulders. "Cora brought it to me. It's for Graduation."

"To wear? On Graduation Day? You can't possibly wear it, Kit, dear. It's perfectly awful!"

Kit's clear, gray eyes regarded her with uncompromising directness. "I have to, Miss Cady," she said firmly. "I'm going to."

12

Graduation Day was as beautiful a June day as one could wish and, as the Seniors filed into the auditorium, they looked suitably solemn and grown up for this occasion. Some of the girls had their hair up for the first time, and the boys, looking a little uncomfortable, were still smart in their unaccustomed stiff-collared shirts, ties, and dark suits.

The hall was full. High school graduation in Meadowridge was an important event since only a few graduates went on to college. This, then, was a special milestone in their lives, the point where they officially stepped into the responsibilities of adulthood. Family and friends had gathered to witness this transition.

As the day warmed outside, so did the interior. Palmetto fans made a rhythmic crackling sound as they were wafted to and fro.

After the singing of the school song, a prayer was offered by Reverend Brewster. Then a few congratulatory words to the graduates were made by Mayor Clinton. Finally, Mr. Henson, the Principal, got up and patting his perspiring bald forehead, first spoke directly to the graduates.

"Many of you may remember being called into my office at some time in the past four years for something or other. Be it a serious matter or less so, I would like to say whatever the reason, it was because I cared for each of you and was deeply interested in you individually. I wanted you to leave Meadowridge High with everything you needed to utilize in your lives thereafter.

"It has been a fine four years. As a class you have been a real asset to our school, and I wish you all well in whatever endeavors you undertake.

"So, on behalf of all the teachers and staff, to each and every Graduate, our best wishes and sincere hope that as you move into the Twentieth Century, you will take with you the highest ideals, the noblest purposes, the purest goals and will each make an individual contribution to the betterment of society, and the world."

Directing his remaining words to the rest of the audience he said, "We have only set them on their paths, equipped them with a sound education, tried to give them the foundations, exposed them to a faith that should strengthen them. We wish them all well on the journey on which they are about to embark, to develop their talents, fulfill their destinies."

The applause was generous and would have lasted longer if Mr. Henson had not held up his hands to halt it.

"Thank you all, but we want to give these young people their chance. First, I give you the Salutatorian of the Class of 1900, Mr. Daniel Brooks."

Dan stepped up to the podium, cleared his throat and began. His voice was husky and low. "Welcome, honored guests, families and friends. We, the Class of 1900, are all well aware of the significance of leaving high school in the dawning year of a new century."

Kit, knowing she had her own speech to give after Dan's, controlled her nervousness by making herself concentrate on every word he was saying. In spite of her intention, it was Dan himself who occupied her thoughts. She saw his body taut with tension leaning on the podium, his hands gripping the sides, and she whispered a little prayer to calm him. She admired the set of his head with its sandy thickness slicked down for this occasion, the profile that would one day be considered distinguished but was still painfully boyish—the nose a little too long, the chin a bit too prominent. But to Kit, Dan was very handsome, had always been.

He would be leaving at the end of the summer to start his medical training, and she, thanks to her scholarship, would be going to Merrivale Teachers College. When would they see each other again?

Unconsciously Kit's eyes moved over to Laurel's cameo-perfect profile, and felt ashamed of the prick of envy she felt for her friend. Laurel was so cherished by the Woodwards. Everything seemed to come to her so easily, especially love. She hardly seemed conscious of Dan's. But Laurel took it all for granted, as if everyone should love her and be loved in return, while for Kit—

Kit pulled herself back to the moment, heard Dan saying something about the "wide path full of opportunities that lies ahead for each of us," and realized that the path ahead of her would be a lonely one, one she must take by herself, with no one to depend on. If only there were someone like Dan to *care,* to hold her hand, to at least walk along beside her, Kit thought wistfully.

No self-pity, she warned herself. Actually, she was terribly lucky. A full four-year scholarship and Miss Cady so willing to help her—It was wrong to envy anyone, to wish things were different.

Hearing Dan's words, "In closing," Kit jerked herself back from her daydreams to listen to his finish.

"May I recite the immortal lines written by the great American poet Henry Wadsworth Longfellow, words it would be well worth our while to take as our talisman and to

inspire us as we start out in the great adventure of life."
Dan's voice deepened dramatically as he quoted: "Lives of
great men all remind us/ We can make our lives sublime/
And departing leave behind us/ Footprints in the sands of
time./Let us then be up and doing/ With a heart for any fate/
Still achieving, still pursuing/ Learn to labour and to wait."

Kit felt her throat swell with emotion. How could her own
speech equal Dan's flowing rhetoric, the high-sounding
phrases, the call to nobility? In comparison, hers seemed
ambitious and self-serving. But there was no chance now to
change it. Soon, the diplomas would be given out and she
would be called up to the podium to speak.

Cora raised her chin, looking over the heads of the people
seated in the row in front of her, and observed Kit with
pride.

If Kit don't look better'n any of them, she thought to herself with satisfaction. Don't care a bit that Jess ranted and
raved over my gettin' that dress for the girl. Was my egg
money anyhow, weren't it? I wasn't about to let that snippy
Miss Cady or the doctor's wife or that high and mighty Miz
Hale think we didn't do right by Kit. After all, it was us who
took her in, sent her to school all these years, except for this
last one. If it hadn't been for us, she might not have even got
to high school. Some of the Orphan Train kids placed out on
farms had to quit school after the Eighth Grade and work
full-time on the fields or in the house. That's what Jess
thought Kit oughta do. But I stood up to him. I knew Kit was
bright, brighter than most, and she oughta have her chance.

She's been a good girl all these years. Couldn't ask for anyone more willin' to lend a hand. She's taken a load off me,
that's fer shure. Come right down to it, I'd have been hard
put to keep things up if it waren't fer Kit's help. 'Specially
with my back and side givin' me fits so much of the time.

And Kit seemed to know when I was feelin' poorly. I never had to say a word. She'd just take over, push me into my room, and tell me to sit a spell. She put up over twenty quarts of berries, canned those peaches, and made applesauce this past fall all by herself. Of course, Seth turned to and give her a hand. Seth really liked Kit. Always did from when she first came. She's helped him with his schoolwork and he's bright, too. Wisht Jess'd see that, and let him keep on in school for a little time longer. But he won't. Not worth talkin' or thinkin' about. Another hand in the field is what Jess wants. If he buys another six acres, he'll need Seth then. Well, since this is probably the only high school Graduation I'll ever go to, I better stop my mind wandering and pay attention to what's goin' on. After all, Kit's going to make a speech.

Yes, I'm sure glad I got her that dress. She looks real fine. I 'spect Miz Woodward and Miz Hale are takin' note of it.

Moonlight streamed through the dimity curtains of Kit's bedroom, making pale squares on the floor. She sat at the window, taking her hairpins out one by one, letting her heavy hair drop over her shoulders. She drew her brush slowly through its silky length. Under her breath she softly hummed the melody of the music she had danced to with Dan.

Graduation had been splendid. Kit had floated all through the day on a kind of suspended cloud. Even having to wear the awful dress seemed unimportant in the overall loveliness of the day. And tonight, had been—practically perfect.

A sigh escaped as Kit allowed herself the luxury of remembering the magical evening. Her mind relived that moment when the band had stopped playing and she had found herself standing opposite Dan in the Paul Jones. To be honest, she had seen a slight expression of disappointment cross Dan's face when he saw Laurel standing next to Kit, only a step away from becoming his partner for the next set. Then he had smiled his warm, pleasant smile and held out his hand to Kit to lead her into the lilting rhythm of the music.

Kit knew all her secret dreams about Dan were foolish. He had never been interested in any other girl but Laurel. Much as she might want to see in Dan's eyes the spark that flared when his gaze was on Laurel, Kit knew it was a futile hope.

They were friends and that was all they would ever be. And Laurel was her friend, too. A dear friend, just as Toddy was. The three of them were bonded by all the things that had happened to them, what they had survived and what was known only to each other. She did not want to covet anything Laurel had. Even Dan's love.

A solitary tear rolled down Kit's face, and she brushed it away impatiently. This was not the night for tears. The summer ahead was going to be a busy one, a summer to work hard, prepare for the fall when she would be going away to Merrivale.

In spite of her longings, Kit knew it was not the right time for romantic fantasies. She had exciting ambitions, plans for the future she must strive to achieve. And then there was her long-held, cherished goal that somehow, some way, someday, she was going to find Jamie and Gwynny. There had always been that empty place in her heart for her little brother and sister.

Kit had no idea how she would go about it, where she would start, how she would trace them. But she knew she was going to, knew she must. It was a promise she had made to herself long ago, one she meant to keep.

13

Laurel was waiting outside the library when Kit got off work at four o'clock.

"Come over for a visit," Laurel begged, slipping her arm through Kit's. "I'm longing to talk to you. I've hardly seen you since Graduation and I have so much to discuss with you."

Kit hesitated slightly. The secret locked in her heart created a barrier between her and her friend, even though Laurel could not possibly know. It bothered Kit that she could not be as open with Laurel as she had always been before, and she longed for the old uncomplicated friendship they had always known.

"You can, can't you, Kit? There's no reason why not, is there?"

"No, I s'pose not," Kit replied, and Laurel gave her arm a little squeeze.

"Good! Papa Lee has taken Mother for a drive in the country so we'll have the whole house to ourselves. I have heaps to tell you."

Kit hoped it wasn't news about Dan. She dreaded hearing Laurel say that she and Dan had exchanged promises about the future. Kit wasn't sure how she could hear that and not betray her own feelings.

When they reached the Woodward house, Laurel stopped in the empty kitchen to fill two glasses with lemonade from a pitcher kept cool in the icebox on the back porch, then placed several thin molasses cookies from a jar on the counter, on a plate, and put everything on a tray for them to carry upstairs to her bedroom.

"Now, isn't this nice?" Laurel asked, smiling as they settled themselves on the window seat that circled the bay window overlooking the garden. "We'll have some privacy for a change."

Sipping the tangy lemonade, Kit's eyes circled the room thoughtfully. The late afternoon sun touched the maple wood bureau and the high spool bed with a golden polish, gave an added luster to the rosy-glass globe of the lamp on the desk, brightened the color of the climbing roses on the trellised wallpaper.

"Oh, Kit, I've been absolutely dying to confide in someone! I think I will burst if I don't tell!" Laurel exclaimed breathlessly. Her eyes were shining, and Kit's heart sank. Surely Laurel was planning to tell her she was in love with Dan! Unconsciously, Kit drew back as if to shield herself from a coming blow.

"And I knew it had to be *you*, Kit. Because, well, actually you're sort of responsible for it."

"Me? How? What am I responsible for?" gasped Kit.

"My decision." Laurel leaned closer. "Kit, I've decided to go away from Meadowridge to study voice! Mr. Fordyce approves, I mean, he told me if I were to go on, that is develop my singing so that I could, perhaps, well, I'm not sure exactly what I will do with it—but he said, I must go to a Conservatory for further training."

Kit's surprise rendered her speechless.

"Yes, I know what you're thinking!" Laurel rushed on. "But wait until I tell you *where* I plan to go! To Boston!

There's a famous Music Conservatory there, and besides, remember *Greystone* is in Massachusetts." Laurel lowered her voice conspiratorially. "I plan to go there, look up my records and then—Kit, I am going to try to find my mother's family!"

With that, Laurel sat back and waited for Kit's reaction. When it did not come immediately, she demanded, "So, what do you think of *that?*"

Kit's clear, gray eyes under the dark, level brows regarded her with unflinching honesty. "I'm wondering what the *Woodwards* think of it," she replied.

A momentary shadow crossed Laurel's face. "Oh, they don't know yet. I haven't told them."

Again Kit's glance traveled the perfectly appointed room—the flowered carpet, the bookcase stocked with all the classics, the ceiling-high armoire stuffed with Laurel's lovely clothes. Laurel was so cherished by the Woodwards. They had made life easy for her, their love evident in every detail of this room planned for her comfort and enjoyment.

As the silence lengthened between them, Laurel said quickly, "Oh, but I'm going to, of course. I intend to. I'm just waiting for the right time."

Instinctively Kit's eyebrows lifted. Would there ever be a right time for Laurel to tell the Woodwards she was leaving? Leaving all this they had provided for her?

"You haven't said what you think, Kit. Don't you see I'm only doing what you urged us all to do in your Valedictory speech?"

Kit took a deep breath. My *speech?* The words she had written and memorized and spoken only a few short weeks ago repeated themselves now in her mind.

"We are all individuals, let us not be poor imitations of anyone, no matter how much we admire them. Let us light our own torches, carry our own standards, fly our own flags.

No one has ever said it better than Shakespeare in *Hamlet,* 'This above all, to thine own self be true, And it must follow, as the night the day, Thou canst not then be false to any man.'"

Laurel's voice brought her back to the moment.

"So you see, Kit. I'm being true to myself—the real self, the one before Greystone or Meadowridge or the Woodwards. I have a family, a history that belongs to *me* and I've got to find it, don't you understand?"

"But, Laurel, you have everything *here!*" protested Kit softly, comparing Laurel's situation to the one she had had all these years with the Hansens. It had only been a matter of chance—two little orphan girls coming to the same town, two families. Laurel had gone to the Woodwards, Kit to the Hansens—Kit threw out both hands in an encompassing gesture, looking about her in puzzled amazement. "How can you leave all this? People who love and care about you, this—?"

"*You're* going away!" Laurel accused. "You're being true to yourself, aren't you?"

"But that's not the same. I'm not leaving anything like this, Laurel. I'm hoping to find something better. Could anything be better than all this?"

"Don't you *really* understand, Kit?" Laurel asked again. "Don't you *really know?* Nothing ever makes up for being an orphan."

Just then they heard the sound of carriage wheels below, and glancing out the window, they saw Dr. Woodward's buggy turn into the driveway. In another minute Mrs. Woodward was calling up the stairs.

"Laurel, darling, are you up there? We're home!"

Kit left soon after in spite of Ava Woodward's gracious invitation to stay for supper. As she walked over to Miss Cady's cottage, Kit's mind was filled with what Laurel had confided in her.

The strangest thing of all was that Laurel had never even mentioned Dan. Did he know her plans? Or would he, too, be told when the "time was right"? Did that mean Laurel did not have any serious feelings for him? Kit was sure Dan loved Laurel. She had seen it in his eyes every time he looked at her. Kit's heart ached for him if Laurel did not return his love. Kit knew too well that kind of pain.

Poor Dr. and Mrs. Woodward. They would be lost without Laurel, who was the center of their lives. But, in a way, Kit *did* understand Laurel's need to leave. There had been times when she had felt the cloying, claustrophobic atmosphere with which the Woodwards surrounded Laurel. With all the best intentions, they had, perhaps, kept Laurel too sheltered, kept her on too tight a string pulled by two kind, but overly protective people.

It was a crippling kind of love. Like a bird whose wings had been clipped to keep it safely within the bounds of an enclosed aviary.

Kit was torn between sympathy for the Woodwards, who would be devastated when they learned of Laurel's plans, and admiration for Laurel, ready to give up all she had to strike out on her own.

Underneath, Kit concluded, all three of them—the Orphan Train trio—were the same. They were all somehow incomplete. There was an emptiness in each of them they longed to fill, even if it was just *knowing* the truth of why they had come to be at Greystone and then put on the Orphan Train, and "placed out." It didn't seem to matter *where* that had been. Just like Laurel had said, "Nothing ever makes up for being an orphan."

14

Kit was packing her trunk. Tomorrow she would be leaving for Merrivale Teachers College. She still almost had to pinch herself to believe it, even though she had received her registration forms, been given her dormitory room assignment as well as the name of her roommate. A Maude Lytle from Myrtle Creek.

She hummed as she laid the five neatly ironed shirtwaists on the top layer of the trunk—two plain white, one blue chambray with white collars and cuffs, a dark blue and green plaid one. She had three skirts—a gray wool, a brown and gold plaid, a black one for Sundays. Miss Cady had given her a lovely, soft knitted coat sweater and matching tam. Mrs. Woodward had gifted her with an elegant teal blue jacket and skirt for very best. She had a half-dozen chemises, camisoles, petticoats as well, stockings and two pairs of shoes—sturdy boots for every day, and high-buttoned black ones with a nice heel for Sundays and any other dress-up occasions there might be.

The school brochure, now worn on the edges from repeated readings, stated: "Merrivale students have many opportunities to attend concerts, plays and other cultural events."

Kit gave a rapturous sigh and twirled around her bedroom a couple of times. As Miss Cady kept saying, it would be a "glorious adventure," as she recalled her own college days.

For the dozenth time Kit checked her train ticket, her purse in which the hard-earned money from her summer job was safely stowed. How could she possibly live through the next few days until she was actually on her way?

The sound of insistent knocking on the front door interrupted Kit's happy occupation and she started down the hall to the front door to answer it. But Miss Cady must have heard it first because she heard her say, "Why, Lonny Hansen, what on earth brings you all the way into town this late in the evening?"

"'Evenin', Miss Cady. Is Kit here?"

"Yes, she is, but what do you want with her?"

"Please, miss, I got to speak to her—"

By this time Kit was standing in the hall behind Miss Cady. Lonny's face looked ghastly pale, the freckles standing out in sharp relief against the unusual pallor of his skin.

"What is it, Lonny?" Kit asked, something in the back of her brain flashing a warning signal.

"Ma's ben took bad, Kit. Doc Woodward's out there now. My pa wants to know if you'll come?"

"What happened, an accident?" Kit asked with stiff lips.

"Some kind of spell. Pa and me found her when we come in from the field. Laid out on the kitchen floor, she were. Eyes all rolled back, hardly breathin', all stiff-like. Pa sent Caspar for the doctor. Then he and me carried her into bed. Her face is all twisted, she can't talk. I dunno, Kit. But can you come?"

Miss Cady turned to Kit. "But of course, you can't go out there now. You're leaving tomorrow! Surely Dr. Woodward can get a district nurse to help out—"

"Kit, I've got the wagon out front," Lonny said, his voice squeaky. "Pa said to ask you to hurry—"

"Lonny, you'll have to tell your father to get someone else. One of the women on the neighboring farm. Surely he can't expect Kit—"

"No, Miss Cady, I have to go," Kit's voice rang out, interrupting her. To Lonny she spoke calmly. "I'll come, Lonny. Just a few minutes till I get some things."

"I'll wait in the wagon. But hurry, Kit, Ma's...well, she's awful sick."

Kit turned and ran back to her bedroom, pulled out her old, battered suitcase from under the bed, and started throwing a few things into it—her hairbrush, nightgown and wrapper.

"Kit, you can't do this. You can't go!" Miss Cady's voice spoke sharply. She had followed Kit and now stood in the doorway.

"Don't you see I have to go?" Kit pleaded. "There is nothing else I *can* do. Cora's done so much for me—"

"Done so much?" Miss Cady's voice rose, her face contorting angrily. "What have they done? Allowed you to do all the menial chores, let you sleep in their attic, be their unpaid slavey all these years? Come to your senses, Kit. You don't owe the Hansens a thing. Or if you ever did, it's been paid a hundred times over."

Kit pressed her lips together but didn't answer.

"Kit, are you listening? Do you hear what I'm saying?"

"Yes, Miss Cady, I do," she replied, folding her blouse and putting it in the suitcase. She shook her head. "I do, but I have to go. You heard what Lonny said, how desperate he looked—"

"Then let that old skinflint, Jess Hansen, pay somebody to come and nurse his wife. It's not up to *you, Kit!* You're on the brink of a whole new wonderful life. You *can't* give that up. If you don't take it, they'll give the scholarship to someone else and who knows if you can get another one."

Kit hung her head, tears gathered stingingly in her eyes. Why couldn't Miss Cady help her? Didn't she see how hard this was? Her hands shook as she closed the lid of her suitcase and snapped the latches.

"I have to go now, Miss Cady. Lonny's waiting."

Miss Cady felt the blood surge into her head, her temples throbbed and her throat hurt as she rasped out the words, "I can't believe you're throwing away everything you worked so hard for. Everything *I* worked to help you achieve! Who knows how long Cora Hansen will live? She may go like that." She snapped her fingers. "Or she might linger for weeks, months, even years! And you'll be trapped. It's not your responsibility, Kit."

But Kit was already at the door, her hand on the knob.

"I'm sorry, Miss Cady, sorry to disappoint you, but I have to go."

Miss Cady lost control then.

"How can you do this? How can you be so unappreciative, after all I've done to bring you this far? I've devoted years to you because I thought you were worth it, and now you're giving it all up!"

Kit's back was to her, but Miss Cady saw the slender shoulders stiffen. Then she opened the door and went out.

For a stunned moment Miss Cady watched the slim straight figure go down the cottage steps out to the waiting wagon. Then she heard herself scream.

"Kit, you'll be sorry! You'll never have another chance like this!"

Kit was climbing up into the wagon. As Miss Cady's voice reached her, she stared straight ahead, willing herself not to give way entirely to the despair and sadness churning within. Lonny clicked the reins and they started forward.

Millicent ran out onto the porch clutching onto one of the posts.

"Ungrateful girl! I taught you everything you know!" she yelled hoarsely after the departing wagon. Then she slumped against the post and began to sob. No, that wasn't true, she admitted to herself. She hadn't taught Kit *everything* she knew. No one could have taught the girl that kind of loyalty and self-sacrifice.

15

Sitting by Cora's bed, Kit could see out the window. October sunshine spilled over the golden fields, now shorn of their harvest, and the maples along the road, turning red and yellow, edged the meadow with brilliant color. Apple trees in the orchard, heavy with crimson fruit ready to be picked, scented the autumn air with a rich winey scent.

The beauty of the Indian summer day filled Kit with a restless yearning to be out under the cloudless blue sky. Unconsciously she sighed, turning to look at the still figure on the bed.

Cora's face was drawn, cheeks sunken, eyelids closed. Her graying hair in plaits lay on the pillow, the once-busy hands inert on the coverlet.

In all the time Kit had known Cora, she had never seen her like this. All her memories of Cora were of constant movement. Pictures of Cora's thin, nervous figure flickered through Kit's mind—bustling at the stove, wielding a broom, bending over the scrubboard, scattering feed to the chickens in the yard, hoeing in the vegetable garden, stretching, reaching, lifting—always working, always in motion.

Now she lay there hour after hour, day after day, barely moving.

"The whole right side is affected," Dr. Woodward had told them that first night when Kit arrived at the farm with

Lonny. "The paralysis may only be temporary. Her speech is impaired, but this, too, may eventually come back. I can't tell how much damage has been done to her brain. We'll just have to wait and see."

Jess's face had looked almost as blank and stiff as Cora's while Dr. Woodward spoke. Kit wasn't even sure he was absorbing what Dr. Woodward was saying. He seemed in a state of shock.

Of course that was understandable. In twenty years Cora had never seemed to have a sick day. She was up and doing within a few days of each of her children's births. Until Kit had come, she had done all the work without any help. Kit felt the seriousness of Cora's illness and the effect it would have on her family had not yet begun to penetrate.

"She'll need to be turned, moved at least three times a day, her limbs gently moved and massaged so the muscles don't atrophy before she gets some flexibility back," Dr. Woodward directed Kit, as if he took for granted that she would be caring for Cora.

That seemed to be what everyone expected. After the first few days, when Cora passed the critical stage and Dr. Woodward said she was out of danger, the Hansen household fell into a routine with Kit managing.

At first, Dr. Woodward had come every day. Then he told Kit that would no longer be necessary. "Now, it is just a matter of time to see if she will recover fully or partially. She may remain like this for a few weeks or a few months or forever." He shook his head. "You simply can't tell with strokes."

Kit had felt her heart sink at this pronouncement.

She had walked with him to the door. Suddenly as if he had just remembered, he turned to her with a frown.

"Weren't you supposed to be off to school, young lady?"

Kit felt herself flinch and she looked away from those kind, concerned eyes.

"Yes, sir, I was, but of course, when Cora was taken sick—"
She let her words fade away, speaking for themselves.

"But you had some sort of a scholarship, didn't you?" he
persisted.

Kit nodded, feeling the ache in her throat with the effort
not to cry at this reminder of what she had given up.

Dr. Woodward stood there for a moment, his face grim,
then shook his head and shifted his medical bag from one
hand to the other.

"Couldn't Jess have gotten someone else in to help?"

"I don't know. I don't think so. I didn't even think—"

Dr. Woodward gave his head another shake.

"What a shame, what a—" He stopped as if wanting to say
something stronger. Then he patted Kit's shoulder. "You're a
good girl, Kit. A fine, courageous young woman."

Kit saw a mixture of sympathy and admiration in his
expression, then he went out the door, down the porch steps,
got into his buggy and drove down the road, accompanied by
curls of dust.

She stood there watching until his buggy became a small
black miniature, moving through the farm gate and along
the road back to town. Dr. Woodward's questions had
brought back all the longing for freedom, the hope she had
known at the prospect of college. For a moment a sharp wave
of regret and despair made her weak, and she clutched the
porch post for support.

But it lasted only a moment. "Never debate in the darkness a decision made in the light." From somewhere within
Kit, those words sprang to mind. They rang in her inner ear
as distinctly as a bell. Echoing within her a turning point
was reached. She would never look back, she promised herself. The fact was that she had sacrificed her own chance for
happiness for a greater, more urgent need. At the time she
had made it, she had acted out of a clear call. And she had
not wavered in her resolution. Nor would she do so now.

As this realization took hold, Kit felt a conscious sensation that she had moved to a higher realm. From out of the past came the teaching in a long ago Sunday school class: "Obey and the blessing follows."

She had to trust that was true. She would wait patiently for the time of the blessing. It didn't matter if anyone else knew or understood. Kit believed if she "trusted in the Lord, He would bring it to pass."

The woman on the bed moaned slightly and Kit rose quickly, bent over her. Cora's lips were parched, and Kit poured water into a tumbler, then dipped a small folded linen cloth into it and held it to Cora's mouth.

Her heart constricted with pity as she looked down at her. It was so sad to see her like this. Kit slipped her arm under Cora's bony shoulders and raised her a little so that she could turn the pillow over to its cooler side. Then she smoothed the sheets again.

Only little more than six weeks ago, Cora had been a healthy, vigorous woman. Kit remembered coming out to help cook for the crew Jess had hired during the haying.

Together they had worked from dawn, hauling buckets of water from the well into the house, carrying in armload after armload of firewood for the stove. They had caught chickens, and Kit, her eyes closed, wincing with every stroke, had held them squawking on the block while Cora chopped off the heads. They had scalded and plucked them, then cut them up into pieces and dropped them on the sizzling cast-iron skillet to fry to a crisp golden-brown. Vegetables had to be gathered fresh and boiled or fried, dough mixed for biscuits, cornbread stirred and pans shoved into the oven. All the time the day was heating up, they continued to cook and bake. Desserts were prepared to take the place of the bread baking in the oven—berry cobbler, gingerbread, peach streudel. Men came in from the fields at noon, sweating and hungry, swilling down gallons of lemonade and cold tea. Kit could recall slumping, limp and ragged into kitchen chairs afterwards for a brief rest, themselves too tired to eat, with only this short break until it was time to start over again getting things ready for supper.

A farm wife's work was never done. It was also thankless. Kit found little satisfaction in all the time, energy, and effort that went into food preparation only to be gobbled down by unthinking men whose only goal was filling their stomachs.

That's why she was so grateful to Miss Cady. Miss Cady had shown her a way out of what might have been an inevitable path for Kit, at the Hansens or as a "hired girl" at some other farm. She had awakened a life of the mind and spirit in Kit that could lift her out of this kind of drudgery, open up a whole new world.

Kit felt a twinge of doubt. Would she ever have another chance? Would Miss Cady ever forgive her?

Kit always experienced a heaviness of heart when she thought of Miss Cady. The loss of this cherished relationship pressed down upon her like a physical weight. She had not seen her former teacher since that awful night she had left the cottage under a barrage of recrimination. Kit had not been able to leave Cora, even on Sunday to go into church, where she might have run into her.

Kit sighed heavily. Miss Cady had no understanding of Kit's sense of obligation to Cora, which, in its way, was nearly as binding as what she felt for Miss Cady. The two had never liked each other, and Kit had always been caught in the trap of divided loyalty. Cora had resented Millicent Cady for all kinds of unnameable reasons, and Miss Cady had deplored Cora's lack of encouragement of Kit's potential. And she actively disliked Jess.

Of course, Miss Cady had been right about Jess. Not by a single word nor gesture had he shown Kit he appreciated her coming. Only a few days after her arrival, she had come down into the kitchen to make some herb tea, hoping to get Cora to sip some much-needed liquid. She had found Jess sitting at his usual place at the table, holding knife and fork in both fists, glowering fiercely.

"When's supper?" he had roared.

Kit had stopped short, the old trepidation of the man's temper gripping her. Then a cold calm overtook her and she faced him unblinkingly.

"I didn't come here to be your hired help, Jess," she said, purposely using his first name. "I am here to look after Cora. She is my priority and my *only* duty," she said firmly, adding, "I suggest if you and the boys want to eat, you either fix it yourselves, or hire a cook."

With that, she had turned around and busied herself filling the kettle from the kitchen pump. She had not waited to see his reaction. She could only imagine the wrath that must have twisted his expression, the color that might have rushed into his mottled face. In spite of some inner trembling, Kit had gone about her task, and when she left the kitchen to go back upstairs, Jess had gone outside.

Not too much later Kit had heard the rattle of pots and pans and raised voices from the kitchen and assumed the Hansen menfolk were muddling their way through supper.

Not long afterward, Dulcie Meekins had been hired to cook. Kit had won her second battle over her fear of Jess Hansen.

Just then the bedroom door squeaked slightly as it was pushed ajar. Around the corner peered the head and curious face of the tiger-striped tabby, Ginger. She put one cautious foot inside, glanced around warily, then seeing Kit, scooted across the room and made a flying leap into her lap. She curled around twice and settled down, meowing contentedly. Kit rubbed the back of the cat's neck, fondled the satiny ears.

The cat's appearance reminded Kit of the first time she had confronted Jess and the outcome. She smiled, remembering how this cat had come to be so comfortably "at home" in the Hansens' house.

The barn cat had a litter of five kittens and Jess had come in the house one day remarking offhandedly "Well, that cat's gettin' pretty old. Reckon this'll be the last litter she'll have. I'll keep one out of the bunch and drown the rest."

Kit nearly dropped the dish she was drying.

"Oh, no, you can't!" she had cried in distress.

Jess turned astonished eyes upon her, dumbfounded that she was opposing something he'd said.

Kit had gone down to the barn a couple of times to view the kittens and found them adorable. The thought that anyone would do anything to them as cruel as Jess proposed was unbearable.

"We don't need more'n one cat," he said, glowering at Kit.

Kit glanced over at Cora for help, but Cora was busy scouring a pot and did not meet her pleading look. Kit screwed up her courage. She was afraid of Jess. She had seen his anger, seen even the agile Caspar and Lonny duck from the back side of his swift hand on more than one occasion, seen them tearfully emerge from the woodshed after an application of his discipline.

But thinking of those dear little furry creatures being tied in a burlap sack weighted with rocks and thrown in the river was too much for Kit's tender heart. Quickly she prayed for inspiration and got it.

"Oh, please, wait! Let me see if I can find homes for them first, before you do anything," she begged. *"Please!"*

To Kit's surprise, Cora broke in. "There ain't no real hurry, is there? Why not let Kit try?"

"We'd have to wait 'til they're weaned if I do that," Jess objected.

"Well, a week or ten days ain't goin' to matter that much, is it?" asked Cora, trying to sound indifferent.

Jess jammed his hands in his overall pockets, made a grunting sound and started back outside mumbling, "Lotta durned foolishness."

"Oh, thank you!" Kit sighed as she let out a long breath. She might even have hugged Cora except that just then, Cora turned to her, frowning.

"You better do like you said, Kit. I don't fancy buckin' Jess when he's set his mind to do somethin'."

Kit nodded happily. She already knew who she was going to suggest to give the kittens a home.

As it turned out the smallest of the litter died and, of the four that were left, Helene and Toddy each wanted one and Laurel, of course, had to have one, too. That left the fourth, the biggest and strongest, at the Hansens.

Before she had put the three others in a basket to deliver them, Kit named them Wynken, Blynken and Nod from a nursery rhyme she had read to Gwynny at bedtime.

The tawny tiger kitten that was left, she named Ginger, and he became Kit's special pet. Unknown to Jess, she carried him up to her loft bedroom every night where he slept, curled up at the foot of her bed.

Smiling at the memory of the episode years ago, Kit realized that was when she and Cora had become allies. After that, there was an unspoken bond between them that remained to this day.

No matter what, Kit would not forsake Cora in her time of need. No matter that Jess was still his surly self and did not deserve her sacrifice. No matter that Miss Cady was angry and had irrevocably abandoned Kit. In her heart Kit knew she had done the right thing—the *only* thing.

16

Kit unlocked the door and stepped into the cottage. She took a few tentative steps down the hall and paused for a minute. From where she stood, she could see into the little parlor and on the other side the dining alcove and just beyond that, the tiny kitchen. Suddenly she realized she was holding her breath, and slowly let it out in a long, contented sigh.

Sometimes dreams *do* come true, she thought. Sometimes prayers *are* answered!

Here she was in the cottage where she had dreamed so many dreams, prayed so many prayers. It had been a long time coming, but everything she had ever hoped for was finally happening.

A place of her own, a job, and for the first time a chance to chart her own future.

Setting down her small suitcase, Kit went out into the kitchen. She took some paper from the stack of newspapers by the stove, crumpled it with a few sticks of kindling from the woodbox, opened the stove door and laid a fire. Striking a long match to it, she had a brisk fire going within minutes. Then, pumping water from the pump near the cast-iron sink, she poured it into the kettle and placed it on the stove. While waiting for the water to boil, Kit looked around her with pleasure.

She moved around slowly, stopping to touch a chair back, smoothing her hand on top of the table, picking up a vase, holding it in her hands for a moment, then putting it down. Everything had happened so fast it was hard to believe.

It had been nearly two years since Cora's stroke, and Kit had gone back to the Hansens to care for her. Her recovery had been slow at first, but little by little Cora had regained the use of her legs; later, she had achieved a halting mobility. Her speech was still garbled but it, too, seemed to be coming back. Dr. Woodward credited this amazing recuperation to Cora's basically strong constitution and to Kit's conscientious nursing. Kit had massaged Cora's limbs, exercised them daily, urged her to push herself, to struggle, not to give in to frustration, to fight to recover her strength and health. This attention had saved Cora from the depression into which so many stroke victims fall by being consistently cheerful and optimistic. Gradually, Kit had helped her to sit up, stand and take those first agonizing steps, holding onto a chair for support and pushing it ahead of her.

Success had been hard-won but, against all odds, Cora was improving.

At the same time, Lonny, the oldest of the Hansen boys, declared he was going to marry Alverna Colby, the daughter of a neighboring farmer. He had been courting Alverna for some time. She was the oldest of eight and capable of taking over at the Hansens without the slightest trouble. Her younger sister would come to give Cora the help she needed in dressing and walking until her recovery was complete.

When Kit realized she was no longer needed and could leave without feeling she was shirking her duty, she felt a sense of unbounded freedom. Almost simultaneously, she heard through Miss Smedley at the library, about the job at the newspaper, the *Meadowridge Monitor* and, armed with references from Mr. Henson and Miss Clemmens, the English teacher, Kit had applied for the position as General Reporter.

The kettle began to whistle, and Kit, knowing just where it was, got down the small, round, brown pottery teapot, found the canister of loose tea, measured it into the pot, then poured in the boiling water, replacing the lid to let it steep. Just the way Miss Cady had taught her, she thought, smiling ruefully.

This was another stroke of luck, a completely unexpected one. The very same day she got the job, she had seen the FOR RENT, FURNISHED sign on the white picket fence in front of the little shingled cottage where she had lived her last year of high school. Miss Cady's cottage.

Millicent Cady had announced to the School Board that she had accepted another teaching position for the next year and would be leaving Meadowridge at the end of the term in June. Now, in August, the little house was vacant and ready for another tenant.

Waiting for *me!* Kit thought to herself.

Her tea ready, she filled a pink and white china cup then sat down at the table, staring out into the garden behind the house.

Who would ever have dreamed things would turn out like this? I must write it all down for Jamie and Gwynny was her next thought.

Writing letters to the little lost brother and sister was something Kit had continued to do all these years.

It had become more a private journal for Kit in which she poured all her private thoughts, feelings, the events and happenings of her life. She had almost discarded the childish hope that they would ever read these "letters" or that she would ever find the children. But writing them gave Kit an anchor in a life that seemed to have lost its moorings.

She finished her tea, rinsed out her cup and placed it on the wooden drainboard, then walked through the cottage again. At the end of the hall she hesitated, wondering which bedroom she should use. The larger one had been Miss Cady's, Kit's the smaller one. But the window in that one looked out back where the apple tree was, where birds nested and where in the spring, the wonderful lilac bushes bloomed in a profusion of pale lavender spears. Without another thought, Kit took her belongings into her old room and began unpacking.

One of the first things she did was to take out the picture she had won as a prize in Sunday school long ago, now framed, and hung it over her bed.

Within weeks Kit was settled in the cottage as though it had always been her own, as much as the cubbyhole at the *Monitor* soon became designated as her "office." She walked the few blocks to the paper every morning, got her assignments for that day. Then, feeling every bit the professional, she went on her rounds, gathering the news items that she would later transfer from her notes into readable material. Afterwards she took it to Mr. Clooney to edit. This process could take a scant twenty minutes, or the piece could remain on his desk for an hour while Kit anxiously awaited his verdict. She would watch him from her vantage point as he read it over. When he laid it aside, it was a signal for her to retrieve it and take the heavily blue-penciled copy back to the composing room for Mac, the printer, to set.

Kit looked forward to each day. She had never felt so alive, so fulfilled, so happy. She loved everything about working at the newspaper. The smell of paper, ink, the sound of the big press on Thursdays when the weekly was "put to bed." When it was printed, she enjoyed opening the fresh new issue, seeing the words she had written in crisp, black print on the crackly white paper.

Granted that, from the beginning, Kit's actual reporting consisted mainly of picking up ad copy from the various Meadowridge stores and businesses and bringing them in for Mr. Clooney to rewrite or lay out for printing. But eventually, with little comment and less direction, he would tell Kit, "Better cover the Town Council meeting tonight," or "Interview Captain Higgins, the Fire Chief, about the possible causes of the barn fire out at the Stratton farm."

As time went on, there were less penciled changes and scratch-throughs on her copy, more grunts and nods as he handed back her copy with a jerk of his thumb, indicating she could deliver it to the back room.

The longer Kit worked at the *Monitor*, the harder it was for her to remember how nervous she had been when applying for the job. Her voice had cracked a little when she asked if the job for a reporter had been filled. Miss Jessica Hadley, who took the classified ads at the high counter at the front, had looked at her with curiously skeptical eyes over her Ben Franklin glasses. Pointing with a pencil she had taken out from behind her ear toward a man with a green eyeshade hunched over a cluttered desk in the corner near the large window that overlooked Main Street she had replied indifferently, "There's Mr. Clooney, the editor. You'll have to see him."

"Never had a woman reporter," Ed Clooney had growled, looking over her letters of recommendation.

Kit had held her breath, hands pressed tightly together, praying that precedent wasn't a prejudice. After all, this was 1902. Women all over the country were working at jobs once held only by men. Besides, Kit had not seen any other applicants lining up outside the *Monitor* building that morning.

At length, he had handed her back the folder with her credentials, saying, "Well, we can give it a try. When can you start?"

And that is how Kit had been hired.

Those first few weeks had been a combination of trepidation and trials. From the noncommunicative editor, the dubious Miss Hadley, the grouchy printer, the prankish Joe, who was a "jack-of-all-trades" and general flunky, no one at the paper seemed overjoyed or enthusiastic about the new employee. For the most part, Kit might as well have been invisible as she came and went, trying hard to do what she thought was expected of a reporter, but with no real guidelines.

Over the months all of them—Mr. Clooney and Miss Hadley, Mac and Joe—had become her friends; more than friends actually. Kit felt she had learned so much from them, not only about newspapers, but what it meant to work as a team, each contributing a part of a combined, worthwhile effort. Miss Hadley seemed to keep the whole operation going. On the day they went to press, she brought a hamper of food as they worked around the clock to get the weekly edition out. She catered to Mr. Clooney's curmudgeon personality, cajoled Mac, the printer, who was inclined to be testy and temperamental; she both bullied and babied young Joe, the printer's "devil," and reassured and commiserated with Kit on the vagaries of getting a newspaper out and maintaining one's sanity week after week.

By the time Kit had worked at the *Monitor* a year she almost felt she had always been there. That was both comforting and a little frightening. Did she want to become a fixture there like Jessica?

Kit wrote in her letter-journal:

> It is fall now in Meadowridge, in some ways the prettiest time of the year here, I think. I love to walk through the fallen leaves along Main Street as I go to

work in the morning, hearing them crunch under my feet, breathe in the crisp winey scent of autumn in the air, the woodsmoke mixed with the sweetness of the newly mown hay drifting in from the fields of farms close to town. Even the sunsets, when I'm coming home late in the October afternoons, seem more brilliant somehow.

Sometimes, all this gives me a peaceful feeling inside and, when I come up the path and into this little house, a sense of belonging. But in a deeper sense I feel restless, a kind of melancholy longing that I can't quite define. It's like hearing a train whistle at night as I lie in bed, and wondering where that train is going and whether I should be on it going—where, I don't know— somewhere where I can find what I'm looking for.

The week of Thanksgiving Kit helped put out the *Monitor* a day early so they could take Thursday off. In the morning she attended the service held at the Meadowridge Community Church. She had so much to be thankful for this year, more than any other year of her life. In all the years she had lived with the Hansens, they had never celebrated anything. But the Colby family had always seemed to be a cheerful, good-natured one. So she hoped young Alverna Colby, now Mrs. Lonny Hansen, would bring some of these ways to her new home.

Coming into the church, Kit took a seat at the end of one of the pews. She returned the nods and smiles of people who recognized her. Most everyone knew her now as "that nice young woman from the newspaper." She was always interested and helpful about getting the Sewing Circle special events in the paper the week before their meeting day, or giving plenty of publicity to the Church Ladies United Christmas Bazaar, as well as spelling all the relatives' names correctly in any writeup of weddings or family reunions on the Social Page. And she could be counted on to write a "lovely obituary" when called upon to do so.

For Kit, it was a good feeling to have found a "place" at last in this town where she had felt an "outsider" for so many years. Then why, more and more, did a vague sense of longing for something else disturb her contentment?

When the organ began playing the opening chords of the first posted hymn, Kit picked up the hymnal and rose with the rest of the congregation to sing, "We gather together to ask the Lord's blessing."

Kit's voice rang out in heartfelt gratitude. The Lord had blessed her with so much, more than she had ever dreamed of, hoped for.

As she sang she became conscious of a sensation of lightness, not only within her, but all around her as though an intense light permeated her body, making her tinglingly aware of everything—the November sunshine slanting through the church windows onto the golden sheaves of wheat along with colorful pumpkins, gourds and Indian corn decoratively arranged in front of the altar rail.

> Come, ye thankful people, come,
> Raise the song of harvest home:
> All is safely gathered in,
> Ere the winter storms begin—

At the close of the hymn, the congregation was seated, settling to hear what their new minister would say. Since the Reverend Brewster's retirement, young Calvin Dinsmore had taken his place in the Meadowridge pulpit. Though the good reverend had recommended him, the Elders had interviewed several other hopefuls, but in the end decided in favor of the man their trusted pastor had suggested. He was still proving himself to the "wait and see" congregation.

"Today is a day we come together with grateful hearts to thank Our Gracious Creator most of all for revealing to us His Son, Jesus Christ. Then we give thanks for His gifts of home, family, friends and bountiful harvest, for the beautiful area in which we live, for minds to think, hearts to love, hands to serve, strength to work, leisure to rest and enjoy. For faithfulness in illness and adversity as well as in prosperity and health.

"On this special day set apart as witness to our gratitude, we acknowledge our dependence on God for all His tender mercies, our thanks for His love, His truth, His forgiveness. Amen."

Seemingly, this brief sermon of a few well-chosen words met with everyone's hearty approval as did his choice of the traditional closing hymn, "Now Thank We All Our God," as at the end of the service, people turned to greet each other with smiles and wishes for the holiday. It was then Kit felt a touch on her shoulder. She turned to see Dan Brooks.

"Dan! What a surprise!" she exclaimed. "What are you doing here?"

He smiled. "I'm spending Thanksgiving with my grandmother and aunts, but, actually I'm on my way to San Francisco."

"San Francisco?"

"Yes, I've been accepted as an intern at a hospital there. I start next week. But it's given me a chance to stop in Meadowridge en route." He paused, looked at her intently. "It's good to see you, Kit. Could we have a cup of coffee somewhere? I'd like to talk. We could go to the coffee shop at Meadowridge Inn, that is, unless you have plans, have to be somewhere?"

"No. I mean, no plans! I'd love to go," Kit said, a warm feeling of pleasure spreading through her.

They left the churchyard and Dan matched his long stride to Kit's. It was a clear, cold, windless day and the fallen leaves that cluttered the sidewalk crunched underfoot as they started for Front Street and the Meadowridge Inn.

"It's so great to see you, Kit," Dan said, smiling down at her. "I wasn't sure any of the old crowd would be around. I felt sort of like a stranger myself when I walked into church this morning. Then, I saw you and somehow I felt—well, not so much—"

"'Among the alien corn'?" Kit suggested, laughing.

"Well, I guess you could say something like that, although I never was as good at quotations as you. So, are you still writing, Kit, poetry and that sort of thing?"

"Not so much poetry any more, but—" she paused then asked, "You know, don't you, that I work for the *Monitor?* And, of course, that means writing, lots of it, every day."

"I guess that's good discipline for a writer. You do still want to be a writer, don't you, Kit?"

"Dan, I *am* a writer! That's what I *do! And* I get paid for it! Every week." She laughed.

"What I meant was—"

"I know what you meant," Kit assured him. "But I really don't know how to answer your question. My job takes up so much of my time, I don't have much left over for the kind of writing I used to do in high school—essays, poetry."

"You were good, Kit, very good. I remember Miss Cady telling us back in grammar school that you were the only one with *real* talent."

The mention of Miss Cady gave Kit's heart a sad little wrench. The rift between them over her going back to the Hansens instead of using her scholarship had never been bridged. Remembering their last painful scene made Kit search for a quick change of subject.

"Well, tell me about *you,* Dan. I think it's very exciting about you going to San Francisco, California. Is it a big hospital?"

"Yes, but the important thing is that it's connected with the University Medical School where they're doing some great research, testing new kinds of treatments."

By this time they had reached the Inn and Dan put his hand on Kit's elbow as they mounted the steps. The Meadowridge Inn had once been a stagecoach stop and had been restored with several new additions over the last several years. The exterior of the rambling clapboard building had a certain rustic charm, but inside it had been refurbished to resemble a fine, modern hotel.

Off the lobby was the restaurant annex where breakfast and lunch were served in a more informal atmosphere than the adjoining elegant dining room provided. They were shown to a table in a sunny corner where they could see out to the town park. A waitress in a crisp blue uniform and ruffled apron brought them coffee and rolls. When she left they both started talking at once.

"I guess you knew—"

"I just heard—"

They stopped, started again. Then, laughing, Dan said, "You first, Kit. You probably know a great deal of what I was going to ask you anyway." He circled his coffee mug with both hands. "Of course, I *do* know Laurel is in Boston. I went by to see Dr. Woodward when I got into town day before yesterday, but he didn't seem to know or at least he did not have much to say about what she was doing or—" he sighed— "when or even *if* she was coming back."

Kit felt that old familiar twinge of yearning as she saw Dan's jaw tighten. He's still in love with Laurel, she thought. Sympathy overrode her own longing. She knew too well how unreturned love felt. Impulsively, she reached over and patted Dan's hand.

"You know, Dan, Laurel always had this need, this obsession, really, to go back to Massachusetts, to Boston, to trace her real family. She talked about it many times when we were alone together. Until that is satisfied, I don't believe Laurel is ready for anything else."

"But, in every way that counts the Woodwards *are* her family," protested Dan, although he spoke without conviction.

Kit nodded. "I know, but she said to me once, 'Nothing ever makes up for being an orphan.'"

"But, *you*—and Toddy, too—" Dan began.

"Both our situations were different." Kit gave a wry little smile. *"Very* different."

"What about Toddy?" he asked. "I went by the Hale house and it was all closed up. There was even a padlock on the front gate. Not a sign of life anywhere."

"Mrs. Hale took them to Europe. They're traveling. I think they've gone to several health resorts. Mrs. Hale keeps hoping to find something, someone who can help poor Helene."

"So, what does that mean for Chris? For Toddy and Chris?"

Slowly Kit shook her head. "I don't know. I'm not sure. I heard Chris left the University his second year, went to South America on a construction job."

The waitress came by with a steaming coffeepot and refilled their mugs. Dan stirred sugar into his coffee thoughtfully.

"Things have sure changed."

"Are you surprised? You've been away three years, Dan. Didn't you expect them to change?"

He looked up, startling her with the intensity of his brown gaze.

Imperceptibly Kit drew in her breath. She thought she had outgrown her feelings for Dan, thought she had blotted them out of her memory. It was too painful to carry her secret yearning, too complicated, too costly to risk the growing barrier between herself and her dear friend Laurel. She thought, also, that she had almost forgotten what he looked like, but she was surprised by the familiarity of his features—the strong chin and sensitive mouth—and alarmingly disturbed when she looked into those searching eyes.

"*You* haven't changed, Kit," he said, then frowned. "Have you?"

"Nothing ever stays the same, Dan," she replied quietly, while her heartbeat quickened, keeping pace with a rising current of excitement.

"I guess you're right." Dan sighed. "Maybe, when you've been away as long as I have—new situations, new people, new challenges—you like the thought that all the things and people left behind—your hometown, the people you grew up with, cared about, loved—are the same, the one constant. Kind of a safety valve. Know what I mean?" Then he shook his head again. "I guess you don't. You didn't leave."

"That doesn't mean that I won't someday. Don't think I plan to stay at the *Monitor* forever," Kit retorted, the color coming into her cheeks.

Dan was startled by the quick reply. He looked at Kit again, scrutinized her face—her complexion now tinged with pink, the smooth high brow, the clear, intelligent eyes. Those eyes! Why hadn't he noticed them before? They were lovely—sort of a silvery-gray and fringed with the most extraordinary dark lashes.

"You know you ought to, Kit," he said slowly, "think seriously about it, I mean. There's a whole big world out there. Lots of newspapers. You could get a job anywhere writing, reporting. Travel around the world, probably, if you wanted to."

"I intend to!" said Kit, feeling a new kind of excitement rise up within her. Until now, she had not had a chance to talk to anyone about her dreams, her ambitions, and as they spilled out to Dan, she realized they had been there all along, needing only a friendly word of encouragement to stir them to life.

They talked on, oblivious to the time, until Kit suddenly noticed the waiters in the dining room, setting up for the midday dinner service. Many Meadowridge families celebrated Thanksgiving by eating out at the Inn and it was nearly noon.

"We'd better be going."

"Yes, I guess so," Dan agreed reluctantly, "I think Grandmother and the aunties plan to serve dinner at one."

Outside on the porch of the Inn, Dan issued an unexpected invitation. "What about you, Kit? Will you come home with me and have Thanksgiving dinner with us?"

"Thank you, Dan, but no. Miss Hadley, at the paper, is cooking dinner for all of the staff—" She paused, laughing a little. "All of us 'orphans' are spending the holiday together. She's alone, and Mr. Clooney's been a widower for years, and I don't know if Mac's ever been married, but I know he lives by himself, and Joe—well, it will be nice for us all." She smiled.

Again Dan thought how radiant Kit looked when she smiled. She was no beauty like Laurel, but this girl had a shining quality about her.

"Well then, I guess this is goodbye, Kit. I'm due out on the early train tomorrow. It's been wonderful seeing you, having a chance to talk. I'm so glad we had this time together."

"I am too, Dan. And I wish you every success. I know you'll make a fine doctor."

They stood there for a minute, not saying anything, each unwilling to make the first move.

"I have to stop by the cottage," Kit said at last, "pick up a salad I made, my contribution to Miss Hadley's dinner, although I'm sure she won't need it. She usually cooks enough for a small army." She hesitated a second longer. "I'd better be on my way."

"Goodbye, Kit."

"Goodbye, Dan. God bless!" she said, then turning up her coat collar, she hurried away.

At the corner, she turned for one last look. Dan was still standing where she had left him. Smiling, she lifted her hand and waved.

17

January 1905

Kit stood next to the editor's desk, anticipating his reaction to her decision. He had turned away from his cluttered oak rolltop and stared silently out onto the town square. Past Mr. Clooney's hunched shoulder, Kit could see out to the dreary winter day. Rain slanted in silvery-blue streaks and streamed down the windowpane.

Finally he swiveled around toward her, the ancient chair squeaking in protest, and scowled at her over his glasses.

"Well, miss, if you've made up your mind to go, I can't stop you," he grunted. "You're not going to find it easy on a big city newspaper, let me tell you that. You're a fine reporter, Kit, I've no complaints. You can cover anything and cover it well. But some editors and reporters still don't accept the idea of 'lady newspaper writers' except for the Society pages or cooking hints!"

He held up his hand, staving off the argument that sprang immediately to her lips. "I know, I know what you're going to say. It's the twentieth century! Just tell that to the managing editor of some city newspaper! If they hire you at all—"

"They *have* hired me, Mr. Clooney!" Kit interrupted, thrusting forward her letter of confirmation received in the morning's mail.

Ignoring it, he went on, "Be that as it may—I still say, *if* they hire you at all, they'll have you out on the worst assignments—interviewing a fireman who had to climb a tree to rescue some old lady's cat, or worse than that, the mother of an ax murderer who claims her son was 'always a good boy'! They'll run you ragged and pay you less than the men, and hope they'll discourage and wear you out enough so you'll quit."

"*You* did that, Mr. Clooney, and it didn't discourage me."

"I did no such thing!" he denied indignantly. "I had you cover what was going on in Meadowridge that day! If that happened to be some scared cat or interviewing some lady who won First Prize for quilting at the County Fair, that was what we assigned you."

Kit didn't argue, just stood there watching Mr. Clooney squirm uncomfortably, rearranging the piles of scattered notes on his desk. At length, he growled. "I suppose you want a recommendation from me?"

"Yes sir, I'd appreciate that."

"Well, I'll think about it. I mean, that's asking a lot, I'd say. Give you a good send-off to another newspaper when I'm losing the best reporter I've ever had."

Kit smiled and said gently, "Thank you, Mr. Clooney."

Turning away to go back to her own desk, Kit paused. "I do want you to know how much this job has meant to me, sir. I've learned so much from you and—"

He waved her away impatiently. "Go on, go on, don't try to sweet-talk your way out of leaving me in a lurch like this! Who am I going to get to replace you? Who that can at least spell and write a readable sentence?"

"I've talked to Mr. Henson at the High School, Mr. Clooney. He has several bright students, all Seniors, who would jump at a chance to work here."

Mr. Clooney pushed his green eyeshade back from his brow.

"You talking about some kid, not dry behind the ears yet? Working here?" he barked. "You trying to push me into an early grave? I got better things to do with my time in this office than conducting spelling bees for kids and correcting compositions!"

Kit hid her amusement at Mr. Clooney's raving. In the more than two years she had worked at the *Monitor*, she had learned that his proverbial bark was worse than his bite. When the pupil was sincere and willing to learn, Ed Clooney was an inspired teacher. The *Monitor* was his life and he took pride in its clean copy and well-written articles. If he had to, he would tirelessly train somebody he thought had the makings of a good newspaperman. Kit had come to respect him, and regarded his prickly temperament with affectionate tolerance. Her training here had provided her with enough confidence to apply to five California newspapers, and get an acceptance from one.

For the next several weeks Kit worked hard to help smooth the transition after her leaving. Mr. Clooney had reluctantly agreed to give two of the Seniors a trial run, and Kit took on the job of tutoring them, initiating them into the routine of newspaper writing. She oversaw their efforts, suggesting changes, correcting copy and encouraging them. The results were much better than Mr. Clooney had expected and, until he could find a full-time reporter, he had agreed to use the two students.

The last two weeks before Kit left for San Francisco were busy ones. There was so much to do to get ready for the long trip, the new life into which she was heading. There were also some old doors to close before she could open the many new ones before her.

One thing she had yet to do was to make a trip out to the Hansen farm to tell Cora goodbye.

One cold February afternoon she borrowed Mr. Clooney's mare, Tilly, and his ramshackle buggy and set out for the farm.

As she rattled over the familiar road, now rutted by winter storms, many memories flooded over Kit. Some were hurtful ones that Kit did not allow herself to explore. She had tried to deal with the pain she had encountered as learning experiences, and she was determined not to let them embitter her.

When she reached the farm, Kit led the horse under the shelter of a lean-to next to the barn. She got a worn horse blanket from under the buggy seat and settled it over Tilly's back to keep the chill off the old mare while she was inside. Then she slipped a feeding bucket of oats over her nose.

After that she hurried through the gray drizzle up to the house. Kit's knock was answered by Cora's daughter-in-law, Alverna. On her hip was a rosy-cheeked baby who looked remarkably like Lonny.

"Oh, come in, Kit," she said. "Cora will be so pleased to see you."

Kit stepped into the warmth of the kitchen and sniffed appreciatively. Something gingery was baking. Starched curtains at the windows and a bright cross-stitched cloth on the table gave the room a cheerful air on this dark winter day. Kit noticed an arrangement of dried statis and straw flowers in a dark blue glass holder on the pine hutch.

"Everything looks so nice, Alverna," she commented, looking around.

"Well, thank you, Kit. You know Lonny's Ma likes things to look nice, so I try to please her."

As Kit followed Alverna up the narrow steps leading to the second floor and to the bedroom Cora now occupied, she remembered her own first attempts at bringing bits of beauty into this stark farmhouse years ago. She recalled how very slow Cora had been to appreciate her efforts and support them.

At the top of the stairs, Alverna knocked at one of the doors, then opened it and leaned in.

"Ma, you've got company. Here's Kit to see you."

Kit entered the room as the woman sitting in the rocker by the window slowly turned her head. Every time she came to see Cora, Kit was shocked to see her gradual decline. After a time of improvement, she had taken a turn for the worse. She was thin now to the point of gauntness. Her hair was nearly white and her eyes sunken into deep sockets in her deeply lined face. The effects of her paralysis still showed in her twisted smile, leaving one side of her face unmoved. Her speech was garbled, and it was necessary to listen very closely to understand her words.

Kit pulled a straight chair over close to Cora and sat down. Taking one gnarled hand in both of hers, she looked into the woman's dull eyes.

"I'm going away, Cora. I have a job with a newspaper in San Francisco, California. So I'm leaving Meadowridge next week."

There was little change in Cora's expression, but she nodded her head so Kit knew she had heard and understood. Kit always tried to make her visits as cheerful as possible, knowing how narrow and limited Cora's existence must be. Since her stroke, she was no longer able to do the work that kept her life busy and full. Kit kept up a lively account of Meadowridge news that might interest Cora, about the town, church and other community events.

After about fifteen minutes, just when Kit was running out of things to say, Alverna reappeared with a tray on which was a pot of tea and a plate of freshly baked gingersnaps.

"Thought you ladies would like a little refreshment," she said, setting the tray on the dresser. She handed Kit a cup and saucer, offered her a cookie then proceeded to place a clean napkin on Cora's lap and pour a small portion of tea into a cup and hold it for Cora to sip. Seeing Alverna's tenderness with her mother-in-law touched Kit and ended any lingering guilt she had felt about leaving the farm and the care of Cora to others.

Cora mumbled something that sounded unintelligible to Kit, but evidently Alverna understood.

"Yes, Ma, I'll show her." And she gave Kit a knowing look. "Wait until you see."

The younger woman went over to a shelf and brought back a thick scrapbook, which she laid on Kit's lap. "Open it," she instructed.

To Kit's amazement, inside on page after page were pasted articles she had written for the *Monitor*, ones printed after Mr. Clooney decided to give her a byline for special features.

Kit felt a lump form in her throat, and she looked over at Cora who seemed to be trying to smile.

"I think Ma's tired, Kit," Alverna whispered as she took the scrapbook away and replaced it on the shelf.

Cora had visibly slumped in her chair, and Kit got to her feet at once. She leaned over and kissed Cora's cheek.

"I have to leave now, Cora. Take care of yourself and I'll see you when I come back to Meadowridge."

Their eyes met, and a kind of communication passed between them, deeper than any words. Cora made a sound, and Kit leaned closer to make it out. Not understanding, she simply nodded and patted Cora's shoulder, feeling the boniness under the calico dress.

At the bedroom door, she turned and looked back and thought she saw a tear trickle slowly down the wrinkled face.

"Ma's kept everything you've written, Kit," Alverna said, on the way downstairs. "Even though she don't read, she recognized your name, Kathleen Ternan."

Riding back into town, Kit began to cry. The tears gathered in her eyes and flowed unchecked.

It seemed implausible that she should be tearful on this eve of her new adventure. She had made the choice. The goal she had set for herself was about to be accomplished; the future, bright. Her life's journey had begun. What lay ahead of her promised all sorts of rewards.

So why was she feeling both sadness and some regret for what she was leaving behind? Could she have done more for Cora? She wasn't sure. All she knew, all she prayed was that, somehow, she had made a difference in her life, after all.

18

San Francisco

Kit had always imagined California as a land of perpetual sunshine, of orange groves and tropical palms. It was rather a shock to discover that San Francisco could be cool with a brisk, ocean-blown breeze, misty mornings, and early evenings of swirling fog.

This was not entirely a disappointment. The fog lent a mysterious aura to a city she found constantly surprising and interesting. Since Kit had always loved the romantic English novels of the wind-tossed moors and fog-bound seaports, San Francisco fascinated her.

Kit arrived in the city on an overcast day with hovering gray clouds, and a sharp, salty wind blowing off the Bay. Upon her arrival she went directly to the newspaper, clutching the letter she had received with confirmation of her employment as a reporter just in case something had happened in the interim and they had forgotten about her.

After a suspenseful, doubt-ridden wait, her hiring was confirmed and she was told to start work the following Monday. She was then handed some forms to fill out. When she ventured the fact she did not as yet have an address to put in the appropriate line, she was sent down to Classified. There a helpful clerk gave Kit a list of room rentals within reasonable distance from the newspaper building.

Armed with these and rather dazed by all the new things
that were happening to her all at once, Kit set out. Her
uncharted future here in this busy metropolis, unpredictable as it seemed, caused some inner apprehension as well
as a certain excitement.

She had to stop and ask directions several times to find
the various addresses given. As she climbed steep hills and
trudged up countless steps to inquire about rooms adver-
tised, she was often told that the place was already rented,
or that the only available room was a double and she would
have to share it, or when she reached it, saw a NO
VACANCY sign in the window. Her suitcase was getting
heavier and heavier each time she had to pick it up and
carry it to the next possibility. With only three more
addresses on her list, Kit began to get discouraged.

Near the end of the day, she rang the bell of a hillside
house, and the door was opened by a sallow-faced woman,
with a suspicious glint in her eyes. She told Kit she had a
room, but warned her before she showed it that she always
required a month's rent in advance.

Weary, but determined not to be intimidated, Kit followed
her up a long staircase to the second floor. She prayed the
room would be decent, clean and acceptable. She was beginning to experience some gnawing anxiety about the big step
she had taken, leaving Meadowridge, coming so far from
the only home she had ever really known.

At the top of the stairs, the woman opened the door and led
the way in.

"Most people like a front room and this one rents for six
dollars a week—*payable in advance*. I rent these rooms by
the month because I don't like people comin' and goin'. I like
my renters permanent. You get a better class of roomers
when you insist on that," she declared. "If they leave before
the month's up, don't matter for what reason, I don't give a

refund. That's my policy. I always tell people beforehand so there's no misunderstanding."

Kit nodded and walked to the center of the room, looking around. There was a brass bed, a washstand with a pitcher and bowl, a bureau with a mirror, a table by the bay window, two straight chairs.

"The bathroom's down the hall...you sign up for baths. The nights or days for this room, Number Four, is Tuesdays and Fridays." The woman leaned against the door frame, arms folded, waiting for Kit's decision.

Suddenly Kit felt exhausted. The long train trip from Meadowridge, with two hectic changes in St. Louis and Chicago, the uncertainty of the new life she was starting, the tiring day-long trek looking for a place to live had all begun to weigh upon her. She was anxious to get settled.

"I'll take it," she said, opening her purse to take out the month's rent.

The woman counted out the bills Kit handed her.

"Well, that's that then," she said when she was satisfied that the money was all there. "I'll give you a receipt when I bring up your clean sheets and towels. By the way, I'm Mrs. Bredesen." And she went out the door, closing it behind her.

Going to the window, Kit drew aside the stiff net curtains and looked down into the busy street below. Judging from the purposeful stride of the pedestrians, everyone seemed to have someplace important to go. Kit felt at once thrilled and threatened. Soon she would be among them, starting her new work, carrying out assignments, getting acquainted. For, of all the people in this vast city, she didn't know a single solitary soul—except for Dan Brooks.

A brisk knock on the door interrupted her thoughts and Mrs. Bredesen reappeared with an armload of sheets and towels.

"You get clean linens once a week, towels twice. There's a laundry chute at the end of the hall. You put your used ones down it on Fridays."

"Thank you," murmured Kit, taking the pile from her.

Then Mrs. Bredesen pointed to a card pasted to the inside of the door. "These here are my rules for roomers. There's to be no cooking of any kind in the rooms. No entertaining or guests of the opposite sex above the first floor. You may receive visitors in the downstairs parlor. The front door is locked at 11 P.M. sharp. I don't open it after that unless for a real emergency. I keep a decent house. I'm a tee-totaler myself, and if my roomers do otherwise that's their business, unless it interferes with mine," she said emphatically. "I keep a decent house and I expect my roomers to obey the rules."

Kit, who wasn't expecting any visitors and certainly had not planned to entertain, listened, nodding solemnly until Mrs. Bredesen finished.

"Well, I guess that's all," the woman concluded. "You won't be taking any meals here, I guess? That's extra, of course. Some of my roomers do. They find it more convenient and more economical than getting it downtown. I serve one meal a day, dinner at six o'clock on the dot. For fifty cents a week extra I put out coffee and rolls in my dining room in the morning. If you want that, you have to sign up."

"I'll let you know, thank you," Kit said quietly, wishing the landlady would leave. She was almost dizzy from fatigue and longed to be alone so she could settle her thoughts and unpack.

Finally the woman was gone and Kit locked the door. She took off her shoes, wiggling her toes, and walked from one small cotton scatter rug to the other over to the bed and sat down. After nearly a week of travel, she felt an enormous sensation of relief to be at last somewhere she could call her own. At least, for a month.

That thought reminded her of the amount just subtracted from her small cash reserve. When she had withdrawn her savings from the Meadowridge Bank, she had felt rich. But, Kit had discovered traveling was costly despite her efforts to be frugal. Besides her one-way ticket to California there had been unexpected expenses en route. She had been delayed twice, with missed connections and late arriving trains and had no alternative than to spend money on food.

Kit emptied the contents of her purse on the bed to count what was left of what had seemed an adequate little nestegg upon her departure from Meadowridge. She felt a small twinge of alarm but refused to allow it to surface. She would be careful, and in two weeks she would collect her first paycheck. Then things would work out.

"Everything works together for good for those who love the Lord and are called to His purpose," Kit reminded herself.

She was putting things back into her purse when she came upon a small square of pink paper. She unfolded it and saw it was Dan's address. Studying it, she remembered the incident with his mother.

One of the last days she had been in Meadowridge, Kit was doing some last-minute shopping. Standing at the counter in the dry goods store, someone had touched her arm.

"Kit? Kathleen Ternan?" the woman at her elbow asked. Kit had not recognized her until she introduced herself. "I'm Vada Brooks," she said. "Daniel Brooks's mother."

"Oh, yes! I'm sorry I—"

"Of course I didn't expect you to know me. We only met that once, at Graduation. You were naturally too excited and happy to remember me. But then you made a great impression on me. On everyone, I should think. Dan always spoke so highly of you." She paused, fidgeting a little nervously as if she wasn't sure what she was going to say next. "And of *all* his friends here, of course. You know he's doing his residency now in a San Francisco hospital?"

Kit had the grace to blush.

"Yes, I know," she replied. "I saw Dan when he was here last Thanksgiving."

"He's doing very well," Mrs. Brooks said in her quick, anxious way, then added, "but he's very lonely. Not that he doesn't have friends among the other young doctors there, the hospital staff. Dan makes friends easily. He is so likable—" her voice trailed off vaguely. "I heard, Miss Ternan, that *you* were leaving Meadowridge yourself, going to work on a newspaper in California, a San Francisco paper."

Kit nodded, wondering what in the world the woman had on her mind.

"Miss Ternan, I was thinking...seeing you and Dan were in the same class, grew up here together...that is, rather *when*, you get to San Francisco...would you let Dan know? I'm sure he would so enjoy seeing somebody from home—an old friend. May I give you his address?" Mrs. Brooks asked, already fumbling in her handbag for a piece of notepaper and a pencil.

Now, as she held the small slip of paper in her hand, Kit read it over. Was that one of those chance encounters, or was there something significant about her running into Dan's mother that day just before she left?

To be truthful, why else had she chosen to apply to newspapers in northern California except on the slim chance that somehow she might see Dan? Kit asked herself. She replaced the note with the scribbled address in the compartment of her handbag, then leaned back against the bed pillows wearily. Slowly her eyes closed and before she knew it she had drifted off into an exhausted sleep.

The next thing she was aware of was the gray light of dawn illuminating the unfamiliar room. Outside, she could hear the sound of wagon wheels on the street below. The city was coming awake, going about its business of the day. And she was part of it, Kit thought, coming slowly awake. She was actually in San Francisco, about to start her career as a journalist.

19

Even though Kit no longer believed that the letters she wrote to Jamie and Gwynny would ever be read by either of them, out of long habit she started her journal entry as she always had:

Dear Jamie and Gwynny,

San Francisco is a big, exciting city. Never in my wildest dreams did I ever imagine anything like it nor did I ever expect to live here.

The city was built on hills, so you will not be surprised to learn that I live in a house on top of a hill. If I lean way out over my windowsill, I can see the Bay and Ferry Building, where the boats come, bringing people from Sausalito, Martinez, Berkeley, and Oakland. From early in the morning, this lower part of Market Street is alive with all sorts of activity—crowds of people, horse-drawn streetcars with clanging bells, carriages and cabs. But the most amazing kind of transportation are the red cable cars. From a distance they look like toys, running up and down the steep hills on rails, pulled by a steel cable which moves in a slot underneath the surface of the street. The first time I rode on one, I was terrified! But you, Jamie, would love them! You always did like scary things—scary stories, being pushed higher and higher on the swings in the park—

Downtown, where I go every morning to my job at the newspaper office, the sidewalks are packed with people, all hurrying somewhere. There is such a variety of them. I love to see the Chinese with their slanted eyes and pale skin, in blue cotton coats and trousers, carrying baskets of vegetables on poles. In contrast are the well-dressed businessmen, in black frock coats, brocaded vests, and gold watch chains. Then there are the miners down from their mines in the Sierra Hills. Usually they have stubby beards, broad-brimmed felt hats, somewhat the worse for wear, flannel shirts and boots. But for all their scraggly appearance, they are some of the richest men in California.

The city, too, has its many faces. On Montgomery Street, the scene changes. Here are expensive shops with all sorts of beautiful things for sale—dress salons and jewelry stores, millinery shops with hats displayed in their windows that must rival those to be found in Paris, fabric stores displaying yards of gorgeous materials—satins, embroidered silks, rich velvets. Here you see the most elegantly dressed people promenading—young men with gold-and-ivory-headed canes and polished hats, escorting ladies in stylish outfits and handsome jewelry.

The buildings here are all several stories high and of every style of architecture, each one seemingly trying to outdo the next in magnificence, size, and splendor. There are mansions like palaces, built by millionaires, in a fashionable section called Nob Hill that are said to be even more incredible inside—marble statues, huge oil paintings, gilded furniture, and treasures gathered from all sorts of exotic places.

There is a contagious undercurrent of excitement here that you can actually feel as you walk along the streets, as if everyone is on the brink of something new, intriguing, or spectacular. One has the sense of expectation, as if anything were possible, that all one's dreams could come true. And why not? You are surrounded by dozens of such examples!

My job, of course, has none of the glamour, the color, the excitement of the city. I don't know really if I expected it to be otherwise. After all, I am lucky to have been taken on with only a small-town weekly newspaper experience. Besides that, I fear, even in 1905, there is a prejudice against the "working woman." My immediate boss, Clem Stoniger, is an "old-timer," a veteran reporter with a wealth of newspaper and life experience behind him. He has had what they call a "checkered career." In his youth he stowed away on a ship and sailed all over the world. Coming around Cape Horn, he landed in California as a kid of sixteen, just about the time the Gold Rush broke. He went with all the others in search of wealth and fortune and he worked a couple of claims, but finally his health broke. Instead of finding gold, he ended up writing about it for eastern newspapers before settling here in San Francisco as a reporter.

He has helped me a great deal. Though most of my duties are dull and routine—checking tax lists, accident reports (these caused mainly by an excess number of vehicles, plus reckless drivers), and obituaries—Mr. Stoniger tells me to be patient. "Your time will come," he tells me. "Sometimes it's just being in the right place at the right time. You never know when you'll get your chance to report the *big* story."

I hope he's right. In the meantime, I try to record my impressions, descriptions of people, incidents I observe. It is all part of becoming a writer, which is what I really want to be—

Dear Jamie and Gwynny,

I have been in San Francisco for three months now, and have grown to love it. This little room seems as if I've always lived here. I've hung the "Guardian Angel" picture—the one I won in Sunday school years ago— over my bed. The afghan Cora gave me is folded at the end.

Each day brings something new. Mr. Stoniger has been giving me small writing assignments, and he hands them back to me heavily blue-penciled with questions like: WHO? WHAT? WHEN? WHERE? WHY? scribbled in the margins. He is teaching me the basics of good reporting. "This isn't Meadowridge or Podunk, Kit. *This* is San Francisco, *this* is the big time. This isn't a country journal, this is a city newspaper," he'll growl at me. At first, I was not only in awe of him, I was afraid of him. But now I realize he is only trying to help me write more accurately.

"You've the makings of a feature writer, Kit," he told me one day when he returned from a longer than usual lunch hour, mellowed, I'm sure, with the help of accompanying liquid refreshment. "Rewrite—that's what makes the difference. Check your facts, then write from the heart."

On my days off, I like to walk. San Francisco is conducive to wandering. I walk down to the Wharf and watch the fishing boats come in and the fishermen unload their catch. There is a kind of beautiful rhythm to their movements. As they work, they call to each other, speaking in Italian, a language with a lilting quality. The fishermen seem a good-natured bunch, evidently loving their jobs, which is, I suppose, the real secret of happiness. To love what you're doing. I certainly do!

I turned a piece in to Mr. Stoniger the other day, a "human interest" story about a miner who had made and lost several fortunes in the gold field, and was going back up to find the "Lost Dutchman" mine. He swore he knew exactly where it was. He was seventy if he was a day, but he still has "gold fever" and was convinced *this* time he was going to overcome all the pitfalls of the past. Mr. Stoniger read it, grunted, and handed it back to me, saying, "You're getting there, Kit, you're getting there," which is about the nicest compliment he's yet paid me.

I've been writing Mr. Clooney and the others at the *Meadowridge Monitor* since I've been here, telling them about San Francisco, describing the sights and scenes. Jessica wrote me that Mr. Clooney wants me to do a regular feature for them. Not only will I be paid for it, but I'll have my own byline—"City Sights and Insights" by Kathleen Ternan.

Dear Jamie and Gwynny,

Guess what? Dan Brooks showed up at the newspaper yesterday, asking for me! One of his aunts had cut out my column in the *Meadowridge Monitor* and sent it to him, so he decided to look me up! My heart nearly stopped when I saw him standing there. He's filled out, and even though he seems taller, he's still the best-looking fellow in our entire graduating class, at least in my opinion. He wanted to make plans for his next day off from the hospital. When I told him the day I would be free, he said he was sure he could switch with one of the other residents.

We didn't have time to exchange much Meadowridge news. I guess we will next Thursday. I started to ask him about Laurel, but something stopped me. Why am I so happy? I shouldn't start to dream about him again. We're just good friends, both alone and lonely in the big city. He was glad to see a familiar face, that's all. Don't get any ideas, Kit Ternan!

Dear Jamie and Gwynny,

It is nearly midnight and I should be in bed since my alarm goes off at six, but I'm too excited to sleep. I have had the most marvelous day, and I want to put it all down before I forget any of it, not that I think I ever shall!

I was ready and waiting when Dan came by to get me about ten o'clock this morning. I was so happy to see him. We both mentioned how strange it is that we ended up in San Francisco, so far from Meadowridge. Maybe more so for me. It's different now that I'm on my own. Dan seems to think it's quite remarkable that I have a job on a big city newspaper and that I seem to know my way around the city. I told him it was all trial and error, that I'd gotten lost plenty of times when learning my way around!

It was a glorious day, the kind San Franciscans like to brag about. Sunny and clear, cloudless skies, a sharp wind off the Bay, making little dancing whitecaps all across the dark blue water. We walked all over, a hundred miles, it seemed! Dan wanted to see everything, go everywhere, said he'd been so cooped up in the hospital on the merciless residents' schedule that he felt as if he'd been let out of prison.

"You haven't changed your mind about wanting to be a doctor, have you?" I asked, a little worried.

"Oh, no, I'm looking forward to being a country doctor. Did I tell you Dr. Woodward has practically promised me that when I finish, I can come and work with him?" Dan asked me.

I felt my heart sink. That meant Dan would be leaving San Francisco at the end of his residency.

"No, you never told me. But, of course, this is the first time we've seen each other since last November."

"That's right," Dan said as we walked on a little further. "I've thought a lot about that Thanksgiving Day, Kit."

I was curious to know *what* he had thought, but that was all he said just then. We were walking up one of these hills that absolutely takes all your breath, so neither of us said much until later.

We walked along the bluffs above the beach. Dan couldn't get enough of the ocean—watching the surf, looking way out to where the big ships glide along the horizon, carrying cargo to ports everywhere in the world. Even where we were, we could feel the salt spray. The wind was blowing so hard, it practically tore the hairpins out of my hair, tossing it into tangles.

Then we went to Chinatown with all its queer little stores, and Dan decided he wanted to try some real Chinese food. He even insisted on eating with chopsticks! I tried, but finally asked the waiter for a fork before I starved to death! Dan struggled stubbornly and managed pretty well.

Afterwards, we wandered in and out of the shops. There were beautiful teakwood screens for sale, boxes, trunks, carved ivory and jade, not just the green kind, but pale pink and lavender, too, jewelry and delicate figurines. Some of the shops are very expensive, others just junk. We had a good time, pretending we had all the money in the world and buying gifts for everyone we knew.

In the late afternoon, we walked down to Fisherman's Wharf. By now it was getting colder, so we stopped at a little café for "espresso," a kind of steamed coffee with a dollop of whipped cream on top. This warmed us up right away. Since Dan didn't have to report back to the hospital until eleven P.M., he insisted on taking me to dinner.

When I hesitated, fearing he didn't know the kind of prices charged at San Francisco restaurants, he seemed to have read my mind. "Don't worry!" he said. "This is on Uncle Ned. He sent me a fifty in his letter today, told me to find a pretty girl and take her out 'on the town.' Those were his exact words! So I've found the pretty girl. Now where shall we go for dinner?"

I didn't say any more, just begged him to let me come by my room and freshen up a bit so we could go out to dine in a style befitting the occasion.

On the way, Dan talked about how good and generous his uncle had been to him all through his college years, med school, and the lean years of interning and residency.

"If it hadn't been for Uncle Ned, I'd never have made it," Dan told me confidentially. Of course Dan himself has done all the usual things to help make ends meet — stoking furnaces, waiting on tables, and mowing lawns. Still it was hardly enough to give him much *extra* money.

"Uncle Ned always seemed to know when I needed it most, and he always came through," Dan said gratefully.

Dan, speaking of his uncle, triggered the memory of an incident when Miss Cady had been disdainful of Ned Morris. I remember particularly one spring evening when Miss Cady and I were walking over to the high school for a combined recital given by the Music and Drama Club and Dan and his uncle had come along in Mr. Morris's open buggy. He stopped immediately and offered us a ride, and Miss Cady had coolly turned him down. After they'd driven off, I'd asked her why she had refused. She seemed indignant that I didn't know.

"We shouldn't be seen in public with a man who runs a pool hall, Kit!"

"Mr. Morris seems as nice as he can be," I said mildly.

"He's no gentleman, or he'd find another line of work!" she snapped.

"Dan told me his uncle is going to put him through college and medical school." I couldn't resist sharing this information since she was being so snobbish. "Dan says he couldn't possibly go if Mr. Morris wasn't paying the fees."

"That has nothing to do with the proper thing for *us* to do, Kit," Miss Cady said, annoyed with me for questioning her action.

I almost reminded her how she had always taught that any kind of work was noble unless it was dishonest. But she seemed so offended by this exchange already that I bit my tongue and decided to let the subject drop. I think it was that incident that made me realize, perhaps for the first time, that Miss Cady was not always right. Just because you admire someone doesn't mean you can't disagree with them.

Anyway, the reason I write this down at all is that, just as I was thinking about Miss Cady, Dan suddenly said, "You know, Uncle Ned was always in love with Millicent Cady. Of course, he knew it was hopeless since she didn't think he was good enough for her, disapproved of his running a pool hall. Actually the poor fellow just sort of fell into it. He had to support his mother and sisters for so many years, started when he was just a kid sweeping floors in there after school for twenty-five cents a week. The owner took a liking to him. Gradually turned the business over to him. Life's funny, isn't it? So much is chance."

But back to our fancy dinner. I felt very special walking into the elegant hotel dining room, where we were shown to a table right by a window with a view of the city. We watched as dusk fell over San Francisco and the gas streetlights winked on. The table was covered with satiny white linen, with big damask napkins folded to look like huge white butterflies. In the center of the table was a bud vase holding a single perfect rose.

A waiter appeared, handing us menus as long and wide as a six-column lead story, and my eyes nearly popped out of my head as I read it! A selection of food that could have been served royalty, I was sure, much of it described in French: *Consomme Fleury* or deviled crabs a la Creole were offered as a first course; a choice of fish or roast lamb with mint sauce or Ragout of filet beef, *a la Bordelaise,* as a second; and there were several choices of salads and vegetables, and a list of desserts that made the choice difficult—*Strawberry Bavaroise, Gateaux a la Royale,* lemon ice cream. After much indecision and whispering, we settled on the same order, which made it easier for Dan to deal with the aloof waiter.

But nothing dampened our pleasure and we ate, talked, enjoyed everything. I don't know how much our dinner cost and did not dare ask Dan as we left. Since he suggested a walk while our dinner settled, I gathered he was not sure he had enough left to take me home in a cab, so I readily agreed that it was a good idea.

Anyway, it gave us more time together. Funny, but we never ran out of things to talk about this whole long day.

As we said good night, Dan squeezed both my hands and said, "Kit, I can't remember when I've had such a good time! Thanks!"

"Well, thank you, Dan," I said, adding, "—and Uncle Ned!"

"How about your next day off?" he asked.

My heart seemed to swell up into my throat, and I could hardly answer. Was it really happening? Dan Brooks wanting to be with *me?*

"Fine," I managed to say, and Dan was off and running to catch the last trolley to the hospital in time to go on duty.

Dear Jamie and Gwynny,

I haven't written in a long time since I've been so busy at work, too tired when I get in at night, and my days off? Well, I've been spending almost every one with Dan. We've explored San Francisco from top to bottom and now have our own special places we like to go, our favorite restaurants. Mostly we walk out along the beach. Like all midwesterners, we're fascinated by the ocean. We also go to Golden Gate Park, sometimes picnic on the grassy knoll, and talk and talk about everything—Dan's work, my job, my writing, his plans. We've even talked some about our families. I've told him all about you two, how I've never really gotten over losing track of you, missing you, and he's told me about his funny, mixed-up life.

His grandmother is dead now and one of his aunts got married, which I know would surprise a lot of people, especially Toddy and Laurel. We always thought of Dan's aunts as typical "old maids," but Leatrice up and married and took off to live in Oregon, Dan says. His other aunt kept the house for a while, then went to live with his mother in Dayton, Ohio. So he really has no more family than I do. It makes you feel closer to someone the more you know about them, about their childhood. We've had so many of the same experiences, the same feelings about—well, being different from other people we knew growing up. Of course, Laurel and Toddy were "Orphan Train" children, too, but their lives were not like mine and Dan's.

He plans to go back to Meadowridge when he finishes. That's the only thing we don't agree on. Somehow I feel San Francisco is where I'm supposed to be, supposed to stay. I don't know exactly why or for how long, but I can't see going back to Meadowridge right now.

Dear Jamie and Gwynny,

The most exciting thing happened today! Leo Hoffman, the entertainment columnist, came by my little cubicle at the paper and put an envelope down on my desk.

"What's this, Leo?" I called after him when he began to walk away.

"Open it and see." He grinned and the cigar he's always chewing on moved from one side of his mouth to the other.

I did and nearly let out a yelp of surprise. Inside were two tickets to the opera! The San Francisco Opera House! For the opening performance of Bizet's *Carmen,* starring the internationally famous Enrico Caruso!

"Oh, Leo, thank you! Why *me?*"

He wrinkled his face into something that looked exactly like one of those rubber dolls you can squeeze into all sorts of contortions, then rubbed his balding head and muttered, "Heard you liked music. Heard you were a good kid! What difference does it make *why?* You've got the tickets, haven't you? Go and enjoy!" he snarled and walked away.

I can hardly believe my luck! The city has been buzzing with excited anticipation ever since Caruso's appearance was announced. He'd already provided the reporters who had met him on his arrival with colorful copy. I've heard the world-renowned tenor travels in a private railway car, lavishly furnished with Oriental rugs and a piano, with his own valet and cook.

The opening of the opera is always one of the most gala events of the San Francisco social season, attended by anyone who *is* anybody in society, the ladies gowned in satin, ermines and glittering with jewels.

What a thrill it will be to be an observer, even if from the third balcony. I can't wait to tell Dan and of course, invite him to use the other ticket!

135

20

Kit turned in her day's copy. Then, sweeping all her notes, clippings, pencils, notebooks, paper clips, odds and ends of the sort that accumulate on most reporters' desks into the drawer, she shoved it closed, locked it, and ran down the steps and out the door of the newspaper building into the April sunshine.

Spring had come suddenly to San Francisco, and Kit felt the welcome warmth of the sun on her shoulders and back as she strolled along. She could not stop smiling every time she thought of the opera tickets and how happy Dan would be when he got the message she had left for him at the hospital. It would be a first experience for both of them, for she knew Dan had never attended the opera either. That they were actually to hear with their own ears the glorious voice that had sung for kings and emperors and sultans seemed too much to believe, and Kit's irrepressible smile appeared again.

Today every person she passed on the street seemed happy, too. Maybe it was the weather—"What is so rare as an *April* day," she misquoted giddily. "If ever there come perfect days," *this* was it.

Everything delighted her—the colorful displays in the store windows she passed, the flower vendors' stalls on nearly every corner, bright with spring flowers. She felt as bouyant as a birthday balloon.

Then, as she was passing a milliner's shop, Kit stopped short. Her heart gave a little leap of recognition. There *it* was in the window, as if just waiting for her, whispering "Buy me, buy me!" She moved closer and leaned against the glass to get a better look.

It was the most beautiful hat Kit had ever seen. Fashioned of soft, pliant pale blue straw, the crown was wrapped with pleated lavender satin ribbon. Nestled in the curve of the brim was a cluster of deep purple silk violets.

Kit's hands tightened on her handbag. Inside was her week's paycheck. Mentally she ticked off the bills she had intended to pay with this week's wages.

The price tag on the hat was turned over. A clever device to lure the interested buyer inside, she thought.

Kit hesitated, her common sense vying with pure feminine desire. Just once to do something impulsive, foolish was tempting. She had never had such a hat. In fact, she had never had many really pretty things. She thought of the evening ahead with Dan—going to the Opera House, hearing Caruso sing the part of Don Jose—a once-in-a-lifetime treat. Surely such a momentous event deserved something special to wear. Kit resisted only a split-second more, then with a small, defiant toss of her head, she opened the door of the shop and went inside.

Twenty minutes later she emerged and, although her heart was racing, the smile was in place. The hat was safely nestled in layers of tissue paper in the smart, round hatbox that bore the proud name of the exclusive millinery establishment.

"In for a penny, in for a pound," Kit thought rashly as she walked further down the street. Once her paycheck had been cashed, something reckless was loosed in Kit. Next she stopped and bought herself a pair of lavender gloves and a lace jabot to wear with her good gray suit. *Real* Chinese lace. Kit had never forgotten Miss Cady's admonition about lace. In the wake of all this extravagance, her pulses were pounding, but before rushing home and out of temptation's way, she made one more stop. A perfumerie shop. Immediately her senses were soothed by a hundred assorted fragrances. Here, under the soft-voiced clerk's dulcet persuasion, she purchased a bar of creamy scented soap, some glycerine and rose water for her complexion, some lavender Eau de Cologne.

When Kit left this last shop, she felt she should, by all rights, be burdened with guilt. Instead, she felt light-hearted and entirely pleased with herself.

It was going to be an extraordinary night, a wonderful night, one she was sure she would always remember, a date she would be able to mark on her calendar as a memorable one—April 17, 1906.

At two hours past midnight on April 18, Kit climbed wearily into bed, the music of *Carmen* still playing in her ears. Tired as she was, she was much too stimulated to go right to sleep. Scenes of the glittering opera house marched in her mind—the promenade of extravagantly gowned women escorted by men in elegant evening clothes up the sweeping staircase, the magnificence of the gilded boxes where the very wealthy sat, settling their furs and capes, fluttering beaded fans, acknowledging other box-holders with nods and bows and smiles, ignoring everyone else.

Kit had observed every detail, thrilling to the experience while making mental notes to include in her letter to Jamie and Gwynny.

As people took their places, there had been a palpable excitement, permeating the opera house from the lofty heights of the tiers of balconies down to the main floor. An air of anticipation rippled through the entire building as the houselights dimmed. Then a hush fell over the audience and there was only a discreet muffled cough and a rustling of programs as people settled down to enjoy the performance. As Bizet's thrilling overture rose from the orchestra pit, the footlights came up, the music swelled, the heavy velvet curtain lifted, and the gaily costumed chorus of singing girls from the cigarette factory danced onto the stage.

The whole evening had been unforgettable. Not least of it all had been the fact that Kit had been there with Dan. He had not known the story of the opera until Kit told it to him, but he seemed to enjoy the color of the production, the glorious music and singing as much as she.

Afterward they had gone to supper, although not one of the lavish champagne and lobster affairs being served the "haute societe" opera-goers of San Francisco at the luxurious St. Francis or Palace Hotel. They dined, instead, at one of their favorite small North Beach restaurants, where they ate pasta with a creamy clam sauce and crusty sourdough bread and discussed every scene of the opera, exchanging impressions and comparing reactions.

Very much later, when the waiters were yawning discreetly and most of the occupants of the other tables had long since disappeared, Dan had walked Kit to her boardinghouse. She had been distressed by the lateness of the hour, knowing he had to go on duty at seven.

"Don't!" he told her firmly. "It was worth it, every minute. It was wonderful. Imagine having lived twenty-six years and never having seen an opera! If I'd known—" he paused. "You know, Kit, you've introduced me to so many experiences I might have missed—authors whose books you recommended to me when you worked at the library, poetry, music, now opera! If it hadn't been for you, well, science and medicine can give a person a kind of dry, narrow-minded—" he paused, searching for the right word.

"Monotony?" she suggested, smiling.

"Exactly!"

They were quiet for a minute, then Dan leaned down and kissed Kit lightly.

"Thanks, Kit, it was one of the greatest evenings of my life."

Taken by surprise, Kit could only stare at him.

Dan grinned and added, "I meant to tell you before. That's the dandiest hat I've ever seen."

Kit stood watching Dan start back down the hill, hands in his pocket, whistling Don Jose's aria. Then, dreamily Kit climbed the stairs to her room, thinking it had all been more than worth it indeed, even if she had to go without lunch for the rest of the week!

Once inside her room, she halted in front of the mirror and tilted her head from one side to the other, admiring her hat from every angle. Then she shook her head at her own image and scolded, "Oh, Kit Ternan, you are an idiot!"

She waltzed around the room, spinning and spinning, flinging her clothes here and there as she undressed. Leaving her hat on till the very last, she took it off and placed it carefully on the bureau where she could see it from the bed. She was still smiling at Dan's remark when, before putting out her lamp, she gave it a last fond glance and drifted off to sleep.

The next thing she knew, she was startled awake by a violent movement. Her bed was rocking as if shaken by a giant fist. She sat up, clinging to the sides of the mattress as the deep, rolling sensation continued.

Outside, she could hear dogs barking, and a rumbling as the whole house seemed to roll. Creaking, groaning, cracking, splintering, crumbling noises surrounded her as she gripped the edge of the bed. She felt like screaming, but nothing came out of her throat as she held on for dear life.

There were sounds of crockery falling, glass breaking, heavy objects crashing to the floor all around her. Her pitcher and washbowl slid off the washstand and broke, pouring water all over. Her toilet articles fell in a jumble, followed by the bureau itself, pitching forward. As the drawers were thrust out, their contents spilled out onto the floor.

The roaring sound seemed to go on forever. Then came one final rough jolt, when the very walls seemed to shudder. Finally everything quivered to a halt and a dreadful silence descended.

Was this the end of the world?

For an endless few minutes, Kit huddled in bed, shivering, straining to listen, braced for what might come next. Then slowly she moved over to the side of the bed and swung her legs over. Her bare feet touched the scatter rug. Still holding onto the bed, she gingerly tested her weight on the floor that tilted crazily. It seemed stable enough. Cautiously she stood up, grabbed her clothes from where she had tossed them on the nearby chair, thankful now she had been too tired to hang them up or put them away the night before. The chest of drawers was upended. Breathing hard, she quickly dragged her nightie over her head and pulled on her underclothes. Her fingers shook so that she fumbled with buttons and hooks. She never knew how, but somehow she managed to get dressed.

Whatever had happened she had to get out, see what it was. She crept over to the window and saw people, in wrappers and robes, pouring out of buildings on both sides of the street. They were shouting and calling to each other. "Earthquake! Earthquake!" Everyone looked as frightened as Kit felt, as though any minute the earth would start moving again.

Kit could hear voices and cries and rushing feet in the hall outside her room. She went to the door and tried to open it. However, the earthquake had twisted the doorframe so that the door was stuck. She could not budge it. She tugged frantically, pulling the knob in vain. With a groan of frustration, she ran back to the open window. Leaning on the sill, she looked down. Could she possibly climb out onto the roof, slide down to the ledge above the porch that fronted the house? Maybe let herself down to the porch railing and to the ground?

The ground was a very long way. Feeling dizzy, she gripped the sill to steady herself. Her heart was hammering, but she knew she had to get out or else be trapped in the house if another quake hit. Kit had heard that sometimes the aftershocks were as bad as the first, and this three-story frame house, teetering as it was on the edge of the hill, had never seemed very substantial to her. She felt faint and closed her eyes, murmuring, "Oh, God, help me!"

Then into her mind came verses she had memorized in Sunday school. Gratefully she repeated them to herself now: "'Fear not, for I am with thee; be not dismayed, for I am thy God. I will strengthen thee, yes, I will help thee. I will uphold thee with My righteous right hand.' Thank you, Lord!" she whispered breathlessly and grabbed her shoes, tied them by their laces around her neck, scooped up her notebook, stuffed it into her handbag, and started out the window.

As she perched on the sill ready to swing herself around, she saw the hat! Her beautiful hat with its satin ribbons and bunch of violets! She hesitated a split-second. It was ridiculous, she knew, but she could not leave it when this building itself might topple any minute. She scrambled back into the room, grabbed it, and jammed it on over her sleep-tousled hair.

The straps of her handbag hung on her arm as she crawled over the roof to the edge. It was then someone in the crowd below looked up and saw her.

"Wait a minute, lady!" a man hollered up to her. "Don't try to climb down by yourself!"

"Thank God!" murmured Kit, and she clung there, trying not to panic as the man hurried over to stand directly below her.

"It's a pretty good drop," he yelled, holding up his arms. "So try to lower yourself slowly, and I'll catch you."

Kit prayed a desperate prayer and then, still hanging on to the gutter with one hand, she lowered herself, let go and fell forward. Her shoes struck her in the mouth as she did so, and she cried out just as she felt strong hands grasp her around her waist. Her weight made the man stagger and sent them both sprawling on the grass, but at least she was safely out of the house.

"Thank you!" she said breathlessly as the man got to his feet, stretched out a hand to pull her up. "That was very brave of you."

"You're a plucky girl."

Standing there in her bare feet in the chill foggy morning, Kit's journalistic instincts surfaced. She dug in her handbag for her notebook and asked, "Could I have your name?"

Even as she scribbled it down and listened to the man telling his *own* earthquake story, something rang in Kit's head. It was Clem's voice, saying, "It's being in the right place at the right time. If you're lucky, you'll recognize it when you're on to a *big* story."

This was the *big story!* Kit knew, and she was right here in the midst of it.

She sat down on the listing steps of the house and, as discreetly as possible, put on her stockings and shoes.Then she took out the small brush she kept in her handbag and swept it through her hair, pinning it up under the inappropriate hat. This was the story of the century, something told her. Writing it would give her unassailable credentials as a journalist.

As the fog lifted, people reacted in surprising ways. An almost carnival atmosphere emerged from the dark terror of the frightening moments before daylight. Then messages began to filter in from other parts of the city—alarming reports of whole blocks collapsing, taking with them buildings full of sleeping occupants, bodies trapped in the suffocating wreckage.

Rumors began to circulate. One horrifying possibility was that the whole of downtown San Francisco had disappeared. Kit wondered about the newspaper building. It was old, with many additions as it had expanded. She thought of the press room with its huge, heavy machinery, and the shelves and shelves of lead typefaces. So near Market Street, that building must have suffered severe damage. And if the composing room was gone, there would be no paper.

Still, she kept on taking notes, moving among the crowd as more and more people from other stricken areas joined the ranks of the hilltop neighborhood. Kit sensed that just under the surface panic simmered as dazed persons wandered through, asking about friends and family members they could not locate. The day became an endless procession of the homeless, dragging their possessions from what remained of the rubble of their houses, searching for a place to stay.

Military personnel from Golden Gate Fort rode in on horseback, taking charge, warning people not to try to go back into the buildings until they were declared safe, offering to escort any who desired shelter to the fort, which was being readied for the refugees.

As it began to grow dark, a strange red glow appeared in the sky. Murmurs rippled through the crowd as people speculated on its cause. Then a kind of unified gasp was heard as word came back that San Francisco was on fire! Fire, started by broken gas mains, devouring the city—house by house, street by street, entire blocks and buildings! Worse still, because of the damage done to water pipes by the quake, there was no water to fight it! San Francisco was doomed!

Angry discussions erupted, people blaming the unknown idiot of an engineer who had planned the city's water supply lines across the path of the San Andreas Fault! Rage, incredulity, fear, panic—every conceivable emotion surfaced as the truth of their predicament dawned on the populace. Then, all emotion spent, they settled in to wait it out—a silence broken only by the occasional cry of a baby, a muffled sob, hushed exclamations of despair.

Hours passed. Kit would try to recall from her notes just what happened then. As it was, she kept working—asking questions, jotting down answers, seeking information from every source she could find. When her stub of a pencil became blunt, she borrowed another and wrote on.

Suddenly Kit heard another sound—a familiar sound no less terrifying because it reminded her of many a Fourth of July in Meadowridge. Like the burst of cherry bombs or fireworks on display came a series of explosions. Rumors spread as fast as the raging fire. Some said the military arsenal had blown up. Others denied it, saying the firemen were dynamiting the fire breaks. And since no one knew for sure, a general anxiety fell over the crowd, as heavy as the pall of smoke now shrouding the city.

As the late afternoon fog began to roll in from the Bay, it hung over the hills and made its usual slow descent, adding its unique gloom. In the dark of early evening the eerie wail of foghorns seemed to be sounding a dirge of destruction.

Here and there small clusters of people settled down to spend the night. Most people had not thought to bring food with them when they fled their houses in panic. As a few small campfires were lighted, a sense of camaraderie moved people to share what little they had. They exchanged their stories and their concerns as well, trying to support what small hope still lingered in worried hearts. Some expressed their anxiety for missing family members, and Kit wondered with a sharp pang where Dan was and if he had survived!

With thousands injured, many still buried in the rubble of demolished buildings, rescue teams worked steadily to bring relief, while all available medical personnel was recruited, doctors and nurses giving aid everywhere. Hospital patients were evacuated and taken to the military compound.

Throughout the long night, the fire swept on like a great dragon, scorching section after section of the city in its hot breath. Embarcadero bluejackets manned pumps with water from the Bay, trying desperately to quench the fire's insatiable thirst.

Her pencil worn to a nub, her body and mind exhausted, Kit shivered in the dampness, more from nerves than from the chill of the night air. So much of what she had seen, heard, experienced this long day could not be immediately recalled. Her emotions seemed deadened, too. A catastrophe of this magnitude was almost incomprehensible, and Kit knew she would have to sort out all the facts, organize her impressions, give herself time to translate this tragedy in terms of human suffering.

Even in her numbed condition Kit slowly began to form her lead. Eventually, she realized, there would be hundreds of stories filed. To be printed hers would have to be outstanding. She needed something dramatic—

"The Ferry Building at the foot of Market Street remained gleaming white among charred telephone poles, cracked cement, piles of rubble, the hands of the clock on its side eerily stopped at exactly 5:15 A.M., the time the earthquake struck—a literal Phoenix rising out of the ashes of a once beautiful city."

As police and military patrolled the streets, word went out that looters were being shot on sight. Rumor or not, it was terrifying for those who had businesses downtown or houses out of which they had rushed, bringing nothing with them but the clothes on their backs.

Kit heard that the big downtown hospital, where Dan was a resident physician, had been hit hard, and rescue parties were trying to find and bring out those who had been injured or trapped in the wreckage. As they dusted off the victims— doctors and nurses and even a few patients—who had suffered nothing more than a severe shaking, these in turn joined the rescue effort. Once out of the damaged building, the hospitalized ill and injured must be transported to a safe location, and the military hospital at the Presidio was designated.

If Dan had survived—and right now she couldn't let herself imagine the alternative—Kit knew he would be among those brave souls who, with no thought for their own safety, would be trying to save others.

Similar acts of unselfish bravery were being repeated all over the city.

As night came on, hundreds of homeless who had not elected to go to the fort were being herded to Golden Gate Park, where tents were already being erected as a temporary shelter.

Kit was undecided as to just what to do when she ran into Nelly Armstrong, a friend from the newspaper, and learned from her that the building itself had been destroyed. They held on to each other, seeing the horror of what had happened reflected in each other's white faces. Kit was relieved to learn messages were being sent over the Postal wire, and reporters were filing their stories from Oakland.

Relief trains had already left Los Angeles with medical supplies, doctors and nurses on their way to help the devastated city. Soup kitchens were being set up to feed the hundreds of people now left without kitchens of their own, food or money to buy it.

Nelly told Kit that her own place, a small one-story house, had somehow managed to escape total disaster. The damage consisted mostly of broken windows, smashed crockery, a few pictures jounced off the walls. She invited Kit to stay with her until Kit could find out if the rooming house would be declared habitable again or at least until she could go back and collect her things.

Gratefully, Kit accepted, and it was sitting at Nelly's kitchen table that Kit began to write the earthquake story that would bring startling changes in her life.

EXCLUSIVE TO *MEADOWRIDGE MONITOR*

From: Kathleen Ternan   Date line: San Francisco, April 18, 1906

At 5:15 A.M. in the gray, foggy dawn of this April morning, disaster struck the beautiful city by the Bay,

San Francisco, California. Citizens were awakened,
roused out of sound sleep by a terrible rumbling noise
followed by a series of strong, jolting shocks that
wrought catastrophic damage on streets and buildings,
as well as causing death and injuries. As buildings top-
pled and walls crumbled, falling bricks and beams
smashed into sidewalks, and huge craters opened in the
streets. Telephone and telegraph poles came crashing
down, splintering in a tangle of wires. No one realized it
at first, but this would serve to cut the city off from all
communication with the outside world for a matter of
hours.

Unless you saw it yourself, it would be impossible to
image the extent of Nature's destruction on this city.

The days that followed the earthquake were formless. A
heavy curtain, like that of the city's smoke, hung over the
people; people who walked like robots, people who looked as
if they were in some kind of trance.

Every day Kit ventured out gathering more material for
her earthquake report. It was the stories of individuals that
interested her most. There were many stories of missing
family members and happier ones of reunions. Over and
over Kit heard people say, "This kind of thing changes your
priorities," "You learn what's important." Bankers stood in
food lines with carpenters, housemaids with their mis-
tresses. A kind of macabre joke, repeated often, was "An
earthquake is a great leveler." Even with all the confusion
and the dreadful destruction, the human spirit proved again
and again to be triumphant, great acts of courage done on
behalf of strangers, kindnesses rendered, generosity
extended.

She knew many fine reporters were writing other kinds of
stories—descriptions of the fires, the destruction of well-
known mansions, hotels, restaurants and commercial buildings, so Kit concentrated on what was known in the trade as
"human interest" stories. And there was no lack of those.

By Friday the fires were pretty well under control. Only smoldering pockets remained here and there, and over all the fine cindery dust and a lingering pall of smoke. Kit had set out early that morning, hoping her PRESS card might get her past the barriers to downtown so that she could see for herself what remained of the once-proud business section, see the skeletons of the luxurious mansions.

She was in the process of convincing one of the policemen to let her through when she heard someone hoarsely shouting her name.

"Kit! Kit Ternan!"

She whirled around and saw Dan, gray-faced, haggard, hollow-eyed, his hair rumpled, wearing a torn, stained, once-white medical jacket over a soiled shirt. He looked as though he had not slept in days, and his stride was slow even as he tried to hurry toward her.

Lifting her skirts over the fallen debris, Kit ran to meet him. In the middle of the ruined street, they hugged, laughing hysterically.

"Oh, Dan, I'm so *glad* to see you!"

"Kit, Kit, I was so worried about you!"

As their words tumbled over each other, they shared scraps of information about what had transpired since they had parted the night of the opera.

"That all seems a hundred years ago!" Kit shook her head in disbelief.

"Another lifetime," agreed Dan. "Everything is gone, Kit. So many hurt, so many dead." His own fiery trial had etched new lines of strength and compassion about Dan's eyes and mouth.

"I know. It's been like a bad dream."

"A nightmare," Dan said solemnly. "I came looking for you, Kit, hoping you'd be in the vicinity of your boardinghouse. When you weren't there, I almost went wild—"

Quickly Kit told him where she was staying.

"I've been ordered to get some sleep," Dan said at last. "We're quartered in the barracks at the Presidio. Then I go back on duty. But I wanted to make sure you were safe before I—" Dan broke off and touched the brim of Kit's hat. He smiled down at her, an amused twinkle glimmering in his tired eyes. "I see you're still attached to your hat!"

Kit laughed, too. She had almost forgotten her beautiful violet-trimmed hat, now much the worse for wear.

Dan put both his hands on either side of her face, then unexpectedly bent down and kissed her on the mouth.

"I still say it's one of the dandiest hats I've ever seen," he said softly.

A month later, Dan was sitting in Nelly Armstrong's kitchen across from Kit, reading one of her articles published about the earthquake and its aftermath. Dan had not seen all the articles, so when he came over on his regular day off to see her at Nelly's, where she was still staying, Kit had shown him her tear-sheets.

"It's good, Kit, really good." Dan looked up from the paper he was holding. "You're quite a writer."

Kit felt a warm flush rise into her cheeks, wash over her face and throat under his admiring glance. She got up and went over to the stove and, lifting the coffeepot, asked, "More?"

Dan shoved his mug toward her and she refilled it.

"Wait until I tell you some exciting news, Dan. It seems my series on the earthquake—the little incidents and interviews I did with people—were picked up by newspapers back East as well. And guess what? I've been offered a chance to write for a woman's magazine. The editor of *Woman's Hearth and Home* wrote to me, asked me if I'd be interested in doing a series of articles for them. She said, *and* I quote—" Kit's voice took on a dramatic tone—"'We'd like to see the same kind of heart-tugging, human interest type stories you did on your series on the San Francisco earthquake.'" Here Kit struck a Napoleonic pose. "I think at last my career is taking off."

"Congratulations, Kit!" Dan said heartily. "That *is* good news! You'll have no trouble getting your old job back at the

Monitor." He grinned. "You're a celebrity in Meadowridge now."

Kit looked puzzled as she sat back down and spooned sugar into her coffee.

"But I have no plans to get my old job back, Dan."

He reached across the table and his hand closed over hers. Looking at her steadily, he said, "Let's go home, Kit."

She stared at him blankly.

"Dr. Woodward's contacted me again, wants me to join his practice," Dan went on. "He's made me a generous offer, Kit. You know I always wanted to be a country doctor, and this would mean stepping into an established practice. Most of all, I'd be working with a man I like and admire. It's a great opportunity."

Kit struggled with several conflicting emotions. Her mouth suddenly dry, she took a swallow of coffee. "That's wonderful, Dan. I'm happy for you."

"Didn't you hear what I said, Kit?" He pressed the hand he was holding. "I said, let's go home, meaning *you and I...together!*"

"I don't understand—" she said haltingly.

"Don't you realize I've fallen in love with you, Kit? I think I've actually loved you for a long time, only I didn't know it. I want us to get married and go back to Meadowridge together."

Kit felt her pulse begin a staccato beat.

Dan regarded her with a mixture of amusement and affection. "You really didn't know I loved you, did you?" His tone was quizzical.

She shook her head. "I always thought we were just—good friends."

"That's the best kind of love, Kit, to begin as good friends." He was smiling, but his eyes were serious as he searched hers for some idea of what she was thinking, feeling. "So, what do you say?"

Longing for him swept through Kit like a strong Bay wind. Could it really be true? Dan, whom she had long ago given up as an impossible dream, offering her his love and life?

As she gazed at him in a kind of stunned bewilderment, he reached for both of her hands and covered them in a strong clasp.

"Kit, you're everything I want in a woman. You're brave and kind and smart and compassionate...and beautiful. I want you to share my life."

Kit swallowed hard, her heart pumping so loudly she was certain it must be audible to Dan's well-trained ear, even without a stethoscope. She struggled to formulate the question she dreaded asking.

"What is it, Kit? Something's troubling you," Dan said, looking anxious. "Maybe being a country doctor's wife isn't your cup of tea."

"No, Dan, it isn't that—although I never really thought about it. But it isn't that at all." She paused, then taking a deep breath, she made the plunge. "What about Laurel, Dan? I know you've always loved her."

A slight shadow darkened Dan's eyes for a moment before he answered. "I did love Laurel, I *do* love her, and I'll always love her. But, Kit, I loved her as a boy loves a sweet young girl, with all those first youthful feelings he thinks will last forever. Of course they don't, and Laurel never loved *me* like that." He hesitated. "Loving Laurel was part of growing up. She is part of my life. Just as you have always been a part of my life, Kit." He paused and, looking at her intently, went on, "But over these past months this feeling for you has been growing until I realized it was there all the time, like a beautiful seed planted that just needed time, exposure, tending, to mature into what it is now—a *man's* love for the woman he wants to spend the rest of his life with.

"I know the difference now. I believe I know what real love is—wanting someone to be with you always, knowing you're understood, knowing that person wants all the things you want for yourself." He paused. "But how can I convince you,

Kit, that my feelings for you are real, that I love you, that I want to marry you?"

Kit returned his anxious look, her eyes shining with astonished happiness. "I *do* believe you, Dan. And I'm honored that you...care for me that way. But...I don't know. I don't know whether I'm ready...I don't know if I want to go back to Meadowridge. You see, it took so long, and I worked so hard to get away, to get a foothold in what I want to do." She halted, then continued slowly, "Because you see, Dan, I *do* want to be a writer, and I don't know if I can marry you and write too."

"But a writer can write anywhere."

"It's not just the place, Dan. It's the time, the energy, the dedication necessary to become a really *good* writer. My heart would be divided. I just don't know if I can—"

"You don't have to give me an answer right away, Kit. I don't finish at the hospital until August, and Dr. Woodward is not expecting me until September." Dan got up, came around the table, and gently drew her up and into his arms. "Just please don't say no."

His touch kindled the long-banked flame of her feelings for him, and they sprang alive within her. Kit leaned against him, and it was a beautiful, safe feeling. As she felt the strength of his arms about her, she was surprised at how natural it felt to be there.

Yet how was it possible to be handed what you had always thought would be your heart's desire and then, when it was offered, not be sure?

"It's an important decision, Dan," she murmured.

"I know. Take all the time you need, Kit. I'm not going to stop loving you."

21

Throughout the next busy months San Francisco vigorously set about rebuilding. The city seemed to have found a new energy, a new spirit, a kind of proud defiance in showing the world it could come back from the brink of annihilation bigger, stronger, more beautiful than ever.

Everywhere in the city could be seen signs of construction. People filled the streets, still under repair, going about their business with renewed purpose. Flower vendors were back at their corners, banks and stores were open for business, restaurants served their customers as if April 18 had been just another day.

The lifeblood of the city throbbed, coursing through every artery of its commerce and industry. Kit was both gratified and disturbed by all this progress. The accelerated pace proved a distraction from the concentration needed for her new writing assignment. Not only that, but night after night she lay awake, pondering the decision for which Dan was patiently waiting before he left for Meadowridge at the end of August.

There was a deep longing in Kit to be cherished, cared for and sheltered by the kind of love Dan was offering. But there was also a fierce ambition to make something of herself, to reach some of her long-held goals, to prove that an orphan can achieve in spite of little encouragement, with only sheer determination and dogged persistence.

Could she have both? Kit tossed and turned endlessly, trying to solve those demanding questions. In her heart, she believed God *had* given her the gift of expressing thoughts and feelings, describing events and people and she had worked hard to develop that gift. She was on the brink of something now that she could not bring herself to give up.

On one of those sleepless nights, a compelling idea for a series of articles came to Kit that brought her wide awake. She realized she had been subconsciously thinking about it for a long time. Now, it seemed the perfect time to write it.

When Kit discussed it with Dan, he encouraged her to go ahead.

"I know it will touch a lot of people, Kit. It's your story. No one else can tell it the way you can. You'll be writing it for Toddy and Laurel and all the children like you three, who were on the Orphan Train."

Night after night, with the light from the oil lamp burning low, Kit emptied her heart through her pen, letting all of it flow through her—the good and bad, the joy and sorrow, the pleasure and pain.

Little Lost Family
by Kathleen Ternan

Within each human heart is a deep longing for a place to belong, not one that must be earned or won or demanded, but is one's right by birth. If that birthright is denied through whatever of circumstance, there is forever a void in that life that nothing else can ever fill.

Twenty years ago in Boston, Massachusetts, this happened to my small brother and sister and me and we became a "little lost family"—

Writing of her experiences as an abandoned child, the remembered feelings of sadness and grief almost overwhelmed her. But Kit wrote on and as she did, allowing her feelings to emerge, her heart was opened to a new understanding, a gentleness, a compassionate understanding for the young, grief-stricken, widowed father who had left the three of them at Greystone Orphanage.

Something else happened during the writing of this article. Until then, Kit had not realized how much she had suppressed, not daring to risk feeling her pain and loss.

At first she thought she might have said too much, revealed too much, opened her inner self too much, knowing this piece would be read by strangers. And yet, after she had put it aside for a week or more, then reread it, Kit discovered a marvelous truth. There was healing power in her creative words—healing for others, for *herself*. It was with a sense of relief that Kit did the final editing and then sent it off to *Woman's Hearth and Home*.

The summer passed swiftly and then it was time for Dan to leave. Reluctantly Kit let him go without an answer.

"I'm willing to wait, Kit," he told her as he kissed her goodbye.

Later Kit wrote in her journal, "How can a city filled with people, with noise and endless activity, be such a lonely place because one person is missing?"

She tried to work hard at the paper during the day so that she would be tired enough to sleep at night. But most nights she stayed up writing. She was like a person possessed, filling page after page with stories, many of them near-forgotten incidents from her childhood.

Every day she checked her mailbox hopefully for a response to her submission to *Woman's Hearth and Home*. Weeks went by, each one seeming longer than the last. She missed Dan more than she had imagined possible and she fretted anxiously about the story she had submitted. Maybe it had been too personal, too sad, oversentimentalized? Maybe she should stick to straight reporting.

Then one day she found a long envelope in her box with the magazine's letterhead. With trembling hands Kit opened it. A check was enclosed. The amount was more than she had expected, twice as much as she had received for her "earthquake" story, and a letter from the editor that Kit read with ever-mounting excitement.

Dear Miss Ternan,

We are impressed with your latest submission, "Little Lost Family," the account of your experiences as an Orphan Train rider. All members of our editorial staff have read it and, I must tell you, it evoked many a heartfelt tear. At our monthly meeting it was unanimously decided to feature this article as the lead story in our December issue—always a popular one with a larger than average readership. I think your story will bring a warm response from our readers.

We are looking forward to having you as a regular contributor to our magazine and hope you will be submitting many more of this type of heart-warming article.

Kit was elated. But with no one to share this exciting news, her joy soon evaporated and the old self-doubts resurfaced.

That night as Kit lay in bed, she was haunted by old memories—nights of lying in the narrow cot in the dormitory at Greystone Orphanage when she felt so abandoned, the nights on the Orphan Train roaring across the dark prairie when she was frightened of what was going to happen to her, wondering if anyone would ever really care about her, and those long nights up in her loft room at the Hansen farm when she would stare into the dark, fighting the fear and loneliness.

It's your own fault, she admonished herself. *You could have gone back to Meadowridge with Dan. Right now you could be in his arms, warm, safe, protected—loved!*

What good was even long-worked-for success if there was no one to share it?

Kit received a complimentary issue of the December *Woman's Hearth and Home* and stared at it, unbelieving. An illustration of a heartbreaking trio of children who looked nothing like her, Jamie, or Gwynny accompanied the article, but even that didn't matter. There was her name, KATHLEEN TERNAN, printed in bold letters in a nationally published periodical!

Kit celebrated Christmas with Nelly and some of the other people from the newspaper who lived too far to go home for the short holiday. Dan sent her a leather writing portfolio, one that could be placed comfortably on her lap. In the enclosed card, he had written, "Just to remind you that it's possible to write *anywhere*, even on a train to Meadowridge!"

Kit's usual optimism was lacking as the New Year was announced by church bells and whistles piercing the foggy midnight. She had turned down an invitation to a party and spent the evening curled up in bed writing in her journal, wondering what 1907 would hold for her.

At the end of January she received a letter from Eleanor Hargrove, the editor of *Woman's Hearth and Home*. In it she told Kit the response to "Little Lost Family" had been staggering. The magazine had been deluged with letters asking for reprints, and she enclosed an additional check, asking permission to comply with their readers' requests.

Miss Hargrove also said the magazine was forwarding, under separate cover, letters that had been addressed personally to the author and that Kit should be receiving them soon. She closed by asking when they could expect another article.

In the same day's mail there was a large manila envelope containing dozens of letters addressed to Kit in care of the magazine. As she read one after the other, Kit had to stop often to wipe her eyes. Then she came upon one envelope whose familiar handwriting and return address surprised her. It was from Miss Cady! The letter began:

I have just read your beautiful story reprinted in our newspaper from *Woman's Hearth and Home*. I have long regretted the circumstances of our parting and blame myself. It was my own pride that dictated you should be an example of my work—*my* accomplishment. Of course, your success is no such thing! You have succeeded through your own diligent effort, your desire to excel. God has a way of bringing about His purpose in a person's life and I can see you have found the unique place He planned for you and are doing the work He has called you to do. Forgive me for not understanding.

Always your friend,
Millicent Cady

Kit read the letter over twice. Never had anything meant so much to her. The unreconciled friendship with Miss Cady had always been an aching bruise in her heart. If nothing else positive came from her article, this alone was sufficient reward.

But there was more to come. Within a week another letter was forwarded to Kit from the magazine. The envelope was of fine, pale gray, deckle-edged stationery; the handwriting, a cultured script.

When Kit opened it and unfolded the letter, a small photograph fell out. She picked it up and looked at it. It was of a beautiful young woman, dressed in an exquisite wedding veil, her dress embroidered with lace and tiny seed pearls.

Puzzled, Kit began to read:

My dear Miss Ternan,

You do not know me, but I have just finished reading your poignant article, "Little Lost Family," in the current issue of *Woman's Hearth and Home* magazine. I was greatly moved. Indeed, almost overcome with emotion. I knew I had to write to you, but I must beg your discretion in the matter I am about to reveal to you.

After ten childless years, my husband and I adopted a beautiful two-year-old baby girl from the Greystone Orphanage. We adored her from the time we set eyes upon her cherubic face, rosy cheeks, big, blue eyes, and masses of ringlets. As I looked upon her that first day, she held out her arms to me, and I clasped her to my heart. It was as if some Higher Power had directed us and we knew instinctively we belonged to each other.

We brought her home and reared her with perfect love and tenderness, seeing that she had every advantage—physical, material, spiritual. She grew up to be a lovely, sweet, talented young lady who never gave us a moment's anxiety and returned the love we lavished upon her.

She has done well in her studies, has a sweet singing voice, and plays the harp. Last year she became engaged to a fine young man, the son of family friends, who has just graduated with a Law Degree and will be joining the distinguished firm of his father and grandfather.

At this point, I must confess, that shortly after the adoption, my husband and I moved to another town where he was to take over the management of a mill, and in this new situation, everyone assumed Gwynny was our own child. We never told her she was adopted. The time never seemed right. She was happy and secure, and the more time that passed, the more we felt it might do great harm if she found out she was not actually our birth child. Let me assure you we consider her such, as if she had been born to us.

But after reading your piece, my heart was deeply touched by *your* suffering, wondering all these years where your baby sister and brother were. That is why I felt compelled to write to tell you about Gwynny.

I have not given you her married name nor where she now resides. I still feel it would be a very disturbing thing for her to find out at this time in her life that she is adopted. I hope and pray you will understand and respect my reasons.

God bless you, my dear. It is my sincere hope that your own life has been as satisfactory as I believe Gwynny would consider hers. You have a God-given gift for expressing the deepest emotions of the human heart and I know you will do a great deal of good with your talent.

The letter was signed only, "A Christian Mother."

The writing blurred before Kit's eyes. Starting from the beginning, she read the letter over again with disbelief. She picked up the small picture, held it, studying each detail. Yes, yes, the eyes, the curls clustered around her forehead, the hint of dimples around the sweetly curved mouth. Even though she was posed with all the demure dignity of a bridal photograph, Kit *could* see the remnants of that precious baby sister.

As she gazed at the face the pain, that had been inside for years, rushed forth in a torrent of tears. But with the pain came release. At last, she knew Gwynny had been safe, beloved, had known a real home, the affectionate care of both parents.

When all Kit's tears were spent, she got out the writing portfolio, dipped her pen in ink and began to write a letter. It was a letter she now felt ready to write. The words came easier than she thought they might. When she came to the end, she signed it, blotted it, got out an envelope and addressed and stamped it. So eager was she that it go out right away that Kit put on her hat and coat and ran to the mailbox at the end of the street. The letter was addressed to Dr. Daniel Brooks of Meadowridge.

22

As the train chugged up the last incline before dipping down into the valley, Kit caught her first sight of Meadowridge in nearly three years. Its rooftops gleaming in the fall sunshine, the spire of the church spiked up into the blue autumn sky, the town lay nestled in rolling hills brilliant with autumn color.

Kit was out of her seat and already moving down the aisle toward the door as the train whistle pierced the air, its engine hissing and its brakes screeching on the rails as it slowed to a stop.

"Meadowridge! Meadowridge, folks!" announced the conductor and Kit's heart leapt. She had a sense of homecoming she had not expected. Then, as she swung down the steps and onto the platform, she saw Dan and tears rushed into her eyes. He was hurrying toward her, long legs covering the distance in record time, waving a bouquet of gold and bronze chrysanthemums.

"Kit, you're here! You're finally here!"

All she could do was nod, her eyes brimming, her heart full.

It wasn't until Dan had given her a hug that nearly left her breathless that Kit saw Dr. and Mrs. Woodward standing behind him at a discreet distance.

As soon as the Woodwards learned of her engagement to Dan and that she was coming home to marry him, Ava had written Kit and told her they would not have it any other way but that she stay with them upon her return to Meadowridge and let them give her wedding.

"You know you are very special to us, as one of the little 'Orphans' who came with our precious Laurel. We always felt you and Toddy were like sisters to Laurel, growing up as you did so close to each other and so much a part of our lives."

Kit read these words over and over, treasuring each one, responding to the love and thoughtfulness that had prompted them.

"Please allow us to do this," Ava had asked.

Dr. Woodward had added his own comments on the invitation by writing Kit to thank her for agreeing to Ava's request.

"Ava looks ten years younger. She is full of excitement and plans. She misses Laurel, as you can imagine, even though both she and Gene have been here for visits. To have a 'daughter' to plan a wedding for has given her a new lease on life. We both are looking forward to your arrival and I want to formally accept with great pleasure the honor you have bestowed on me in asking me to give you away on your great day."

Dr. Woodward had added a P.S. that delighted Kit: "I hope Dan realizes what a lucky young man he is that you have given him your promise to love, cherish and so on! If not, I shall take him aside promptly and inform him of the fact. However, I do not think that will be necessary. He is wandering around Meadowridge with quite an absent expression on his face, frequently forgets things, stares into space, answers in a distracted manner any questions put to him. I would be concerned about him, if I did not know better, for his condition is quite alarming. But having suffered from the same ailment myself thirty-some years ago, I easily recognize that. Dan is love-sick, lonely and anxious. These symptoms will only subside when the only known cure is administered, one Kathleen Ternan arriving in Meadowridge."

Now, they both stood waiting their turn to embrace Kit and welcome her back.

At the Woodwards' house, Kit was warmly greeted by Ella who served them all fresh coffee and cinnamon rolls right out of the oven as they gathered around the dining room table to discuss wedding plans. Dan, who could not seem to take his eyes off Kit, was singularly vague when asked for an opinion or suggestion.

Finally, Dr. Woodward got to his feet and said with a chuckle, "Well, Dan, I think we should leave the ladies to settle the details. You don't seem to be offering much help, and I certainly know nothing about decorations for the church or what kind of punch to serve at the reception. Besides, we have patients to see, my boy."

When the men left, Ava, her arm around Kit's waist, took her upstairs to Laurel's old bedroom to get settled.

"I can't tell you what it means to have you here, Kit," she said giving her a little squeeze. "And I have wonderful news. Laurel is definitely coming for the wedding! We hope she will sing! And we've written to Toddy but she is not sure whether or not she can get time off from her nursing duties. But even if she can't make it, Mrs. Hale insists on having the reception."

"Oh, Mrs. Woodward!" Kit exclaimed. "I never thought — never dreamed — this could all happen!"

Ava looked pleased. "Well, it *is* happening! And no one could deserve it more than you, my dear girl," she said, patting Kit's shoulder affectionately.

Ava left Kit alone in the lovely pink and white bedroom that she had envied in years past. She always loved visiting her friend here where they had shared so many girlish confidences. On the rare occasions she had been allowed by Cora Hansen to stay overnight, Kit secretly used to pretend, before going to sleep, that *this* was *her* room! Now she was to stay here, live in the Woodwards' charming home for two whole weeks before her wedding day.

She walked around, admiring the flowered wallpaper, her hand trailing along the footboard of the polished maple bed, pausing to examine the dainty appointments on the dressing table, the embroidered dresser scarf on the mirrored bureau. Kit recalled that evening, the summer after graduation, when Laurel had met her outside the library after Kit finished work. They had come up here so they could talk in private. That was when Laurel told Kit she was planning to go away. Taken off guard, Kit had asked her, "But how can you leave all this?"

Kit had never forgotten Laurel's reply. "Don't you *really* understand, Kit? Don't you really *know?* Nothing makes up for being an orphan."

Now Kit understood better what Laurel meant. The wounds—of being abandoned, whatever the circumstances, left to fend for oneself in the impersonal atmosphere of an orphanage, daily face the uncertainty of the future—went deep. Maybe they were never really healed, no matter where one was "placed out." The scar tissue remained, and ever after, the pain of that loss surfaced.

Involuntarily Kit shuddered. The worst damage was that she could never quite believe that lasting happiness was possible, that whatever she had might be snatched away without warning. As a result she had learned not to cling to people, not to expect things to last, not to expect happiness. Maybe, that's why it had taken her so long to believe Dan really loved her, wanted her to marry him.

In a rush of gratitude, Kit slipped onto her knees beside the bed, and put her head down upon her clasped hands.

"Dear Lord," she prayed, "help me to trust Your love, Your kindness to me. I know You have brought Dan into my life for a purpose. Make me worthy of his love, help me to accept it and him as Your gracious gift to me. Please help me to become a good wife to him. And, Lord, thank You—"

Before Kit got up from her knees she whispered the words with which she always closed her prayers. "And bless Gwynny and Jamie, wherever they are."

That evening Dan came for supper and afterwards he and Kit took a long walk along familiar streets in the lingering light of the early autumn evening. Almost unconsciously they ended up at the playground of the old Meadowridge Grammar School. They sat down on adjacent swings and, as they idly pushed back and forth, they talked.

"It seems like a dream to be back here," Kit said. "This brings back so many memories, doesn't it?"

"Yes, but I'd really rather look forward to the future—*our* future. I didn't think it was possible to be this happy," Dan said, twisting his swing around so that he was facing her. "I love you so much, Kit."

His eyes held such tenderness that again Kit felt the start of tears. Trying to make light of them, she said, "I don't know what's wrong with me, doctor, I feel so emotional—"

"Emotions are natural. If we didn't have them, how would we know we're alive?" Dan smiled. Then he got up, held out his hand to her and pulled her to her feet and into his arms. Then, hand in hand, they strolled down toward Meadowridge Park.

It was still light enough to see the ducks skimming on the water at the edge of the lake, making little ripples on its silvery surface.

"I have something for you, Kit." Dan drew a small jewelry box from his coat pocket. He took Kit's hand and placed it in her palm. "Open it."

She looked at him, then down at the rounded velvet box and pressed the spring that lifted the lid. A single luminous pearl shimmered against the deep blue plush lining.

Kit drew in her breath.

"I wasn't sure what kind of engagement ring you might want. Then, when I went to look at them, I knew right away what kind you should have. A pearl seemed to me to represent *you*, Kit—pure, serene, with a deep inner radiance." Dan looked a little embarrassed. "I'm no poet—I wish I could think of something really eloquent to say at a time like this—"

For one who had never owned any jewelry this was the grandest ring she had ever seen, and she felt the surge of tears once more as she took the ring out of the box. "This says it all, Dan. Please, put it on my finger." And she held up her left hand.

"Now, it's official," he said with a grin when the ring was in place.

Mrs. Danby, a little bent but as sharp-tongued and skilled with a needle as ever, arrived at the Woodwards the following morning, ready to do the final fitting on Kit's wedding dress.

A few weeks before Ava had asked Kit to send her measurements so that Mrs. Danby could get started on her wedding gown, which was to be Ava's gift to her. Knowing she could not possibly afford anything as lovely as Mrs. Woodward would be sure to feel was appropriate, Kit gave in.

As she stood being pinned, tucked, and turned while Mrs. Danby, under Ava's close supervision, marked the hem of the cream-colored satin, Kit recalled the debacle of her graduation dress. The design of *this* dress was faultless, perfect for her tall, willowy figure. Remembering that other occasion naturally brought Cora Hansen to mind.

She and Dan rode out to the farm soon after Kit's return to see Cora, show her ring and tell their wedding plans. It saddened Kit to see Cora had slipped further and although she seemed to recognize Kit, her eyes were vacant and her manner lethargic.

On the way back to town, Kit wept a little and Dan tried to comfort her.

"She's in no pain, Kit, and her daughter-in-law is taking good care of her. Mrs. Hansen's had a hard life. Probably this is the most restful period of her entire life. I think she's contented and, whether or not she showed it, I am sure it pleased her very much to see you."

"I don't know." Kit sighed as she wiped her eyes. "I wish, somehow, I could have done more to make her happy."

"You can't be responsible for another person's happiness, Kit. You did more than you know to make Cora Hansen's life brighter, better, happier." He reached for her hand, drew it through his arm to hold it along with the buggy reins. "You do that for everyone whose life you touch, Kit."

Two days before the wedding Laurel arrived.

The two young women hugged, laughing and crying and exclaiming all at once when they saw each other.

"You look wonderful! Prettier than ever!" declared Kit, holding her friend at arm's length.

"And *you*, Kit! You were always beautiful! But *now*—" She shook her head. "Love! If they could only bottle it and sell it, it would make someone a fortune!"

They both giggled and hugged again and ran upstairs to Laurel's bedroom, where Kit was happily ensconced. Settling down together on the windowseat like old times, they exchanged news, reminiscing and chatting as easily and naturally if they had never been apart. There was so much to share.

Ava almost hated to break in on the marathon conversation to tell them supper was ready. Afterward, Dan came by to welcome Laurel, then left again to let the two friends continue their reunion, uninterrupted.

Later, while getting ready for bed, Kit paused in front of the dressing table mirror. Putting down her hairbrush, she turned and looked her friend in the eye.

"The truth, Laurel?"

Laurel seemed surprised. "The truth? Well, of course. What is the question, Kit?"

"I—I know you loved Dan at one time—"

"Yes, I did." Laurel spoke decisively. "And I *still* do!"

Kit gave an involuntary gasp.

"But not the way you must be thinking," she hastened to say. "I love Dan as a sister loves a brother."

Still holding her breath, Kit pressed. "But tonight— when you saw him—were there any—well, any regrets?"

"Regrets? About *Dan?* Heavens no, Kit!" Laurel exclaimed. "I'm so happy for you both. Really and truly," she said earnestly, then went on. "If you knew Gene, you wouldn't have had to ask. Gene is exactly right for me just as Dan and you are exactly right for each other."

"It's just that when we were all in high school—" Kit blushed.

"Dear Kit, that was years ago! It seems a hundred now. Besides, if I had stayed here, not gone to Boston, I'd never have met Gene! That seems impossible now, but it's true. I wouldn't have found my grandmother either. And of course, it was through Gene that I was able to put together all the pieces of my life, find out about my real father."

Laurel came over and gave Kit a hug. "Ah, no, Kit, no regrets about anything. God had it all planned out for each of us. I believe that, don't you? And the way Dan looks at you, Kit, you should never have any doubts about *him*. I'm sure *he* has no regrets."

Kit returned her friend's hug gratefully. "I guess it's because I never really expected to have something this wonderful happen to me," she said slowly. "And lately so many good things have happened—I've had some success with my writing and now, Dan. It's almost too good to be true."

"I know, I used to feel that way at first about Gene. I kept pinching myself to make sure I wasn't asleep and that I'd wake up and find I'd dreamed it all." Her eyes sparkled, then her lovely face grew serious. "It may have something to do with our being orphans, Kit. In the orphanage you're made to feel you're not important, you're just a number, a place in line, a cot in the dormitory—and then that awful thing of being paraded out in front of people, to be inspected like cattle!" She halted and for a moment they both relived that dreadful experience of the Orphan Train. Then with a little shudder Laurel went on.

"I *know* I was lucky being 'placed out' with the Woodwards, Kit. But you know it wasn't all easy. Mother was mourning their own daughter, Dorie, and I always felt I had to be better, brighter, nicer in order to be accepted. Even as a little girl I felt that pressure. And you know something else, Kit?" Here Laurel hesitated.

"What?"

"I was always afraid they'd send me back, that I'd do something terrible and have to go back to the orphanage!"

Kit shook her head slowly. "No, I didn't exactly worry about that, although I'm sure Jess might have been glad to get rid of me. In fact, I *hoped* sometimes that I *would* get sent back and maybe be 'placed out' somewhere else—especially when I saw the kind of homes you and Toddy had. Or, maybe, that my father would come looking for all of us—my little sister and brother—and we'd be a family again." Kit sighed. "I can't remember exactly when I gave up that dream!"

Laurel nodded sympathetically.

Kit wiped away the few tears that came and said brightly, "Oh, I haven't told you what happened after my article

'Little Lost Family' was published in *Woman's Hearth and Home* magazine, have I?"

She got out the letter from the woman who had adopted Gwynny, and let Laurel read it. They were just in the midst of an animated discussion when the bedroom door burst open unceremoniously and a voice sang out, "Surprise!"

Startled, they both turned and saw her standing in the doorway.

"Toddy!" they screamed in unison.

23

With the arrival of Toddy, the trio was complete. It was long after midnight when the three of them finally gave in to fatigue after the long day filled with excitement. Toddy departed for the Hale house, promising to be back early in the morning, and Laurel and Kit fell into bed and were instantly asleep.

The following afternoon, while Laurel practiced the solos she had been asked to sing at the ceremony, Toddy and Kit walked over to decorate the church for the wedding the next day. Both the Woodward and Hale gardens had supplied an abundance of brilliant fall flowers for them to use.

As they went up and down the aisles, tying wide satin white and gold ribbons in bows on the ends of each pew, Toddy and Kit had a chance to talk.

"I was so sorry to hear about Helene," Kit said softly.

"I know," Toddy replied. It was still hard for her to think about her adopted sister's death. "Of course, we all knew that it could happen any time. Her health was so delicate. But I don't think I believed it until it actually happened."

"It's easy to deny something you don't want to accept," agreed Kit, thinking of her own denial that her father had willingly abandoned them, chosen not to return, let them all be adopted. "But, in the end, life forces us to face even the unpleasant things."

"Yes." Toddy nodded, swallowing the hard lump that rose in her throat when she spoke of Helene. "Her death did make me come to some important decisions about my future. If she had lived, I don't think I would ever have gone into nursing. Mrs. Hale made everything so easy for us—"

"Is your training very difficult?" Kit asked, remembering the endless hard work of caring for Cora Hansen when she was ill.

"Yes, *very*. If I didn't feel it was what I was supposed to do, that it *was* my vocation, I don't think I could have gotten through the last two years. Now, I love it. It's given me a sense of purpose. The fact that I'm actually helping people who need me makes me feel worthwhile."

"And what about Chris, Toddy?" Kit asked gently.

Toddy took a long time arranging the bow she was tying before answering. "I sent him away, Kit. I didn't think it was fair to keep him dangling. Chris wanted me to run away with him and get married, in spite of his parents' objections. But knowing Helene might have only a short time to live— well, I'd already determined to devote the rest of my life to her."

"And you haven't been in touch with Chris since Helene died?"

Toddy shook her head. "I didn't give him any hope, Kit. I couldn't. I told him to find someone else—" She took out another length of ribbon. "Three years is a long time to wait for someone—"

"But you don't know that for sure, Toddy. Have you seen his mother?"

"Oh, Mrs. Blanchard!" Toddy shrugged, remembering the scene in the visitors' parlor at the Nursing School, and from under the layers of self-protection, the buried humiliation and hurt surfaced. "No, and I certainly don't expect to. She would go to great lengths to avoid seeing me, Kit. She believes Chris is better off without me. And she may be right."

With that, Toddy picked up the box of ribbons and moved to the next pew.

In the tone of her friend's voice, Kit heard the edge of pain, and felt Toddy wanted the subject closed. But her sympathetic heart prayed that some day her friend would know the same kind of happiness she was experiencing. If not with Chris Blanchard, then with someone else who could love Toddy and whose love Toddy could return.

They finished decorating the rest of the church, then speaking of happier things, the two friends walked back to the Woodwards together.

Coming up the walk, Kit and Toddy heard Laurel's clear soprano voice ringing out. "Joy unspeakable and full of glory!"

Entering the house, they found Laurel at the piano in the parlor.

She looked up as they came in and greeted them gaily. "What other song do you want sung before the processional, Kit? 'O Perfect Love,' or—"

"What about 'The Lord's Prayer?'" Kit suggested. "I've heard you sing it and you do it so beautifully."

That evening the three gathered again up in Laurel's room. They were all rather quiet, knowing that this would be the last time they would be together in this particular way. Laurel would be returning to Boston, and Toddy had to leave right after the reception to go back to nursing school.

Suddenly Toddy broke the silence. "Do you remember what we promised each other when we were on the Orphan Train?"

"Of course!" Laurel exclaimed.

"That we'd be friends forever," Kit supplied.

"No matter what!" Toddy added.

"And we will," Laurel said firmly.

"Yes, but we're all going our separate ways now. Our lives are changing and expanding. Somehow we've got to find a way to stay in touch, not lose each other."

"Well, there are always letters."

"Yes, but it's so easy to put off writing, or even answering a letter. Time goes by, then it seems too much of an effort to try to catch up on everything that happens and gradually you let it slip by—" continued Toddy.

"What do you suggest then?" asked Kit, who found writing letters no task at all.

"I was thinking of a kind of round-robin letter," Toddy said. "We'd each write regularly, just jot down things we want to share, keep a sort of diary or journal. For example, I'd start it, say, when I get back to St. Louis, then mail it to Laurel in Boston. She'd add what she's been doing, then mail it to Kit here in Meadowridge. Kit would add her part and mail it back to me!"

"Wouldn't it get too long and bulky?" Laurel seemed puzzled.

"No, because when I receive Kit's version, I'll delete my first entry, add a new one, and mail it on to you in Boston. I think it would work."

Each of them realizing how important it was to hold on to their oldest and dearest friendships, they agreed to give it a try.

Meadowridge Community Church was filled to capacity the following afternoon. An air of hushed expectancy stirred among the people who had crowded in to witness the marriage of their "young Doc" and his bride, one of their own.

As Kit, looking pale but radiant, came inside on Dr. Woodward's arm, they heard Laurel's sweet soprano raised in the words of the beautiful prayer set to music: "Our Father, which art in heaven, hallowed be Thy name—"

"Are you all right?" Dr. Woodward asked Kit anxiously, patting her hand.

"Yes, I'm fine," she reassured him.

Earlier, however, she had awakened, trembling with apprehension. For a few moments she lay in bed, staring at the early morning sunlight streaming into the room. It promised to be a lovely autumn day. Her wedding day!

Just then she heard a skittering sound and sat bolt upright as a few pebbles hit the windowpane and scattered onto the floor. She threw back the covers, jumped out of bed, and ran over to the window. There below, standing in the garden, was Dan.

Kit leaned on the windowsill and demanded in a stage whisper, "Dan! What are you doing here?"

"I couldn't sleep." He grinned up at her.

"But we're not supposed to see each other before the wedding. It's an old tradition."

"I had to come. See if you were really here. Do you love me? Are you going to marry me today?"

Kit suppressed the laughter bubbling up inside her and pressed both hands against her mouth. "Yes! I love you. And I am going to marry you today! Just *be* there," she called back to him.

"Just wanted to be sure." Dan chuckled, then blew her a kiss, and hands in his pocket, went whistling out through the gate.

That was the surprising, boyishly endearing side of Dan that few people saw in the usually serious young doctor. It was the part of him Kit loved most, knowing that she alone was allowed to see it. Dan had his own old childhood insecurities. But Kit knew they were both getting over the things that might have crippled them emotionally. Together they were learning to love and trust and depend on each other.

After that early morning secret encounter with Dan, all Kit's nervousness vanished. Ava, helping her dress, remarked that she had never seen a bride so serene and composed.

At the first chords of the classic wedding march, dozens of friendly, smiling faces turned to watch as Kit and Dr. Woodward started up the aisle.

Dan, looking tall and splendid in a dark suit, a boutonniere in his lapel, held out his hand to receive Kit as Dr. Woodward left her at the altar.

"O promise me that someday you and I—" Laurel sang as Kit placed her hand in Dan's and they moved together to join the Reverend Dinsmore.

Dr. Woodward stepped back and took his seat beside Ava, sitting in the first pew on the left, the place usually occupied by the bride's family. Well, that's what they were, *practically*, Dr. Woodward thought to himself, recalling vividly that moment of hesitation twenty-some years ago when he had stood with Laurel and seen Jess Hansen sign the adoption paper for Kit. He would never forget the forlorn look on the child's face, those big gray eyes wide with terror, as she had stood there holding her small cardboard suitcase. For one moment Lee's and Kit's eyes had met, hers in a mute plea for help. He remembered the strong urge he had felt to walk up to Jess and tell him he couldn't have Kit, that *he* was taking both little girls home with *him*. And then the thought of Ava and her reaction had he returned with, instead of the *boy* she had agreed to adopt, *two* little girls.

He had often regretted his lack of courage. Laurel had brought them so much happiness. Having Kit might have doubled it. Well, no use looking back. Kit had turned out well in spite of her joyless existence at the Hansens. And somehow he and Ava had been able to give her some of the love she may have lacked in that cold family.

_ And Dan, well if he couldn't have him as Laurel's husband, his *real* son-in-law, he was getting him as Kit's and as his associate in his practice, as well. Yes, God had blessed him mightily and he was grateful. Lee Woodward folded his arms and sat back to enjoy the ceremony.

Olivia Hale, seated right behind the Woodwards, looked admiringly at the petite figure of the maid-of-honor, charmingly dressed in apricot taffeta trimmed with velvet, perfect with Toddy's bright hair and coloring. Then her approving glance moved over to Kit. She was certainly a stunning bride. The Brussels lace Olivia had brought back from France and given Kit for her veil was exquisite over her gleaming dark hair. Her eyes returned to Toddy. What a blessing the girl was, she sighed. Maybe she had taken her in out of pity and for the purpose of giving her invalid granddaughter a companion, but Toddy had proved so much more than that. Olivia recalled the trepidation with which she had brought Zephronia Victorine Todd from the station the day the Orphan Train had come. But she had been paid back a hundredfold. Her heart gave a small twinge as she thought that Toddy would have to leave on the evening train. Toddy was always a proverbial "ray of sunshine." Even after these few days, Olivia knew she would miss her. After only one more year of nurses' training, however, she would be back for good, Olivia hoped. She planned to make a large endowment to Meadowridge Hospital, where they needed to update the facilities and purchase new equipment. Perhaps that would prove an incentive to Toddy to practice her profession in a small town.

Gazing at Toddy's profile turned toward Kit and Dan as they took their vows, Olivia thought there was something wistful in her expression. Was it possible she still had romantic feelings for young Chris Blanchard? *No,* Olivia told herself comfortably. *I'm sure that was over before we left for Europe.*

From her vantage point in the choir loft, Laurel took in the entire scenario—the rapt well-wishers sitting in the pews, the lovely sanctuary transformed into a late-summer garden, the couple standing at the altar.

Her heart swelled with happiness for Kit. And Dan. Laurel was so grateful that he had found someone worthy of him, someone strong and independent and loving to be his helpmate and life's companion.

She hoped she had reassured Kit about any lingering feelings between Dan and herself. Laurel had never returned Dan's youthful infatuation for her. She had accepted it, enjoyed it, and cared for him as the brother she would never have. But she always felt as if she were waiting for her "real life" to begin, even though it was a vague, dreamlike vision of a far-away future. Dan's devotion had sheltered her as completely as the Woodwards' protective love. Neither, however, had prepared her very well for being on her own. That had taken courage that Laurel had called forth from some deep, hidden source within herself.

Remembering her Grandmother Maynard's description of her real mother, Lillian, as "sweet-natured but strong-willed," Laurel had to smile. That could just as well describe *her!* It had hurt Papa Lee and Mother to discover that, but they had finally accepted it. She looked over at them affectionately and saw they were holding hands as they listened to the minister's words.

"Wilt thou have this man to be thy wedded husband, to live together according to God's ordinance in the holy estate of matrimony?"

Unconsciously Laurel's lips formed the words, recalling adoringly how Gene had gazed at her, repeating that very same vow nearly two years ago. How lucky she was to have found him! Laurel thought, rejoicing. It was like finding the other part of herself. Together they were one, inseparable. "To love, honor and cherish, in sickness and in health, for richer or poorer, and forsaking all others, as long as you both shall live."

Suddenly Laurel couldn't wait to go "home" to Boston, to Gene. He had not been able to leave his teaching post at the Music Conservatory to accompany her on this trip to Meadowridge. It was lovely to be with Papa Lee and Mother, and to see Toddy, and be part of Kit's wedding, but Laurel knew her real place was with Gene.

"To have and to hold from this day forward—" Toddy looked down into the flowers of Kit's bridal bouquet she was holding during the ceremony, so that Kit's hands would be free when the couple exchanged rings.

It was Ava who had selected the combination of flowers for Kit to carry—white and yellow chrysanthemums, blue forget-me-nots, surrounded by myrtle leaves, arranged in a ruffle of tulle and tied with white satin streamers. Each flower had its own meaning—Ava had chosen them to represent Kit's special qualities of truthfulness, loyalty, constancy, and love.

"Having given each other a ring, the symbol of eternal love, and pledged to one another mutual respect, faithfulness and devotion before God and this congregation, I now pronounce you husband and wife."

A smiling Kit and Dan turned around, and Toddy handed Kit back her bouquet. At the sight of Kit's shining eyes, her look of absolute bliss, Toddy's heart turned over. Would *she* ever know such happiness?

Even though Kit was adept at putting emotions into words as a writer, she would have found it hard to express the deep feelings of that moment. After Dan slipped the wide, gold band on her finger and she heard Reverend Dinsmore's solemn pronouncement, Kit felt exalted. Her feet simply did not seem to touch the floor as they started back down the aisle of the church.

Before her, she saw a sea of smiling faces. Many pairs of eyes, some of them brimming with tears, regarded her with warmth. She felt the flow of good wishes for her happiness sweeping toward her, enveloping her. Her throat ached with emotion.

Kit thought down all the long, lonely years that had led her to this moment and was overwhelmed with wonder and thankfulness. From somewhere in the back of her mind came the scriptural promise that was being fulfilled in her life today: "I will restore the years the locusts have eaten."

She felt the pressure of Dan's touch on her arm as they halted at the door of the church. "They want to take a picture of us here, darling."

Dazedly Kit looked down the steps where a man stood beside a cloth-draped camera on a tripod.

"That's wonderful! Stand right there, if you will. I want to get it just like that if you'll hold still for just one minute and keep smiling!"

Keep smiling? Kit felt as if she could never stop! There was an exploding sound as the photographer pressed his bulb.

"One more to be sure." They held still another minute. Then the man said, "Perfect! Thank you, Dr. and Mrs. Brooks."

The first time they had been addressed as "Dr. and Mrs. Brooks" registered in Kit's mind just as indelibly as the camera recorded the image of their first few moments as husband and wife on the steps of Meadowridge Church.

24

Kit looked up from her desk at the *Meadowridge Monitor* and took a deep breath. The wind blowing in from the open window was refreshingly fragrant with the smell of new spring blooms that had just begun to cautiously unfold in the park across the street from the old brick newspaper building.

She smiled to herself. After San Francisco, Meadowridge was a small town indeed, and coming back had not been all that easy for Kit. There were things about a rural setting she had not missed, but neither had she found in the city the things she *had* missed. Of course, in the end, it was because of Dan she had come back. She knew she loved him and wanted to spend the rest of her life with him. Now, a half year later, she had not regretted for a minute her decision to return.

Leaning her chin upon her hand, Kit tapped her teeth with the tip of her pencil and indulged in a little reminiscing.

They had not taken a wedding trip, but had gone after the reception at the Hale's to the repainted, refurbished house Dan's grandmother had left him. Ava had overseen the work, and every sparkling window, shining floor, polished surface welcomed Kit.

It still did not quite seem possible that all her dreams and hopes had come true, Kit sighed. The man she loved, a charming house, rewarding work. Life was altogether satisfactory and fulfilling.

Kit spent three afternoons a week at the *Monitor* and worked on her other writing at home. Since Dan was taking over more and more of Dr. Woodward's patients, especially those in the outlying areas and farms around Meadowridge, his hours were long and unpredictable. Kit could spend considerable time working on her writing without neglecting her new husband, his comfort or needs.

Her thoughts were interrupted by the arrival of the day's mail. Mr. Pennfold placed a stack of letters on her desk, tipping his cap and greeting her cheerfully.

"'Morning, Mizz Brooks. Lorna over at the Post Office says you get more mail than anyone in Meadowridge. Reckon it's all that writing you do." He chuckled as he went out the door.

Kit shuffled through the envelopes. Most of them were notices sent by the various clubs and social groups, or from church secretaries wanting publicity for their bazaar or bake sale or special meeting. There were several forwarded to her from the magazine. She was still hearing from readers about the "Orphan Train" story as well as some of her newer pieces published by *Woman's Hearth and Home*. It was gratifying to know that what she wrote was reaching so many people.

She often thought of the woman who had adopted Gwynny and written to her. She had shared the letter with Dan, and the photograph of her grown-up sister was mounted in a lovely silver frame and put in a place of honor on the mantle in their parlor.

Of course Jamie was still a question mark, and Kit often thought about her brother and prayed he was well and happy.

One afternoon, Kit was working alone in the office at the *Monitor*. It was Thursday, and since the paper had come out that morning, everyone else had gone home to a well-deserved rest. Kit, bent over the article she was writing, did not look up when she heard the front door open. It was probably Mr. Clooney, who found it hard to stay away from the newspaper more than a few hours, or perhaps Jessica, coming to check on something she'd forgotten.

It wasn't until a large shadow fell across her desk, blocking the sunlight, that Kit lifted her head.

Standing at a little distance from her was a man of medium height and muscular build, staring at her curiously. He wore a rough blue cotton shirt open at the neck, a many-pocketed sleeveless vest, faded indigo pants tucked into well-worn, dusty boots. Whipping off a battered, billed tweed cap, he shook back tousled sandy-colored hair and, ducking his head shyly, asked, "'Scuse me, miss, but are you Miss Ternan?"

Kit frowned. She didn't recognize the fellow although there was something familiar about him.

"Yes."

He reached in his pocket, pulled out a folded paper, slowly opened its many-creased length and smoothing it out, held it up to her.

"You wrote this?"

Kit saw the head, "Little Lost Family," and nodded.

"Well…Kit, it's me. Jamie." A grin tugged at the corners of the rather cynical mouth in the weatherbeaten face, wrinkled the corners of the eyes that were too old for twenty-five.

"Jamie?" she repeated.

"The same." The grin widened.

The pencil in Kit's fingers snapped and broke as her grip spasmed and she staggered, stumbling to her feet, holding onto the edges of the desk for support.

Suddenly came a rush of emotion, so powerful it stunned her. A torrent of feeling so intense she did not think she could contain it shuddered through her body, leaving her weak and shaking. After all her longing, all her pathetic wondering about her brother, here he was standing in front of her.

"Jamie! Jamie, how did you find me? Oh, Jamie!" she cried hoarsely.

"I was in St. Louis," he began. "And I seen this in the newspaper, reprinted it said from some magazine called *Woman's Hearth and Home*. I couldn't hardly believe it when I read it and realized it was about *us* and that you had written it!"

"Oh, Jamie, this is so wonderful! To think you found *me* when I've been praying for so long to find *you!*" Tears streamed down Kit's face and she held out both hands to him, wondering if he would mind if she hugged him.

His hands were workman's hands—calloused, the knuckles swollen and scarred, nails broken. Feeling their roughness, Kit wondered what kind of work Jamie did. But, first, there were other more important things.

"Come on, Jamie. We have so much to talk about, so much to catch up on—You must come home with me. I want you to meet my husband—"

"You married? But this byline says 'Ternan.'"

"That's my professional name, Jamie, the name I write under. But, yes, I'm married to someone I've known practically all my life. He's a doctor and we live just a few blocks over." Kit put on her sweater, picked up her hat, then tucked her arm through Jamie's. "Oh, I have so much to ask you, so many questions."

Soon they were seated in Kit's sunny kitchen. She put on the kettle to make coffee and sliced a large piece of apple pie for Jamie as she listened to his story.

"I was adopted out of Greystone by a nice, older couple who didn't have any kids of their own. They had a little farm upstate and I stayed with them about three years. I went to a country school and I even had a little pony to ride, chickens to feed. My chore was to gather the eggs every day. I liked it just fine." Jamie leaned his elbows on the table, one hand holding a forkful of apple pie, ready to pop into his mouth. "And...I guess you could say that was the end of the good times."

"What do you mean, Jamie?"

"Well, Mr. Heffner died and the old lady got real peaked and nervouslike, said she couldn't keep things goin' by herself. So a neighborin' farmer, a fellow named Gordon, bought her out lock, stock and barrel and took me along in the bargain. He didn't care nothin' about kids, just wanted extra hands, ones he didn't have to pay." Jamie scowled. "Worst thing that could have happened. If I'da known what it was gonna be like, I woulda run away right then."

"But what about Mrs. Heffner? Why didn't you go with her wherever she was going?"

"She felt bad about it, cried somethin' awful. She was gonna live with her sister and they already had four kids of their own, didn't want no more."

"So, then what happened?"

Jamie took another mouthful of pie before answering.

"I run away."

"When you were only...what...nine or ten? Oh, Jamie—"

"I don't know just how old I was at the time, but it wasn't too long after I stayed as long as I could take it at the Gordons. Talk about mean, Kit." Jamie shook his head. "And it weren't just me. He had another kid there workin' for him. He was about fifteen, and he'd been plannin' to escape— yeah, that's what he called it—like from a prison! He'd been stowin' stuff away for months, gettin' ready to do it. And I begged him to take me with him."

"This Gordon—what did he do?"

"You don't want to know, Kit." Jamie shook his head. "If I took my shirt off, you could see some of the scars 'cross my back where he used a buggy whip on me! I kicked and fought him but—" Jamie shrugged. "Well, what could a scrawny kid do against a growed man? He'd beat Tom a lot, too. That's why Tom was leavin.'"

"And so...did you?"

"Yep, we planned it real careful, tried it out a coupla times. We knowed when the freight train passed down at the edge of his farm, just when it slowed for the crossin'—"

"You rode the freight cars, Jamie?" gasped Kit.

"Plenty of times." He grinned, and curling his little finger daintily as he picked up the cup of coffee Kit had just refilled, Jamie put on an affected air. "In fact, I'd say it was my most frequent mode of transportation!"

"Oh, Jamie, what a life you've had. For a little boy to be alone, on his own like that—" She sighed, looking at him.

"Aw, it wasn't all bad, Kit. Sure it was tough, but there were other guys ridin' the rails. Some of 'em helped us out, taught us some of the tricks to survive, and me and Tom stuck together."

"So, you didn't get to go to school at all then, Jamie?"

"Not after I left the Heffners. But I've got along. One summer Tom and me got jobs with a carney—a travelin' carnival, doin' all sorts of odd jobs. We went all over, stayin' just a couple of days in every town, then movin' on. Got to see a lot of the country, Kit. I liked it a lot. So, that's what I do, Kit. I'm a carney roustabout. It's a good life."

Kit's hands were clasped tightly in front of her on the table. Her throat felt hot and tight. She remembered the little brother whom she had taught his letters, and how to print before he was even five. She thought of the bright, inquisitive mind, how quickly he caught on to things, how much he had wanted to learn to read for himself, but loved for Kit to read to him. Jamie was smart. If he'd had an education, no telling how far he could have gone, what he might have become.

When Dan appeared, he welcomed Jamie warmly, said this certainly called for a celebration, and left again to go to the pharmacy and bring back a quart of ice cream for dessert. Kit was already preparing vegetables to go with the pot roast she had started earlier. The three of them sat around the kitchen table talking. Dan and Kit listened to Jamie's recital of his vagabond years, the interesting world of the carnival people of whom they knew nothing.

Dan was finally forced to leave them, saying he had surgery early in the morning, but Kit suspected he was tactfully leaving brother and sister alone for some more intimate sharing.

"I hope you plan to stay with us for a while, Jamie," Dan said as he shook his hand heartily before leaving the room.

Kit poured more coffee for each of them, then she and Jamie moved into the little parlor. She tossed some large pillows on the floor and they settled down in front of the fireplace where a small fire glowed cheerfully. Kit showed him Gwynny's picture and the letter from their sister's adoptive mother.

He read it through and when he handed it back, his eyes were glistening.

"Well, it looks like things turned out just fine for her. I'm glad." They were both silent for a long moment, staring into the fire. Then not looking at Kit, Jamie slowly began to speak. "I found Da, Kit."

"You *did!* How, Jamie? Where?"

"When Mrs. Heffner packed me up to go over to the Gordon farm, she put in my adoption papers and I kept them. On them, they had Da's name and his address, at least what it was when he signed the release papers for me and Gwynny to be adopted. So, I just took a chance he might still be livin' in that area, near Brockton."

"So did you see him?"

"Yeah, I saw him." Jamie sounded grim. "I mean, I went by his house and found out where he worked. I'd seed some kids outside and thought maybe they wouldn't be too pleased for another kid—especially one who'd been ridin' the rails and didn't look so great—showin' up like that. So I waited for the end of his shift at the shoe factory and—"

"You spoke to him?"

"Sure. I recognized him but he didn't know me. Not at first, anyhow. I was pretty big, even at fourteen. It took him by surprise, that was for sure. He got kind of pale, then sort of started explainin' why he'd left us at Greystone, agreed to us gettin' adopted."

"Did he ask about Gwynny, or me?" Kit asked tentatively.

"He was sort of embarrassed, Kit, so I let him off the hook. I had thought of askin' him if I could spend the night at his house. A good home-cooked meal and a warm bed would have come in handy just then. But he stumbled around and said he'd married and there were some little kids—"

They were both quiet. Kit reached over and squeezed Jamie's big, rough hand.

"I guess there's nothin' to do but forgive him, Jamie."

"Sure, why not?" Jamie shrugged. "Poor guy. I guess he was up against it—out of work, three mouths to feed—Who's to say what anyone would have done?"

The clock on the mantle struck two before the brother and sister at last said good night. Kit had made up the bed in the downstairs bedroom that used to be Dan's when he was a boy and had lived here with his grandmother and aunts.

Kit hugged him before she went upstairs.

"I hope you will stay for a while, Jamie. I've just found you. I don't want to lose you again."

Jamie smiled but didn't say anything but, "Thanks, Kit, good night."

When Kit awakened the next morning, the room was full of sunshine. She knew she must have overslept because the house was very still and quiet. She lay there for a minute, realizing Dan must have slipped out early to go to the hospital without waking her. And Jamie! In a rush of remembering all that had taken place the day before, Kit jumped out of bed, threw on her wrapper, and went down the stairway, tying her sash as she did.

"Jamie!" she called, looking for him first in the kitchen. Then she ran down the hall. The downstairs bedroom door was open, the bed stripped, the sheets and blankets neatly folded at the bottom. "Jamie!" Kit called again and her voice echoed through the empty house.

Slowly she walked back through the house and went into the parlor where they had sat and talked together for hours. On the mantle, propped up against the clock, was a folded paper. With a growing feeling of certainty, Kit went over and picked it up.

> Dear Kit,
> It was sure great to see you. I didn't want to say anthing last night, but I had to leave at dawn to catch the train to where the carney is going to be next week. Don't be sad. Now that I know where you are, I'll be turning up again like that bad penny they talk about. You can count on it. You're some cook, Kit! Before too long I'll be seeing you.
>
> Your brother,
Jamie
> P.S. You got a fine husband. Tell him so long for me and thanks for everything.

Kit slipped the note into her pocket and went into the kitchen. Automatically she filled the kettle with water and put it on the stove to boil. She moved stiffly like someone in physical pain. Then suddenly great racking sobs welled up from deep inside her and she put her face in her hands and wept.

She wept for Jamie, for herself, for Gwynny, for all the lost years they might have had together, all that they might have given each other—the caring, the love, that irreplaceable threefold cord that bound them forever as a family.

The kettle's hissing alerted her that it had boiled dry. How many minutes had passed, Kit wasn't sure. She only knew that after the storm of weeping was over, a kind of calm settled over her. She lifted the kettle from the sizzling burner and refilled it.

Looking out the kitchen window into the backyard, she saw that the old apple tree had, seemingly overnight, put forth tiny pale green leaves. A full-breasted robin balanced on one bough. Spring's first promise.

As she stood there in the stillness, Kit realized her tears had done their healing work. Yes, it was only natural to grieve for what had been lost. But she knew in the fullness of her spirit, that every experience is for a purpose, and no matter how wrong or sad or tragic the original circumstances, God could use it for her good. Jamie had his path, Gwynny hers, Kit hers.

Suddenly it was as if Kit were seeing everything with new eyes. She realized she possessed all the essentials of happiness within the small sphere of this house, the beckoning garden, the bright April day. It would be ungrateful to a gracious Creator not to enjoy every minute allotted to her.

Kit took a deep breath, whispered a thankful prayer. The day stretched before her with countless opportunities for service, love and happiness.

She spent the morning planting vegetables for summer harvest. In the afternoon she took a favorite book of poetry outside and read, something she had not done in a very long time. Later she picked jonquils and grape hyacinths from

Dan's grandmother's old-fashioned garden and arranged them in a Blue Willow pitcher and placed them on the dinner table. Then she fixed a casserole and salad, ready to serve whenever Dan arrived.

She had just done up her hair, put on a fresh blouse when she heard Dan's footstep on the porch and the front door open. As he stepped inside, he called, "Kit, Kit, I'm home!"

With a heart newly sure, she called back, "So am I! So am I!" and ran to meet him.